SAGA OF THE SWEDISH WATER SPIRIT

Caroline Helenasdotter

Förlaget Annasdotter

Förlaget
Annasdotter

ISBN-978-91-527-8560-7

"I deem it unfitting to make myself less than I am"

Free translation of the quote;

"Det anstår mig icke att göra mig mindre än jag är"

EDITH SÖDERGRAN

CONTENTS

CHAPTER 1

As the earliest sunbeams caressed the Earth's bosom, Liv stirred from her peaceful dreams, enraptured by the dulcet serenade of the rooster's call resonating across the boundless horizon. With a gentle grace, her eyes unveiled the panorama before her, a realm adorned in the tender glow of morning's gilded clasp. An orchestral ensemble of melodious birdsong and the gentle rustle of leaves bestowed upon her rousing, entwining seamlessly with the symphony of her heart's rhythmic dance.

Though Liv's mortal form exuded vigour and vitality, a fatigue permeated the recesses of her essence, draping her spirit in a cloak of weariness. It descended upon her like a heavy mantle, veiling the brilliance that once kindled her inner flame. The relentless march of time and the crucibles of existence had etched their enduring imprints upon her, dimming the brilliance that once gleamed within the depths of her gaze.

Yet, amidst this universe of contradictions—the vitality of her corporeal form and the weariness of her soul—she discovered solace within the mild clasp of the summer dawn. The atmosphere, saturated with the heady perfume of blooming blossoms and dew-laden meadows, brushed against her skin, enlivening her senses with its caress, warm and delicate. Soft zephyrs whispered clandestine secrets, carrying the whispered vows of a pristine day, beckoning her weary spirit to yield to the serene currents of optimism and renewal.

Liv, immersed in the tender promise of this enchanting morn, could not resist the allure of the profound magnificence unfurling before her. The heavens, a curtain of sapphire blue, adorned with heavenly tendrils of diaphanous clouds, mirrored the depths of her desires and yearnings. The sun, now fully ascended, suffused the world with its resplendent presence, casting a divine luminescence upon all it graced, as if imparting an affectionate caress upon the very essence of creation.

In this profound realm, where nature's symphony entwines with the nuances of her own heart, Liv found herself suspended betwixt wakefulness and reverie, existing within the delicate equilibrium of a transcendent moment. She discerned the innate harmony in the convergence of her earthly vessel and spiritual essence, an opulent gear wheel that resonated with the ceaseless voyage of her being.

Embracing the endearing fondling of this balmy summer morn, accompanied by the melodic proclamation of the rooster's crow, Liv acknowledged her resilient physique and her wearied yet tenacious soul, understanding that within the embrace of each nascent day resided the potential to rekindle the radiant spark that glimmered within her, eagerly awaiting reawakening through life's choreography of poetic enchantment.

With graceful fluidity, the sun ascended the celestial stage, unfurling its tender gaze upon the rolling hills of their ancestral Swedish homestead, as though revealing an eternal pageantry for the eyes of 1623 to behold. Its ascent bore an unhurried cadence, savouring each passing moment, adorning the heavens with streams of liquid gold and apricot, infusing the atmosphere with a gentle, otherworldly radiance.

Within this sanctified dawn, an undeniable calm held sway,

saturating the very essence of the land. A serene tranquillity draped the earth, as though the soil itself froze in an expectant stillness in sacred reverence, and the pulse of existence reverberated in hushed murmurs. Amidst this symphony of serenity, the leaves whispered with a shy fragility, their gentle waltz punctuating the calm air. Their graceful pirouettes formed a tender duet with the distant chorus of birds, their melodious voices carried upon the breeze, creating a blend of harmonious sounds that transcended both temporal and spatial realms. Perched on ancient boughs, these avian minstrels composed nature's sonnet on the canvas of the awakening day, their trills and chirrups evoking a profound sense of awe and tranquillity.

Enshrouded by the verdant touch of the landscape, the farmhouse stood strong, an emblem of resilience echoing through generations. Its grandeur lay in its unpretentious simplicity, emanating an aura of rustic grace, its weathered visage whispering untold tales. Nestled at the very heart of the fields, it emerged as a sanctuary amidst a sea of swaying grasses and wild blooms, their vibrant hues reaching skyward in an unabashed ode to celebration.

Within its steadfast walls, secrets of life and love found sanctuary, dreams embedded deeply within its timbers. Time, with its gentle touch, had etched its story upon the proud facade, a patina of history marking the passage of days, seasons, and centuries. It seemed to embody the very spirit of the land, a silent witness to the eternal flow of life's sublime dance.

As the sun's hopeful touch painted the landscape with a golden embrace, the undulating hills, the hushed atmosphere, and the ancestral farmhouse melded harmoniously into a peaceful existence. In this harmonious communion, the layers of time unfurled, merging the realms of yore and present into a moment that rose above the constraints of mere chronology. And as the sun reigned over their cherished Swedish homestead, the indomitable legacy of their ancestors resonated in the rustling of the gale, echoing the timeless tales of love, resilience, and longing intricately fitted into the building blocks of their expansive family estate.

In the distance, a contented herd of cows grazed gracefully, their gentle lowing carried upon the breeze. The fragrance of freshly cut hay lingered in the air, a poignant reminder of the tireless toil that had prepared the fields for the season's arrival.

With languid grace, Liv rose from her bed and rubbed her sleepy eyes, still concealed in the remnants of deep slumber. Gazing through the small window, her eyes met the sun's ascent, casting its radiant glow over the vast expanse of fields that enveloped their cherished farmstead.

In the realm of a rustic farm, positioned among expansive meadows kissed by the sun's gentle caress, Liv's journey unfolded like the unfurling petals of a resilient blossom. More than two decades had passed since her arrival, at the tender age of fifteen. It was upon this idyllic farm that she took her first strides into the realm of matrimony, bound to a man named Finn.

In those early days, when the world seemed like an infinite smorgasbord of boundless potential, Liv's heart danced with the purest love for her chosen partner. Finn, an eighteen-year-old, exuded an aura of strength and self-assurance that enchanted her very core. Their union, forged in the crucible of parental arrangements and the promise of prosperity, bestowed upon Liv a sense of gratitude and contentment. Her parents, custodians of tradition and guardians of security, had orchestrated this union, rejoicing in the discovery of a prosperous household for their cherished daughter.

In the sun-drenched fields where their souls entwined amidst toil and shared aspirations, Liv believed she had discovered her life's everlasting companion. Yet, as time delicately claimed days of their shared existence, whispers of discontent and unrest began to take hold within the chambers of her heart. The once-vibrant love that had blossomed within her now seemed to wilt, leaving behind a bittersweet tinge of melancholy.

The weight of two decades bore witness to a metamorphosis, as the gossamer threads of Liv's youthful hopes intertwined with the raw realities of her being. The farm, once an emblem of promised joy, now stood as a silent witness to the nuanced layers of her odyssey. Every weathered line etched upon her visage and every strand of silver adorning her hair held untold tales, a testament to the relentless passage of time and the whispered yearnings that resided within her soul.

Liv, the sovereign of her own fate, stood at the crossroads where her emotions converged. Memories of a once ardent love, now evaporated like dewdrops in the warmth of the day, swirled within her mind. In the depths of her being, a yearning for something indefinable, something elusive, began to stir. It was an unrest that beckoned her to explore the untraveled realms of her soul, to find solace in the arms of an intangible yet magnetic force that called out to her.

Amidst the undulating cornfields, swaying beneath the golden kiss of the sun, Liv found herself longing for a connection that eclipsed the boundaries of convention and expectations. It was a primal yearning that whispered of untamed desires and uncharted territories, an invitation to venture beyond the confines of her known world. Within the secret chambers of her heart, a seed of curiosity was planted, waiting for the gentle showers of destiny to coax it into bloom. She ardently longed for the moment when she might again heed the whispers of her heart, revealing the map to her authentic passions.

Within the realm of the countryside, where rich fields stretched like woven threads of gold, Finn's lineage presided over the grandest manor in the entire county. Their ancestral farm, located a mere twenty minutes' sojourn from the nearest village, stood as a beacon of opulence and abundance. In those bygone days, when the Swedish lands remained sparsely populated, the privilege of having a village nearby was a rarity, bestowed upon only the most fortuitous few.

Within the expansive borders of this majestic realm, Finn's lineage thrived, creating a myriad of interconnected lives. Svante, his brother bound by blood, and Greta, his sister, shared the sanctified grounds of their ancestral farm. Svante, a guardian of ancestral heritage, nurtured his own household alongside his beloved wife, Tyra. Four precious children, the living embodiment of their union, adorned the land with their laughter and unblemished purity. Their harmonious haven found solace within the fertile enclosure of the farm's productive cradle.

Greta, a widow touched by the cruel hand of war, sought refuge within the familiar safety of her childhood home. The echoes of loss reverberated through the depths of her heart, for her beloved spouse had perished to the ravages of battle. Yet, adorned in the armour of resilience, Greta discovered strength in her three cherished children, remnants of a love that once blossomed vividly. Together, they forged an unbreakable bond, their spirits entwined within the walls of their ancestral dwelling.

In the union of Finn's ancestral lineage, the pillars of his heritage stood resolute. His progenitors, guardians of custom and custodians of the land, graced the farm with their sagacity and guidance. With each dawn's awakening, their weathered hands embraced the toil of labour, their souls entwined with the very spirit of the land they called their own. Their presence, a witness to enduring devotion and unwavering fortitude, bestowed a sense of continuity upon the ever-evolving cycles of life that adorned the terrain.

Thus, amid this diversity of intertwined lives and shared encounters, the farm pulsed with the cadence of existence. The calloused palms of labour and the whispered chronicles of generations melded together, weaving a narrative that spoke of heritage, perseverance, and the unbreakable bonds of kinship. As the seasons danced upon the land, the echoes of joyous laughter, hushed confidences, and the tender embrace of familial affection lingered within the joyful halls of their primordial dwelling.

In this serene countryside, where whispers of ancient wisdom rode the winds, the farm blossomed as a mighty garden, a place where family roots entwined with the fertile soil. Every nook, every path, held memories etched into the very essence of the land. It was a place where laughter harmonized with the rustle of leaves, where the weight of duty waltzed with the joy of shared abundance.

Amid the comforting hold of their shared home, Finn's family sought solace and drew strength, their spirits nourished by the rich history of their heritage. Bound by a connection forged through labour and loyalty, they remained tethered to the earth that cradled their existence. And as the sun, an artist of radiance, brushed the fields with its golden strokes, casting a luminous embrace upon their abode, the farm stood tall in affirmation of the enduring legacy of a united family, nurtured by the blessings of the land and the echoes of their ancestors.

From the cradle of ancestral whispers, Finn emerged as the elder sibling, a son of the soil deeply attuned to the rhythms of the land. Within his veins coursed the patrimonial currents, intricately woven into the fabric of his being. The farm, a firm symbol of heritage, had stood as an unwavering companion to

Finn's kin since time immemorial. Its fertile soil bore witness to the unpredictability of life, and Finn, as a guardian of tradition, awaited the day when he would inherit the vast territory of their cherished land.

In the hallways of time, Finn's footsteps resounded with purpose, guided by the whispers of his forebears. Each furrowed field, each weathered oak, told stories of toil and triumph, etching upon his heart a profound reverence for the wisdom passed down by his forefathers. He embodied the steward of their sacred realm, a custodian of their treasured heritage.

Since his earliest days, Finn breathed in the sweet perfume of the earth, his hands moulded by the tender caress of the soil. The contours of the land imprinted upon his soul, forging a profound bond with the spacious domain that stretched towards the horizon. He beheld the graceful dance of seasons, observed the eternal cycles of birth and renewal, and acknowledged the symbiotic harmony between man and land.

His parents, keepers of the farm's legacy, nurtured Finn's affinity for the fertile earth, weaving tales of struggle and resilience into his upbringing. They guided his steps along well-trodden paths, imparting archaic wisdom with each passing year. Finn's spirit intertwined with the land, his destiny interwoven with the fields that extended beyond the limits of sight.

Amidst time's capricious grip, Finn thrived, his spirit connected to the weight of progenitorial aspirations. His hands, once soft and untested, matured into resilient tools, etched with the marks of toil that perpetuated through the ages. As the seasons changed, he honed the art of harmonizing with the earth's mysteries. The land yielded to his stern touch, offering abundant harvests as if spellbound by the link between man and nature.

Thus, Finn stood as the bridge between epochs, a vessel through which ancestral whispers resonated. The flame of heritage burned bright within his soul, casting its radiant glow upon the path he trod. The mantle of inheritance beckoned, a weighty responsibility he clung to with devoted allegiance.

Within the ruthless hands of time, the farm stood firm, an anchor of constancy, its fields an infinite canvas where Finn's lineage unfurled. Each dawn carried the land's whispered reminders, a reminder of its enduring legacy. And in his humble role as guardian, Finn vowed to safeguard the blessings bestowed by his forefathers. Enclosed by the earth's hold dwelled the essence of his kin, a timeless tribute to their resilience and boundless love for the consecrated soil.

Within the hopeful bond of their union, Liv's heart bloomed like a resplendent flower, intoxicated by the essence of Finn's steadfast presence. He, a paragon of unyielding resolve and solid devotion, personified strength and resilience. Each passing day unravelled new depths in Liv's affection, her very soul entwined with his straightforward spirit.

Finn, a stalwart pillar, carried the weight of the world upon his broad shoulders. His hands, weathered by the toil of the land, whispered tales of uncompromised commitment to their shared life. Liv admired his respectable fidelity, his tireless dedication to shaping their future. In his constancy, she sought solace and assurance, believing Finn would be her guardian and provider for all eternity.

Yet, as the seasons passed, Liv unearthed a yearning in her heart, an ache that echoed through her every breath. She yearned for gentle caresses and stolen glances, for whispered words of love that would ignite the dormant embers of passion within her soul. Deep within her being, she longed for a touch that would heal the fragmented pieces of her heart, nurturing a love that transcended the boundaries of mere obligation.

In the secret refuge of her dreams and fantasies, Liv adorned her thoughts with the delicate petals of hope, yearning for a nexus of entwined hearts. She craved to be swept away on the wings of love, embraced by the gentle whispers of affection. No longer content with being a mere companion in Finn's journey, she yearned to be treasured as an esteemed soul who kindled the flames within his spirit.

Alas, Liv's dreams collided with the harsh reality of Finn's stoic nature. His gaze remained fixed upon the arduous toil that filled their days, a symbol of his resolute allegiance to the land and its abundant bounty. Love, it seemed, was a distant melody, overshadowed by Finn's practicality.

Liv, her heart ablaze with longing, yearned for the tender touch that could bridge the divide between them. She yearned for whispered words that would paint their love with vibrant shades of affection. Yet, as the days unfolded, she found herself adrift in the shadows of unspoken desires, yearning for a connection that slipped through their fingers like fine sand.

In the solace of her solitude, Liv would cast her gaze upon Finn, his steadfast stare fixated on the tasks that demanded his attention, his shoulders burdened by the weight of their world. She wondered if he, too, yearned for the ephemeral dance of love, concealed beneath the fortress of his stoic facade. Her heart trembled with longing, for the connection they once shared had faded, the vibrant spark of their early days now dimmed by the shadows of unrequited desire.

With each passing sun, Liv grappled with the enigma of Finn's emotional fortress. She questioned why the depths of her love remained unexplored, yearning for the touch that could reawaken hibernating sparks of passion within their intertwined souls. As her spirit swayed between hope and despair, she sought answers in the secrets carried by the breeze, praying for the gentle transformation that would reignite the fires of their love.

Liv's heart hungered for an affection that transcended the boundaries of duty and obligation. She craved a love that would weave their souls together, breathing life into the forgotten chambers of their hearts. With every beat, she longed for the tender touch that would bridge the gap between their separate worlds, whispering the unspoken love, and she thirsted for the day when Finn's heart would find its way to hers.

Under the moon's gentle glow, Finn was bound by the weight of lineal expectation, his duty to carry forward their lineage echoing through the corridors of his mind. Like the steadfast rhythm of the seasons, he would have sex with Liv, twice a month. Yet, in those blissful moments of union, a veil of detachment shrouded his countenance, masking the depths of his emotions.

Liv, the eternal seeker of love's seductive hold, ached for their shared space to reverberate with the lilt of affection. But Finn, a stoic figure, seldom spoke the language of passion, his words carried away like murmurs on the wind. Their kisses, fleeting and evanescent, offered mere glimpses of an intimacy that lay dormant, while his touch, bound by necessity, faltered in its passionate caress.

In the hush of their union, Liv wondered if the fire of their love would forever remain smothered, stifled by the obligations that entwined them. Her heart, adorned with vulnerable petals of hope, longed for the flames of desire to ignite their souls, to exceed the barriers of duty and kindle a love that defied expectations.

Finn, burdened by the weight of tradition, understood the necessity of heirs, the substantial responsibility resting upon his steady shoulders. In those passionate moments, he would merge his destiny with Liv's, their bodies becoming vessels for the legacy they were destined to weave.

As their bodies intertwined, Liv felt the chill of obligation, the whispers of duty tainting the air. She yearned for words that would stir the repressed desires, for kisses that would kindle the flames of love's intoxication. But Finn, shackled by the grip of custom, struggled to unleash the fervour concealed beneath his stoic facade, his touch confined to the realm of procreation.

Liv, her heart ablaze with unfulfilled desires, gazed upon the distant stars, seeking answers in their peaceful radiance. She craved the passion that danced between their souls, the raw vulnerability that would render their bodies a canvas for the strokes of ardour. In the stillness of their encounters, she pondered if their love would forever remain confined to the realm of duty, forever yearning for the liberation that true passion could bestow.

Their nights remained veiled in echoes of longing, the untold tales of passion yearning to find voice. Liv, with each shared moment, whispered silent prayers to the moonlit skies, beseeching the gods to awaken the subdued fires within Finn's heart. For she knew that their love, restrained by the cords of obligation, sought to break free, to soar upon the wings of unfettered passion and reclaim the realm of sexual union.

Liv, a dreamer adorned with the dainty petals of romance, carried within her a world teeming with vibrant imagination. Her spirit danced amidst the realms of adventure and love, weaving embroidery of grandeur in her dreams. Since the dawn of memory, Liv had yearned for a love that would consume her, a love that would extend beyond the passage of time and etch its mark upon the texture of eternity.

In the early days of their relationship, Liv's heart blossomed with hope, a garden of aspirations nurtured by love's promising touch. She longed for a symphony of joy and boundless happiness, where their intimacy would become an orchestra of passion and tenderness, each note resonating with the depths of their souls. Yet, as the days waned and the seasons passed, a veil of discontent settled upon her, casting shadows upon the flickering flame of her dreams.

Liv, caught in the grip of physical proximity, found herself lost in an infinite deep of emptiness, her desires unquenched, her soul yearning for more. What once triggered her fervour now whispered echoes of discontent, as the act that should have kindled their love became a mere routine. The fading glimmers of her passion dwindled, suffocated by the chains of duty and monotony, leaving her adrift in a world devoid of enchantment.

A hollow void gnawed at the core of Liv, an emptiness that her husband's provisions could not fill. Though grateful for the shelter, sustenance, and stability Finn provided, her heart dreamed of a connection that transcended practicality. The wisdom of her mother's words, a legacy passed down through generations, had warned her that marriage was an alliance forged in the fires of necessity, a union driven by practical considerations. Yet, the rebellious echoes that once resounded within Liv's spirit had faded, replaced by the hollowness of unfulfilled visions.

Hope, once a radiant star guiding her path, now seemed distant and far reached, a flickering beacon swallowed by the hallow darkness of the night. Liv's chest reverberated with an ache, a void that whispered of untamed dreams and unfulfilled passions. The fairy tales of eternal love that once filled her dreams now appeared distant, their enchantment fading amidst the trials of reality.

Nevertheless, Liv concealed her discontent like a secret veiled beneath her delicate facade, fearful of betraying her gratitude and the security bestowed upon her by marriage. She battled the turmoil within, torn between the longing for a love that surpassed the mundane and the desire to honour the practical bonds that held them together. In the depths of her being, hope withered, its petals scattered by the winds of disillusionment.

Echoes of her dreams resounded in the hidden chambers of her heart, craving a love that defied time and waltzed among the stars. Yet, as she peered into the abyss within, hope flickered like a distant flame, its glow dimmed by the harsh realities of her marriage, leaving her to wander in a realm where dreams faded into mere echoes of the night.

In the tender embrace of motherhood's cradle, Liv, at the tender age of sixteen, welcomed her firstborn son, Oscar, a child adorned with vitality and a spirit that knew no bounds. A year later, the gift of life graced her once more, and she brought forth Melker, a son carrying the strength of ancient oaks within him. As Liv blossomed into her eighteenth year, twin boys joined their growing family, their arrival heralding a symphony of new beginnings. Yet, as the branches of their family tree multiplied, Finn's gaze wandered astray, like a ship lost upon a desolate sea. The tender bonds of affection and love that once entwined their souls now faded into echoes, mere vanishing reminiscences within the pages of their shared history. Finn's touch, withered into scarce encounters, fragments of a fire long extinguished.

Within Liv's heart, a tempest raged, its stormy winds tearing at the resilient centre of her being. Her children, like beacons in the night, illuminated her path and saved her from surrendering to the abyss that beckoned. For it was their laughter, their innocent eyes mirroring her own, that breathed life into her peculiar spirit.

Yet, as the cycles of nature unfolded and cast longer shadows, Liv, akin to a spectre haunting her own existence, envisaged a love that had eluded her. In the depths of her soul, she teetered on the precipice of losing herself, her dreams flickering like a dying candle. But the flame of maternal devotion, fierce and unwavering, sustained her. It was for her children, the treasures born from her very essence, that Liv held fast, finding solace in their presence, even as the love between her and Finn dwindled to mere fragments of remembrance. In their laughter and the purity of their embrace, she caught glimpses of hope, frail blooms scattered amidst the hardships she endured.

Thus, with each passing day, Liv clung to the segments of her spirit, discovering respite in the beauty of her children, their existence a tribute to the love she once shared with Finn. Though the bond between husband and wife had all but vanished, the eternal flame of a mother's love burned brightly, illuminating the path that lay ahead.

Deep within her heart, Liv envisioned a love that would rejoice her spirit, awaken the dormant heat of her ardour and guide her out of the labyrinthine darkness. Yet, for now, she remained anchored to her children, resolute in her role as their guiding light, embracing the bittersweet symphony of motherhood's duality, even as her own desires flickered in the concealed corners of her being.

In the twilight of Liv's twenty-first year, a delicate bud of life took root within her, bearing with it the weight of an arduous journey. The strains of previous childbirths had tested her resilience, yet this time, her enduring body appeared to yield. The pain of labor descended upon her, each contraction a tempest that ravaged her tired frame.

Within the hushed chamber, bathed in the soft glow of flickering candles, shadows danced upon the faces of anxious witnesses. The midwife, a beacon of knowledge and compassion, had exhausted every resource to alleviate Liv's suffering, but the path to birth remained shrouded in uncertainty. The baby, nestled within, defied the natural order, presenting itself feet first.

Liv's painful cries infected the room like a merciless virus, a lament of anguish and fear, as tears cascaded down her pained countenance. In the depths of despair, the spectre of mortality loomed, threatening to sever the ties that bound her to her beloved children. Crimson rivers flowed, staining the very essence of her being, and a somber conviction gripped her, as though her precious child had already embarked on a voyage to the next life without ever truly entering this one.

Grief, akin to a poison, seeped into the depths of her heart and soul, overshadowing the waning hope that clung to her spirit. Yet, through the darkness, a glimmer of resilience grew, enkindling the burning strength of her willpower.

At last, the baby's feet emerged, a beacon of advancement in the obscure depths of labour's labyrinth. The midwife implored Liv to summon every ounce of her strength, to push forward with a resolve forged in desperation. Time stretched and distorted, extending into infinity, as the struggle reached its zenith. Finally, the essence of life within Liv, intermingled with the midwife's steadfast diligence, yielded a delicate triumph. The baby emerged, a still figure cradled in the hands of destiny. The midwife, swift and determined, wove her enchantment, coaxing vitality back into the fragile vessel. Breath, a celestial hymn, whispered its return, stirring the undying embers of hope.

Cradled in blankets woven with affection and tender care, the child found solace in the arms of Greta, Finn's younger sister. Tears of gratitude streamed from Liv's eyes, carving paths of relief upon her weary cheeks. In that life altering moment, the flame of life's forceful fire was ignited anew, as the room resounded with the harmony of rejuvenation and the chorus of renewed hope.

In the realm between dreams and awakening, Liv's consciousness unfurled. The midwife, guided her back to the realm of the living, quenching her thirst with gentle sips of water and wiping away the remnants of travail. Though pain and turmoil lingered in the chambers of her memory, a resilient smile graced Liv's lips as she beheld her newborn daughter.

Days wove themselves into weeks, and with the passage of time, Liv's strength returned gradually, the sparks of her vitality glowing with a tempered brilliance. Yet, as the seasons transformed, the realization descended upon her like a whispered secret — the possibility of conceiving new life had been irrevocably stolen away.

The baby, a seraphic embodiment of promise and resilience, nestled within the cradle of Liv's arms. Gunn, a name chosen with tenderness and hope, became the centrepiece of a love that surpassed all else in life. Guided by maternal instinct and fortified by the support of her devoted companion, Liv nurtured the burgeoning spirit with tenderness and devotion.

Together, they initiated a concurrent adventure of growth and revelation, where the sinfonia of love unfolded in every gentle touch and whispered lullaby. Amidst the rustic reality of farm life, Liv's heart found peace in the blessings bestowed upon her. She relinquished the ache of lost dreams, for she cradled in her arms the precious gifts of five beloved souls. Time, akin to an ardent lover, slipped through their fingers, bearing them along the currents of seasons. Yet, even as Liv embraced the simplicity of her existence, the dormant embers of longing and yearning resisted being extinguished. They whispered with a gentle persistence, tattooed into every corner her being. Dreams of love's ardour and the allure of untamed adventures beckoned to her, though their fires flickered dimly beneath the weight of resignation.

Life in the countryside flowed in an enchanting choreography, a mixture of daily rituals and ties that bound kinship. Finn, an unyielding statue hewn from complacency, remained impervious to the depths of Liv's yearnings. In the quiet hours, her heart ached for a love that transcended duty's chains and obligation's grasp, seeking a torch that could awaken the resting zeal nestled within her very soul.

In fleeting moments of audacious bravery, Liv dared to raise her voice, unveiling the whispered secrets of her heart to Finn. Alas, his response came as an icy gust of disapproval, casting a shadow upon her cherished hopes. He denounced her yearnings as impure, dismissing her desires as unsuitable. Perplexed, Liv questioned the teachings of their faith, for had they not extolled the sanctity of love within the sacred bonds of wedlock? How could the yearning for her spouse's affection be stained with sin?

Her spirit, wounded yet unyielding, clung tenaciously to the twinkling glimmer of hope. Deep within her core, she held steadfast to the transformative power of love, yearning for the day when Finn would unlock the depths of his heart and shower upon her the love, she so ardently craved. For Liv comprehended that genuine bliss lay nestled within an embrace that surpassed mere duty, where ardour and gentleness merged in a timeless waltz of intertwined souls. As the ruthless shadow of time claimed days, slowly stealing hours, bringing her life closer to death, Liv, akin to a solitary wanderer, found herself surrendering the tendrils of hope that once enlaced her heart. The flames of yearning and dreams of fervent passion and unconditional love flickered, waning against the ceaseless currents of her reality. Yet, within the depths of her essence, a whispering fragment of faith endured—a gleam that adamantly refused to be extinguished.

Her love for her offspring, those precious spirits birthed from her very essence, became the radiant beacon that illuminated her path. They transformed into steadfast anchors, grounding her to the realm of the living, infusing her spirit with undeniable strength that defied the weight of unfulfilled aspirations. With each tender embrace, with every ripple of laughter that resounded through the corridors of their home, Liv's heart blossomed with a courage bestowed by maternal devotion.

In the resplendent gleam of their innocent gazes, she discovered the audacity to tread the labyrinthine passages of her existence. They epitomized resilience, a confirmation of her enduring love, and in their presence, Liv found strength and a newfound sense of purpose. Through nights devoid of sleep and days brimming with tireless toil, she nurtured their growth and guarded their innocence, building a universe with love and devotion.

Yet, beneath the surface, the yearning persisted—a wild flame that danced defiantly within her soul. It whispered tales of impassioned embraces, of a love that surmounted the confines of her plain life. Liv clung to the hopeful seeds of her dreams, believing that one day fate would conspire to uncover the myriad of unconstrained affection that eluded her grasp.

Though the world around her lay cloaked in the shadows of resignation, Liv clasped onto her hope with the fervour of an ardent believer. She understood that within the endless space of existence, the realms of possibility were boundless. Thus, in the tranquil moments of solitude, she would cast her gaze heavenward, allowing her yearning to entwine with the celestial mysteries, trusting that destiny's hand would guide her toward the shores of uncharted ardor.

Deep within her essence, a wondrous transformation began. With every gentle inhale, Liv grew braver, her very soul flourishing with sanguine hope. In the recesses of a mother's affection, she unearthed her own reservoir of courage, unyielding fortitude, and indomitable strength. Day by day, she relinquished the burden of desolation, adorning herself instead with the armour of faith and optimistic perseverance, traversing life's labyrinthine paths with a heart resolute.

For Liv understood that as long as the vigorous sparks of yearning danced within her, she would stride upon the hallowed realms of reverie, embracing the burning fire of her existence and treasuring the immeasurable love she bestowed upon her cherished offspring.

CHAPTER 2

As the sands of time trickled through the hourglass, the years spun a tale of transformation and parting. One by one, Liv's sons embarked on their own quests, lured by distant horizons and urban allure. They explored new paths, etching their destinies upon the labyrinthine streets of city life. The empty spaces reverberated with their absence, a poignant reminder of the passage of fleeting moments.

Yet, amid the footprints of their departed footfalls, there remained a diamond of hope, a cherished treasure that danced within the walls of their homestead abode. It was Gunn, Liv's daughter, who lingered amidst the familiar ground of their shared existence. Within the depths of Liv's heart, a triumph of adoration played, resonating with the rise and fall of a connection that transcended earthly realms.

Gunn, akin to a radiant star gracing the midnight sky, bestowed upon Liv's world an effervescent luminescence. In the depths of their bond, words fell short, incapable of capturing the essence of their profound union. It was a celestial melody that whispered secrets of love, inscribing itself upon their souls in a language comprehended solely by kindred spirits.

Through tender caresses and unspoken verses, Liv and Gunn danced within the sphere of profound understanding, their hearts intertwined in a harmonious embrace. In Gunn, Liv discovered a mirror reflecting her deepest aspirations, dreams, and unuttered longings. Their spirits intermingled, bound by a predestined thread that surpassed the boundaries of comprehension.

As the seasons gracefully turned their pages upon the stage of their lives, Liv found immense joy and fulfilment in the presence of her beloved daughter. Together, they revelled in the abundance of shared memories, painting the canvas of their days with tints of laughter, tears, and unspoken gestures of love. Their connection surpassed the transient nature of time, as if their souls had traversed countless lifetimes side by side, entwined in an eternal dance.

Liv cherished all her children with a boundless intensity, yet it was Gunn who stirred the deepest currents within her being. In the depths of their intertwined existence, they unearthed a love that transcended earthly confines, a love that whispered of the infinite. For within Gunn's tender gaze, Liv caught a fleeting glimpse of her own spiritual essence, and in her daughter's presence, she discovered the quintessence of her own existence.

Within the deep foundation of their bond, Liv found hope, purpose, and a reaffirmation of a love that defied the constraints of mortality. They were kindred spirits, perpetually entwined in life's theatrical act, forever intermingled in a love that murmured echoes of eternity.

As the slumber loosened its gentle grip, Liv unfurled her graceful limbs, greeting the caress of a cool zephyr upon her countenance. She cast her gaze upon her home, a chamber adorned with bespoke furnishings and artistry meticulously woven by her nimble hands. She had adorned her room with tapestries and intricately embroidered fabrics, each thread carrying a fragment of her creative essence. A nascent dawn beckoned, heralding the arrival of another challenging day, awaiting her diligent labour. Clad in simplicity, Liv enveloped herself in a plain dress, a garment that whispered of humility and grace. With each tender strand that enclosed her form, she embodied the timeless elegance of a life devoted to nurturing and toiling in harmonious accord with nature's interplay. In the stillness of her preparations, Liv's musings wandered like a gentle brook, meandering through the fertile landscapes of her thoughts. With every delicate stitch and tender tie, her heart overflowed with anticipation for the day that lay before her.

Her footsteps, as silent as murmured prayers, guided her to the stable, to the sentient souls whose presence illuminated her days. There, in the security of the barn, Liv would tend to their needs, embracing the sacred obligation of nurturing their spirits and safeguarding their well-being. With hands that bore the imprints of both labour and compassion, she would nourish the bond between caretaker and creature, an ageless connection forged in the fires of empathy and responsibility.

As the sun bestowed its benevolent caress upon the earth, Liv's path would lead her to the rustic coop, where the feathered poultries awaited her gentle ministrations. She would scatter their world with golden kernels of sustenance, their grateful clucks resonating as a hymn of appreciation for the nourishment bestowed upon them. With each morsel she shared, a pattern of interdependence would emerge, painting a portrait of harmony between guardian and feathered ward.

Guided by the rhythm of nature's breath, Liv's hands would find tranquillity in the peaceful calmness of the cows, their majestic presence radiating serenity. With practiced grace, she would coax life's elixir from their benevolent udders, the symphony of their milk filling the pails with sustenance and nourishment. In this intimate exchange, a profound bond would be forged as she expressed her gratitude for the bountiful gifts of sustenance, they selflessly bestowed.

And when the earthly chores were fulfilled, Liv would venture into the enchanting hold of the forest's verdant mystery. There, amidst the emerald canopy, she would embark on a devoted pilgrimage, seeking the wisdom of ancient herbs that whispered secrets to those who listened with reverence. With brisk fingers, she would pluck the leaves and petals that held the essence of healing and knowledge, a demonstration of the indescribable wisdom that nature tenderly share with those who seek.

Within this blend of daily rituals and habitual duties, Liv found herself intertwined within the essence of the forest's beating heart. Her modest dress and apron became emblems of her devotion as she danced in harmony with the circle of life. With each act of respect and every nurturing touch, she engraved her mark upon the world, imprinting the narrative of her purpose upon the sacred canvas of time.

Within the deepest corners of Liv's heart, the forest held a cherished cornerstone, an oasis of solace where her spirit sought refuge amidst the verdant magic. Beneath the ethereal canopy, dappled sunlight wove intricate patterns upon the forest floor, painting a mosaic of whispered enchantment. It was within this seductive realm that she communed with nature's tender melodies, where tranquility enfolded her like a soft, mossy shawl.

The enchantment of herbs and their mystical alchemy beckoned Liv, a flame kindled by the skilful hand of her own mother, whose wisdom had traversed generations. Together, they had moulded a monument of knowledge and reverence, unveiling the secrets of the healing arts. With each step, she became the guardian of nature's apothecary, a messenger between the earthly realm and the ethereal domain of remedies.

In the heart of the forest, where the rustling leaves whispered ancestral lullabies, Liv began her exploration. Her agile fingers danced upon the delicate foliage, tracing the veins that carried the life force of ancient wisdom. With veneration, she plucked the leaves and petals, unveiling the fragrant masterpiece of nature's medicine cabinet, each one a precious chest of healing potency and spiritual resonance.

Within the depths of her soul, Liv cherished the antediluvian covenant between plant and human, a profound connection that crossed over time and space. With every inhalation, she absorbed the forest's curative breath, as if the very air whispered tales of restoration and rejuvenation. The vibrant chromaticities of leaves and blossoms mirrored the kaleidoscope of emotions within her, offering solace and serenity amidst the tumultuous journey of life.

As she communed with nature's abundance, Liv's heart swelled with gratitude, paying homage to the wisdom imparted by her mother's guiding touch. It was an honoured inheritance, a symbol of the intergenerational interconnectedness, a reminder that love and wisdom are timeless gifts passed down through the maternal lineage.

In the heart of the forest, Liv discovered refuge from the clamour of the world, surrendering to the tranquil whispers that resonated in every rustle and sigh. And as her gait graced the enchanted paths, her spirit soared on the wings of ancient wisdom, embracing the healing power of herbs with reverence and devotion. For within this realm of verdant abundance, she unearthed not only the potency of nature's remedies but also the profound healing that took place when one's heart harmonized with the melodies of the earth.

Within the uncompromising chambers of the church, the disapproval of the priest cast its shadow upon Liv's cherished pursuit, like an autumnal gust that sought to extinguish the flame of her passion. His stern gaze, shrouded in sanctimony, failed to fathom the depth of her devotion, and in his judgment, he endeavoured to confine the expansiveness of her spirit.

Yet, amidst the echoing whispers of ecclesiastical piety, Liv found support in the approval of her husband's acceptance. Finn recognized the radiance of her inner flame; he remained true in his unwavering support. He embraced the kaleidoscope of her being, where her avocation was not merely a pastime but an affirmation to the boundless capacity of the human heart to seek solace and purpose in unconventional realms.

In the ornate balance between faith and individuality, Liv's journey veered away from the narrow corridors of religious convention. Her husband's fidelity served as an anchor, steadying her amidst the tumultuous winds of societal expectations. With him, she discovered the liberty to express the complexity of her soul, undeterred by the disapproval that sought to confine her spirit.

Within their marriage Liv's passion for herbs blossomed like a rare and vibrant flower, embraced by Finn's approbation and nurtured by the gentle rain of empathy. In this acceptance, her pursuit advanced, flourishing in defiant brilliance.

Amidst the dissonance of judgment and acceptance, Liv's heart remained a safe space of cherished authenticity. Deep within her, she held the profound realization that societal censure could not extinguish the transformative power of her chosen path. For within her, a flame blazed, resplendent and unwavering, illuminating the depths of her being, a symbol of the sacred realm forged by reverence, where her husband's unswerving acceptance embraced the entirety of her essence.

In the depths of Liv's being resided an insatiable fascination, ignited by the legends and tales whispered by the memories of time. These ethereal murmurs beckoned her toward the enigmatic forest and the nearby lake, where the spirit of the Swedish waters, Näcken, was said to dwell. A figure of myth and mystery, Näcken's reputation, akin to the veiled depths of the lake, swathed in trepidation and awe.

Liv, although her path had never intersected with that of Näcken, found herself entwined in the myriad of legends told by the villagers, whose words painted him as a perilous force of nature. They spoke of his allure, his enchanting melodies that ensnared unsuspecting souls, and the danger concealed within his realm. Yet, beneath the surface of their admonitions, Liv sensed a yearning, un undying spark of curiosity that whispered tales of audacity and enchantment in her heart.

In her reveries, Liv often found herself gazing upon the tranquil lake, its mirrored surface reflecting the enigmas that gracefully danced upon its liquid canvas. Her thoughts wandered, weaving a narrative of what it would be like to encounter Näcken, to stand upon the precipice where reality and the supernatural entwined. She longed to witness the magic he possessed, to delve into the enigma of his presence, and to take part in the ethereal melodies that flowed from his fingertips.

For Liv, Näcken symbolized more than mere folklore; he embodied the threshold where fear and fascination converged, where danger and beauty entwined in a mysterious balance. It was a beckoning that resonated deeply within her, awakening a hungry curiosity that yearned to unravel the secrets whispered by ancient trees and reflected in the depths of the lake. She sought not only to witness Näcken's enchantment but to fathom the essence of his existence, to catch a glimpse of the interplay between light and shadow that sashayed along the spectrum of his being.

In the depths of her heart's yearning, Liv dared to imagine dreams of an encounter, an erotic moment where Näcken's seductive essence would envelop her mortal being. She longed to witness the sublime enchantment that danced within his eyes, to feel the delicate tendrils of his bewitching melodies caress her very soul and his strong hands ignite her passionate fantasy. It was an erotic dream that transcended caution, for deep within her, she sensed that Näcken held the key to unlock the gates of wonder and illuminate the veiled realms that lay hidden beneath the surface of the world.

With every breath that carried her hopes and aspirations, Liv's spirit teetered on the edge of possibility, her heart open to the enigmatic mysteries held within the grip of the forest and the lake. For within her, a flame burned, fuelled by the desire to give in to a journey where the ordinary intertwined with the extraordinary, where mortal and ethereal danced in harmony, and where the encounter with Näcken would expose a chapter of existence infused with magic and profound transformation.

Amidst the ebony depths of time's tortuous creation, Liv's eyes glimpsed the elusive Skogsrået, a mystical entity draped in enigma. With each ethereal encounter, the villagers' hearts quivered in the grip of fear, for Skogsrået's presence carried the weight of ancient legends and whispered secrets. The priest, cloaked in his mantle of authority, and his faithful entourage started an inexorable quest to capture the elusive spirit, their pursuit spanning decades like a fleeting dance with destiny.

In the hidden recesses of Liv's memories, fragments of unworldly beauty intertwined with primal trepidation, painting a portrait of Skogsrået's irresistible magnetism and the terror it invoked. The villagers, bound by the chains of superstition, sought solace in the shelter of their trembling hearts, wary of the enigmatic truths that the creature held. Whispers of Skogsrået's mischievous enchantments echoed through generations, birthing cautionary tales that whispered through moonlit nights and rustled within the leaves. Yet, amidst the currents of fear and the relentless chase, Liv's soul remained suspended in the realm of curiosity and wonder. Her gaze, untouched by trepidation, beheld the transformative potential that lay within the gift of Skogsrået's spirit. In its shadowed countenance, she sensed a muse of forbidden knowledge, a conduit to realms where the veil between reality and fantasy shimmered, tempting intrepid souls to unravel the hidden truths that eluded mortal comprehension.

The priest, accompanied by his fervent seekers, carved a path paved with obsessed resolve and possessed determination, driven by an ardent desire to capture the essence of Skogsrået. Decades melded into an unending crusade, their pursuit an embodiment of both mania and reverence, their hearts ablaze with the mission of discovering secrets that transcended the moral boundaries of the church.

In this elaborate dance between seekers and the sought, between fear and fascination, Skogsrået emerged as a symbol of liberation from the confines of the mortal realm. Her elusiveness served as a gentle reminder of the intrinsic mysteries that intertwine with existence, beckoning souls to transcend the boundaries of the known and embrace the realms of the arcane. For Liv, the tales of Skogsrået ignited a flicker of illumination within her, a yearning to venture into liminal spaces where the interplay of light and shadow birthed the transformative enchantment of revelation.

Hence, as the eons spun their tales, Liv's spirit blossomed like an oasis of boundless curiosity amid the trembling hearts of the villagers. Within her, Skogsrået's presence ignited a mixture of emotions, blending awe and trepidation into a profound orchestration of existence. And amidst the fading echoes of the priest's futile hunt, Liv's soul remained a beacon of contemplation, welcoming the ineffable allure of the Skogsrået's essence, yearning to unravel the veiled wisdom that shimmered within her mesmerizing eyes.

Within the sanctuary of the priest's convictions, Näcken and Skogsrået were cast as ethereal beings cloaked in darkness, their genesis intertwined with the origin of fallen angels and malevolent demons. The priest, his voice resounding with fervour, spun tales of malice and damnation, cautioning against the seductive presence of these entities. His words, akin to the toll of a somber distant bell, reverberated in Liv's ears, attempting to bind her spirit with chains of fear.

Yet, amidst the tendrils of caution that sought to ensnare her, Liv's heart remained a steadfast rock of profound insight. She, with eyes that saw beyond ecclesiastical ideals, grasped the truth that eluded the priest's impassioned proclamations. Skogsrået, in the depths of its mysterious existence, was not a harbinger of evil, but a guardian spirit sprung from the very heart of the forest itself. A sentinel of whispers, she manifested the sacred duty of preserving the woodland's secrets, her gentle presence reserving her wrath solely for those harbouring ill intentions against the sanctity of her realm.

Like the harmonious interplay of sunlight through ancient branches, Liv's understanding illuminated her path through the labyrinthine maze of beliefs. She acknowledged the duality that resided within the narratives spun by the priest, recognizing the existence of shadows while refusing to let them overshadow the radiance of truth. For within her soul, a symphony of compassion and reverence played, tuning her heart to the rhythm of nature's wisdom, unveiling the symbiotic dance between Skogsrået and the domain she vowed to safeguard.

With each step that carried Liv deeper into the forest's realm, she walked unburdened by the specter of fear. Her spirit resonated with the whispers carried by the murmuring greenery, attuned to the ancient hymns sung by the woodland's guardian. She knew that the essence of Skogsrået was linked with the composition of harmony, her divine presence echoing the composition of life that pulsed through every corner of the forest's soul.

In the unspoken union of Liv's understanding and the guardian of the woods, a pact of reciprocity was forged. She, with her gentle intentions and reverent footsteps, traversed the forest as a humble guest, an emissary of harmony and communion. Skogsrået, recognizing Liv's pure intent, accepted her presence, allowing her to bear witness to the hidden wonders that blossomed beneath the verdant canopy. For Liv, the forest transformed into a cathedral of hidden truths, a world where the divine dance between protector and protected grew fiercely, and where the symbiotic bond between guardian and guardianess bloomed in resplendent unity.

Thus, as Liv ventured deeper into the heart of the forest, her steps uttered the language of trust and understanding. With every inhalation of the forest's magical breath, she honoured the unspoken covenant between Skogsrået and her chosen protector. For within Liv, a profound knowing nestled, guiding her through the labyrinthine paths of beliefs, unmasking the luminescent truth that only those with harmful intentions should fear.

Whispers of enchantment, carried upon magical breezes, embraced Näcken's haunting melodies, tales spun with a touch of melancholy and longing. The fabled lake stood as a portal to a realm tinged with tragedy, where young hearts, lured by Näcken's captivating allure, surrendered to its depths, vanishing from the world above. Liv, her spirit adorned by the graceful hand of time, treaded cautiously in the lake's vicinity, no longer a youthful maiden but wise to the enigmatic ways of the ethereal spirit.

Within her heart, a belief blossomed like a mysterious flower, urging her to ward off Näcken's shadowed intentions. Clad in a protective shroud of silver, woven by whispered wisdom and intuition, Liv embraced the radiant mantle, thought to fend off the nefarious charms that resided within Näcken's mesmerizing melodies. With each step she took, her distance from the lake's edge embodied the weight of wisdom, evidence of her understanding that the passage of time had woven a shield around her soul, rendering her immune to the spirit's enchanting call.

When the echoes of their vows still lingered in the air, Finn had unveiled a web of caution, revealing the myriad perils that adorned the depths of the forest. The tale of predatory creatures and vengeful spirits resonated through their bond, intertwining with their vows of love and commitment. Liv, skilled in the art of the hunt, carried within her the teachings of her father, etched upon her spirit like ancient wisdom's sacred glyphs. In his parting, her father had bequeathed to her his cherished rifle, a talisman of survival, a testament to her resilience in the face of adversity.

Yet, within the ancient dance between predator and prey, Liv's spirit discovered harmony. The echo of her father's teachings reverberated not as a call to dominion, but as a covenant of respect. The rifle, an emblem of empowerment, embodied the essence of balance and stewardship. It became a conduit through which she channelled her reverence for life, a means to secure her survival while safeguarding the sanctity of the animal realm.

Her skilled aim, honed through countless hours of dedication, carried the essence of compassion within its trajectory. Liv, with her heart attuned to the pulsating rhythms of nature, would never take more than was needed. In each pursuit, her reverence for the cycle of life resounded, an offering of gratitude to the creatures that shared their existence with her. Her deft touch and empathetic spirit became a display of the complex balance of harmony and symbiosis, where the dance between predator and prey wove together admiration and understanding.

Within the essence of Liv, a sonata of survival and compassion intertwined. The tales of Näcken and the forest's perils played like melodies upon the strings of her consciousness, harmonizing with her innate comprehension of the interconnection among all beings. In her footsteps, the wisdom of experience grew deep, guided by the gentle pulse of respect and the realization that true mastery lay not in conquest, but in the delicate equilibrium between necessity and veneration.

As Liv ventured through the gateway where survival and symbiosis intertwined, her essence graced the forest with strokes of tender compassion. The spirits of the land, the creatures that graced its hallowed expanse, bore witness to the sanctity that radiated from her very being. For within her, the delicate play of existence flourished, where the symphony of survival and reverence intertwined, a hushed ode to the eternal connection between the human soul and the resplendent embodiment of nature's grandeur.

CHAPTER 3

Surrounded by dawn's radiant glow, Liv wandered the path that led her to her rustic home, her soul intertwined with the pulsing rhythms of the awakening world. Amidst the harmonious orchestra of emergence, her eyes beheld Finn, tending to the majestic creatures that bridged the divide between reality and the realm of dreams. In his presence, Liv discerned the morality coursing through his veins, yet a shadow of melancholy haunted their love, dimming its once-vibrant flame.

Within the hidden chambers of her being, Liv harboured the bitter-sweet awareness that time's tender course had transformed the essence of their love. The colours that once blossomed in resplendent unity now whispered with faded echoes, a graveyard of forgotten vows and unspoken yearnings. The moments of their shared existence had shaped a landscape where contentment lingered like a nostalgic sigh, and Liv, yearned for the fragments that haunted her memory.

Yet, amidst the shadows that danced upon her longing, Liv summoned the fortitude to silence the waves of discontent that threatened to consume her. She clutched at the threads of gratitude, engraving them into the foundation of her thoughts, reminding herself that the life she lived on the farm held blessings to be treasured. Clad in the denial of her dreams and wishes, she sought solace in the embrace of duty, for within the realm of her daily toil resided a semblance of fulfillment she dared not overlook.

As she tended to the creatures that blessed their abode, a tender ache of yearning resonated within the corners of her heart. It sang the melody of untamed dreams, of uncharted paths beckoning her spirit toward the allure of adventure and the promise of love's true awakening. Though she had never savored the sweet elixir of such passions, their enticement whispered seductively, leaving breadcrumbs of possibility into the core of her existence.

But the gentle reverie was shattered by the intrusion of reality. Finn, the guardian of her waking hours, stirred her from the enchantment of her daydreams. His presence, a sturdy anchor to the mundane world, served as a heartfelt reminder of the delicate equilibrium she maintained between yearning and acceptance. With a fleeting glance, Liv locked away the ephemeral fantasies that danced within her, refocusing her gaze upon the path that stretched ahead, adorned with the fragments of the life she had chosen.

Liv, with unshakable determination, sought to hide her countenance in a masquerade of bliss and satisfaction, though tempestuous sentiments laid siege to her innermost being. As dawn enshrouded the world in its tender embrace, moments before surrendering to slumber's gentle clasp, she summoned the audacity to enthral Finn once more, unwilling to yield to a bond devoid of ardour and tenderness. A glimmer of hope ignited within her heart, yearning for the convergence of their souls once more.

With each step, Liv navigated the sublime waltz between the yearnings nestled within her heart and the acceptance of her chosen path. And as the sun ascended to its zenith, the farm stirred with fervour, for summer had sprinkled its beauty upon the land. Unspoken burdens etched upon Finn's visage, his words danced as somber refrains carried by the gentle whispers of his gaze.

"The season demands much from us. The hay must be gathered ere autumn's rains arrive," he spoke, his voice a solemn melody graced by the winds of understanding.

"Indeed, the creatures hunger and the crops beckon for care," Liv replied, her words embracing the symphony of duty and responsibility.

"True, and the fence on the northern pasture needs tending, for the cows wander astray," Finn continued.

"Svante, perhaps, can lend his skill with hammer and nails," Liv suggested, her tranquil gaze traversing the sacred expanse of their domain, finding solace in the unity of their shared purpose.

"It is a fine idea. We must also prepare to preserve our bountiful harvest, that we may endure the winter's embrace," Finn confessed, concern veiling his countenance like the delicate veil of falling snow, hiding whispers of uncertainties within its spirit.

"I know. Soon we shall gather the berries and make jam. Your mother implores me to join her in this endeavour," Liv's voice quivered, a fragile hope blossoming within her words.

"A wise notion. We may sell our creations at the town's market," Finn acknowledged.

"Yes, that would be delightful. And perchance, we could steal away to the tranquil shores of the lake, if only for a day," Liv's gaze, gentle as the caress of moonlight, lingered upon her beloved, her eyes kindling the fires of understanding and unspoken desires.

"I fear our time may be scarce for such pleasures. The weight of labour presses upon us," Finn dissolved into introspection's labyrinth, his presence engulfed by the enigmatic tapestry of contemplation.

"But, Finn, we must pause and catch our breath. Our toil cannot consume every moment. We, too, deserve the joys of summer, for it has been too long since we basked in the radiance of our unity," Liv's voice trembled like a hopeful breeze, adorned in the vestments of optimism.

"I comprehend, Liv. Yet, the farm is our lifeblood. We must ensure our tasks find completion," Finn's fidelity resonated through his unwavering words, loyalty's melody swelling within their steadfast cadence.

"I understand, but sometimes it seems our existence is nothing but hard work. We must find moments of respite together," Liv pleaded.

"I know, Liv, and I apologize. The time for such solace shall come when our labours relent," Finn embarked on his path, a solitary wanderer captivated by the allure of duty's embrace, each step a poetic rhythm marking the beginning of his sacred tasks.

"I hope so, Finn. I really do." Before proceeding, Liv inhaled deeply, allowing the air to fill her lungs and infuse her very being with renewed composure. In that breath, one could perceive the gathering of strength and determination, as she prepared herself for what lay ahead. "I struggle to find the words, but...I sense a waning of your affection for me."

Finn's countenance softened as he leaned closer. "Liv, you know my care for you runs deep. We have traversed a long journey together, tending to our family and nurturing our land. We simply lack the luxury of time for what you deem as love. Such desires belong to the young, to those untainted by the harsh realities of existence. Our life is prosperous, why does it not satiate your soul?" A flicker of irritation danced fleetingly across Finn's face, betraying his frustration as the subject was broached once again. It manifested in the subtle tightening of his features, a transient shadow that momentarily eclipsed his countenance. In that instant, the weight of repetition became tangible, a reminder of the weariness accompanying the revisiting of this topic. Though he endeavoured to veil his vexation, the underlying exasperation could not be wholly concealed. It offered a fleeting glimpse into his inner landscape, where patience grew thin and the yearning for fresh discourse prevailed.

A wellspring of tears brimmed in Liv's eyes, threatening to spill forth, as she vehemently shook her head. The unshed droplets shimmered like fragile dew, reflecting the anguish resonating deep within her soul. It was a significant moment, where words seemed inadequate to convey the depth of her sentiments. The sorrow etched upon her visage bore the weight of unspoken anguish, evoking profound empathy in those who bore witness. In her tearful gaze and the gentle motion of her head, a multitude of untold tales unfurled, unveiling the turmoil that tugged at her heartstrings. "Yet I yearn for love, Finn. I yearn for the days of yore, when our hearts were ablaze with love I feel as though we merely tread the path of routine now, and it wounds me to my core."

A gentle breeze stirred the tendrils of Finn's tired soul, carrying with it the weight of weariness that had settled upon his shoulders. As though burdened by the immense expanse of existence, his hand traversed the tousled terrain of his hair, caught in a dance of frustration and contemplation. Within the elaborate threads, a reflection of his tangled thoughts emerged, a web of complexity mirroring the disarray within. In that fleeting instant, a tempest of emotions swirled, and his dishevelled locks bore witness to the chaos of his inner turmoil. It was a gesture seeking solace, a feeble attempt to find clarity amidst the labyrinthine maze of his mind. Through the sigh and the gentle caress of his hair, Finn unveiled a vulnerability, an unspoken plea for respite from the trials that beset his path. "Liv, I comprehend your perspective. Yet, we have built a life together, with obligations we must honour. It is not always simple, but we persist."

Lifting her gaze to meet Finn's, Liv's eyes transformed into windows to her soul, silently imploring understanding and empathy. Within their depths, an explosion of emotions danced —a delicate fusion of vulnerability, yearning, and an insatiable thirst for connection. Her unvoiced supplication tugged at heartstrings, resonating with an urgency that knew no bounds. In that moment of wordless entreaty, Liv beseeched Finn to truly perceive her, to ponder the depths of her unspoken sentiments, and to respond with the compassion and warmth she so fervently craved. "Yet, do you not believe we can also nurture our love? It holds significance for me, Finn. I yearn not to traverse this existence feeling uncherished and desolate."

Finn's gaze lingered upon Liv, his eyes tracing the contours of her countenance, capturing the very essence of her presence in that fleeting juncture. Silence spun its delicate threads between them, filled with anticipation, as he seized a moment to collect his thoughts, allowing the weight of his words to take form. "I hear your words, Liv. I shall strive to be more attuned to your emotions. Yet, I cannot promise an immediate transformation. The farm demands much from us, as does our family."

A subtle nod escaped Liv, a small gesture that bore a flicker of hope, however feeble. In that understated motion, a glimmer of confusion pirouetted within her, casting a shadow upon her weary heart. "I understand, Finn. I yearn for the day when our paths converge once more."

Across the expansive tableau of the field, Finn's hand reached out, as if traversing the realms of distance, to converge with Liv's in a touch of tenderness. Their fingers delicately intertwined, birthing a connection forged through decades. "We shall endure, my dear Liv. I give you my solemn word." However, the hollow echoes of Finn's promise failed to find solace within Liv's embrace. They reverberated through the corridors of her consciousness, the remnants of assurances unfulfilled. The relentless absence of moments dedicated to her own aspirations and desires cast an ominous shadow of doubt upon her longing heart. Within the depths of her being, a tempest brewed, a swirling maelstrom of fury and discontent, its tempestuous winds threatening to unleash the pent-up torrent of her emotions.

In the tender aftermath of Finn's departure, Liv's hushed yearning whispered delicately on the breeze, a fragile entreaty adorned with unspoken depths. Her gaze, enraptured by the sprawling vista of their cherished farm, drank in the graceful essence of summer, its fair touch caressing her lungs with gentle grace.

Imbued with purpose's call, Liv headed toward the verdant sanctuary of the vegetable garden. There, amidst the fertile soil, the seeds of hope for the forthcoming season awaited their tender embrace.

As Liv's footsteps danced to the rhythm of the earth's heartbeat, she was greeted by Greta's genuine smile, radiant as sunlight's warm embrace. In that fleeting moment, their spirits entwined, surrendering themselves to the laborious task that beckoned,

Their voices, harmonizing like mythical sirens, sung melodies that transcended the earthly realm, infusing their toil with the elixir of joy. With every passing hour, the sheen of sweat adorned their brows, an offering of tireless effort and unwavering devotion to the task at hand.

Since the destined day when Liv crossed the threshold of the rustic abode, intertwining her life with the sacred union of Greta's brother, Finn, an unbreakable bond of camaraderie flourished betwixt the souls of Liv and Greta. Time, like the patient gardener tending to its blossoms, nurtured their friendship with skilful hands. Diligent as the sun-soaked fields they toiled upon, these kindred spirits laboured side by side, their hands weathered yet undeterred, their spirits attuned to the same rhythm of perseverance.

Liv, with a heart brimming with reverence, beheld the indomitable spirit that resided within Greta's being, a fortitude that shimmered like a rare gem amid the tempestuous currents of life. In the face of tribulations that cast their shadows upon her path, Greta emerged as a beacon of tenacity, an embodiment of strength that inspired Liv's own aspirations. With each shared hardship, they embraced the solace of understanding, their unspoken language echoing in the silent spaces of their souls.

In the wake of a desolate battlefield that swallowed Greta's beloved husband, a valiant soul sacrificed to the ravages of war, the weight of bereavement cloaked her like a shroud, casting shadows that danced in somber rhythms. Alone she stood, entrusted with the solemn duty of nurturing their children, a tribute to her solitary strength amidst the ceaseless tides of adversity. Yet, amidst the echoes of her anguish, Liv emerged as a trustworthy guardian, extending her benevolent hand to guide and nurture the innocent hearts left in Greta's care.

In the realm of their sisterly bond, forged in the crucible of shared tribulations, these kindred spirits became pillars of solace for one another. As the weight of Greta's responsibilities pressed upon her weary frame, Liv, a harbinger of compassion, was the steadfast presence that soothed the furrowed lines etched upon her countenance. With hands entwined, they traversed the labyrinthine corridors of life, finding solace in the symphony of whispered confidences and unspoken support.

In the core of their devotion, the burdens of a world too heavy to bear alone were gently carried upon the shoulders of their intertwined souls. Through good and bad days, their bond remained unyielding, like a steadfast lighthouse piercing through the fog of desolation. In the depths of Greta's weary gaze, Liv beheld the reflection of a shattered spirit, adrift amidst the tempestuous sea of grief. Bereft of solace, she sat in solitude, her countenance etched with a storm of tears that cascaded like silent rivers of anguish. The weight of her sorrow, suffused the atmosphere, transforming the very molecules into somber notes that harmonized with the ache of her soul.

With an empathetic knowing, as ancient as the constellations that adorned the heavens, Liv understood the depths of love that had intertwined Greta's heart with her departed husband's. She, too, had witnessed the divine symbiosis of their affection, a love story born out of deep devotion, now shattered into fractured fragments. The threads of empathy that bound their spirits in sisterhood absorbed the sorrow that hung like a mist, bridging the chasm between their souls.

"I'm so sorry for your loss, Greta," Her footsteps resonated with a rhythmic cadence, a tender symphony in sync with the melody of her caring heart. "I can't even imagine what you're going through."

"Thank you, Liv. It's been really hard. I just can't believe he's gone." With a heart tormented by anguish and sorrow, Greta succumbed to the depths of her emotions, tears cascading like a torrential downpour from her glistening eyes. Each teardrop bore the weight of a thousand unspoken pains, painting a portrait of her shattered soul. The echoes of her cries reverberated through the universe, as if pleading for solace, for an embrace that could mend the fragments of her wounded spirit.

"I understand, for life's scales often tip unjustly," whispered Liv, her countenance adorned with a veil of melancholy that cast a soft shadow upon her features. Within the depths of her eyes, a tempest of sorrow swirled, as if the weight of the world had settled upon her delicate shoulders. Her face transformed into a living canvas, inviting empathy and compassion to offer solace in the face of life's relentless trials. "Yet, I want you to know that I am a steadfast presence in your life. I am here for you, ready to listen, no matter the hour or circumstance." With tenderness and devotion intertwined, Liv gently clasped Greta's hand, their fingers interlacing in a delicate bond of connection. In this gesture of unwavering support, she settled gracefully by Greta's side, their souls finding solace in the shared proximity of their presence.

"I am deeply moved," Greta whispered, her voice a delicate veil concealing the tempest within her heart. She summoned her inner strength, coaxing a smile to grace her lips, though it trembled like a fragile butterfly's wings. Her visage, adorned with courage's fragile armour, bore witness to the indomitable spirit that dwelled within. "The path ahead without him feels insurmountable. We were destined to weather the years together."

"Scarcely do people savour the luxury of growing old," Liv intoned, her gaze mirroring the depth of sorrow that swelled within her. Each word she spoke carried the weight of melancholic melodies, permeating the air like a haunting lament. Her eyes, windows to untold stories and unspoken desires, yearned for understanding. It was a silent plea, a craving to be seen and enveloped within a sea of empathetic understanding, as overwhelming sadness threatened to consume her very essence. "Your children, dear Greta, now rely upon your devoted care. Their need for you surpasses all else."

"You speak the truth. I must gather strength for them. Yet, the weight feels overwhelming," Greta confessed. But within the depths of her gaze, a spark of hopeful resilience ignited like a radiant beacon. The burdens of her past struggles and present trials metamorphosed into embers of determination, illuminating her eyes with an undoubted resolve. Her gaze transformed into a window to an indomitable spirit, unyielding in the face of life's trials.

"I share in your sentiment," Liv spoke softly, her voice a mixture of compassion and understanding. Her words flowed with tender kindness, offering support in times of anguish. Like a healing balm, her utterances soothed wounded souls, creating a haven for connection. Her compassionate voice pierced through the darkness, a beacon that assured others of their cherished presence within a community of unwavering support. "But fear not, for you are never alone in this journey. I shall forever stand beside you, as will our entire community. Whatever you require, I shall be there, an unwavering pillar of strength and compassion."

"Thank you, dear Liv. In your friendship, I find solace," Greta spoke softly, her touch tender as she wiped away the tears that adorned her cheeks. Each stroke of her hand carried a delicate vulnerability, leaving behind a trail of emotions etched upon her skin. Their gazes locked, intertwining like threads of understanding and shared experiences.

"Of course, dear friend. Remember, should you require anything, simply voice your need. It is natural to mourn, to feel sadness and weakness for a time. Just be wary of losing yourself in the depths of sorrow."

"I shall heed your words. Thank you for your comforting presence. Finn, when he was here, appeared discomforted by my grief."

"Finn has never been one to navigate the realm of emotions," Liv whispered softly, her voice barely audible, carried upon a melancholic breeze. Her murmurs held a depth that hinted at the intricacies of her inner world, an invitation to introspection and profound longing. In that faint utterance, her emotions became tangible, arousing curiosity and a yearning to unravel the enigma concealed within her whispers. From the recesses of memory, where Liv lingered in the tender embrace of nostalgia's gentle kiss, a canine voice ruptured the veil of her reverie, an ephemeral bark that severed the fragile threads of her past.

"The dog's bark echoes through the forest once more," Greta expressed concern. "Creatures lurk nearby. The priest spoke of Skogsrået after Sunday's mass, claiming she draws nearer to the fields, her baldness becoming more apparent."

"Fear not, for Skogsrået holds no power over you," Liv's voice flowed like a soothing melody, a gentle caress that enveloped Greta's being. "While she may lure men to their demise for trespassing, I have yet to hear a tale of harm befalling a woman under Skogsrået's influence." As Liv's words washed over Greta's receptive heart, a serene calmness settled upon her like a tranquil oasis amidst stormy seas. The weight of her fears dissipated, replaced by a sense of tranquillity and renewed hope.

"Have tidings reached your ears of your cherished twins?" Greta's voice resonated with genuine curiosity and a thirst for knowledge as she posed her question.

"No," Liv's response carried a weighty sorrow, shrouded in unspoken words that seemed to elude expression. The depths of her sadness nestled within, elusive to the outside world. Her answer held unspoken layers, whispering of a grief that transcended mere language.

In the years of Liv's maternal lineage, a poignant chapter unfolded—a tale of her youngest progenies venturing forth from the familial nest like courageous sparrows taking flight. Their destinies intertwined with the martial tempest of a bygone era. The year whispered upon the lips of time, a distant echo of 1623, when Sweden, a resolute nation ascending celestial heights, witnessed the grandeur of its own ascendance.

The kingdom found itself enmeshed in protracted conflicts, locked in a dance of strife with neighbouring powers—Denmark, Poland, and Russia. Yet, from the crucible of adversity, Sweden emerged as a triumphant phoenix, etching its victories upon the annals of history, painted upon the canvas of countless battles won.

Amidst the backdrop of a nation's ascent and the resounding harmonies of war chants, Liv, an unyielding protector, emerged as a matriarch. Her nurturing essence intricately bound with the destinies of her beloved sons, seamlessly melded into the complex composition of a land wrestling with both adversity and victory, emerging from a crucible of tumultuous eras. Within Europe's tumultuous canvas, war unfurled its wings, casting an ominous cloak that veiled the heavens. A tempest of destruction and desolation swept across the land, drenching the continent in sorrow's somber palette. Countless souls, a symphony of lives lost, danced amidst the wreckage, as cities and hamlets, once vibrant and resplendent, crumbled like fragments of shattered dreams. Amidst this symphony of sorrow, Sweden, akin to a resolute sentinel, marched forth undeterred, its brave warriors and vital provisions a steadfast offering to steadfast allies, embroiled in battles waged on myriad fronts, their resolve unyielding.

Yet, in the depths of Liv's being, amidst the sanctuary of her humble farm, the complexities of worldly politics and conflicts felt distant, muffled by the symphony of maternal fears that echoed within her. Her sons, her valiant emissaries of bravery, stirred an anguish that kept her restless under the starlit canopy of sleepless nights. Pride swelled within her breast, yet mingled with the ceaseless tides of apprehension, an ever-present spectre that haunted her waking hours. In the solitude of her thoughts, she contemplated the capricious nature of fate, her heart entwined with the uncertain thread of their existence. Would a dreaded letter, borne on sorrow's wings, bring forth the searing truth of their demise? Her weary soul oscillated between the delicate flicker of hope's glow and the engulfing shadows of despair.

Then, as if carried on a wind's breath, a letter arrived, its secrets whispered from afar. It bore the awaited touch of her sons' words, a fleeting connection amidst the colossal range of uncertainty. Liv's heart bridged the chasm of distance, thirstily drinking from the wellspring of solace that their words conveyed. The world beyond her farm, with all its tumult and splendour, momentarily dimmed, eclipsed by the precious gift of a mother's respite, cradled within the ink-stained parchment.

Dearest Mother,

May this heartfelt missive find you enveloped in tranquillity. How we yearn for the embrace of your presence and the cherished sanctuary of our humble farm. Alas, fate has led us down an unforeseen path, wherein we find ourselves immersed in the crucible of battle, defending our nation with pride. The magnitude of this responsibility is not lost upon us; it is an honour beyond measure to serve alongside our comrades-in-arms, united in purpose.

Life in the army proves arduous, demanding every ounce of our mettle. Yet, we stand resolute, determined to conquer the challenges that assail us. Amidst the trials, we hold steadfast to the memories that anchor us to home. Father's absence is keenly felt, and we hope that his days are filled with good health and fortune.

We beseech you, dear Mother, to release the tendrils of worry that entwine your soul. Know that our spirits remain unyielding, our bodies robust. Our bond as brothers serves as an unbreakable shield, strengthening us in the face of adversity. Rest assured, we shall grace the parchment once more, sharing tales of valour and perseverance.

With an abundance of affection that transcends the boundaries of ink and parchment,

Erik and Per

With a gentle grace, Greta sensed the delicate currents of Liv's emotions, like whispers on the breeze, hinting at the depths of her maternal love. The weight of unspoken worries cast a subtle shadow upon Liv's countenance, veiling the mention of her beloved sons, a sacred realm best left untouched. In the quiet spaces between their shared breaths, Greta perceived the uncharted territories of Liv's heart, where love and concern intertwined in a tender dance.

"It is time for us to retreat within," Greta whispered, her voice carrying the melody of unwavering resolve. Liv, acknowledging the significance of Greta's words, responded with a gentle nod, their unspoken agreement a testament to their unbreakable bond. In this shared understanding, their presence united, they embraced the trials and triumphs that awaited them, fortified by the unwavering support they found in each other's company.

"Let us seek solace within, for Gunn shall soon grace us with his presence," Greta spoke, her voice a soothing balm that caressed their souls, as they walked the path that led them homeward.

CHAPTER 4

On a melancholic eve, veiled in misty drapes, Liv sought joy in Gunn's beautiful smile, their weary frames seeking solace after a day of toil. Together, they perched upon the fertile earth they nurtured, gazing into the boundless horizon.

With a heartfelt breath, Gunn shared her innermost desires, "Dearest mother, my dreams beckon me. I yearn to wander to the bustling city and become a guardian of new life." Casting a cautious glance, trepidation resonating within her, she awaited her mother's response.

Liv's countenance softened, a tender smile adorning her face as she whispered, "That dream dances with grace, my dear Gunn. Your talents and compassion are boundless, and as a midwife, you shall shine. I am filled with pride, and I shall move mountains to aid your quest." With gentle caresses, she graced her daughter's hair, a touch dripping with affection. "I recall your days as a resilient child, your spirit ablaze. May your desired destiny be yours to embrace," Liv conveyed, her heart bathed in comfort and joy in her cherished daughter's presence.

Gunn nodded, acknowledging her mother's words, yet an inkling of unease clung to her as she added, "However, father wishes for me to wed a villager, a farmer. He fails to comprehend my dreams." A tinge of sorrow coloured her voice, revealing the burden she carried.

Sympathy graced Liv's visage as she regarded her daughter, her words a gentle yet unwavering current. "In times when family fail to fathom our aspirations, the true compass lies within, Gunn. A valiant woman like you shall forge her path, and soon you shall hold the reins of your own destiny."

"But my defiance will stoke father's ire," Gunn lamented, her tone tinged with frustration. Sensing her daughter's despair, Liv drew closer, seeking solace to bestow.

"He shall not harbour hatred. Allow me to converse with him. Though understanding may elude him, hatred shall not claim his heart. Your elder brothers have already carved their lives within the city walls. Perhaps we can correspond with them, and they may offer aid and shelter, or perchance, I can approach the village's revered midwife, beseeching her to accept an apprentice?" Liv proposed, her voice an infusion of hope. She refused to witness Gunn forsaking her dreams, yielding to appease her father, withering away on the rustic farmstead.

"But the farm requires my presence, burdened with unrelenting tasks, and summer's advent nears," Gunn uttered, a touch of resignation painting her words.

"Here, my child, you are not enchained," Liv ardently proclaimed, her unwavering gaze upon her daughter. "Your path shall be unbound, and I shall be your staunch ally, battling for your dreams. We shall thrive, even in your absence. Worry not, dear one. Fabrications to retain you shall not impede your flight. Follow your heart, forsaking not your desires to placate your father. Though stern, his hold cannot determine your fate."

"I merely yearn to elicit his pride," Gunn confided, her gaze averted. "He ardently desires a union with a villager in close quarters."

"He fears losing you," Liv unveiled, her smile resolute. "Per and Eric venture into the throes of war, while Oscar and Melker find solace in distant city lights. By wedding a villager, your father can keep you near, for you are his sole daughter."

A wistful lament surfaced from the depths of Gunn's troubled soul, whispering, "Yet, I feel as though I shall disappoint him."

"Do not worry, for I pledge it shall not be so," Liv proclaimed, intertwining her trembling fingers with Gunn's. "Unconditional love and unwavering pride shall forever accompany you, regardless of the path you tread. I have strived to raise spirited souls, independent and inquisitive, forging their own truths. I know your strength, I trust your prowess, and I shall exhaust all efforts to aid you. Tomorrow, after mass, I shall converse with your father, and approach the town midwife. Together, we shall pen letters to your brothers, exploring the endless possibilities of your dreams."

"But if he refuses?" Gunn's gaze, tinged with trepidation, implored her mother.

"I shall unearth persuasive means, and if thwarted, we shall find a passage to the city, where your brothers reside. Yet, fear not, my beloved daughter, for such measures shall not come to pass. Know this: I stand forever by your side, a stalwart defender, an unwavering support. Joy permeates my very being through your existence," Liv vowed, her smile tender, her devotion unyielding.

Gunn, overflowing with gratitude, bestowed upon Liv a smile brimming with profound appreciation, softly whispering, "Thank you, mother. Your words possess the magic to soothe my soul."

"My sole purpose is to give my children my utmost," Liv declared, determination ablaze.

Sensing a hint of lingering sorrow within her mother's eyes, Gunn gently inquired, "Yet, did you not harbour dreams of your own?" A loving smile veiled Liv's countenance, concealing the tapestry of hidden melancholy that weighed upon her response.

"My life has been blessed, enfolding five wondrous and splendid children, whom I cherish beyond measure. To call myself your mother fills me with immense pride. You have bestowed meaning upon my existence, illuminating the darkest of nights. Fear not, my child, for I shall endure. Now, it is your time to embrace the path that lies ahead," Liv confided, her voice a tender melody.

Gunn's voice quivered with longing, "Your absence shall leave an indelible void."

"And I shall miss you dearly. Yet, no matter where you wander, my love and support shall forever enfold you. I shall visit as often as I can, but the time has come for you to forge your own destiny. Such is the circle of life. Cast not guilt upon your heart for departing from us. Come, now, dusk approaches. Let us venture indoors," Liv whispered softly, rising from their perch, extending a helping hand to guide Gunn along their journey.

CHAPTER 5

Beside her daughter's side, Liv sat consumed by sorrow, drowning in a sea of hopelessness, clasping Gunn's fragile hand as a lifeline. A veil of sadness clouded her thoughts, seeping into her very core. Time's harsh touch had inflicted Gunn with a treacherous affliction, an insidious malady that evaded Liv's devoted care. Despite her tireless endeavours, hope dwindled with each passing day. Gunn, the essence of Liv's existence, occupied an irreplaceable space in her heart—a daughter whose absence would extinguish the flame of purpose within her.

Guided by desperate determination, Liv ventured into the lush depths of the forest, gathering enchanted herbs and crafting remedies of ancient lore. She sought counsel from the village's wise healer, putting hope in their wisdom. Yet, the ailment retained its relentless grip, a suffocating hopelessness ensnaring Gunn in its horrific grasp. A fever blazed within her, and her mind succumbed to delirious pain. Liv, her spirit fading, stood at the precipice of helplessness and fear, with her daughter's destiny hanging in balance. In her desperation, she beseeched the divine, offering her own life as a sacrifice, surrendering anything to safeguard her daughter's fading existence. Alas, her pleas fell upon deaf ears, and the heavens appeared indifferent to her supplication. Anguish and frustration swelled within Liv, an unrestrained tempest of despair and anger. Powerless and motivated by a mother's love, she yearned to rescue her cherished daughter from impending doom.

As Liv diligently watched over Gunn's weakened form, her mind wandered back to the wondrous day of her birth. In that moment, Gunn had been a fragile blossom, yet Liv's love transcended the boundaries of reason. Gunn, a radiant sun amidst life's cruel battles, had ignited a purposeful fire within her heart. Though Liv's love for all her children burned with intensity, the bond shared with Gunn, her only daughter, possessed an otherworldly essence, an unbreakable thread that spanned unseen realms.

With tear-stained eyes, Liv refocused her gaze upon the present. With a tender caress, she stroked Gunn's hair, whispering words of solace into the fragile air. She vowed that healing would come, that one day they would look back upon this trial as a testament to their resilience. In their entwined hands, Liv found comfort amidst the tempest of despair that haunted her anxious frame.

As the hours stretched into an unforgiving night, Gunn's life force flickered, her breaths fading into debilitated whispers. Time's relentless march urged Liv toward a fateful decision, for she knew that swift action alone might salvage her daughter's diminishing essence. Gathering her resolve, she took a steadying breath and embraced a perilous remedy, whispered tales from the lips of a wandering healer. A blend of potent herbs and mystical ingredients took shape under Liv's skilled hands—a potent elixir that teetered on the brink of salvation.

With trembling determination, Liv administered the remedy to Gunn, clutching her daughter's hand as though bound by an unspoken pact. Her voice, filled with everlasting devotion, entwined with supplications to unseen spirits and benevolent deities, beseeching their intervention, their mercy. In this critical moment, Liv begged God to grant her daughter a second chance, to bestow upon her the gift of renewal and life.

In the forceful reign of the moonlit hours, Liv stood as a guardian, never faltering, by her daughter's side. Time itself seemed to stretch, wrapping the veil of darkness around their intertwined destinies. Each delicate breath that escaped Gunn's lips grew softer, a fleeting melody on the edge of silence. As the first rays of dawn kissed the sky, Gunn released her mortal coil, her spirit departing with tranquil grace from this earthly realm. Liv's heart shattered, burdened by an indescribable ache that draped over her like an eternal mantle. Her beloved daughter, the very essence of her being, slipped away, leaving behind a chasm of inconsolable sorrow. The tendrils of grief ensnared Liv's spirit, piercing her with a wound that time could never heal. For there exists no agony more profound, no destiny more merciless, than the loss of a cherished child.

In the realm of emotions that rend the heart, the sorrow that accompanied the departure of a deeply cherished soul resided as a profound and melancholic ache within the depths of Liv's being. It was a sorrow that transcended the realm of language, for it wove a mournful symphony of anguish that resonated in the chambers of her soul.

In the moment of departure, the world lost its vibrance, as if all colours had dulled into a somber palette. Each breath became a laborious task, as if the weight of grief permeated the very air, stifling any trace of serenity. Time lost its meaning, as days merged into a seamless, desolate expanse, each passing moment echoing the pain that had engulfed the heart.

The absence of her beloved daughter became an abyss that engulfed the spirit, leaving behind a void that could never be filled. It was as though a star had been extinguished in the night sky, leaving an eternal darkness that obscured any glimmer of hope. The world transformed into a desolate landscape, with memories of shared laughter and affection haunting every corner, bitter reminders of what once was.

Liv's mind became a labyrinth of bittersweet recollections, where cherished moments interwove with the piercing realization of their irretrievable loss. Each memory, once a source of solace, now served as a double-edged sword, evoking both joy and sorrow in equal measure. The understanding that there would be no more shared moments, no more tender embraces, shattered her heart into fragments that could never be made whole again.

Grief became an ever-present companion, a spectre that clung to the essence of existence. It wove itself into the fabric of everyday life, casting a shadow over even the simplest of tasks. The world's joys and triumphs, once celebrated together, now appeared hollow and devoid of meaning. Liv’s heart longed to reach out, to bask in the warmth of affection once more, only to be met with a harrowing emptiness.

Amidst the depths of this profound sorrow, tears flowed down Liv’s face as a manifestation of her soul's anguish. They cascaded like a sorrowful river, each droplet a symbol of love that remained unfulfilled and yearning. The ache in her chest became an unrelenting burden, a constant reminder of the profound connection that had been severed. It was a pain that surpassed the physical realm, permeating every fibre of one's being.

The tendrils of sorrow lingered, forever entwined with the very essence of existence, an ever-present whisper of the profound and irreplaceable presence that had slipped away.

CHAPTER 6

Liv, immersed in an ocean of despair, had been pouring forth tears without respite, as if time itself had ceased its relentless march. Neither slumber nor sustenance could find solace within the confines of her anguished existence, for sorrow had permeated and infected every recess of her being, tarnishing the very essence of her soul. In the face of such devastating loss, all remnants of hope crumbled, reduced to mere fragments of a forgotten dream. To lose a precious child, the cruellest stroke of fate, tore at the delicate fabric of Liv's existence. She stood at the precipice of a desolate realm, questioning how she could endure the unbearable void left by Gunn's absence. Hopelessness gnawed at her spirit, rendering her a captive in the depths of desolation.

Desperate and hollow, Liv called out to Finn, seeking support in his arms amidst this tragic ordeal. Yet, Finn, too, retreated into the recesses of his own sorrow, immersing himself in toil to evade the piercing thoughts of their grievous loss. The world around them had transformed into a realm of futility, where the very essence of life had been extinguished. Their beloved daughter, forever lost, would never grace their presence again. In this merciless and unjust existence, Liv seethed with an inner fire, tormented by the relentless grip of death. Why, in the name of all that is righteous, had God not claimed her instead? Liv, veiled in the nebulous realm betwixt life and death, yearned for Gunn's youthful innocence, brimming with dreams and aspirations for a future bathed in serenity.

Enveloped in anger, Liv confronted Finn, her query reverberating through the silent abyss. Why did God, in their divine wisdom, choose to snatch away their beloved daughter? Finn, a vessel of faith, responded with words that offered no solace to her wounded heart. The machinations of the Divine remained an enigma, transcending mortal minds. In hushed whispers, Finn implored Liv to have faith, to trust that all would be set right, for God's presence was ever constant, unwavering in their support. This response, a bitter elixir to swallow, proved intolerable to Liv. What kind of deity would allow the untimely departure of an innocent child while a wretched, lifeless husk of a woman continued to draw breath? The scales of justice teetered askew, igniting the fires of righteous indignation within Liv.

In her desperation, Liv sought to negotiate with the heavens, yet her pleas resounded in empty echoes. She would have willingly bartered her own existence to salvage her beloved Gunn, for her own life paled in comparison to the radiant light that had been extinguished. Alas, the painful conclusion she was forced to embrace was that God harboured no concern for their subjects. Despite her fervent supplications, God remained unmoved, their benevolence nowhere to be found. Liv had wagered her very soul, emptying her being in a futile attempt to reverse the irreversible. And yet, her cries were met with naught but silence, an eerie proof of her shattered faith and a reminder of a God who appeared deaf to her anguished entreaties.

Under the shroud of night, when the world was swathed in ebony hues, elysian guardians adorned the celestial expanse. The moon and stars emerged as radiant sentinels, their ethereal luminescence casting a shimmering glow upon the crystalline firmament above. In this nocturnal enchantment, Liv, fortified by unflinching resolve, ventured forth from the haven of her countryside abode, her heart resounding with the poignant strains of destiny's melodic song. The fragrance of summer danced upon the gentle wind, while a warm and sultry atmosphere enveloped her being, cradling her in its tender caress.

Immersed in an abyss of night's dominion, Liv remained dauntless, her spirit anchored to an unwavering purpose. Within her deepest self, she clung to a resolute understanding that her final act would dissolve all suffering into the void. Boundless liberation beckoned, and the torrents of pain would fade into fleeting whispers within the realm of the living. Every fibre of her being recognized this somber pilgrimage as the rightful path to tread.

A nurturing breeze caressed her cheek, its touch akin to a lover's caring kiss, while the resplendent moon, brimming with its magical glow, bestowed upon the forest floor a pale luminescence, casting an otherworldly spell.

Amidst the prison of solitude, Liv discerned the haunting echoes of the wolves' melancholic serenade, their mournful cries carried upon the winds that traversed the expansive realm of the forest. These wild guardians embodied the primal essence of nature's chakra. Even if the feral beasts were to descend upon her, their sharp fangs sinking into her soft flesh, the searing torment would be but a transient interlude, a fleeting pang in comparison to the relentless ache already entrenched within her dying spirit. The Swedish Forest enveloped her, a realm of exquisite enchantment, a homage to nature's abundant majesty. Liv, intimately acquainted with its grand presence, had found solace and inspiration within its tranquil bosom since her youth. The forest, a home for her restless soul, offered solace and kindled her creative spirit in equal measure.

A symphony of life thrived amidst the verdant empire of the woodland, where a diverse assembly of creatures, both mundane and magical, sought refuge. Each inhabitant, a marvel in its own right, painted the forest's tableau with vibrant strokes of mystique. Towering sentinels, ancient and wise, stood with rugged bark etched by countless ages, their gnarled branches reaching heavenward as if beseeching the divine. Leaves, delicate emissaries of the arboreal realm, whispered secrets upon the breeze, their rustling melodies composing a gentle lullaby.

Through the cathedral-like canopy, beams of moonlight streamed down, their gentle caress crafting a mosaic of warm, golden radiance upon the hallowed forest floor. Light and shadow waltzed upon the earthly canvas, illuminating the intricate interplay of flora and fauna, an opulent tapestry painted by the moon's talented brushstrokes.

Amidst her meandering journey through the dense depths of the forest, Liv beheld a tableau of wondrous beings, an orchestra of life harmonizing with the sacred realm. Graceful deer, adorned in coats of russet and obsidian, cast their gentle gaze upon the meadows kissed by moonlight, their eyes shimmering with the wisdom of ancient woods. Squirrels, nimble acrobats of the arboreal stage, frolicked among the green landscape, their tails a display of fluid motion as they exchanged spirited chatter in a language known only to them.

In the presence of such marvels, Liv's spirit humbled itself, acknowledging the forest as a realm pulsating with magic and boundless enchantment. Each creature, a sacred emissary of the woods, ignited reverence within her soul, inspiring an unwavering commitment to their preservation and protection. She understood that these wild denizens were vessels of ancient wisdom, deserving utmost respect and guardianship.

Silent footsteps traced the path of solitude, guiding Liv through the heart of the forest, her being resonating with profound tranquillity. An ocean of peace unfurled before her, interwoven with nature's symphony, a melody that stirred her soul. Within the depths of this magical place, Liv sensed the veil of secrets adorning ancient trees, the enigmatic allure whispering amidst the foliage. It was a privilege bestowed upon her, this ephemeral encounter with the realm's bewitching inhabitants, as she embarked upon the ethereal threshold for one final rendezvous.

Gradually, the forest unveiled its treasure, revealing a pristine lake, its cerulean surface aglow with a gentle luminescence that bestowed serenity upon the surrounding woods. In the stillness of the air, an owl's haunting hoot resonated from a nearby tree, an emotive melody echoing through the reverential expanse. Deep within her heart, a wellspring of conviction surged forth unburdened by hesitation, for Liv recognized this sacrosanct juncture as her eternal resting place, where the whispers of the forest and the harmony of the lake would cradle her soul in everlasting repose. Embarking upon her aqueous journey, she surrendered herself to the lake's powerful hands. Though the water held a hint of coolness, it failed to stir discomfort, for she treaded a realm where worldly sensations held no power. Unversed in the art of swimming, she yielded to nature's fate, welcoming the final voyage that would soon entwine her mortal existence.

In the twilight of her journey, as the depths enveloped her, Liv found herself captivated by the enigma of death's tangible presence. A dimension of questions unfurled within her consciousness, yearning to discern the secrets that lay beyond this life. Would cosmic currents reunite her with Gunn, her precious kin, amidst the realms beyond mortal existence?

As the aqueous cloak enshrouded Liv's weary head, an ephemeral flicker of trepidation danced through her essence, yet she summoned the strength to persevere. The chill of the water cascaded upon her tender skin, an icy embrace contrasting with the fervour of her determination. With audacious resolve, she unveiled her eyes, surrendering to the depths and the mysteries they held. As vital air released its grasp upon her lungs, the embroidery of life gradually unravelled, its threads slipping away from her mortal form.

In the misty depths, a revelation stirred within Liv's fading consciousness. Like a ghostly apparition emerging from cloaked recesses, a figure appeared, gliding with purposeful grace a few meters ahead. Below the surface, a man materialized, his features contorted by a wild and untamed visage. With powerful arms, he seized Liv in his commanding hold, guiding her towards the refuge of solid ground. Coughs erupted from Liv's being, her nervous system valiantly striving to revive the flickering flame of life. As she turned to face her rescuer, a profound realization dawned upon her trembling heart—this was no ordinary mortal, but a creature of the depths, a water spirit dwelling within the abyssal realms of the lake. It was Näcken, the harbinger of aqueous realms.

Within the realm of local legends, he existed as a masterpiece crafted with threads of both extraordinary power and captivating allure, a fusion of beauty and peril. Whispers swept through the village, their elusive tendrils carrying tales of his existence, each narrative an echo of his enigmatic nature. Legends unfurled like ancient manuscripts, inscribed with stories of his seductive melodies, luring unsuspecting souls into the watery abyss, their lives extinguished amidst the mesmerizing strains of his music.

In the realm of folklore, Näcken, the elusive water spirit, was whispered to possess a profound gift for metamorphosis, assuming the guise of a youthful man, his hair cascading like strands of moonlight, his voice an empyrean lamentation that lingered in mortal hearts. Along the tranquil shores of the lake, he would seek solace, cradling his violin with skilful hands, summoning melodies that intertwined and crafted a fabric of enchantment.

Those who chanced upon Näcken's melodic strains found themselves ensnared within a captivating trance, their senses bewitched, their spirits entangled in the hypnotic dance of his music. Spellbound and bereft of volition, they succumbed to the allure of the watery depths, drawn inexorably towards the siren's aquarius kingdom, their earthly existence swallowed by the shadowy waters. While trepidation surrounded Näcken's essence, many could not help but be entranced by his paradisiacal beauty and his mastery over the symphony of his violin. Whispers spoke of his otherworldly prowess, tales weaving the belief that he, the enchanter of sound, could grant wishes and bestow blessings upon those deemed worthy.

Liv, since her childhood days, had been immersed in the lore surrounding Näcken, a mosaic of caution and wonder that painted her perceptions. Though she had never glimpsed him, his melodies, carried by the nocturnal breeze, had graced her senses on moonlit nights, stirring both fascination and apprehension within her soul.

Liv, a blend of caution and curiosity, held within her a profound awareness of Näcken's formidable power and perilous nature. Yet, amidst the tendrils of trepidation, a strange enchantment stirred, birthing a fascination that defied understanding. Her thoughts, like fluttering secrets in the air, wove intricate patterns of speculation, yearning to unravel the enigma that cloaked Näcken's essence.

In the depths of her consciousness, a delicate interplay of fear and allure intertwined, performing a graceful dance. She quivered in the face of his might, the weight of his existence casting an indomitable shadow upon her soul. And yet, the ineffable magnetism of his numinous beauty pulled at her heartstrings, luring her to explore the enigmatic depths of his allure. Within her, a dichotomy arose, where fear and curiosity entwined in a refined waltz, weaving a tapestry of mystery.

Through the corridors of her memories, Liv retraced the tendrils of her youth, when she, wide-eyed with wonder, first encountered the whispers of Näcken's power. Even then, an inexplicable force, unfathomable yet undeniable, drew her towards him, forging an invisible bond that united their spirits in a realm beyond comprehension. In the recesses of her contemplation, Liv pondered Näcken's esoteric nature, musing upon the delicate equilibrium between taming the tempestuous storm of his essence and his eternal role as a harbinger of danger to humanity. A universe of caution etched itself upon her thoughts, reminding her of the vigilance required should their paths intertwine, for his mastery possessed the ability to enchant and ensnare the unwary.

Yet, beneath the shroud of trepidation, a tender ember of admiration glimmered, shedding light on the sacredness of Näcken's place within the intricate web of existence. Her heart, intertwined with reverence, embraced the majesty of his gifts, acknowledging his divine position in the symphony of life.

Despite the ever-present spectre of peril that cloaked Näcken, Liv found herself spellbound by the nebulous coils of his mystical power, simultaneously terrifying and irresistible. A profound resonance reverberated within her spirit, harmonizing with the knowledge that his legends would endure through the heartbeats of time, whispered in hushed tones to generations yet to come. This everlasting testament bore witness to the eternal allure, enigma, and marvel that resided within the embrace of the natural world.

In a suspended moment that straddled the realms of myth and reality, Näcken, the ethereal entity of lore, materialized before Liv, a manifestation of resplendent grandeur. A divine creation of magnificence unfurled, revealing the most captivating vision she had ever witnessed. His hairs, cascading in a lustrous ebony hue, exuded a vibrant energy that seemed to breathe life itself. Each strand, akin to midnight's silk, swayed with an untamed vitality, emanating an aura of strength and allure. It was as though his locks concealed a hidden wellspring of power, a testament to the force coursing through his very essence. Those raven-black tendrils whispered tales of mystique and passion, inviting others to marvel at the enchanting spell they cast. With each graceful motion, his hair transformed into a living proof of the untamed spirit that dwelled within him, captivating hearts and igniting the imagination of all who beheld it. His eyes, adorned with the beauty of emerald depths, shimmered like precious gems, reflecting the vastness of eternity itself.

Amidst the dissolution of the world around Liv, a sacred hush enfolded their encounter, time itself yielding to the profound presence of Näcken. The heavens, stirred by his celestial magnetism, unveiled an intensified luminosity, adorning the heavenly canvas with a brilliance crafted solely to grace his elysian embodiment. Liv, betwixt realms, questioned the very fabric of her existence, her senses immersed in a sublime ecstasy. For in Näcken's resplendent appeal, the eloquence of words and verses faltered, their meanings eclipsed by the sheer magnitude of his transcendent essence. He existed beyond the mortal confines of life and death, a celestial entity dwelling in a realm uniquely his own.

Within this otherworldly encounter, Liv's heart quivered with an overwhelming adoration, her soul drawn into the orbit of Näcken's iridescent splendour. The boundaries of mortal perception dissolved, leaving behind an insatiable yearning to be consumed by the ineffable grace emanating from him. Näcken, the embodiment of awe-inspiring majesty, kindled a fire within her spirit that defied mortal understanding, beckoning her to partake in the essence of his enchanting realm. Enthralled by Näcken's sublime captivation and the dreamlike ballet of his celestial grace, Liv found herself entangled in the strands of an irresistible attraction. A tempestuous whirlwind of emotions swept through her being, paralyzed her senses with a forbidden longing. She remained acutely aware of the inherent impropriety, for Näcken belonged to the enchanted realm of the forest, an entity unbound by the shackles of humanity, while she, a mere mortal, remained tethered to the earthly domain.

Yet, amidst the rational whispers that urged her to resist, Liv could not deny the fervent cadence resonating within her very core. Näcken's essence, akin to an elixir of enchantment, wove its spirals into her spirit, infusing it with an intoxicating ardour that surpassed the limitations of life and death. With each glance bestowed upon his divine form, she found herself inexorably drawn deeper into the labyrinthine realms of possibility, questioning the very essence of her existence.

In Näcken's presence, the boundaries of reality dissolved, and Liv questioned if she had strayed into the realm of fables, a realm where fantasy surpassed the limitations of the living. The enchantment that radiated from Näcken kindled within her a flicker of hope, an unyielding yearning to transcend mortal boundaries and sway in the moonlit embrace of an extraordinary passion. Liv's heart dared to believe that, perhaps, within the interplay of the mortal and the fable, their destinies could intertwine, composing a symphony of ardour that reverberated across the currents of existence.

Within the depths of Näcken's being, a stirring of curiosity unfurled like an ancient melody, resonating with the vibrancy of Liv's unwavering allure. For in her presence, he beheld a mortal soul adorned with courage and a resolute fearlessness that defied the ordinary boundaries of human existence. A mysterious connection, intangible yet profound, whispered its secrets through the hidden realms.

Näcken, who had traversed countless encounters with mortals, both male and female, found himself ensnared by the essence of Liv. There was an enigmatic fascination in her spirit that beckoned to him, a familiarity that evoked a haunting resonance within his own being. It was a magnetic force, unseen yet tangible, a mysterious connection that outstripped cognition.

In Liv, Näcken discovered a kindred spirit, a spiritual dance partner who dared to venture into the depths of his presence without trepidation. She awakened within him an intrigue that triumphed mere curiosity, stirring the embers of a shared destiny veiled in the enigmatic threads of their encounter. Though unable to decipher the riddle of their connection, Näcken's heart embraced the notion that their union held the potential to unravel the mysteries of their intertwined souls, an alchemical fusion of the mortal and the ethereal that harmonized with the flow of the cosmos.

As rivulets of water cascaded down their entwined forms, Liv was consumed by a profound and fervent yearning for Näcken. Bound in an embrace of vulnerability and desire, they beheld one another with eyes that mirrored the flames of an untamed passion. Näcken, standing before her all naked, in a state of primal vulnerability, wordlessly bared his soul in its purest essence. His physique, sculpted and lithely refined, exuded an aura both primal and untamed—a force that stirred the depths of her being.

Within Näcken, Liv beheld the epitome of strength, an embodiment of raw power that surged through the depths of his being. She was acutely aware that his touch possessed the ability to kindle her soul with fiery ardour or extinguish her life with effortless ease. It was this knowledge, this delicate dance upon the precipice of danger, that set ablaze a flame of eroticism within her very essence. The allure of the unknown, the capricious nature of Näcken's desires, held a seductive appeal that surpassed logical understanding.

In their clandestine connection, Liv yearned for the merging of their desires, a convergence of passion and vulnerability that welcomed the fragility of mortality and the euphoria of surrender. As their gazes locked in an unspoken covenant, they plunged into the abyss of the forbidden, where yearning intertwined with the electric currents of imminent peril. It was within this union of intensity and longing that Liv dared to relinquish herself, yielding to the enigmatic depths of Näcken's mystique. Enveloped in a passion that exceeded human confines, she gave in to the intoxicating ecstasy of the unknown, venturing where few dared to tread.

Näcken's sexual physique loomed large and robust, captivating Liv's gaze. Within her being, a fierce conflagration blazed, an inferno of ardour that defied reason. Though the notion seemed inconceivable, she remained powerless against the surging emotions welling up inside her. Liv's longing for Näcken exceeding any previous encounters, surpassing the bounds of her wildest dreams, transcending mere infatuation. This allure, this magnetic pull, ignited a passion that enveloped her entire existence, rendering her helpless in the face of its intoxicating hold. Amidst the whispering waves, Liv's heart yearned for Näcken's penis to enter her body on that very shore. Her soul, like a fragile blossom, quivered in anticipation, craving the touch of his mouth and fingers against her yearning body. The moonlight danced upon the rippling water, casting a spell of enchantment upon their clandestine rendezvous. In that suspended moment, the cosmic ballet froze in time, as if sensing the profound significance of their imminent union. It was a longing that exceeded the boundaries of time and space, a longing that craved the communion of their souls, intertwining in a celestial symphony of passion and love. In the depths of her being, Liv yearned for Näcken to ignite a blaze of passion that would consume them both, an ardent union of bodies and souls that rose above mere physicality. She yearned for him to traverse the realms of tender caresses and fevered kisses, to intertwine their essences in a symphony of desire. With every beat of her heart, the magnetic pull between them intensified, drawing them closer to the precipice of ecstasy.

Imagining Näcken's hands tracing the contours of her body, his fingertips painting trails of fire upon her skin, Liv's senses ached with a hunger that could not be contained. She longed for his lips to map a constellation of desire upon her flesh, igniting a kaleidoscope of sensations that would leave her breathless and trembling. Each breath she took was filled with the heady anticipation of their bodies entwined, surrendering to the sacred dance of pleasure and surrender.

In her deepest fantasies, she could feel the weight of his gaze, the heat of his breath mingling with hers, as they became one in a passionate fantasy. The world around them would fade into oblivion, leaving only the rhythm of their desire, the melody of their fervent union, echoing in their souls. Liv's very essence quivered with the sheer intensity of her yearning, craving Näcken's touch as a vessel seeks the ocean, longing for their beings to merge in a cataclysm of sexual desire and euphoria.

For Liv, this longing outshone the confines of physicality, moving into the hidden realm of the soul. It was not merely the union of their bodies she yearned for, but the merging of their spirits—a sacred bond that would forever shape their fates. In the depths of her being, she knew that Näcken held the key to unlocking a profound connection, one that would leave an indelible mark upon her destiny.

Within Näcken's mystical being, a timeless battle raged between caution and desire. He, an entity of unparalleled power and enigmatic grace, comprehended the weight of his actions and the far-reaching consequences they could unleash upon their intertwined worlds. Yet, like a celestial moth drawn irresistibly to the flame, he found himself irresistibly pulled towards the radiant luminescence emanating from the depths of Liv's soul.

Näcken, the embodiment of untamed forces that stirred the very fabric of reality, trod upon the precipice of their connection with delicate steps. Every movement he made carried the cosmic weight of responsibility, for he possessed the potential to unravel the creation of mortal lives. The tendrils of caution coiled around his essence, whispering tales of the chaos that could ensue if he surrendered completely to his desires.

And yet, despite his immutable awareness of his own potency, Näcken discovered himself ensnared in unique whispers of Liv's essence. It was a captivating force, an alluring magnetism that infected his bloodstream. Her presence called to him, summoning the depths of his own enigmatic nature, and he yearned to traverse the uncharted territories of their profound connection.

With measured steps and a heart burdened by the gravity of

his actions, Näcken danced upon the tightrope of possibility. He understood the delicate balance between restraint and surrender, fully aware of the fragility of their liaison—the fragrant bloom of passion teetering on the edge of the abyss. The irresistible seduction of Liv's essence stirred within him an insatiable thirst, an unyielding pull that defied the constraints of caution. In the core of Näcken's being, the intricate interplay between restraint and surrender carved a path of profound introspection. He recognized the necessity to navigate the realm of their connection with utmost care, for their encounter possessed the potential to ignite an inferno of consequences. And yet, the celestial yearning entwining their souls proved an indomitable force, an irresistible current propelling him toward the precipice where their intertwined destinies awaited.

"Why have you saved me?" Liv finally uttered, her voice trembling yet filled with awe, as she stood before Näcken in silent admiration.

"Nay, fair enchantress, you harbourest no fear within your heart," Näcken declared, his voice resonating like a sonorous melody that pierced the surrounding silence, as he closed the ethereal distance between them. "Pray tell, what keeps you unshackled from the grip of trepidation?" Liv, captivated by the profound depths of Näcken's eyes, delved into their ancient reservoirs, where eons of wisdom and enchantment resided.

"You possess the power to manipulate me as you desire; I do not harbour any fear towards you. Engage in whatever actions you please, for I shall not give in to fear. You may choose to slay me or subject me to the most exquisite torments, yet still, my spirit shall stand unyielding " Liv replied bravely, her voice was poised to confront any peril that might arise.

"I possess the capacity to extinguish your life, to inflict torment upon you, to sow the seeds of anguish," Näcken's voice resounded with a ferocious intensity, his words carrying the weight of a tempest's fury. "Do you not comprehend the depths of my being? Why, then, do you stand unyielding, unafraid?" In the face of Näcken's formidable presence, Liv met his gaze with courage, her own eyes shimmering with an untold tale. The threads of her spirit danced with an inner radiance, an essence both wild and serene.

"I know who you are. I shall face whatever lay ahead of me," Liv said courageously, her words echoing with a steadfast determination. As Näcken's lips curved into an enigmatic smile, a cascade of secrets and unspoken desires unfurled within that bewitching curve. His smile, akin to moonlight dancing upon a midnight lake, held the promise of a thousand whispered confessions and hidden yearnings. It was a smile that transcended the confines of ordinary comprehension, a radiant enigma that stirred Liv's soul and set her heart ablaze.

Time itself seemed to pause, held captive by Näcken's beguiling countenance. Every crease and dimple, every fleeting glimmer in his eyes, imparted a trove of knowledge regarding a world unseen, a realm where passion and mystique coalesced into an intoxicating elixir. Like a siren's call, his smile beckoned her deeper into the depths of his captivating presence, inviting her to surrender to the currents of a radiant connection.

With every subtle curve of his lips, Näcken spun an intricate web of longing and anticipation, a masterpiece that engulfed Liv's senses and ignited her passions. It was a smile that whispered of eternal promises and stolen moments, of stolen glances and clandestine embraces. In that bewitching smile, she glimpsed the tempestuous secrets of his soul, a realm teeming with unspoken passions and forbidden ecstasies. As his mysterious smile illuminated the space between them, Liv felt a hypnotic attraction, an irresistible force that drew her closer to the depths of his magical essence. Within the confines of that smile, she sensed the power to unravel the intricacies of her own desires, to traverse the ethereal realm where vulnerability and rapture converged. It was a smile that held the key to unlocking the hidden chambers of her heart, unravelling the layers of her being with each enigmatic flicker.

In the presence of Näcken's mysterious smile, Liv's own world became a realm of possibilities, where boundaries blurred and inhibitions dissolved. She longed to decipher the secrets etched upon his lips, to delve into the depths of his enigma and discover the profound connection that awaited them both. It was in that divine smile that Liv found solace and courage, for it whispered of a union that transcended the ordinary, a union destined to ignite a fervent passion that would send their inner flames soaring.

"Reveal my identity," Näcken urged, his voice a whisper carried on the wind, echoing through the enchanted depths.

"You are Näcken," Liv answered without hesitation.

"Pray, enlighten me," he inquired, his words caressing the air like a gentle breeze. "What tempestuous currents led you to seek death beneath the water's embrace, what reason have you to commit suicide?"

"I have lost my child," a melancholy melody wove itself into the cadence of Liv's voice, though sorrow no longer reigned over her spirit. As she stood before Näcken, the ache of her heart seemed to recede, diluted by a paradisiacal presence.

"In the realm of my dominion, it is I who guides souls to the watery depths," Näcken intoned, his voice a tenebrous masterpiece that echoed through the hallowed space. With an air of darkness and dominion, he posed the query, "Does the desire for oblivion and death still linger within you?"

"There is something about you," Liv uttered, her tones like a delicate question woven into the air, a melody of wonderment dancing on her lips "My pain has subsided now in your presence."

"I am an ancient entity, intertwined within the core of the lake and the forest, my essence resonating with the timeless enchantment that imbues these realms," Näcken revealed, his words swirling with a divine power. With each measured step, he drew nearer to Liv, their proximity reaching a breath's width, where his every exhalation caressed her senses, carrying with it an intoxicating allure. In the closeness of their encounter, Liv perceived Näcken's essence, a scent unbound by human constraints, redolent with the essence of mystery and allure. Her heart, like a captive bird, fluttered with an accelerated rhythm within her chest, while a tingling current coursed through the very fabric of her being, awakening dormant heartbeats of longing and fascination.

Amidst the grip of crepuscule 's amorous hues, Liv and Näcken entwined like serpents in a dance of fire and longing, sexual desire exploded within her body. Their bodies, drawn together by an all-consuming allurement, swayed to the rhythm of a forbidden fairytale, a melody that whispered of lust and unbridled yearning.

Näcken, a shadow cast in masculine elegance, led with a firm yet tender hand. His fingers traced the contours of her body, a silent proclamation of possession and protection. With a gaze as intense as a smouldering ember, he commanded her presence, a silent plea to surrender to the inebriating tides of their shared passion.

Liv, a vision of sensuous grace, responded to his touch as though their souls were connected by an invisible thread. Her every movement echoed the cadence of his lead, a dance of vulnerability and trust imbibed like ink on the parchment of their identity. Her eyes, like twin stars, burned with an ardour that exceeded the boundaries of language, inviting him to explore the depths of her sexual longing while he started to kiss her neck with soft lips.

Liv closed her eyes and enjoyed Näcken's elysian touch, his movements, a symphony of contrasts, played out in harmonious discord. With each calculated brush of thigh against thigh, a spark ignited, fanning the flames of an incendiary chaos that consumed reason and restraint. Their chests brushed against one another, a collision of hearts that beat in unison, a rhythm only they could comprehend. His hands coiled her body like a venomous snake playing with its dying pray.

He spun her, a tempest of silk and lace, their bodies locked in a magnetic rotation that soared like a comet, oblivious to gravity's constraints. Her breathless moans filled the air, a melody that harmonized with the pulsating rhythm of their hearts. She surrendered herself to his guidance, an act of trust that spoke of a connection that ran deeper than life and death. In the seductive clasp of the present, Liv surrendered the entirety of her being, allowing herself to be enveloped by the irresistible force of his hold. With a vulnerability that mirrored dawn's fingers coaxing the hidden charm of a flower into view, she immersed herself in the depths of his grasp, a willing captive to the currents of their shared existence. Her essence, akin to a delicate snowflake settling on a still winter's night, melded seamlessly with his touch, as if they were two notes in a harmonious symphony, dancing in a timeless ballet of souls.

Liv moaned in a crescendo of desire, when Näcken started to touch her breasts, their bodies pressed together in an intimate tango, a melding of spirits that soared beyond the material plane. His lips and her nipples, drawn together by the gravity of their passion, met in a fervent kiss that tasted of shared dreams and unspoken promises. It was a moment trapped in eternity, an illustration of the potent alchemy of two souls dancing to the rhythm of passion and longing. The pleasure consumed her while she gave in to temptation.

Liv sensed the horniness seeping into her bones, and with each breath, a symphony of longing and passion swelled within her body. With a grace befitting a celestial being, Näcken tenderly lifted Liv from the earth's embrace and gently set her down upon the green ground, a symphony of desires began to unravel, she yearned to feel him inside of her body.

As Näcken's nimble hands gingerly unravelled the fabric that adorned her, an erotic unveiling commenced. With each layer removed, a vulnerable beauty emerged, radiant in her nakedness. Lips that had thirsted for the taste of his kiss were once again granted the fervent caress of his mouth. Their mouths converged in an ardent union, a dance of tongues that melded passion and playfulness, teasing the boundaries of ecstasy.

Liv's senses awakened to a profound connection, as if the very pulse of life coursed through her veins. The rustle of leaves, the gentle whispers of the wind, and the symphony of birdsong formed a harmonious chorus, bearing witness to their clandestine communion. She lay bared and vulnerable, her essence entwined with the sacred energies of the forest, imbued with a serenity that wrapped around her like a lover's embrace.

The forest enveloped Liv, cradling her with the benevolence of ancient trees and moss-kissed earth. She felt the pulse of life echoing within her, a vibrant rhythm that intertwined with her own heartbeat. As Näcken's lips traced delicate trails upon her skin, her very essence merged with the essence of nature, harmonizing in a sublime union of sensuality, erotism and serenity.

Liv surrendered to the sensual symphony of the forest, an immersive experience that surpassed the physical realm. The forest became a witness, its ancient wisdom whispering reassurance, as if guiding their passionate union.

Exposed beneath the verdant canopy, Liv became a vessel for the enchantment of nature's caress, her body a canvas upon which the elements of desire and liberation danced in perfect harmony. The forest breathed alongside her, as if attuned to the heartbeat of their shared ardour, infusing her being with a serene and profound connection to all that surrounded her.

With every stolen kiss and every whispered sigh, Liv and Näcken merged in a dance of sensual exploration, their spirits mingling with the soulful energies of the forest. It was a moment where time ceased to exist, where the boundaries of self-dissolved, and the sacredness of their union was amplified by the ancient echoes of the woods. In the languid embrace of their ardour, Näcken delicately parted the veil of Liv's legs, unveiling a realm where passion and intimacy converged. It was a moment teeming with anticipation, as if time itself stopped to watch their meeting, honouring the sacred unveiling of desires yet unspoken. As the boundaries of their physical beings dissolved, a symphony of vulnerability and trust unfurled, weaving them together in an intimate dance.

Within that sacred space, where their souls entwined, Liv's essence bloomed like a fragrant blossom, petals unfurling to the touch of Näcken's hands. It was a tender act of reverence, an exploration guided by both tenderness and desire. With every gentle touch, his fingertips mapped a trail of pleasure upon her skin, awakening nerve endings to a chorus of exquisite sensations that danced along her spine.

In the depths of their connection, Liv felt a profound vulnerability mingled with a passionate yearning. It was a moment of surrender, an act of trust where inhibitions melted away like dewdrops under the caress of the morning sun. Näcken's touch, so reverent and knowing, traversed the landscapes of her desires, leaving trails of fire in its wake.

As Näcken's hands journeyed, their fingertips became poetic instruments, playing melodies of desire upon Liv's flesh. With each delicate stroke and whispered caress, he unveiled the hidden symphony that resided within her, awakening notes of pleasure that reverberated through her core. Their intimacy became an exquisite dance, a choreography of passion and vulnerability, where every movement held the power to ignite a wildfire of sensation.

In that intimate communion, Liv felt the profound interconnectedness of their souls, a fusion that transcended the physical realm. It was a moment of unity, where boundaries blurred, and their essences merged in a cosmic embrace. The unveiling of her body became a testament to the depths of their connection, a testament to the infinite layers of passion and desire that bound them together.

With each breath, the air crackled with an electric intensity, as if the universe itself leaned in, enraptured by the intimate tableau unfolding before it. Liv, with her every nerve alive and every sense heightened, surrendered to the intricate tapestry of passion and trust woven between them. It was a passion that surpassed mere physicality, transcending into the realm of spiritual intimacy, where their souls danced to the rhythm of their shared desires.

In the erotic act of Näcken parting Liv's legs, their bodies became vessels for the poetry of passion and desire, a canvas upon which their deepest longings were painted. In that moment, they embarked on an intimate journey, where vulnerability and pleasure merged, their spirits entwined like vines embracing the sun. It was a tender exploration of intimacy, an intimate symphony composed of whispers, sighs, and the rhythm of their entangled breaths.

Both gentle and forceful, like an unpredictable ocean, Näcken started to lick her clitoris. Liv moaned loudly in pleasure. His tongue moved like a whirlwind sweeping the landscape, sending pleasure through her senses. Her being became a vessel wherein desire and pleasure intermingled, their fervent union igniting an inferno that surged through the intricate channels of her veins. A symphony of sensations coursed through her very essence, resonating with a profound intensity that defied the confines of mere existence. Each heartbeat reverberated with a fervour akin to the thunderous waves crashing upon a shore, while her breaths whispered secrets of longing and anticipation.

In this tempestuous dance of desire, the vines of passion created a mixture of emotions, intertwining with the essence of her soul. Every fibre of her being yearned for connection, an ardent craving that pulsed within her like a celestial beacon. The world around her faded into insignificance as her senses succumbed to the intoxicating spell of ecstasy.

Within her, the flame of ardour flickered and swelled, radiating a luminosity that outshone the brightest stars. Its incandescent glow transformed her into a vessel of sensuality, her very presence a magnet that drew the cosmos closer. The universe itself bore witness to the grand spectacle unfolding within her, as desire and pleasure cascaded like shimmering stardust, caressing the contours of her existence.

Her heart, once a mere organ of life, now beat with the rhythm of passion's symphony. With each pulsation, she offered herself willingly to the symphony's crescendo, surrendering to the irresistible pull of desire's allure. The notes of this melodic yearning intertwined, harmonizing with her deepest desires, as her soul reached out, seeking its divine counterpart.

In the realm of this euphoric rapture, time ceased to exist, and the boundaries of her mortal coil melted away. She became a vessel of unadulterated passion, an embodiment of unrestrained fervour. No longer bound by earthly constraints, she soared upon the wings of a resplendent ardour, transcending the ordinary and embracing the sublime.

In this transcendence, desire and pleasure became entwined in a love affair of cosmic proportions. Their union was proof of the raw power of passionate connection, a wild flame that burned with an intensity capable of lighting the darkest corners of existence, her veins pulsed with the essence of this fiery passion.

Näcken's tongue felt warm and moist, like a blissful summer breeze, on her pulsating clitoris. He let his tongue move with a kaleidoscope of speeds, a tempestuous whirlwind of motion that defied the boundaries of time. Each lick carried him forward, propelled by a symphony of velocities that painted a vivid portrait of his indomitable spirit. With each playful move with his mouth, he metamorphosed, seamlessly shifting between realms of swiftness and leisure, power and tenderness, an ever-evolving embodiment of dynamic motion. Näcken's tongue initiated explosions within that shook Liv's core like a merciless earthquake.

His tongue dance embraced the dichotomy of velocity, an intricate ballet of contrasting rhythms. At times, he surged forth with the fury of a tempest, his muscles propelling him forward with an unstoppable force, like a wild stallion unleashed upon the world. In those moments, his movements were a blur, his determination etched upon the very air he displaced, leaving a trail of fervour in his wake.

Yet, amidst this torrent of speed, there were interludes of respite, where his flow transformed into a caress, a delicate touch upon Liv's exposed clitoris. His movements became gentle whispers, as if he tiptoed upon the petals of a blooming rose, careful not to disturb the delicate beauty of her body. Time seemed to slow, and his every movement bore the weight of reverence, as if he sought to honour the sanctity of existence with each measured breath.

Within the depths of her being, Liv was consumed by a pleasure so profound, it eclipsed the boundaries of her previous experiences. It was as if the bedrock of her being had been created with strands of ecstasy, unfurling in exquisite waves that caressed her senses with tender insistence. With each whispering touch, every exquisite stroke, Liv's body became a symphony of sensations, orchestrating a melody of pleasure that resonated through her every nerve. It was a dance of heightened awareness, where her skin became a canvas yearning to be painted with the brushstrokes of bliss.

As the currents of pleasure coursed through her, Liv felt her soul awaken, as if the dormant embers of desire had been ignited into a passionate inferno. It was a symphony of heightened sensations, a blend of fervour and vulnerability that unfurled within her like a wild ocean. In this sacred moment of rapture, Liv transcended the ordinary, her spirit soaring on the wings of a passion she had never fathomed before. It was a blissful surrender, a delicate surrender to the symphony of her desires, harmonizing with the rhythm of her lover's touch.

Within the realms of this newfound pleasure, time ceased to exist, replaced by a timeless expanse where only the symphony of their union held sway. Liv's every breath, every gasp, was infused with the euphoria of this enchanting encounter, as if her very essence had merged with the melody of the universe itself. In this delicate dance of pleasure, Liv discovered a new dimension of intimacy, where her pleasure was cherished and celebrated. It was a revelation that shattered the confines of her past, freeing her to explore the boundless expanse of her desires, unfettered and unapologetic.

As Liv surrendered to the depths of this intoxicating pleasure, she became a vessel of passion, her essence entwined with the celestial symphony of ecstasy. It was a symphony that crescendoed within her, rising and falling like the tides, as she journeyed to realms of pleasure she had only dreamed of before. In the wake of this profound pleasure, Liv was forever transformed, her spirit ignited with the fire of newfound liberation. The tendrils of this rapture lingered upon her clitoris, an indelible mark that whispered of a passion unbound, forever etched in the embodiment of her existence. As Liv immersed herself in this uncharted terrain of passion, she embraced the divine chaos that unfolded within her. The sensations that coursed through her veins were electric, each touch setting off a cascade of rapture that reverberated through her core. She marvelled at the boundless capacity of her own heart, her very being a vessel for this euphoric crescendo.

With a commanding presence, Näcken enfolded Liv's torso within the sanctuary of his robust grasp, passionately he let his tongue slip inside of Liv, eating her essence from within.

His hands radiating an intensity that stirred her very essence. The weight of his touch bore witness to a strength that both grounded and empowered, leaving Liv breathless with a heady mixture of anticipation and surrender. In the embrace of his strong hands, Liv felt an undeniable magnetism, a fusion of masculine power and tender devotion that kindled a chorus of experiences within her. Each touch, deliberate and purposeful, told passionate stories of Näcken's desire to claim her, to navigate the labyrinthine contours of her being with a reverence that bordered on the divine. The dichotomy of his strength and gentleness sent ripples of electrifying awareness through her, as if the meeting of their energies created a sublime alchemy that transcended the boundaries of mortal touch. As Näcken's hands enveloped her torso, Liv was enveloped in a symphony of sensations that pulsed with a fierce tenderness. The convergence of their energies wove an intricate explosion of pleasure and connection, each touch an intimate caress that echoed through the chambers of her soul. In this embrace, she felt seen, desired, and cherished—a profound affirmation of her existence amidst the boundless scope of the universe.

Näcken moved in perfect synchrony with the cadence of Liv's body. In this exquisite union of movement, Näcken became the embodiment of intuition and connection, his every gesture a manifestation of his profound understanding of Liv's desires. Their bodies became instruments, their movements composing a medley of passion and pleasure, orchestrated by an invisible force that pulsed through their veins. With every breath shared, every shared gaze and every nuanced touch, Näcken's presence melded with Liv's essence, fusing them into a seamless whole. In this divine choreography, Näcken moved with grace and reverence, as if guided by an ancient wisdom that transcended time itself. His touch, like a brushstroke upon a canvas, painted trails of sensation upon Liv's skin, eliciting a myriad of gasps and shivers that echoed through the depths of their beings. In this harmonious interplay, the passage of time paused, allowing them to savour every moment, every fleeting touch. Näcken's movements were a language spoken in the dialect of desire, each motion whispering tales of adoration and longing. It was as if the universe itself conspired to choreograph this symphony of passion, granting them a glimpse into the divine unity of their souls. In the seamless fusion of their bodies, Näcken and Liv transcended the boundaries of the mundane, transcended into a realm where passion and connection merged. Their dance became an ode to the sacred union of hearts and bodies, an exploration of the limitless depths of pleasure and intimacy.

As they moved in perfect harmony, Näcken and Liv became vessels of divine expression, channels through which the raw and primal energy of desire flowed. Their bodies entwined like vines, their spirits entangled in a cosmic embrace, and together they embarked on a journey where their every movement was imbued with a transcendent beauty that defied words. When Liv climaxed, Näcken forcefully put his whole mouth over her clitoris just to feel her come in his mouth.

In that moment, Liv's essence intermingled with the immense cosmos, her spirit merging harmoniously with the very fabric of the forest, every creature and soul flowing through her veins. Serenity, like a gentle river, coursed through her heart, bestowing upon her a profound sense of security and solace. Näcken, in his enigmatic might, lifted Liv effortlessly, cradling her in his arms, an unspoken promise of guidance and protection.

Through the dappled shadows and whispering leaves, Näcken treaded with grace, traversing the mystical depths of the forest, a silent communion of souls. Liv's gaze, brimming with gratitude and a deep sense of indebtedness, remained fixed upon Näcken's countenance, for she recognized the profound significance of their encounter. Aware of the transformative power of their union, she treaded with caution upon this perilous precipice, a realm where longing and desire intertwined.

While the ache of her loss still lingered, constricting her heart and paralyzing her veins, a flicker of hope stirred within the depths of Liv's soul. Once dormant dreams and passions began to reclaim territory within her very bloodstream, weaving intricate patterns of resurgence and revival. The tenuous threads of connection to life, frayed by grief, started to knit anew, their delicate threads reaching out, entwining with the echo of existence.

Näcken's mysterious gaze, fixed upon the forest and its mystical realms, illuminated the path they traversed, as nature itself recognized his potent magic. The destination remained a mystery to Liv, yet she found solace in Näcken's embrace, an embrace that whispered of sanctuary and trust. In solemn silence, they journeyed, until the forest yielded to the enfoldment of open horizons. With a gentle grace, Näcken set Liv's feet upon the tender ground, as if bestowing a gift of belonging to the world anew.

"The forest, in its nocturnal embrace, becomes a perilous realm for a lone human," he murmured, his voice carrying the weight of shadows and the allure of forbidden secrets.

"All the animals and creatures seemed to keep their distance from you, and yet your magic strengthened the forest," Liv's eyes, filled with a longing that transcended mortal desires, met Näcken's gaze.

"I am more than a mere being," Näcken whispered, his voice a melody that resonated with ancient wisdom. "I am a spirit, a creature, a guardian, entrusted with the delicate balance of the forest's ethereal realms. Those who dare defy me shall know the might of nature, for in my presence, the very essence of the forest and its inhabitants thrives, imbued with a potent enchantment."

"I feel a connection with you," as Liv inched closer to Näcken, she found herself lost in the depths of his enigmatic eyes.

"In my presence," Näcken began, his voice a whisper carried

on the wind, "the emotions of all beings intertwine, forming a tempest of intricate and profound experiences. None can escape unscathed after crossing paths with me. Some meet their demise in a haunting dance, while others unearth hidden gifts and talents that transcend mortal limitations. The majority quiver with fear, for they know not what path I shall tread."

There was a momentary pause, as Näcken's words hung in the air like dew-kissed petals. Then, with a curious inflection, he questioned, "Do you still yearn for the touch of darkness and death, dear one?"

"It is a strange feeling," Liv's gaze remained fixed upon Näcken, her heart stirred by a profound yearning, an echo of desire that penetrated her soul. Her very essence seemed to ache for the surrender to his commanding presence, to bask in the allure of his unfathomable power.

"It is as if life itself now burns inside of me, and I no longer seek to find death," Liv confessed, her voice carrying the weight of a newfound revelation.

With a deliberate turn, Näcken directed his gaze towards Liv, their eyes locking in a shared moment of understanding. His voice, infused with both solemnity and grace, echoed through the silent night.

"Indeed, I am an arbiter of fate, a weaver of destinies," Näcken spoke, his words infused with a mixture of solemnity and benevolence. "While for some, I bring forth change and transformation, for others, I grant wishes and aspirations. In your case, instead of extinguishing your life's flame, I have planted a fragment of my ethereal essence deep within your being. I have saved you from the depths of despair, and in return, restored the radiance of your existence."

Liv's gaze, a swirling tempest of desire, fixated upon Näcken's intense scrutiny of the distant farm. Within the depths of her being, a wildfire of longing blazed, beckoning her to abandon herself to Näcken's commanding presence, to willingly surrender to his irresistible will and untamed potency.

In that enchanting moment, time stood still, as if held captive by the alchemy of their desires. Liv felt her soul quiver, like a delicate bird yearning to take flight, as Näcken's aura entwined with hers, crafting a sophisticated composition of forbidden allure and limitless yearning.

The airy connection between them transcended the tangible realm, a celestial dance of intertwined destinies. Liv sensed Näcken's power, like a primal force coursing through her veins, awakening dormant desires and igniting her spirit with the intoxicating possibilities that lay before her.

In the depths of her heart, Liv knew that surrendering to Näcken's will meant acing a world unknown, a realm where mortal boundaries blurred, and passion intertwined with the otherworldly. The mere thought sent tremors of anticipation rippling through her, casting aside the veil of caution and inviting her to embrace the enigmatic enchantment that Näcken embodied.

With every breath and heartbeat, Liv yearned to dissolve into Näcken's essence, to lose herself within the currents of his potent charm. Their gazes locked in an unspoken covenant, an uncharted journey awaiting their steps, as if the universe awaited the future, aware of the profound connection that bound their souls together.

Näcken's eyes, deep and ancient, met Liv's with an intensity that stirred her very core. A profound stillness settled upon them, as if time lingered in anticipation of Näcken's words.

"Then behold, my gift to you," Näcken whispered, his voice a melodic blend of mystery and power. "For some, I am the herald of transformation and upheaval, while for others, I am the weaver of dreams and aspirations. In your darkest hour, instead of claiming your life, I have reignited the flame of your existence. I plucked you from the depths of despair, breathing new life into your very essence."

His words resonated within Liv's soul, echoing through the cells of her body. She felt the weight of Näcken's benevolent enchantment coursing through her veins, a subtle yet palpable current of vitality that whispered promises of a life reborn. In his act of salvation, Näcken had bestowed upon her a profound gift, a transformative touch that surmounted earthly restrictions.

As Näcken's gaze lingered upon Liv, she felt the gentle touch of destiny's hand upon her shoulder. Her path had forever veered, interlaced with the heavenly enchantment Näcken embodied. With gratitude emanating from the depths of her being, Liv cherished the bestowed gift, an affirmation of Näcken's immeasurable compassion and otherworldly grace.

Liv's voice quivered with longing as she spoke, her words carrying the weight of unspoken desires. "Tell me, Näcken," she implored, her voice a soft gust of wind that caressed the air, "May our paths intertwine once more?"

A mysterious smile graced Näcken's lips as he reached out, his fingertips delicately tracing the strands of her hair. The touch ignited a dormant fire within her soul, electric like moonlight's whispered touch upon her skin.

No words were needed, for Näcken's touch revealed a chronicle of infinite sagas. It held promises of hidden mysteries and forbidden yearnings, of a realm where boundaries dissolved, and mortal constraints faded into insignificance. In that simple gesture, Liv felt an intoxicating blend of vulnerability and liberation, as if her very essence had become entwined with the threads of Näcken's captivating presence.

The air around them hummed with unseen energy, as the ancient melodies of the forest whispered their secrets to the enraptured pair. Näcken's touch lingered, a gentle caress that stirred the embers of longing within Liv's heart. It was a tender invitation to delve into the depths of their connection, a silent affirmation that the path they tread was one of shared destiny.

Liv surrendered herself to the enchantment of Näcken's touch, her hair an intricate masterpiece, inviting his fingers to interlace within its strands. The world around them faded into insignificance, leaving only the pulsating current of their shared presence. Bound by an unspoken pact, their hearts danced in synchrony, attuned to the rhythm of an existence suffused with Näcken's captivating touch.

"If it is your desire," Näcken replied, his voice a powerful symphony of intrigue and passion. "You have ignited a flicker of curiosity within me, a flame seldom sparked by mortal presence." Liv caught a subtle trace of disdain woven within his words, an unspoken reminder of the vast chasm that separated their worlds. "You need not search far, for your presence shall be felt in the currents of existence."

With each backward step Näcken took into the depths of the forest, Liv's heart quickened, the weight of his piercing gaze lingering upon her like a tempest in the night. As darkness consumed his silhouette, a palpable void settled in the wake of his departure, momentarily leaving Liv breathless. Hastening her pace, she retraced her steps, longing to return to the familiar grounds of the farm.

A flutter of unease swept through her as Liv became aware of the predicament in which she found herself. Forgotten garments lay scattered amidst the verdant woods, a potential catalyst for scandalous whispers if stumbled upon by unsuspecting eyes. What judgments would Finn, her family, and the villagers cast upon her if they were to chance upon her unclothed form darting through the shadows? Accusations of sorcery and pacts with the netherworld would surely ignite, while the disapproving gaze of the village priest would magnify their torment.

Yet, fortune smiled upon her, as the slumbering house welcomed her return in blissful oblivion. Swiftly, Liv adorned herself with attire, the fabric becoming a veil that concealed both her nakedness and the extraordinary encounter that had transpired beneath the moonlit canopy. As she settled into her bed, a profound sense of contentment washed over her, interwoven with a euphoria that danced within her veins.

In the realm of dreams, Liv's consciousness embarked on mystical voyages, where Näcken's enigmatic presence lingered within the depths of her imagination. It was a voyage of exploration and enchantment, a mixture of curiosity and longing. And as slumber enfolded her, Liv surrendered to the intoxicating waltz between reality and fantasy, cherishing the moments shared with Näcken as treasures concealed from the judgmental gaze of the world.

Deep within her soul, Liv recognized the indebtedness she bore to Näcken, a debt she could never truly repay. With a solemn vow etched upon her heart, she pledged to honour him in the sacred recesses of her existence. Her eyelids gently closed, surrendering to the embrace of darkness, as a profound sense of wonder washed over her.

Within the labyrinthine depths of the forest, Näcken's divine essence had kindled a fervent flame within her, illuminating the path to a realm where enigmas and miracles intertwined. The touch of his celestial presence lingered upon her skin, a delicate caress of otherworldly grace that left her breathless.

And though she had ventured into the abyss, traversing the veils of uncertainty, Liv unearthed a treasure untouched by the shroud of night. It was not merely a fleeting encounter, but an enduring connection that resonated deep within her core. In Näcken's presence, she found solace, beauty, and an elusive sense of purpose.

As the world slumbered, Liv revelled in the enigma of their shared secret, cherishing the preciousness she had discovered in the embrace of darkness. And with each passing moment, her spirit unfurled like a delicate blossom, illuminated by the radiant touch of Näcken and the beguiling mysteries of the forest, forever entwined at the heart of her being.

CHAPTER 7

As the gentle blush of dawn caressed the sky, awakening the world with its tender touch, Liv stirred from her dreams, serenaded by the chorus of canines. With a soft exhale, she welcomed the newborn day, its arrival accompanied by a hopeful whisper that caressed her ears. Resolute and steadfast, Liv began her daily toil upon the fruitful earth, labouring diligently with unfaltering loyalty. The cadence of her endeavours entwined with the pulsating heart of the land, entwined in a delicate dance of existence. While outwardly the scene remained unaltered, within the depths of her being, an imperceptible evolution had unfurled.

The world, once familiar, had undergone a profound transformation beneath the surface of her perception. In the aftermath of her encounter with Näcken, the ordinary facade of existence now shimmered with newfound profundity and resonance. It was as though a curtain had been raised, revealing a realm of enchantment seamlessly integrated into the very essence of reality.

Amidst the symphony of her toil, a subtle radiance emanated from her core, casting a gentle glow upon her countenance. Her family, astute observers of her spirit's ebb and flow, discerned the subtle shift in her demeanour. A hint of tranquillity graced her features, akin to a whispered secret of contentment dancing within her eyes.

Though the world carried on its bustling affairs, for Liv, the horizons of possibility had expanded, and the commonplace held concealed enchantments yearning to be discovered. And as she persisted in tending to the chores of the farm, she carried within her the profound realization that the world had irreversibly changed, forever adorned with the hues of a whispered encounter that had transformed the quintessence of her innermost being.

"I am pleased to have your presence, Liv," Greta spoke as the sun cast its gentle radiance through the windows, illuminating the room in a soft glow. Greta and Liv engaged in the quiet rhythm of tidying, their laughter intertwined with the sweeping of brooms and the gentle swish of cloth against polished surfaces.

With each deliberate motion, Greta's smile blossomed, mirroring the warmth and camaraderie shared between kindred spirits. Their friendship, a sanctuary amidst the tumult of the world, sought solace in the simple act of restoring order and harmony to their shared dwelling.

As they banished the remnants of yesterday's footsteps and tenderly erased the traces of life's passage, their hearts sang with joy, for in that moment, their connection transcended the ordinary. They comprehended the profound beauty that resides within the textured artwork of everyday life, within the act of nurturing their home with tenderness and devotion.

Their laughter reverberated through the corridors, breathing vitality into the sacred spaces they cultivated together. A sense of unity settled upon them, intertwining their souls in a bond woven with shared memories and unspoken comprehension.

In that tranquil interlude, as they adorned their lives with order, Greta and Liv unearthed the sanctity of their bond.

With each stroke of the cloth and each exchange of laughter, Greta's smile whispered a silent gratitude, acknowledging the precious treasure of friendship and the alchemical power of shared moments, even in the simplest of endeavours.

"You appear to be finding strength amidst this tribulation," Greta voiced, her prayers lending support to Liv's weary spirit.

"Life's burdens are harsh and inequitable," Liv began, her voice a tender lament, "yet, I must not wallow in sorrow any longer. There is much to be done. Gunn will forever dwell within my heart and soul, though regrettably absent from my side. However, I possess an unwavering belief that our paths will intertwine once again."

"She waits for you in heavenly realms," Greta offered with conviction. In the depths of her being, where grief and hope coexisted, Liv grappled with life's enigmatic dance of mortality and beyond. Uncertain of the mysteries that lay behind the final breath of life, she clung steadfastly to a belief that exceeded human understanding.

Though Gunn, her cherished daughter, had departed this earthly plane, Liv clutched onto an unshakable conviction. It murmured to her soul, a fragile melody of solace and reassurance, assuring her that their souls would converge once more in realms that eluded mortal grasp.

In the face of the unknown, where questions loomed like shadows and doubts encroached like tendrils of mist, Liv embraced a hopeful faith. It defied the boundaries of reason, imbuing her consciousness with hues of unyielding devotion. She dared to envision a reunion, a sacred encounter amidst uncharted realms.

For Liv, the afterlife remained an enigma, veiled in whispers of ancient tales and uttered prayers. Yet, within her heart, she harboured an immovable belief that the boundless realm of eternity would offer solace, born of love and reunion. With each breath, she nurtured this flickering flame of faith, fanning it against the winds of uncertainty.

In tender moments of solitude, when the moon cast its silvery glow upon her tear-stained visage, Liv whispered promises to her departed child. She vowed to traverse dimensions, guided by the compass of unconditional love, until they were united once more. She found reconciliation in the conviction that their connection transcended the limited confines of earthly existence.

Thus, with every beat of her grieving heart, Liv carried the torch of hope. Within the elaborate design of the beyond, where souls ventured beyond the limits of mortality, she remained resolute in her belief. Tethered by a mother's love, she embarked on her quest, unyielding, forever trusting that love would illuminate their path towards an eternal harmony.

In the cradle of night's calming hush, Liv existed betwixt realms, suspended in the soothing dance of reality and reverie. The echoes of her encounter with Näcken quivered within her innermost self, entwining with the nocturnal symphony that whispered outside her window. As the moon poured its luminescent glow upon her restless form, Liv's thoughts waltzed with fragments of enchantment and longing. Näcken's essence, akin to a celestial melody, meandered through the intricate network of her mind, leaving an indelible imprint upon her senses. She gently closed her eyes, surrendering herself to the vivid tableau of memories that painted the canvas of her mind. Näcken's touch, bearing resemblance to a divine caress, still lingered upon her delicate skin, provoking a symposium of reactions that resonated deep within the wellspring of her soul. His voice, a melodious invitation, whispered secrets and desires, entwining their very essence, enmeshed in the fibres of her being. Its seductive timbre floated within her, an enchanting rhythm that echoed across the thresholds of time. The scent of him, an intoxicating fusion of earth and allure, intoxicated her senses, leaving her spellbound in its lingering presence. It kindled a fire of yearning, entwining her thoughts and igniting an unquenchable flame of longing.

In the tranquil embrace of the night, Liv revelled in the memories of Näcken's countenance, a timeless enigma that rebelled against ordinary conventions. His otherworldly allure, a tempest of contradictions, captivated her imagination, etching his presence indelibly upon the foundation of her heart. With each breath, she revisited their encounter, every detail etched upon her consciousness with meticulous artistry. The weight of their connection, a profound resonance that transcended the boundaries of mundane existence, remained forever etched upon the sacred walls of her being.

As the night serenaded her with its lullabies and the stars bestowed their celestial light upon the world, Liv luxuriated in the sanctuary of her thoughts, enraptured by the memory of Näcken. His essence, a bewitching enchantment clinging to her very core, continued to mesmerize her, suffusing her nocturnal solitude with a heady concoction of desire and wonder. In that realm where wakeful dreams unfurled, where reality and fantasy entwined, Liv surrendered to the seductive remembrance of Näcken's touch, his voice, his scent. Amidst the nocturnal symphony, she found solace in the knowing that their encounter had imprinted upon her the indelible mark of an extraordinary connection.

The symphony of her memory intermingled seamlessly with the kaleidoscope of her boundless imagination. The remembrance of that unforgettable night kindled an ardent fire within her, igniting the embers of longing that still smouldered within her soul. Within the corridors of her imagination, Liv savoured the tender caresses and whispered secrets exchanged beneath the moonlit canopy. The spirit of the lake emerged as a radiant muse, inspiring her thoughts to soar on the wings of possibility, unburdened by the shackles of reality.

In the realm of dreams, where imagination spins its narratives, Liv found solace in the indefinable bond she had forged with Näcken. It was a spiritual relationship that went above the mundane, a meeting of souls beyond the realm of ordinary encounters. Within the realms of her fantasies, the memory of their connection permeated her being, prompting a whirlwind of yearning and anticipation, a seductive storm that plucked the strings of her heart with each reimagined touch. What an unforgettable experience it was letting him pleasure her!

Within Liv, Näcken had kindled a flame, a fervour that blazed with an ardour defying comprehension. The memory of their celestial encounter beckoned her, luring her towards uncharted realms of longing, where the limits of her desires expanded beyond the horizons of what she once deemed possible. In the domain of her musings, Liv luxuriated in the intoxicating interplay between memory and reverie, where the spirit of the lake burned as an everlasting beacon, illuminating her path towards a future adorned with untamed ardency and profound union. Her thoughts danced in perfect harmony with the vivid tableau of her recollections, a variegation of passion and yearning, sculpting an enchanting panorama upon the canvas of her soul. Liv started to feel her pulse rising and a radiant fire burning in her cells. A longing, deep and unyielding, stirred within Liv's soul, craving the touch of Näcken that had awakened a profound desire within her.

Yet, a delicate dance of yearning and hesitation unfolded within the chambers of Liv's heart, entwining her in the safety of her haven, cautious of the risks entangled in the spirit of the lake's embrace. The spectre of exposure cast its shadow upon Liv's musings, a gentle hand restraining her from the precipice of surrender. It whispered prudence, reminding her of the consequences lurking should she dare to venture into the realm of Näcken's profound encounters. Fear of discovery bound her to the comfort of familiarity, guarding her against the mystery that lay beyond.

Yet in the midst of the mosaic of uncertainty, a beam of eagerness flickered, refusing to be extinguished. It danced within her depths, casting a seductive glow upon the tantalizing possibilities nestling in Näcken's touch. The allure of an uncharted expedition beckoned, urging her to take that audacious leap into the chasm of passion nestled within Näcken's grasp.

In the innermost recesses of her being, Liv wrestled with desires, torn betwixt the sanctuary of her bed and the siren call that resonated from the recesses of her longing. The interplay of yearning and trepidation wove an intricate pattern of emotions, each strand pulling her closer to the precipice of surrender, yet anchoring her with a tether of caution.

In the refuge of her musings, Liv yearned for the transformative caress that Näcken could bestow upon her, envisioning the fathomless depths of experience unfurling in his wake. It was an invitation to explore uncharted territories of pleasure and intimacy, to transcend the confines of the familiar and plunge into the realms of rapture nestled within Näcken's embrace.

Thus, as Liv wrapped herself in the warmth of her bed, she grappled with desires, her heart suspended betwixt the longing for Näcken's touch and the tremors of consequence that awaited her. In this delicate waltz of yearning and reservation, she contemplated the risks and rewards that lingered beyond her sanctuary, her resolve poised upon the edge of ambiguity.

For now, she remained enfolded in the familiar embrace of her haven, cocooned by its protective shelter. Yet the spark of curiosity within her continued to glow, a flame that whispered of liberation and profound connection. It murmured of a time when she would summon the fortitude to venture forth and seek the bountiful experiences Näcken could unveil, defying the constraints of fear and surrendering to the spellbinding euphoria that awaited her in his touch.

A warm and pleasant feeling, like an awaited rain in the desert, started to grow around her crotch, her clitoris seemed to be aching when thought of Näcken invaded her mind. With a delicate grace, Liv allowed her hand to glide down towards her clitoris, guided by an invisible current of desire. Each movement was a reflection of her burgeoning passion, an exploration of sensations that resonated deep within her being. As her fingertips traversed the landscape of her own longing, they became the vessels of her desires, tracing a path of anticipation upon her skin. The atmosphere appeared charged with electric tension, as if the entirety of creation paused, enthralled by the intimate dance between Liv and her own yearning.

With every stroke and caress, Liv unravelled the layers of inhibition that had confined her, liberating herself in the wake of her own audacity. The touch of her hand, both tender and commanding, waking a crescendo of pleasure that cascaded through her veins, awakening dormant senses with an intoxicating fervour.

In this exquisite act of self-discovery, Liv basked in her own sensuality, revelling in the depths of her desires that unfolded beneath the smooth touch of her hand. It was a journey of self-revelation, a dance of vulnerability and empowerment, where the boundaries of pleasure blurred and merged into a tapestry of pure ecstasy.

As her hand continued its descent, Liv felt a stirring of primal energy, a connection to the core of her being that transcended the confines of the physical. Her touch became an affirmation of her own desires, an invitation to revel in the pleasure that resided within her, and to honour the profound beauty of her own sensual nature.

With each movement, Liv delved deeper into the unknown territories of her own sensuality, unearthing hidden desires and unveiling layers of passion that had long been dormant. Her hand became a conduit for liberation, a homage to her own autonomy and the fierce embrace of her own pleasure.

In this private moment of self-exploration, Liv celebrated the sovereignty of her body, revelling in the intoxicating symphony that reverberated through her every nerve ending. Her hand, an instrument of both tenderness and audacity, inscribed a tale of self-empowerment upon her skin, leaving an indelible mark of liberation and unbridled passion.

In the fluidity of her touch, she found solace, as her hand

became an extension of her own untamed spirit, guiding her towards a realm where pleasure and self-acceptance converged in a glorious union.

In the depths of her yearning, Liv cast aside the weight of societal expectations and the judgment of the priest. In that moment, the boundaries that confined her desires faded into insignificance, eclipsed by the intensity of her emotions. The thought of having intercourse with an ungodly creature, heightened her sense even more. Her longing and passion for Näcken was forbidden, a sinful act that society would condemn and outcast her for. Moreover, she had broken the sixth commandment of engaging in sexual act with someone other than her spouse.

In the veiled embrace of secrecy, Liv comprehended the looming danger that lay in the revelation of her clandestine bond with Näcken. The repercussions, grave and unyielding, poised to devour not only her mere existence but the essence of her being. The burden of impending judgment pressed upon her with the force of an untamed ocean, for she recognized the tempest of disgrace that would engulf her family's name.

Yet, nestled within the depths of her soul, Liv remained untainted by the smouldering flames of guilt. She defied the notion of being branded a sinner, for her heart had guided her along a luminous trail adorned with Näcken's irresistible allure. In yielding to that enchantment, she unearthed a liberation that soared beyond the confines of societal norms and expectations. The essence of her existence throbbed with a newfound emancipation, as if she had chanced upon a secret verity that propelled her into an elevated realm of consciousness and breathtaking splendour.

With gentle touch, like a bee tending to a flower, Liv stroke her clitoris in circles, while she focused all her energy on Näcken's magnific body and captivating mind. Within her yearning flesh she felt the sexual energy bursting up inside of her, something had awakened, something that could not be denied but demanded attention and undivided loyalty, like a tsunami impossible to control. An unworldly passion forced itself through her blood, leaving unforgettable marks in her arteries.

In the hallowed hush of shadows, Liv turned inward, a tempest of willpower churning within her. With fervent determination, she suppressed the primal urge to let forth her moaning, a symphony of silence galloping through her soul.

In the absence of Näcken's physical presence, Liv poured forth the depths of her energy, dedicating every essence of her being to him. With each breath, she surrendered herself to the profound connection they shared, confident that Näcken could perceive the fervent homage she offered. Though physically apart, Liv's energy pulsed with an undeniable force, bridging the gap between their beings. She trusted that Näcken, with his supernatural essence, could sense the magnitude of her offering, the intensity of her passion that exceeded the limitations of the tangible world.

All worlds and all the realms came together in her act of self-pleasure. Liv's love for herself and her yearning for Näcken converged within her and poured out into the universe at a rapid speed.

In the cradle of her desire and yearning, a wave of indescribable pleasure washed over Liv, cascading through her being like a torrential downpour of liberation.Every filament of her existence hummed with an exquisite harmony, as she melded effortlessly with the abyss of her yearnings. She welcomed her longings unreservedly, allowing them to enfold her in a seraphic caress, a ballet of vulnerability and empowerment that roused a powerful enthusiasm within her soul. In the fierce tango upon the edge of her own yearning, Liv luxuriated in the heady emancipation that enveloped her. She yielded to the profound depths of her desires, welcoming the euphoria that coursed through her veins, a homage the unbridled ardour pulsating within her.

A vivid display of Näcken's unforgettable penis took a firm grip of her thoughts, his limb held a perfect size. Anticipation surged through Liv's veins, like a symphony of fluttering butterflies. Her heart quickened, matching the rhythm of her breath, as she yearned for the gentle caress of Näcken's breath upon her neck and his pulsating penis within her. The mere thought of his warm exhales and his strong limb playing roughly inside her body, sent shivers of delight cascading down her spine.

Every fibre of her being quivered in delicious anticipation, as she painted vivid fantasies in her mind's eye. The whispered promises of Näcken's breath, like a tantalizing breeze, told secrets of pleasure and intimacy, igniting a wildfire of desire within her. In her daydreams, she could almost feel the tantalizing proximity of his lips, brushing against her neck. Imagining the softness of his breath, she surrendered to the wonderful dance of sensation and longing, craving the electrifying connection that would ignite their souls.

She yearned for the intoxicating dance of Näcken's breath against her skin, his penis filling every inch of her, the wild whispers of his presence that would send tremors of pleasure coursing through every cell of her exited body.In the fervent ache of yearning, Liv revelled in the imminent convergence of their souls, eagerly anticipating the sacred fusion that would render them breathless, forever transformed.

The mere thought of Näcken's breath upon her neck orchestrated a symphony of longing, a prelude to the symmetrical union that beckoned. Thus, she steeled herself for the seductive bliss that lay in wait, aware that Näcken's whispered breath, akin to a pledge of devotion, would ignite a resplendent odyssey into realms where passion and fulfilment intertwine in harmonious rapture.

She was willing to let Näcken do anything to her, no task was too arduous, no boundary too daunting. Liv stood ready, like a willing acolyte, to explore the new territories of their shared desires. In this intense dance of dominance and submission, Liv discovered a new sense of purpose. Her willingness to fulfil Näcken's desires became an affirmation of her own inner strength and her unyielding commitment to their bond. It was an illustration of the extraordinary lengths she would go to nourish their connection and quench the insatiable thirst of their shared passion. She continued to rub her clitoris harder with her fingers. A stream of pleasure advanced within her system. She could feel herself getting closer to orgasm. Liv focused on Näcken and imagined him taking her wildly from behind, just like the untamed best he was.

In the depths of her imagination, Liv conjured vivid images of Näcken's primal nature, a raw and feral essence that stirred her senses. She marvelled at the untapped ferocity that lay dormant within him, eagerly anticipating their next encounter and the unrestrained passion it would unleash while he devoured her from behind. The thought of his perfect hands on her bulbous nipples made Liv touched herself faster and faster, her entire body tuned in with her longing, she was getting close to finishing.

When Liv climaxed, she felt a wave of light, energy and pleasure bursting through her system as she put her entire hand over her clitoris. She had dedicated this moment to herself and to the desirable creature of the lake.

After pleasuring herself, a blissful warmth immersed Liv, caressing her being with a gentle tease, as she luxuriated in the afterglow of her Näcken-inspired fantasies.

A radiant smile graced her lips, illuminating the room with a glow born of pure contentment and joy. Her sexual fantasies about Näcken subsides and she felt content for the night.

Encased by the tender promise of slumber, Liv embarked on a voyage where dreams took wing. Deep within her heart, a flickering ember of hope twirled, casting a gentle radiance upon her serene face.

As she surrendered to the tranquil depths of the night, a sense of elation unfurled within her being. It spoke soft, melodic assurances of the yet-unseen, crafting a blend of anticipation and tranquillity.

In the cradle of her reveries, Liv's spirit soared with unwavering optimism, carrying her across imaginative landscapes of the subconscious. Within this realm of limitless marvels, hope bloomed like a resplendent blossom, infusing her dreams with vivacious vigour.

As the stars swept their celestial brushstrokes across the heavens, Liv's dreams became a canvas where her buoyant aspirations unfurled. With each untroubled breath, her spirit bathed in the boundless expanse of possibilities, where every tomorrow held the potential for enchantment and fulfilment.

In the sweet enfoldment of the night's gentle hold, Liv slept calmly, her heart buoyed by the whispers of a brighter dawn. In that ethereal realm between wakefulness and slumber, her soul veered to the cadence of hope, nurturing the seeds of potential that blossomed within her dreams.

CHAPTER 8

Days melted like honey under the sun's gentle caress, while Näcken's unforgettable presence whispered softly, entwining its ethereal tendrils around Liv's every musing. His essence, a haunting elixir, had intruded itself into her very essence, etching an everlasting sigil upon her resilient soul. Deep within, an insatiable flame danced, its fervour feeding her daydreams, dissolving the boundaries of her reality. Amidst the warmth of a dazzling Sunday morning, when the heavens brushed the sky with strokes of molten gold and the air shimmered with an alluring hug, Liv and her family gathered at the village church. Clad in garments woven with devotion and reverence, they adorned their earthly forms, mere mortals draped in sacred raiments. Within the sanctified church, a chorus of voices melded, their harmonies ascending towards celestial realms, entwining with the sanctity of the consecrated space.

Yet, amid the melodies and pious rites, Liv found herself entangled in a ceaseless struggle with her own musings, her heart's yearnings ensnared within Näcken's enchanting clasp. Though her gaze remained fixed upon the altar, she beheld naught but the paradisiacal spectre of his presence, a phantasmal echo that whispered deep within her spirit. The sacred hymns mingled with the rhythm of her racing pulse, as she grappled with the dichotomy of her existence—enveloped in the corporeal realm of the church, forever tethered to Näcken's mystic magnetism.

While the congregation sought solace and divine communion, Liv's mind wandered through different realms, chasing the lingering echoes of Näcken's haunting melodies. The sacred hymns became a distant refrain, eclipsed by the symphony of her own fervent desires. And as the prayers swirled through the air, Liv's thoughts reached out to Näcken, traversing the threshold between devotion and an insatiable yearning for a reunion fated to elude her grasp. Within the untrodden abyss of Liv's soul, a timeless struggle unfolded—a battle waged between her earthly obligations and the irresistible charm of Näcken's otherworldly allure. Oblivious to the tempest brewing beneath her composed visage, her kin sought answers in familiar rituals, while Liv wrestled with the ever-deepening chasm that separated her reality from the enigmatic realm she had been drawn into.

In the aftermath of that hallowed Sunday, Liv carried within her a tumultuous sea of thoughts and desires. Though the world may have continued its customary stride, within her, a tempest raged—a tempest fuelled by Näcken's essence, forever altering the course of her existence.

Within the gentle folds of the church pews, Liv nestled herself between Lars and Karin, Greta's youngest children, while the steadfast presence of Finn and his family formed an unbreakable bond in the row just behind. As the congregation swayed to the cadence of prayers, Liv closed her eyes, permitting her mind to wander through the labyrinthine corridors of her existence, tracing the footprints that had led her to this definitive moment.

In the midst of the sacred ambiance, where the fragrance of incense mingled with fervent whispers of devotion, Liv ventured on an inner quest within her thoughts. The rituals of the mass held scant allure for her, for deep within her being, she held the belief that divinity, if it existed, would rejoice in the liberation and jubilation of humanity. True worship, to her, entailed accepting the freedom to follow the compass of the heart, adorning the world with acts of compassion and love, rather than seeking solace in mundane prayers within the confines of a lacklustre sanctuary, where the priest's voice sought to burden the faithful with sin and shame.

Liv's faith took root in a different soil, one that celebrated life's splendid diversity and beckoned the soul to unravel the boundless possibilities it bestowed. The church's dogmas felt constricting to her spirit, akin to a captive bird yearning to soar amidst the immense scope of the sky. For Liv, the path of devotion transcended the boundaries of rigid doctrines, reaching towards the sun-drenched horizons where kindness, acceptance, and limitless love reigned supreme.

In the tranquil pew, as the hymns cascaded through the air like gentle sighs of devotion, Liv held steadfast to her convictions. Her eyes remained sealed, guarding the colourful mosaic of her convictions from the prying gazes of the faithful surrounding her. She found strength in her silent rebellion, guided by the compass of her conscience, in symphony with the pulsating rhythms of life itself.

In the presence of the zealous invocations and respectful gestures, Liv carved her own asylum within the depths of her being, a retreat that met the world with open arms, cherishing the sacredness in every breath and every beating heart. For her, the true essence of worship resided in the profound connection with the roots of existence, fortified by the threads of empathy, compassion, and an unwavering pursuit of truth.

Näcken's magical whispers reverberated through her, entwined with her breath, quickening her pulse. The world had undergone an irrevocable change, and Liv stood at the precipice of choice—a choice between the path of duty and the irresistible siren calls of a connection that exceeded the grasp of mortal comprehension. While the churchgoers dispersed, entranced in their own contemplations, Liv stood firm in her faith, cognizant that her values danced to a distinct rhythm—one that celebrated life's grand symphony and beckoned the soul to explore its boundless and awe-inspiring territories

In the arms of the church pew, amidst the hushed mumbles of devotion, Liv remained true to her path—a path that exalted life's rich palette of shades, championed the emancipation of the spirit, and welcomed the beauty dwelling within every soul she encountered. And as she unveiled her eyes to the world, she carried her faith, unyielding and resplendent, a flame burning luminous within her, enlivening her adventure upon a road less traversed.

Within the firm walls of the sanctuary, as the mass gracefully came to an end, Liv sat in poised silence, her ears graciously receiving the priest's sermon. Yet, her heart and mind initiated a clandestine voyage to a realm far beyond, a realm adorned with dreams and wild musings. Swift as a startled deer, she swiftly retreated from those forbidden reveries, conscious of the priest's watchful gaze upon her. His eyes, stern and penetrating, pierced through her veil of devotion, sensing the wanderings of her spirit.

Liv was intimately acquainted with the priest's indifference towards her, a chilly barrier erected between them from the very beginning. Prudently, she had learned not to provoke or challenge his authority, for she was acutely aware of the precarious position in which women found themselves. Her interactions with the clergyman were reduced to mere nods and carefully measured words, a dance of cautious steps and restrained gestures. Liv understood all too well the perils that awaited those daring women who exhibited too much resilience, their strength perceived as a threat to the established order.

With each fleeting moment in the pew, Liv enveloped herself in a shroud of discretion, concealing her inner world beneath the mask of compliance. Behind her measured nods and guarded silence, a tempest of thoughts and desires thrived, wild and yearning for emancipation. But within the confines of the hallowed space, she dared not unfurl the wings of her spirit too widely, fearful of attracting the attention of those who sought to suppress her.

In the priest's gaze, Liv glimpsed the disapproval that had tainted their encounters, an unspoken message signalling that her individuality and strength were unwelcome within the boundaries of their interactions. It was an implicit understanding, one that underscored the delicate dance she was compelled to perform, adroitly navigating the treacherous waters of subservience while silently nurturing the flame of her inner resilience.

The weight of societal expectations bore down upon her, an incessant reminder of the hazards that awaited those women who dared to defy the norms. And so, Liv cloaked her voice in restraint, veiled her thoughts, concealing the profound depths of her spirit in a dance of self-preservation. In a world where whispers could swiftly transform into cries of accusation, she clung to the potency of silence, allowing her actions to resound eloquently as she mastered the art of navigating treacherous terrains.

As the mass neared its culmination, and the congregation dispersed like dandelion seeds in the wind, Liv rose in unison with the flock, her outward demeanour a mirror of conformity, her heart a labyrinth of conflicting emotions. Yet, deep within her being, the flame of her indomitable will burned brightly, a quiet rebellion against the constraints imposed upon her. With each step she took, she carried the weight of a history teeming with silenced voices and oppressed souls, vowing to honour their arduous struggle by treading delicately along the precarious line that delineated survival from self-expression.

Amidst the fading echoes of church hymns, Liv emerged from the embrace of the sanctuary, burdened by the unspoken truths that resided within her. And as she departed from the hallowed abode, her eyes met the priest's stern gaze one final time, an exchange bearing with profound meaning—defiance cloaked in compliance, resilience veiled in submission, an unheard concerto resonating across the centuries.

The congregation strewn like flowers carried by a mild wind, seeking solace in the shared warmth outside the church. Liv and her family mingled amid the colourful composition of conversation, exchanging pleasantries and savouring fragments of the day's tales. With grace and tenderness, Liv adorned her countenance with a friendly smile, gracefully partaking in the exchange of polite discourse with each neighbour, ever mindful of the weight of societal expectations delicately poised upon her shoulders.

Amidst the bustling symphony that followed the service's conclusion, the sun-kissed congregation gradually dispersed, bidding fond farewells and embarking on their homeward journeys. Liv, together with her family, meandered along the familiar path that led them back to their cherished home. As per the enduring beliefs of Finn's father, an unwavering champion of Sunday's sanctity, the male members of the family sought respite, while the women and children gracefully assumed their roles as guardians of hearth and kinship.

Within their humble dwelling, the womenfolk embarked on a tender ballet of culinary craftsmanship, their nimble hands and affectionate hearts weaving an orchestration of tantalizing aromas and exquisite flavours. Laughter's melodies and the harmonious chorus of clinking utensils resounded through the air, as the family embraced the patriarchal traditions. Amidst the rhythmic cadence of domesticity, Liv, ever attuned to the customs bestowed upon her, dutifully tended to her responsibilities, her hands an extension of devotion and duty for those who shared her life on the farm.

As the sun painted the sky with strokes of amber and gold,

the chiming echoes of church bells faded into the distant ether. It was within their cherished dwelling that Liv and her kin sought solace and rejuvenation, nourishing both body and soul. And as the tantalizing aroma of a lavish meal enveloped the space, an undeniable sense of unity and gratitude imbued the atmosphere, casting an enchanting spell of tranquillity upon all who sought solace within those homestead walls.

In the rhythmic cadence of their labour, in the collective understanding of their contemporary roles, Liv and the women of the household honoured the essence of family and tradition. Each task executed with intention and imbued with strength, their harmonious symphony resonated with the intricate threads that wove them together as one. And while the men reclined in repose, their spirits replenished, the women's unwavering dedication radiated the obligations of their duties, their quiet fortitude a testament to the profound resilience coursing through their veins.

As the hands of the clock swirled in a dance across the face of time, the culmination of the nourishing feast drew near. The fruits of their labour, both tangible and solid, stood as a reminder to the rhythm of their lives, a constellation of hard labour and dedication interlaced with every morsel gracing the table. And as the enticing aroma of their collective efforts enveloped the abode, the air came alive with shared laughter and whispered conversations, casting a gentle, inviting glow upon their cherished home. As the family converged around the table, their hearts brimming with affection, they revelled in the sustenance that transcended the mere fare before them. For within those hallowed walls, affection, ancestral customs, and the sturdy promise of kinship illuminated the fundamental nature of their being, enkindling eternal flames of gratitude that danced ceaselessly within their souls.

After dinner, when everyone had fallen asleep in their beds, under the shroud of night, as the world succumbed to the mantles of darkness, Liv's restless spirit stirred within her. A primal yearning, fierce and irresistible, tugged at the strings of her heart, beckoning her to seek Näcken once more. Yet, trepidation held her captive, spinning a tangled web of fear that entwined her every thought. Dread clawed at her being, for she knew all too well the consequences that awaited should her absence be discovered. The mere spectre of Finn's wrath, his tempestuous fury, cast a sinister pall over her resolve.

In the hushed depths of solitude, Liv wrestled with her desires, her mind a battlefield of choices. She pondered the feeble excuses that could be woven, should prying eyes inquire about her nocturnal sojourn. A tale of hunting or foraging for wild berries held a semblance of plausibility, yet its fragility threatened to crumble beneath the scrutiny of discerning gazes. For Finn possessed an uncanny intuition, a knowing that delved far beneath the surface. To him, a woman slipping into the night harboured a singular purpose, one that no artifice or deceit could cloak.

Still, the flames of passion blazed unabated within her, their intensity consuming her very essence. And so, she confronted the eternal quandary that plagued her existence. Was she to endure a half-life, enchained by the shackles of convention and fear, for the sake of transient security? Or should she, with bated breath and a heart pounding like a captive bird, seize the opportunity to relish in happiness, even if it meant courting danger and the uncharted? The scales of her heart teetered, whispering a resolute answer that reverberated deep within her soul.

In the chambers of her spirit, the fear of mortality held little sway, its grip weakened by the spectre of an unfulfilled life. Liv, with a flicker of defiance, resolved to seize the elusive strands of joy that had eluded her for far too long. The clandestine tryst with Näcken beckoned, its allure promising emancipation from the fetters that bound her. And so, with a resolve forged in the crucible of longing, she dared to venture into the night, guided by the magnetic pull of desire.

Silently, like a phantom moving through the haze, Liv slipped away, her footsteps cautious yet resolute, as if eluding the vigilant sentinels guarding her existence. Each breath carried a potent mixture of anticipation and trepidation, an intoxicating blend that swirled within her. The risk weighed heavily upon her shoulders, the delicate equilibrium between liberation and the consequences of discovery poised precariously. Yet, fuelled by the fierce yearning that blazed within her, she cast off the cloak of fear and embraced the unknown with audacity born of desire and longing.

For Liv knew that the embrace of Näcken held the promise of an existence unburdened by the restraints of her present reality. In his presence, her spirit soared, unshackled from the chains that threatened to confine her. And so, with a heart filled with yearning, she commenced a clandestine path, defying the manacles of convention and destiny.

In the moonlit realm, where whispers danced in the midst of the shadows of darkness, Liv set out upon her maiden stride towards the enigmatic Näcken, led by the luminous flame of her yearnings. The night became her closest confidant, encircling her in its midnight grasp, as she boldly ventured into the realm where dreams took shape. And in that audacious quest for forbidden rapture, Liv blossomed like a resplendent phoenix, rising from the remnants of conformity, giving in to the delicate allure of a life created on her own terms.

With careful grace, Liv walked into the mysterious night. As she approached the edge of the forest, a sight awaited her that ignited her very essence. Näcken stood there, an otherworldly presence adorned in the splendour of moonlight. Her heart danced to an erratic rhythm, in sync with the pulse of the universe. In his presence, the forest stirred, its secrets whispered upon the wind, while a celestial luminescence illuminated the path ahead.

Tall and slender he stood, draped in the honesty of his being, his countenance resembling a constellation of glistening diamonds. His porcelain skin, caressed by the gentle touch of starlight, held her gaze captive, reflecting the moon's soft glow with a resplendent shimmer. As Liv's eyes met Näcken's lustrous locks, her heart quickened, for within that enchanting hue, she glimpsed a reflection of the enigmatic depths that lay within him. His hair, like a bewitching secret shared by woodland sprites, beckoned her closer to the essence of his soul, urging her to unravel the mysteries hidden within.

Within his eyes, celestial spheres converged, casting a cosmic radiance that surpassed finite intellect. Ancient wisdom, woven through the fabric of countless eons, resonated in the chambers of his mind, calling to Liv to delve into their unfathomable depths.

In his enigmatic presence, an indomitable strength emanated, defying comprehension. Yet, enmeshed with this boundless power, a profound sorrow cascaded, tugging at Liv's heartstrings. It was a sorrow that bore witness to the weight of existence, echoing the whispers of forgotten tales and lost ages. Within Näcken's essence, she encountered a paradox—a symphony of light and darkness, strength and vulnerability, interlinked within the threadwork of his being.

Together, they stood on the threshold of possibility, their destinies entwined by the cosmic dance of two souls enraptured in the enigma of existence. In the tranquil stillness of the night, as the forest shared its secrets in hushed whispers, Liv surrendered herself to the hypnotic influence of Näcken's aura, knowing that within this extraordinary encounter lay the potential for both ecstasy and despair.

"You are here, you have come to meet me," Liv observed.

"Your yearning reverberated within the heart of existence," Näcken responded, his voice a symphony of shadows and echoes. "I could not resist the call, for I longed to be your guardian, navigating you through the enchanting depths of the forest." His words carried weight, dripping with a haunting resonance that stirred the depths of Liv's soul.

"So, it is true that you can perceive my emotions?" Liv's hesitation, like a fleeting shadow, danced across her soft face. Yet, deep within her being, a spark of newfound courage ignited. It illuminated her eyes with a resolute gleam, casting aside any lingering doubts.

"In the realm of judgment, shame and guilt are but mortal constructs," Näcken's voice resounded with ancient wisdom. His eyes, oceans of time-honoured knowledge, held no condemnation, only acceptance. "I am not here to confine or alter your essence. I exist beyond the confines of human perception, liberated from the chains of imposed morality. It is your untamed and unapologetic true nature that calls to me." His words echoed through the night, carrying a profound truth that inflamed her heart and soul. In Näcken's presence, she felt liberated, held by an acceptance that surpassed human bias. Näcken's piercing gaze met Liv's, entwining their souls in an unbreakable connection. Within his words, there existed an untamed freedom, a release from the guilt of shame and judgment. In his presence, Liv found release, as if the weight of societal expectations had dissipated. She understood that her desires were not to be condemned or hidden away, but to be cherished and celebrated. Näcken's words resonated deep within her, urging her to surrender to the passions that stirred her heart.

"But I am wedded to another," Liv's voice, a mere whisper, carried her words like a delicate breeze through the night. Vulnerability and longing intertwined within her voice, floating toward Näcken like a fragile melody.

"In the realm of existence, the truth of your life unfurls, born from choice and possibility. A delicate crossroad stands before you, inviting you to decide. Should you yearn to return to the embrace of your husband, fear not, for I shall cast no shadows upon your decision," Näcken uttered with serene cadence.

Revealing the depths of his soul, he confessed, "Jealousy finds no dwelling within my ethereal being, for it belongs to the realm of fleeting mortals. The bond that ties you to another man holds no sway over my essence. I do not seek to possess you as humans covet their beloved, like an imprisoned bird. Nay, I yearn for your liberation, to traverse the labyrinth of your unique journey, to be wholly and authentically yourself. Grant me the privilege to accompany you on this profound voyage, for I long to be your guide, unveiling the enigma of your deepest desires. Together, we shall unravel the intricacies of your essence, unearthing every secret longing and unearthly passion that resides within your being."

"Your eyes bear a different hue this night," Liv's gaze rested upon Näcken's otherworldly form, a being born from the annals of ancient folklore. His countenance, a symphony of ethereal grace, transcended temporal confines and cosmic realms alike. His beauty, an enigmatic force, wove its way through the tapestry of existence, whispering tales of enchantment and wonderment.

"In the limitless magnitude of existence," he whispered, his voice a gentle caress, "I possess the power to assume any semblance that mirrors the depths of your longing. Within the realm of your emotions, your dreams, and your cravings, I resonate and breathe. My very essence entwines with your being, intimately entangled within the intricate fibres of your desires."

With a celestial smile, he continued, his words kindling a modest inferno of potential and indecision. "Behold, for my enchantments know no bounds. I possess the power to shape-shift, traversing the spectrum of forms, assuming the guise that ignites the flames of your deepest yearnings. This arcane magic grants me the freedom to aid, to ensnare, to captivate, to impart wisdom, to dispense justice, or even to allure the very essence of your mortal existence. In every realm, with each soul, a unique perception unravels, painting a portrait of who I shall become, " he pondered. "Within the canvas of your desires, I perceive the flickering candles of anticipation. In this delicate dance, I hold the ability to shape destiny, carefully interlacing strands of your aspirations and determining their ultimate fate."

"What would you have me do this eve?" Liv inquired, her voice trembling with longing.

"Within the depths of our shared realm," a proclamation echoed from Näcken's lips, resonating with a supernatural promise. "I am but a vessel for your deepest desires," he murmured, his voice a celestial melody, "a willing servant to your unspoken whims. No plea need escape your lips, for my essence perceives the silent cadence of your heart."

In the realm of unity, Näcken embraced Liv, his touch a declaration of unwavering devotion. Carried by his strength, they travelled through the sacred woodland, where whispers of ancient spirits intertwined with the whispering leaves. Amidst dappled hues of emerald and gold, their journey spoke of voiceless harmony, an uncharted path laid by their entangled destinies.

With a graceful embrace, Näcken effortlessly swept Liv off her feet, carrying her through the lush expanse of the forest. Amidst the ancient sentinels of towering trees, they undertook their journey, guided by the unseen hand of destiny. Until, at last, they emerged into a beautiful clearing, where time itself seemed to pause in awe.

Arriving at a sanctified clearing, bathed in the radiant glow of moonlit rays, Näcken tenderly seated Liv upon a rustic throne, a steadfast log of nature's grandeur. It was here, in the stillness of nature's breath, that their passions would grow uninhibited, like flowers revealing their beauty to be kissed by the sun's gentle touch.

With an ardor that transcended the mortal realm, Näcken's impassioned lips sought Liv's, igniting a blaze of desires that engulfed them both. Their souls entwined in a passionate ballet, their bodies vessels of celestial yearning. Through every tender caress, every passionate dance of sensation, Näcken traversed the map of her essence, his touch an artist's brush upon the canvas of her being.

In a realm where desires interweave, Näcken's passion soared through the air, an unspoken pledge hidden in his voice. Without plea or supplication, his very essence discerned the unspoken longings that stirred within Liv's heart. It was as if the vines of her wishes whispered their secrets to his soul, uniting their destinies in an enchanting puzzle.

Their lips collided in a fervent union, an intoxicating blend of passion and longing. His hands, guided by an unyielding confidence, roamed the curves of her body, a sensuous dance of exploration and connection. Every caress, every whisper of touch, awakened a melodic array of sensations. their bodies entwined in a rhapsody of ecstasy.

A surge of exhilaration swept through Liv's veins, leaving her breathless and yearning for more. As Näcken's hands journeyed through the shape of her form, a cacophony of reactions erupted, resonating with a perfect harmony that sent shivers of pleasure coursing through her every fiber.

In Näcken's touch, Liv discovered a profound connection, a delicate dance of intimacy and desire that left her gasping for the sweet oxygen of passion. With each caress, his hands moved with a purposeful strength, starting an avalanche that conquered every single cell in her body, with an intensity she had never known.

In a moment of raw vulnerability, Liv felt her inhibitions melt away like snow giving in to spring’s cruel touch, as Näcken expertly unveiled the layers that adorned her, removing the garments that shielded her from the world. His touch was both tender and commanding, a recognition of his understanding of her deepest desires and the profound trust that bound them together.

With every article of clothing cast aside, Liv stood exposed, basking in the freedom of vulnerability. Näcken's strength, both physical and emotional, morphed into a place of protection, where she could fully surrender to the magical currents of their connection.

As Näcken's hands explored the landscape of her skin, Liv surrendered herself to the flow of pleasure that consumed her. In his touch, she found a resonance, an affirmation that they were indeed meant to trek this path together. The power of Näcken's touch awakened dormant desires within her, stirring a passionate flame that burned with an insatiable hunger. As Näcken's hands moved with purpose and grace, Liv surrendered to the beguiling dance of their desires. In their passionate union, she discovered a profound liberation, a place where the weight of the world dissolved and she could revel in the pure ecstasy of being alive, entwined with Näcken in a medley of pleasure and bliss.

Liv moaned out to the universe in ecstatic pleasure, the undeniable truth of him being a spirit of the lake faded into oblivion, his touch felt like a divine blessing upon her aroused body. The forbidden nature of their affair set off a primal wildfire within Liv, intensifying her desire with each passing moment. With a resolute determination, Näcken's lips descended upon Liv's quivering belly and hips, bestowing a trail of passionate kisses that left her craving for more.

In that hidden domain, where societal veils dissolved and conventions were but whispers, Liv became ensnared in a potent elixir of desire and elation. The awareness of their forbidden union only amplified her yearning, starting an incontrollable hurricane, defying all logic.

As Näcken's lips made contact with her supple skin, a mixture of electric perceptions coursed through Liv's body, igniting a cascade of pleasurable tremors that vibrated to the very centre of her self. His kisses, tender yet fervent, traced a path of ecstasy along her belly and hips, leaving an indelible imprint upon her soul. In each deliberate movement, Näcken revelled in the illicit nature of their connection, understanding the entrancing power that lay within the forbidden fruit. His lips, like a prohibited elixir, bestowed upon Liv a feast of unbridled pleasure, further entwining their souls in a dance of longing and surrender.

With every kiss, Näcken stoked the embers of Liv's desire, awakening a hunger that grew insatiable with each passing moment. The forbidden nature of their affair infused their union with a heightened sense of urgency and a seductive blend of danger and ecstasy.

Decisively Näcken moved his muscular arms down over Liv's trembling body and spread her legs, lust was taking over his mind and bewitched her with intriguing pleasure.

As Näcken's lips ventured beyond her mouth, they traversed the expanse of her skin, leaving a trail of zealous affection in their wake. From the curve of her neck to the gentle slope of her collarbone, his kisses were an artful exploration, as if he sought to map the contours of her essence with his tender touch.

As Liv perched upon the log, an oasis of their shared desire, Näcken's lips became the catalyst for an enchanting interplay between their souls. With a tender reverence, he leaned in closer, his breath mingling with hers, and bestowed upon her a series of delicate kisses upon her clitoris that opened the floodgates of sensations within her being.

With each brush of Näcken's lips against her expanding clitoris, Liv felt the world around them dissolve into a magical realm, where time stood still and the only reality that mattered was the enticing connection they shared. Each kiss upon her coveting clitoris carried a weight of longing, a token of their shared desires and the unspoken language of passion that flowed between them. Näcken's tongue played intensely with her clitoris while his hands caressed her legs.

With a tender determination, Näcken's lips delved into the depths of seduction, leaving a trail of feathery kisses along the delicate expanse of Liv's inner thighs. Each caress was a whisper of desire, a tantalizing exploration that sent waves of anticipation coursing through her deepest corners.

As Näcken's kisses gradually ascended, tracing an exquisite path up the landscape of her body, Liv's her senses erupted like a geyser in a dormant landscape, her skin electrified by the erotic touch of his lips. Each press of his mouth against her flesh was proof of his reverence and adoration, a token of the depth of his passion.

With a blend of gentleness and intensity, Näcken continued his ascent, bestowing kisses upon Liv's torso, his lips a hallowed melody of devotion and pleasure. Each lingering kiss stoked the fires of her longing, drawing her ever closer to the precipice of ecstasy. In the sensuous dance between Näcken's lips and Liv's supple skin, time ceased to exist. Their connection transcended the physical realm, building a bridge of profound intimacy and shared vulnerability. With each tender exploration, Näcken unravelled the layers of her desire, disentangling her inhibitions and awakening a passion that radiated like a scorching sun within her.

As Näcken's kisses traced their way upward, Liv surrendered herself to the rapture of their union. Each soft press of his lips against her flesh was an invitation to surrender, an invitation to delve deeper into the boundless realms of pleasure that awaited them.

In that sacred exchange of lips and skin, Näcken revelled in the artistry of seduction, evoking sensations that eclipsed the mundane and eclipsed the ordinary. It was a dance of passion and surrender, where Näcken's lips became the vessel through which Liv's desires were set free, elevating their connection to a realm of unrivalled intimacy.

Näcken kissed Liv's breasts and nipples like precious treasures hidden away from the worlds prying eyes, slowly he let his wet tongue and mouth embrace the gentle and fragile curves of her petit body.

With a tender yet commanding hold, Näcken effortlessly raised Liv, enfolding her in his arms as if she were a priceless gem adored by the cosmos. With deliberate elegance, he settled upon a weathered log, placing Liv upon his lap, creating a seductive place where their spirits could entwine in erotic unity.

In a choreography of desire, Näcken's lips descended upon Liv's neck, imprinting a trail of tender kisses that flared up like a torch in the darkness. The gentle brush of his lips against her sensitive flesh sent shivers of anticipation cascading down her spine, awakening a primal hunger that swelled within her core.

As his lips caressed her skin with featherlight precision, his fingertips forged a destiny of their own, tracing the contours of feminine origin. Gently Näcken slipped two fingers inside of Liv while his thumb caressed her clitoris. His fingers moved with purpose and intention, unleashing a storm of sensations that brought Liv to the precipice of ecstasy. In perfect harmony, Näcken's lips and fingertips led a rhythmic symposium of pleasure, their movements intertwining in a sensual dance that defied boundaries and ascended to higher realms, when they entered Liv. Each caress on her yearning clitoris unravelled the layers of Liv's desire, evoking a riotous yearning that demanded to be set free.

Liv surrendered herself to the tempting union of his touch upon her female parts. The exquisite fusion of his kisses and the graceful dance of his fingertips over her most sensitive areas, enveloped her in a world where time's sands no longer fell, and nothing mattered except the heated union of their desires. Näcken became both artist and poet, using his lips and fingertips to compose an opus of pleasure upon Liv's receptive canvas.

As if attuned to the very rhythm of her being, Näcken possessed an innate ability to anticipate Liv's every inclination, always one step ahead in their intricate dance of desire. It was as though their souls were embraced like two flames dancing in the wind, building an unspoken tie that extended across the realms of time and space.

With an uncanny intuition, Näcken effortlessly flowed with Liv's movements, a masterful partner in their intimate choreography. Whether it was a subtle shift in posture or a fleeting glance, he met her needs and desires with a profound understanding that left her breathless. With every nuanced movement, he unleashed the torrential currents of her dreams, effortlessly fulfilling her unspoken wishes, and leaving her in awe of the sublime union they shared.

With a sensuous rhythm, Liv's hips began to sway, an instinctive response to the bewitching magnetism between her and Näcken. In impeccable cohesiveness, Näcken drew her closer, their bodies merging in a seamless embrace, their hearts beating in unison while he touched the inside and outside of her body. As their upper bodies became enwrapped in a passionate tangle of limbs, Näcken's touch remained an ever-present caress upon Liv's skin. His hands, guided by an innate understanding of her desires, roamed her body with a reverent exploration, sparking infernos of yearning that engulfed their souls.

In the fortress of Näcken's kiss, Liv discovered serenity and a safeguarding shield that encompassed her whole being. His lips, wild and devoted, spoke a language of reassurance, whispering promises of unwavering protection and eternal presence. As their lips met in an intimate clinch, Liv knew deep within her soul that Näcken would never let her go.

With an innate understanding, Liv's hands ventured down the contours of Näcken's muscular back, tracing the vigorous landscape with a delicate touch. Her fingers, guided by a mixture of desire and trust, explored the stronghold that resided within him, revelling in the sensation of his warm, solid form beneath her touch. Näcken's arms were a refuge from the world's turmoil, a sanctuary where she could surrender herself completely, knowing that he would shield her from any harm.

While Näcken's lips caressed the tender shells of Liv's ears, his hands started to move faster. The poundings sensation of her looming climax filled the air. In the fiery grip of Näcken's commanding presence, Liv willingly surrendered to the dance of their desires. His confident demeanour and magnetic allure sparked a fire within her, igniting a profound sense of blissful surrender. She found solace in relinquishing control, knowing that Näcken's guiding dominance would lead them to untold heights of pleasure. As she gave in to his dominance, she discovered a freedom that hummed a joyous tune in her essence, unleashing a wellspring of unbridled passion and uninhibited longing.

While Liv climaxed, she uttered words of pleasure, Näcken pulled her closer, within his arms Liv felt shielded from the dangers of the world. Upon the rustic log, they sought solace in each other's arms, experiencing a timeless moment of profound connection. With intuitive acknowledgment, Näcken and Liv lingered in the embrace, their bodies melding together in predestined harmony. The hands of time paused their motion, as they sat, enveloped in the warmth of their shared presence.

"Why did you stop?" Liv's voice trembled, drawing Näcken's gaze into a cosmic reverie. Within the depths of his eyes, the whirlpool of infinite lives swirled, each fragment a luminescent memory, like a ripple spreading through the river of ages. The theatre of life opened its curtains to reveal its captivating acts, their entwining threads weaving a captivating drama of ancient wisdom, joys, and sorrows. The weight of ages and forgotten whispers converged, casting a spell that whispered of ancient secrets and profound connection.

"I will only proceed as your heart truly desires," Näcken responded, his words a dance of intrigue and anticipation.

"But it is you that I yearn for," Liv's voice, a gentle sigh, released her innermost secrets to the universe itself. The words, like dainty flowers, swaying with the softest touch, carried the weight of vulnerability and a trace of longing. In that whispered revelation, Liv bared a glimpse of her soul, sharing a part of herself hidden from the world.

"Yes," Näcken murmured, his voice a gentle rain, nourishing the seeds of her spirit., "yet within your longing lies the essence of our union." With effortless strength, he lifted her from the earth's embrace, cradling her in his arms. Together, like planets orbiting the sun, caught in an eternal cosmic dance, they descended from the realm of enchantment, guided by an unseen force.

Hand in hand, Näcken and Liv, ventured forth on a twilight odyssey, guided by the moon's magical glow, their footfalls weaving a vibrant symphony upon nature's blissful tapestry. The nocturnal whispers bore witness to their fiery union, a portrait painted by destiny's skilled hand, capturing the essence of life's journey, their souls entangled like vines in a dense forest.

Amidst the ebbing darkness, they tread the path that led to the farm, each step affirming their shared existence. In this nocturnal pilgrimage, Näcken's touch conveyed an unspoken promise, a vow to walk alongside her in the realm of the ordinary.

Together, united by a celestial filament, linking their souls with an unbreakable bond, they progressed homeward, their hands intertwined, guiding them through the labyrinthine passages of the night. As the moon bathed their path in a soft, silver glow, they journeyed through the enchanted labyrinth of their destiny, like heroes in an epic tale, surrendering to the whispers of the stars above.

"Are there others like you?" Liv's voice, a soft whisper, carried the curiosity of a thousand moonlit nights.

"In every shimmering lake, beneath nature's verdant veil, my kindred spirits lie, their ethereal presence a reflection of the sacred script written on the parchment of the universe's secrets. Once, the woodlands flourished with mystical beings, a celestial menagerie that graced the sacred stage of the earth, each playing its unique note in the orchestra of the universe. But as humanity's dominion expanded, the towering canopies trembled, felled by the relentless blades of progress, while waters turned bitter with the venom of indifference. With each passing sun, our numbers dwindle, fading like whispered enchantments that once held sway over mortal hearts. Where once we reigned as sovereigns of land and water, now fear taints the footsteps of humanity, for they dare not tread upon the realm we called our own. Yet, the shadow of oblivion looms ever closer, casting its pall upon our ethereal existence," Näcken responded, his voice a lament tinged with sorrow, echoing the mournful demise of a once-revered realm destined to fade into the realm of myth, its majesty like a fading star, once shining brightly but now dimmed by time.

"For how long have you dwelled here?" Liv's words, gentle as a breeze, sought to unveil the depths of Näcken's ancient existence.

"I am as ancient as the very soul of this lake," he replied, his words bearing the marks of time's indomitable flow, like scars on a weathered rock. Like a whispered incantation borne upon the wind, his words intertwined with the essence of primordial waters. Throughout epochs untold, his being had become entwined with the ebb and flow of the lake's ever-changing tides, their destinies forever entangled in a dance of ages. His voice held the wisdom gathered from forgotten realms and secrets whispered by ancient currents.

"What will become of you if the forest is felled, and the lake dries out?" Liv's voice trembled, her words like wisps of smoke, dissipating in the winds of doubt. Fear tinged her every syllable, revealing the vulnerability of her heart.

Näcken, peering into the depths of her being, beheld the melancholy that swelled within her eyes. Empathy flowed from his soul, a soft rain of insight, nourishing the seeds of understanding. "Weep not for my sake," he murmured, his words a soothing balm to her sorrow. "Neither shelter nor solace do I require, for I am the guardian of my own existence, standing unyielding amidst the currents of fate."

In his proclamation, Näcken unveiled a steadfast resolve, a lionheart, fearless in the face of obstacles, roaring with determination. Clad in the armour of unwavering strength, he embraced life's tumultuous currents, unburdened by the fragile cloak of vulnerability, a diamond, forged under pressure, reflecting the brilliance of his warrior spirit. Neither sympathy's allure nor protection's embrace could sway him, for his essence remained rooted in unyielding resilience, untouched by mortal desires.

"I yearn to keep our connection, yet I fear the discovery of my husband and the villagers," Liv confessed, her voice a delicate tremor, carrying the weight of her worries and apprehensions.

Upon Näcken's lips bloomed a vow, like steel, tempered in the furnace of truthful dedication. "As the guardian of your heart, I shall shield you from harm's ravages," he proclaimed, his voice a symphony of steadfast loyalty. In the depths of his resolute gaze, a flicker of protective ardour ignited, a flame that danced with eternal vigilance.

Like a sentinel of passion, he stood tall amidst the tempests that threatened their connection, his presence an unyielding bastion against darkness' onslaught. With every fibre of his ethereal being, he pledged to keep her safe from malevolence's grasp, drawing strength from the wellspring of his enduring loyalty.

Through untamed realms and uncharted trials, he would be her forever champion, shielding her soul from the arrows of adversity. No harm, no threat, no shadowed peril would befall her, for his devotion would stand as an impenetrable fortress, resolute and unwavering.

"You misunderstand, my concern lies not with my own safety, but with yours. I have witnessed the cruelty of the priest, his ruthlessness, and the villagers possess the means to hunt you down and kill you. I do not want your life to be forfeit because of our connection," Liv's voice quivered, laden with worry, as she shared her fears and anxieties with the ether. Her voice painted a portrait of trepidation, the creases of concern engraved on her visage, like ancient runes telling her tale.

With persistent valour coursing through his veins, Näcken spoke, his voice an unwavering anthem resonating through the sacred expanse. "Let them arise," he declared, undeterred by the encroaching spectres of danger. Like a beacon of hope in the midst of darkness, he welcomed the perils that awaited, standing tall like a mountain peak, rising above the clouds of doubt and uncertainty.

In the face of adversity, he vowed to confront each threat head-on, resolute in his determination. No retreat would mar his path, for he knew that within his very being dwelled the strength to defy any assault. With every fibre of his ethereal essence, he would rise to defend his existence, harnessing every tool at his disposal, summoning the forces of his divine might.

And if the final requiem beckoned, if the rivers of time carved their path through the landscape of destiny, he would not falter in despair. Amidst the veils of transition, he would stand resolute, his spirit unbroken, his existence transcending mortal fate. For even in his final breath, his essence would linger, a whisper upon the wind, an eternal testament to his unconquerable spirit.

"Maybe it is for the best to bid farewell," Liv whispered, her voice a delicate ripple upon the surface of her soul. Within the depths of her being, conflicting emotions swirled, a tempestuous symphony that played out the dance of their love. In its intricate melodies, she sensed the haunting notes of inevitable anguish and irreparable dissolution. The tapestry of fate, like a poet's pen, wrote a poetic verse of destiny, foretelling a journey laden with pain, destruction, and the looming spectre of mortality.

Trepidation's tendrils, like slender branches, entwined her heart, whispering cautionary tales of the sorrows that awaited them. She cast her gaze upon the path they walked, aware that the flames of their passion, though ablaze with brilliance, would eventually consume all in their wake, leaving only smouldering embers as remnants.

In this fragile moment, Liv stood at the precipice of truth, her heart caught in the uncertain dance of hope and fear. She recognized that their love, while radiant with intensity, carried within its core the seeds of inevitable suffering and the whispered dirges of their mortal frames.

Yet, amidst the thunderous clouds of uncertainty, the flicker of their connection beckoned her to tread the path of transcendence. For even in the face of impending tragedy, the allure of their connection, akin to a siren's song, held the promise of an experience so profound that it leaped over mortal boundaries.

In the hushed corridors of her consciousness, Liv grappled with the paradox of their romance, where love and agony coexisted. And within that delicate balance, she must choose between surrendering to the inevitable sorrows or embracing the ephemeral ecstasy that could only bloom in the shadow of their impending fate.

"Should your conviction align with such a choice, I shall honour it with utmost reverence," Näcken spoke, his voice a celestial chant that filled the sacred enclosure. With chivalrous grace, he stood, his countenance serene and undisturbed. Like a serene pond mirroring the gentle gleam of the moon, he replicated her decision with a profound understanding that transcended human frailties. Deep within his soul, a resolute acceptance unfolded, free from the shackles of anger or disappointment.

In his boundless wisdom, Näcken recognized the sanctity of choice, honouring the sovereignty of her heart's decree. With noble grace befitting an ethereal being, he pledged to hold her decision as sacred as the most cherished verse, enshrining its essence in the sanctum of his soul.

No trace of resentment tainted his visage, for his respect was born of a rare purity that extended beyond possessiveness. It flowed as gracefully as a river's stream, guided by the call of liberty's course, unencumbered by the chains of expectation. Thus, he exhaled his devotion, casting it upon the winds of acceptance, where it danced amidst the heavens, a tranquil offering to the symphony of cosmic fate.

In Näcken's tranquil surrender, he went above and beyond mortal limitations, embracing the enigmatic dance of human desires and the puzzling design of destiny. With gallant grace, he relinquished all attachments, allowing the devotional pulse of her heart to guide their conjoined paths.

In this noble offering, Näcken bestowed upon her the precious gift of autonomy, the freedom to chart her course amidst the infinite universes of possibilities. And in the absence of anger or disappointment, he created a hermitage for her to flourish, a radiant blossom in the grand garden of existence.

From the depths of his mellifluous voice, Näcken spoke a note of profound surrender, his words bearing the gravity of timeless commitment. "The power to shape your own destiny lies solely within your hands," he whispered, his voice a gentle caress upon the currents of the air. Yet, in the mystical chamber of his being, a vow blossomed, a whispered promise resonating with courteous constancy.

"Should the winds of fate ever guide you toward a precipice of need, I pledge my unwavering presence, a sentinel poised at the threshold of your call. " With a forbearance beyond mortal understanding, he stood steadfast, an immovable beacon of solace, ready to immerse himself in the tempest of her world.

Within the depths of his enigmatic soul, curiosity awakened, a fervid flame that danced with insatiable hunger for the treasures hidden within her being. With magnanimous ardour, he offered himself as a champion, a warrior ready to protect and defend his chosen queen.

He sought not to whisk her away from the life she knew, instead, he yearned for her to acquaint herself with the boundless expanse of her being, to traverse the realms of possibility without inhibition or constraint. In this unique union, Näcken aimed to be Liv's enduring ally, a rising sun that brought hope and purpose to each step of self-discovery and unbridled bliss.

In his steadfast loyalty and insatiable curiosity, he embodied a love that transcended the boundaries of time, patiently awaiting her return and embracing the symphony of her dreams.

With a touch that pulsated like an immortal aria, Näcken gently clasped Liv's hand, their connection a courageous bridge between realms. As their steps entwined, he guided her along the path that led to her rustic home, his presence a faithful protector amid the unfading undulation of life's ebb. "Within the embrace of time's memory, I shall patiently abide," his voice, adorned with a timeless resonance, whispered into the ether. Releasing her hand, his form melded with the depths of the sylvan realm, a guardian forever present, awaiting the call of her heart.

Enveloped in a veil of uncertainty, Liv retraced her steps with a hastened pace, returning to the farm. Within those mundane walls, a world slumbered, unaware of the enchanting encounter that had unfolded beneath the celestial tapestry of the starlit sky.

Yet, the lingering echoes of Näcken's words resided in her mind, like a divine hymn whispering in the depths of her soul. The weight of his undying promise settled upon Liv's heart, drawing hope from the shadows of confusion. Within the quiet solitude of her abode, she pondered the enigmatic dance of fate that had briefly intertwined their mortal lives, and within the depths of her being, she carried the seeds of a newfound longing, an ache that echoed with the signature of his unflinching devotion.

As dawn's light spread across the world, a new chapter of nature's artwork began, Liv stood amidst the dawning light, a blend of uncertainty and burgeoning anticipation. Even in the stillness of her slumbering farm, Näcken's ethereal promise remained, a wild sea that surged into the defining chapter of her existence.

CHAPTER 9

Fate's fingers danced like a puppeteer, guiding the grand performance of life, weeks unfolded like fleeting dreams, and Liv, burdened by the ache of yearning, ventured forth upon her familiar farmstead's ground. Yet, an inner void persisted, an undeniable yearning that eluded her attempts to banish it from her soul's core.

Amid the security of her daily toil, she sought refuge, immersing herself in the rhythmic dance of labour and the intimate communion with the earth. Her hands, weathered and hardened, moved tirelessly through fields and stables, weaving threads of purpose and dedication. In her devotion's depths, she sought comfort from the lingering murmurs of an elusive daydream that resisted the grasp of time's passage.

Each passing day, Liv immersed herself in the embrace of the farmstead, a bid to anchor her thoughts to the tangible world that surrounded her. Yet, no matter how diligently she surrendered to her responsibilities, an intangible presence tugged at her consciousness, reminding her of a realm beyond the veil of her reality.

An elusive enchantment haunted her, a mirage shimmering on the edges of perception, refusing to fade away. It whispered of untamed realms and unexplored possibilities, leaving traces of wonder in its wake. Her heart, laden with unfulfilled dreams, craved the touch of that enchanting fortress, longing for a connection beyond the limits of the mundane.

In moments of solitude, Liv wrestled with the paradox of existence—the ordinary entwined with the exceptional, the farmstead's tether pulling her towards earth, while the alluring fantasy beckoned from a celestial realm. She found herself caught in a dance of duality, where the weight of her responsibilities grounded her, yet the spectre of unfulfilled desires danced on, casting its enchantments upon her spirit.

With every breath, she teetered on the precipice between acceptance and yearning, forever mindful of the lingering call of a tireless fantasy that dances with the stars in the vastness of the mind. Amidst the labyrinthine corridors of her conflicted soul, Liv grappled with the immutable truth that intertwined her heart with longing and dread. Romance with a being from another realm loomed before her, its shadows hinting at a fate that could sow seeds of anguish and despair.

Yet, as she slipped further from the mysterious caress of the woodland's arms, her yearning blazed like wildfire, threatening to consume her fragile resolve. A perilous desire she knew it to be, for mercenaries roamed the land, driven by zealous convictions and disdain for the magical beings dwelling beyond the mortal realms.

Whispers of fear echoed in the villagers' hearts, stifling them in silence. The priest, the embodiment of fanatical conviction, deemed the fabled beings as malevolent, demanding their eradication. In this realm of enchantment and danger, Liv's heart beat with conflicting emotions, torn between the forbidden allure of passion and the perilous consequences that lay in wait.

In the depths of her being, Liv understood the formidable nature of the priest, his unwavering zeal propelling him towards his inexorable mission. She dared not give him cause to unleash his fury upon Näcken, fully aware of the dire consequences that would follow. If the mercenaries were to vanquish the mythical creature, their path of vengeance would inevitably lead to her, subjecting her to the clutches of death's grasp, accused of consorting with what was deemed wicked.

This treacherous quandary weighed heavily upon Liv, her heart torn asunder by the harrowing prospect of Näcken's demise and her own condemnatory fate. Within her, a tumultuous dance of yearning and guilt intertwined, threatening to shatter her very soul. Lost amidst the tempest of her inner turmoil, her agony remained hidden, etched upon her visage, concealed within the intricate chambers of her solitary heart.

No solace could be found in the arms of confidants, as the complex nature of her struggle defied easy comprehension. Thus, she carried the burden of her torment, an inferno of secrecy burning beneath the facade of her outward existence. Her soul, like a forbidden symphony, reverberated with conflicting desires, a melody unheard by the world.

Within the confines of her secluded heart, Liv remained adrift, a vessel sailing upon a sea of yearning, her tears unseen, her anguish a silent requiem echoing through the winding pathways of her essence.

In their shared life on the farm, Finn perceived a change unfolding, a subtle transformation cloaking his beloved wife in enigmatic veils. Her once vibrant words, threads that wove their tapestry of conversation, now withered upon the vine of silence. The incessant clamour for his attention, once a passionate plea that danced upon his ears, now resided in a realm of hushed respite. He welcomed this break, as its absence granted him space to breathe and exist as an individual. Yet, beneath the surface of this newfound tranquillity, Finn discerned the shadows of discontent that obscured Liv's face.

Though Finn often regarded Liv as a tempestuous force, a complex being immersed in her own dreamscape, his love for her was deep and solid. The sight of her melancholy pierced his soul, as if a fading ember extinguished its light within her very essence. At times, he pondered whether her sorrow stemmed from the depths of their daughter's death or if the disquietude seeped from the crevices of their marriage, eroded by the relentless passage of time.

Witnessing Liv toil tirelessly, a manifestation of resilience and selflessness, Finn's heart brimmed with remorse. The weight of gratitude settled upon his weary shoulders, as he yearned to convey his appreciation for her ceaseless endeavours. Yet, the language of romance eluded him, a forgotten dialect rendered obsolete by the hands of time. They had traversed the arrangement of wedlock for countless years, and the vigour to court her after arduous days of labour seemed elusive, especially now that their children had reached adulthood. Although her beauty still captivated him, Finn found himself lacking the will and fortitude to engage in intimate entanglements as frequently as Liv desired.

At the epicentre of his identity, Finn acknowledged the profound contrasts that set him apart from his beloved. Yet, amidst the expanse of their differences, a flame of resolve kindled within him. He yearned to bridge the divide, to cross the depths that separated their souls. This very night, despite the weariness that burdened him, Finn vowed to honour her desires, to offer himself in a gesture of love and unity. For he believed that such a display of affection, however humble it may seem, would ignite the embers of her happiness and rekindle the passion that once illuminated their shared journey.

As dusk's soft curtain fell upon the landscape, the hour of clandestine rendezvous summoned Finn to Liv's bed. Night spread its wings, covering the world in obsidian hues, while he, patient and determined, awaited the slumber that embraced every weary soul. Finally, his horny footsteps guided him to her side, where Liv lay nestled in the sanctuary of dreams.

Within the chamber's dimly lit dimension, Finn stood hidden in the darkness, his heart ablaze with a heady blend of admiration and fervour. Time had left its traces upon Liv's visage, for the years of toil had imprinted their marks upon her features. At the age of thirty-six, some may perceive her as weathered, yet she remained a paragon of beauty. Amidst the ebony strands of her hair, the silver whispers of wisdom danced, while gentle lines near her eyes spoke of the myriad tales she had lived. The effervescence of youth had faded, but in its place bloomed a mature appeal, its fragrant petals radiating an enchanting luminosity that rivalled the stars above.

In the realm of blessed unions, Finn considered himself a fortunate soul, for Liv, his cherished wife, graced his existence. Ages ago, when their vows entwined their destinies, she had been hailed as the embodiment of exquisiteness, casting an enchanting spell upon all who beheld her. Now, two decades later, the unrelenting touch of time had left its undeniable mark upon her appearances infusing her with a radiance that surpassed mere age. The labour of tending to the earth's abundant fields had bestowed upon her face lines of wisdom, marking the passage of years with whispered tales.

Yet, even as the sands of time whispered their unyielding passage, Finn beheld Liv through a lens of adoration. The symphony of her look resonated within his being, a bewitching potion brewed by the hands of fate. True, the ceaseless demands of their agrarian existence left little room for the art of courtship, causing their connection to flicker like a distant star. And in those moments when her pleas for his undivided attention reverberated in his ears, he recoiled, seeking solace in the sanctuary of solitude. As Finn stood amidst the undeniable beauty of his wife, an enchanting aura enveloped his senses, kindling a profound sentiment within his body, he could feel his himself getting an erection.

A deep longing stirred within his soul, resounding with the delicate body of his beloved's wife. The very essence of her feminine body, tugged at his core, igniting an ardent desire to part her legs and to hear her moan in pleasure. Oh, how he yearned to fill her inside with his penis! Liv had always bestowed upon Finn a symphony of devotion, but now she seemed to wander amidst the endless horizon of her thoughts, leaving him adrift in a sea of sexual longing. Yet, paradoxically, this newfound space between them only fueled the embers of his unwavering sexual desire, lighting a torch of fervent passion to immerse himself in her body. The absence of her tender breasts haunted him, as he yearned to rekindle the blooming fire that had once burned with their sexual act. As Liv's enthusiasm for love and affection fades, Finn found himself drawn even closer to her feminine essence.

In the realm of their life's evolution, the echoes of their last sexual encounter drifted like a cloud in the sky, fading into the recesses of time. For what seemed like an eternity, Finn had ceased to yearn for the taste of her aroused body.

Yet, in this moment, a breathtaking symphony of desire swelled within his erected penis, like a tempestuous wave crashing upon the shore of his soul. Standing there, amidst the infinite expanse of sexual longing, he was ready to surrender to the enchantment of their once shared passion.

Finn approached the bed where Liv lay in peaceful slumber, gently he started to caress her body with yearnful fingers. As the tender sprouts of awakening touched Liv's slumbering soul, her eyes fluttered open like a sail catching the first breath of the morning breeze, greeted by the presence of her horny husband. Silent questions drifted through her mind, like whispered secrets carried on a curious breeze. Startled by Finn's presence, a symphony of surprise danced within Liv's gaze, mirroring the delicate hues of dawn breaking upon a meadow. A hurricane of emotions swirled within her, weaving a mosaic of uncertainty and curiosity, unsure of how to surrender to the view that enveloped her waking world. Yet, to Finn, her wavering hesitation was a sign of Liv's emotional soul. Finn reached out his hand, extending it towards Liv, caressing her petit body.

Finn's hand found its way under Liv's garments. As his hand settled upon Liv's breasts, massaging them gently, a palpable energy coursed through his veins, an electric current that mirrored the surge of emotions swirling within his heart.

As Finn's fingertips eagerly embraced the gentle curve of Liv's breasts, a wild current of sensation coursed through his veins, igniting a pounding passion within his penis, in the sanctuary of his thoughts, there existed but one luminous fixation.

Across the expanse of their shared history, Liv had yearned for the tender affections of her beloved husband, an ache that echoed within the chambers of her heart. For far too long, the tendrils of romance had eluded their embrace, leaving a void that yearned to be filled. And now, in the soft retreat of their home, he was sitting in her bed with a big erection, rubbing her breasts.

In the nascent moments, a glimmer of hope unfurled within Liv's heart. Perhaps, this juncture held the promise of a fresh dawn, an earnest desire to bestow upon her the depths of what her soul yearned for. For a very long time, Liv's sole desire had been to receive her husband's attention, Finn seldom did any effort to invite her into sexual encounters.

In the depths of her spirit, Liv felt a bittersweet hesitation, an unvoiced yearning that struck deep within the core of her being. Countless moments had she silently craved the tender gaze of her beloved, seeking solace in the warmth of his affectionate presence. Yet, an enchanting twist of destiny had ignited an indescribable flame within her, transforming her heart into a sanctuary for another. Amidst this swirling tempest of emotions and uncertainties, a tumultuous battle raged within Liv's soul. Loyalty and devotion tugged at her heartstrings, vying for supremacy against the intoxicating allure of this newfound obsession. In the dimness of her uncertainties, she stood at the brink of affection and duty, her fragile heart caught betwixt two worlds.

Within her conflicted soul, a tempest brewed, for Liv's heart longed to utter the forbidden word "no," yet the weight of obligation bound her to silent acquiescence. Conventions, laws, and societal customs held dominion, her spirit shackled to the unyielding duty of obeying her husband's will. The ever-changing dance of time whispered its secrets upon the wind, carrying echoes of societal expectations and the burdensome chains of subservience. A resolute understanding settled within Liv, one that spoke of the sacrifices demanded to navigate the labyrinthine maze of a bygone era.

The desires that surged within her, like a turbulent sea yearning to break its confines, remained muffled beneath the suffocating veil of obedience. She, like countless women before her, found herself ensnared within the labyrinth of an epoch where her voice was but a whisper, eclipsed by the resounding decree of her husband's authority. The yearning within her, an incandescent flame flickering in the hidden recesses of her heart, dared not defy the societal chains that ensnared her. Fear of the priest's wrath paralyzed her spirit, for she knew not the extent of his retribution.

With each breath, she swallowed the bitter pill of obligation, her heart burdened by the unspoken sacrifices she bore. In the depths of her gaze, a silent plea shimmered like a lone star in the night sky, yearning to be seen, to be heard amidst the deafening silence of compliance.

Thus, with a heart weighed down and a soul burdened by unspoken yearnings, Liv succumbed to the relentless cadence of her era and allowed Finn to touch her. The ache of her desires mingled with the melancholy of surrender, as she wove her existence into the texture of submissiveness, yearning for a time when her spirit would find liberation in the battle cries for autonomy. Within the boundaries of societal norms, a chilling reality cast a shadow over Liv's existence, for the law bestowed upon her husband the audacious privilege of reigning over her very essence. A quiver moved through the graceful arc of her spine, as she confronted the stark truth that her autonomy was a fragile illusion, trapped by the manacles of a legal decree. In this somber realm where shadows entwined with the delicate petals of her femininity, the cloak of power draped itself unyieldingly upon her form. Bound by archaic statutes that favoured masculine authority, her body and soul became subservient, her dreams and desires concealed beneath the veil of enforced compliance. Liv's inner self, once sacred and untouchable, was violated by the cruel hand of the law, granting her husband unrestricted dominion to shape her destiny, moulding her into a mere vessel of his will. The tender essence of her womanhood became an object of possession, her dreams fading beneath the weight of his entitlement.

Yet, amidst this desolate landscape of sanctioned oppression, a flicker of defiance danced within the depths of her spirit. It was the undying flame of her resilience, the eternal ember that refused to be extinguished. In the recesses of her soul, she nurtured the seeds of courage, finding endurance in the knowledge that the human spirit, though suppressed, possessed an unwavering strength.

In the depths of Liv's reminiscences, the echoes of Näcken's words resurfaced, a soothing breeze that wrapped around her soul with its unyielding serenade. Each syllable etched itself upon her soul, a sacred vow that echoed like the whispers of the past in the present. For in his protective arms, he pledged to never wield the chains of control, to never impose his will upon her unique essence.

The memory enfolded her, like a soft breeze caressing her weary spirit, as she recalled the moment their souls intertwined in harmonious unity. In the depths of his gaze, he beheld her with rare clarity, seeing beyond the wall that concealed her imperfections. He saw her, not solely for what she appeared to be, but for the essence that danced within her, a wild light that radiated from the depths of her being.

As Finn nestled beside Liv, a sexual tempest brewed within his aroused gaze, his eyes alight with a passionate fire that sent shivers cascading through her form. From the depths of his primal soul, an intense coldness emanated, stirring the air around them, a potent juxtaposition to the fervent heat that simmered beneath his exterior. With unwavering determination, he locked his gaze onto hers, his eyes engaging in an intimate dance, his depths intertwining in a symphony of unspoken desires, as his hands worked their way over her entire body.

In the realm of surrender, Liv yielded to Finn's commanding touch, her essence engulfed in a tempest. With every caress of his hands, she found herself enveloped in a symphony of repulsiveness.

At the root of her being, a subtle tremor resonated, for Liv's heart no longer yearned for the touch of Finn. The vivid threads that once intertwined their souls had faded into the distant recesses of memory, adrift in the passage of time's tides. The flame that once ignited her spirit had dimmed, replaced by an ardent longing for the safety and solace found within Näcken's spirit. In the core of her being, a symphony of yearning reverberated, each melodic note an ode to the love she had discovered in Näcken's unwavering devotion. It was a fervour that enfolded her in unyielding protection, casting aside the doubts that plagued her delicate heart. With every breath she drew, she pined for the security of his arms, a place where her restless soul could find respite.

Within the confines of her reflections, fragments of their encounter cascaded like celestial stardust, illuminating the path she yearned to tread. Finn's unwary touch had lost its radiant gleam, overshadowed by the gravitational pull of Näcken's steadfast presence. It was with him that she discovered the strength to confront the uncertainties of the world, his words serving as a refuge that shielded her from the tempestuous winds of doubt.

In the realm of closed eyes, Liv delved into a realm where daydreams spun webs of wonder and magic, dissolving the boundaries of reality and unveiling the inexplicable essence of love. With a delicate flutter of her lashes, she surrendered herself to the dance of her mind, conjuring an image where Finn turned into the embodiment of Näcken's fiery touch.

In the obscurity behind her closed eyes, she painted a portrait of passion, a vibrant tableau of the emotions she once shared with Näcken. With each breath she took, she beckoned his presence to envelop her, to fill the void that Finn's touch could not assuage. Within the depths of her consciousness, she recreated the tenderness of Näcken's caress, an alchemical fusion of cherished memories and fervent desire that coursed through her veins like liquid fire.

Sexual fire consumed his soul, taking over his senses. In a whimsical gesture, Finn's fingertips roughly slipped into the embrace of Liv's vagina. She winced, experiencing discomfort, but tried her best to act indifferent. In an instant of electrifying motion, Finn spun Liv around and bent her down on all four. With a surge of raw, primal desire, Finn forced his penis inside of Liv's hesitative body. Within the ferocity of Finn's violent move, Liv felt unease, unable to refuse his sexual invitation. In the depths of her being, Liv experienced a profound mix of unpleasure and uncertainty. Finn stepped forward, assuming the mantle of command, compelling her undivided attention. Uncertainty danced in her eyes, twinkling like distant fireflies in the darkness, as she unwillingly surrendered to the forceful power that Finn exuded. With a resolute force, Finn entered her body from behind, every push resonating with a potent strength that commanded attention. He moved with an untamed force, acting like a wild animal.

Liv peered into the abyss of her very essence, her heart murmuring truths that reverberated through the chambers of every cell of her body. With a profound lucidity, she grasped the insufficiency of their current marital union in appeasing the insatiable yearnings within her. Within the depths of her weary heart, hope waned like a dying ember, its radiant glow diminishing amidst the chilling depths of her disenchantment. The foundation of their once-vibrant matrimony had unravelled, ensnaring her within a labyrinth of fragmented dreams and fading vows.

Liv endeavored to turn around, but Finn kept a high and intense speed. Like a delicate songbird yearning to escape its gilded cage, Liv fluttered her wings, desperate to break free from the confining grasp of her circumstances. As Liv yearned to break free into the embrace of freedom, Finn stood as an unwavering pillar, halting her delicate movements with an authoritative touch.

In a sturdy continuation of his purpose, Finn pressed forward on his resolute path of achieving climax. After what seemed like an eternity, Finn finally reached his orgasm. In a violent surrender to the embrace of sexual release, Finn reclined, his body finding solace amidst the soft sheets that cradled him next to Liv.

A flicker of discontent tinged Liv's soul, a flame of vexation that gracefully pirouetted upon the surface of her being. Deep within the holy recesses of her heart, a pang of disillusionment reverberated. The unmistakable truth wafted through the air, a bitter zephyr slicing through the delicate fibres of her emotions. It became painfully clear that her desires held no weight in his realm, that his apathy had constructed an impregnable fortress between their souls. The realization descended upon her like a dense fog, veiling the twinkling sparks of hope that once adorned her spirit. The void engendered by his indifference resonated within her, pulsating with the echoes of unfulfilled yearning and the poignant ache of unrequited longing.

In the bloom of her youth, Liv clandestinely embarked on a journey into the arcane realm of self-pleasure, reaching orgasms beneath the shroud of secrecy, she did not care about the church's attempts to convince her that engaging in the act of self-pleasure would lead to hell, or that it was considered very sinful for women to experiment on their bodies. Liv pleasured herself as an act of empowerment and love, once she married Finn, she sought to experience the same pleasure she had achieved on her own, this time with him.

As Finn yielded to sleep's affectionate hold, his breaths a melodic cadence beside her, Liv found herself swallowed by a colossal ocean of perplexity. The mantle of darkness mirrored the mysterious terrain of her inner world., concealing her heart in a labyrinth of uncertainty. Her longing for hope, for the rekindling of the luminous flame that once enlightened their union, battled against the gnawing void that persisted within her. It clawed at the fringes of her soul, an incessant ache that left her yearning for something elusive, slipping through her fingertips like whispers in the wind.

In the hush of the nocturnal realm, where the murmurs of the world dissolved into distance, Liv wrestled with the depths of her inner tumult. Her heart sought relief in the memory of the connection she had once shared with Näcken, a bond that ignited her spirit and strengthened her life force.

Yet now, in the presence of Finn, she questioned if that same spark could ever be rekindled. Doubt loomed over her, casting shadows upon her dreams and desires. Would she ever encounter that profound passion, that soul-stirring union, within this labyrinth of uncertainties?

Restless, she lay awake, her thoughts a tempestuous symphony reverberating in the silence. Her heart yearned for clarity, for a guiding light to illuminate the path leading to fulfilment. Yet, as she listened to the nocturnal whispers enveloping her, she remained adrift upon a sea of indecision, uncertain of the next step.

In the depths of the night, where dreams intermingle with reality, Liv sought peace within the tranquil stillness. She yearned for the answers that eluded her, for the whisper of guidance that would unveil her destined course. As the night waned, and the moon cast its gentle luminescence upon her restless form, Liv's heart lingered in a state of liminality. It clung to the flicker of hope, believing in love's transformative and healing power, while simultaneously grappling with the unsatiated void that dwelled within her.

CHAPTER 10

The following day bloomed with a gentle sigh, wrapped in Liv's resilient soul. An unrest, like a fleeting mist, subtly coiled its creepers through her musings, stirring waves of restlessness in her impassioned mind. The shimmering spark of hope, once aflame for Liv and Finn, now ceased its dance, leaving an empty space within her very being. In that moment of clarity, Liv discovered that Finn could never truly grasp the depths of her essence, nor offer the love and admiration she yearned for with unwavering ardour. She had spent endless days sculpting herself, moulding her identity to fit his expectations, desperately yearning for a day when he would shower upon her the affection she craved. Yet, now, she comprehended the futility of her endeavours, for Finn was unchanging, bound to the confines of his own existence. This realization pierced her heart, for she knew deep within her soul that it was unjust to demand transformation from another, to cling to an illusion of metamorphosis, or to surrender her love to the mirage of an unrealized potential. Although aware of this truth, it did not soothe the ache of her discontent. The knowledge that Finn would forever remain unchanged merely magnified her sorrow. The previous night had bestowed upon her a revelation, shattering her hopes for a miracle and exposing the harsh reality that her dreams with Finn would forever be a fleeting fantasy. Solitude coiled around her, squeezing her spirit, leaving her breathless and adrift. The weight of her misplaced hope pressed upon her like a burdensome yoke, making her feel naught but a foolish dreamer for investing her heart so deeply throughout countless years. In that moment, the obscurity was dispelled, revealing the illusion that ensnared her, forcing her to confront the stark truth of her unfulfilled yearnings.

Quiet and motionless, Liv treaded through the hours of the day, her lips withholding the words that danced upon the edge of her tongue. Nightfall descended, casting its obsidian shroud upon the world, yet sleep eluded her, and she lay enmeshed in the embroidery of her turbulent thoughts. Within the perplexing maze of her thoughts, the presence of Näcken loomed large, his essence entwining with the very fabric of her existence. A relentless yearning, mysterious and profound, coiled deep within her core, its origin elusive and enigmatic. It whispered spells in the depths of her soul, riddles she could not decipher or fathom. Never before had such an irresistible longing ensnared her, an inexplicable tug that defied logical explanation. Its intensity unsettled her, stirring a fragile fear in her heart, for it hinted at a vulnerability she had never known. As she lay there, gazing upward at the ceiling, she attempted to translate her emotions into words. In the realm of her thoughts, Liv dwelled upon the ethereal splendour that adorned Näcken, his countenance radiant beneath the moon's tender touch. She marvelled at the celestial gleam that graced his eyes, shimmering like starlit crystals in the vast expanse of the nocturnal heavens. Her imagination crafted a song of enchantment that whispered secrets only the moon could comprehend. The memory of his caress lingered upon her senses, an irresistible symphony of sensation, as his embrace had rescued her from the depths of desolate despair. She pondered upon his elegance, an embodiment of graceful majesty, traversing the woods with a primal allure, akin to a wild creature in harmonious communion with its emerald realm.

Yet, in the farthest recesses of her spirit, no words could ever spin the intricate tapestry of her yearning for Näcken. It surpassed the boundaries of mortal speech, an indescribable force that swept her into a tempest of euphoria and apprehension. Her heart throbbed with an insatiable hunger for Näcken's essence, an unquenchable thirst for the depths of his existence. The intensity of her longing defied all explanation, a dance between yearning and surrender that dwelled in a realm beyond comprehension. Näcken, as a wild creature of nature, comprehended the depths of her desires, and against all odds, he chose to grant her the rapture she sought, defying the constraints of human caution.

For she had been chosen by the untamed, an otherworldly being of darkness and desire. From the depths of his primal soul, he cast his gaze upon her, singling her out amid the boundless scope of the universe. In his enigmatic wisdom, he saw in her a kindred spirit, a flame that mirrored his own untamed passions. With a haunting allure, he claimed her as his own, transcending the boundaries of the familiar world. A mortal entwined with an ethereal divinity, she stood at the precipice of a forbidden union, where the boundaries between reality and fantasy blurred into a kaleidoscope of primal enchantment. Lost in contemplation, Liv heard a faint sound outside her window. Stepping out of bed, she peered into the night, and there, nestled in the arms of moonlight, stood Näcken, a being with enchanting enigma. His presence, a convergence of dreams and actuality, danced on the edge of her perception. Was this a fleeting vision born from the desires of her slumbering mind? Or did he truly materialize before her, a spectre from the magical realms? Uncertainty enveloped her like whispers of forgotten melodies, as the boundaries between wakefulness and reverie blurred, beckoning her to surrender to the mystical realm that called out to her.

Liv's heart, akin to a soaring bird, took flight on the wings of untamed longing. In a rush of fervent yearning, she flung open the window, a portal to their clandestine union. Näcken, a sworn denizen of the night, heeded her summons, effortlessly ascending, defying the pull of gravity. His form, a silhouette against the backdrop of moonlit hues, emanated an aura of otherworldly grace. Together, they embraced the realm between forbidden enchantment and cherished surrender, as their souls entwined in a dance of passion and destiny.

"Are you but a figment of dreams?" she whispered, her words, gentle as fluttering flower petals in the air.

"I am but a murmuring twilight, a guardian of your desires," Näcken responded, his voice bearing the weight of ancient vows, his words flowing forth like whispered secrets carried on the breeze.

"Why have you come?" Liv's voice trembled with bewilderment.

"In the depths of your soul, I heard your silent plea," Näcken murmured, his voice a melodic echo of the night. As he stood there, bathed in the ethereal glow of the moon, Liv beheld the transformation of his hair, flowing like strands of midnight silk in the gentle caress of the wind. And his eyes, once shrouded in darkness and mystery, now shimmered with a profound azure, reflecting the enigmas of the cosmos.

"Why do I yearn for you?" Liv's voice trembled with anticipation. Näcken, embodying an enticing riddle, advanced with deliberate grace, bridging the physical and metaphysical distance that separated them. "You must depart, my husband will uncover the truth, the villagers will bring you harm, they will kill you!" Fear laced her cautionary plea, her voice delicate with the intent to shield him from imminent danger.

"I would traverse uncharted realms, facing unknown perils, to answer your call whenever it beckons. No adversary shall hinder my devotion, for I am resolved to stand as your faithful guardian, eternally by your side," Näcken pledged, his voice resounding with steadfast determination.

"Why did the hounds not sense you, why did they not bark?" Liv inquired, her voice gentle and filled with curiosity.

"They are creatures of the wild, their spirits entwined with my enchantment," Näcken replied, his gaze penetrating Liv's eyes, revealing a fearless ardour that set her soul ablaze.

"How can you depart from the lake? Will you not perish here?" Concern tinged her voice, carrying the weight of her worries on fragile wings.

"Though my strength diminishes beyond my realm, I remain unwavering, ready to traverse countless realms to be with you," Näcken vowed, his words shimmering with pure devotion.

"Yesterday, my husband violated me in this very bed," Liv's gaze fell upon the bed, disappointment veiling her eyes with a shroud of sorrow.

"In the realm of mortal laws, his claim as your husband may hold sway, yet my heart dissents, for human customs often elude my comprehension," Näcken's resolute gaze remained fixed upon Liv, his eyes exuding serenity and reassurance. "But I, unlike him, would never impose my will upon you against your desires. Though the power to vanquish an entire village lies within my grasp, I would never inflict harm upon you in any manner."

"Why not? What sets me apart?" Liv's words slipped from her lips in a near-whisper, carrying a hint of vulnerability. "I am no longer a young woman, my beauty has begun to fade, and my hair is touched by strands of grey."

"You, a mere mortal, have captivated my attention, a rarity in itself. There is an enigma surrounding you, a mystique that eludes my grasp, yet compels me. And I vow, with all that I am, to shield you from harm, to safeguard your existence with unflinching loyalty."

"By law, my husband possesses the right to claim me whenever he desires." The melancholic timbre of Liv's voice resonated with profound sorrow, carrying an emotional depth that seemed to weigh heavily upon her spirit.

"I am aware of your marital bond, and I reiterate my stance

of not seeking possession or dominion over you. My desire is to witness your freedom, to witness you unburdened by obligations. If your heart inclines towards remaining with your husband, then follow its course. And if it is your wish for me to depart, let the words escape your lips, for I shall never inflict harm upon you," Näcken assured with a solemn vow, his voice overflowing with earnestness and loyalty.

"And what of you? Are there other women you seduce more than me?" Liv concealed her unease with utmost delicacy.

"As long as our souls intertwine, my loyalty shall remain steadfast, devoted solely to you. In your presence, I discover a sense of wholeness, and no other shall capture the gaze of my heart." Näcken fixed his deep gaze upon her, his eyes emanating an unshakable assurance and resolute confidence.

"Why do you submerge people beneath the water?" Liv's voice trembled with an undercurrent of fear as she voiced her query.

With solemnity and composure, Näcken addressed Liv's concerns, his voice resonating with quiet strength. "Indeed, I possess great power, and within me lies the potential for violence. Yet, I am not driven by an insatiable thirst for harm or violence. I derive no pleasure from causing suffering. However, if pushed to the brink, I will defend myself with every ounce of my being, even if it means fighting until the end, slaying every creature in front of me. Do not be swayed by the whispers and tales woven among your kind. I am not a being ruled by impulsive wrath or unchecked fury. Such notions are but malicious fabrications, mere falsehoods crafted to instil fear. Rest assured, dear one, for your worries do not go unnoticed, and I shall do everything within my power to alleviate them."

"Please, keep your voice low, lest you awaken my entire family," she expressed her concern with a tremor of worry in her words.

"They slumber under my enchantment, fear not, for their dreams shield them from harm," Näcken's voice resounded with a dark and profound tone, instilling in Liv a sense of security and sanctuary. "Humans have told deceitful tales about me since their intrusion into the sacred woods. They brand me as their adversary, yet I merely exist within my rightful realm, safeguarding the lake, the woodland, and its wondrous inhabitants. To humans, I may appear as their foe, but to the mystical beings born of these ancient woods, I am their saviour from a greater malevolence that relentlessly preys upon them, seeking to obliterate their sanctuary. My essence morphs depending on whom you inquire, for perception paints me with diverse strokes."

"Why does your memory persistently linger in my mind?" Liv inquired, her voice filled with curiosity.

"Do you desire my departure, that I should recede like a waning moon, vanishing into the veiled depths of night? Shall I fade away, relinquishing the tendrils of our connection, allowing solitude to engulf us? Speak your truth, and I shall heed the melody that resonates within your soul." Näcken spoke with tranquil composure and a voice imbued with empathetic wisdom.

"No," she whispered softly, her voice carrying a gentle touch of tenderness.

"We share an enigmatic bond, forged in realms beyond comprehension. I sense an ethereal tether between us, woven on that fateful night when I plucked you from the clutches of danger. Yet, fear not, for my enchantments can captivate the hearts of many, should I choose to do so. However, with you, it is different. I have not sought to bewitch or ensnare, but rather, I have been enraptured by your soul, and now, your essence lingers within the corridors of my being."

"What shall you do?" Liv's voice, gentle as a whispered breeze, caressed the air. Näcken, guided by an unspoken understanding, enfolded her within his arms, merging their essences into an embrace of profound unity.

In the midst of moonlit charm, Näcken's lips descended upon

Liv's with a fervour that ignited the celestial realms. His commanding presence urged her to arch, stretching her neck to meet the formidable caress of his divine touch. Within his powerful embrace, Liv succumbed to a tempestuous whirlwind of longing and yearning, surrendering herself to the courteous dance of passion and desire.

But as swiftly as the passionate flame had ignited, Näcken withdrew, yet held firmly onto her delicate hands. The air hummed with anticipation, and Liv's body radiated a passionate heat that reflected the fervour of her yearnings.

"Why did you cease?" Liv's voice, infused with desire, resonated through the hush. A gentle smile graced Näcken's countenance, his eyes ablaze with devotion.

"I have answered your yearnings, to grant you all that your heart desires. In you, I discover a connection that surpasses time, a devotion that knows no boundaries. My loyalty to you shall endure beyond mortal realms, for I am bound to your essence, eternally devoted to your existence."

Näcken's words lingered in the air, suffused with unbreakable sincerity. Liv's heart, torn between desire and moral quandary, throbbed with an uncertain rhythm. The exquisite moonlight cast a spell upon them, enshrouding them within a domain where choices bore unimaginable consequences.

"Should you yearn for your husband's demise or death, for liberation from the chains that confine you, utter the words, and I shall move mountains and vanquish all adversaries to bestow your happiness," Näcken's voice resonated with committed devotion.

Liv's breath quivered as she contemplated the proposition, torn between the allure of freedom and the morality that clung to her soul. The weight of responsibility pressed upon her conscience, for within the depths of her desires lay the potential unravelling of lives.

Näcken's gaze held a profound understanding, his eyes reflecting the profundity of their shared dilemma. With a tender touch, he reassured her, "Fear not, for we shall navigate this labyrinth of emotions with utmost care. Your happiness is my unwavering pursuit, even if it necessitates sacrificing my own desires."

"I do not wish for you to bring harm upon my husband!" Liv's voice trembled with a mixture of fear and disbelief, escaping her lips in a horrified whisper. The weight of Näcken's proposition settled upon her like a haunting shadow, distressing the very core of her being.

"I comprehend," Näcken responded, his voice carrying a tender yet resolute cadence. "Yet, it is vital for you to understand that your desires hold sway over me, should you choose to pursue them. On the morrow, I shall await your arrival with immovable patience. For you, my dearest, possess a singular essence, unlike any other."

With those words, like a whispered oath, hanging delicately in the air, Näcken gently released Liv's hand and gracefully descended from the window ledge. As he turned for a final glance, his eyes conveyed a depth of devotion unreachable by human minds. Silently, he melded into the embrace of the enchanting night, leaving Liv to confront the profound choices that lay ahead.

Overwhelmed by a blend of apprehension and fascination, Liv went back to sleep, serenaded by the nocturnal whispers of the forest. The rhythm of her heart matched the mystical melodies that wove through her mind—a symphony of longing and uncertainty. Liv acknowledged that her yearning for Näcken defied explanation, defied reason. Yet, it remained an undeniable truth, a force that stirred the depths of her being like nothing else. Resting her head upon the pillow, Liv surrendered to sleep, her dreams entwined with elusive harmonies and ethereal murmurs. In the realm of dreams, Näcken's presence lingered, an ever-present reminder of the extraordinary connection they shared.

CHAPTER 11

As the sundown's mellow curtain fell, veiling the weary dwelling in a sweet clench, Liv's restless spirit paced fervently within the confines of her longing. Her heart yearned for the whispered lullabies that could release her into the enchanting cradle of the woods. Throughout the passing day, her thoughts waltzed to the haunting melodies of the unseen musician, entangled in a dangerous dance of allure and desire. Aware of the peril coursing through her veins, Liv found herself unable to withstand the irresistible pull that beckoned from the depths of her soul. The remnants of hope for her fading marriage had dissipated, granting her the sweet liberation from enslaving bonds.

And so it came to pass, as if the very essence of her dreams converged at the edge of the woods, the bewildering entity patiently awaited her arrival. A mythical spectre, adorned with supernatural grace, poised amidst the interplay of moonlit beams and elusive shadows. As Liv beheld this otherworldly being, her heart surrendered to the hypnotic rapture that coursed through her veins, each beat bearing witness to the enchanting spell woven by Näckens's presence. He was at one with the woods, yet he surpassed the very stars above. He was a vivid reverie, yet a blessed reality. He was a captivating mirage, yet a transcendent verity.

In the heart of ancient groves, he stood as a vessel of unity, his essence intertwining seamlessly with the spirit of nature—a celestial symphony eclipsing the stars that graced the midnight sky. He existed as a vibrant mirage, teasing the fringes of her slumbering desires, and as an ethereal reality, a divine blessing bestowed upon her mortal existence. He ensnared her senses with luminous enchantment, his allure surpassing worldly constrains, for within him resided a truth that transcended ephemeral illusions.

Their souls, inexplicably entwined, whispered a concealed bond that swept through the avenues of time, as if the universe had crafted their destinies in the celestial dimension long before their earthly paths intertwined. Liv, her spirit now surrendered to the inescapable embrace of their encounter, found solace in the irrepressible dance of fate.

In the intimate realm where souls conversed, an unspoken familiarity camouflaged her soul, as if she had always carried the knowledge of their destined encounter deep within her heart. Now, in the face of their inevitable union, she found herself bereft of choice, willingly surrendering herself to the bewitching magnetism of their shared destinies. With a touch that evoked a symphony of impressions within her, Näcken claimed Liv's hand as if it were a time-honoured pact, and together they began walking through the enchanting depths of the woods. The night, adorned with an endless sea of stars, unveiled its unforgettable radiance wherever Näcken tread. The woods, stirred by the presence of this ethereal companion, shimmered in the celestial glow, displaying a hidden realm of enchantment and marvel that mirrored the intensity of their connection.

"You radiate illumination wherever your footsteps touch the earth," Liv whispered, her voice a gentle murmur, touched by the reverence that danced within her gaze.

"I am the ember of light that banishes the abyss, the shadow that twirls in harmony with the moon's tender caress. I embody nature's breath, a timeless spirit integrated at the heart of existence. From ancient woods, I draw strength, my purpose resonating in symbiotic harmony with the sacred boundaries I safeguard."

"But isn't that the duty of Skogsrået?" Liv inquired.

"She is my celestial kin, crafted by the same hands, our souls united by destiny's touch. We both wander these realms, traversing shared domains and revelling in the radiance of harmonious realms," Näcken revealed.

"I do not even know your name," Liv confessed.

"It is Lythandir, but few know me by that name. To the creatures in this forest and these waters, I am simply Näcken," he replied.

"Lythandir " Liv repeated. " How come you know my name?" Liv asked.

"In that pivotal moment when cosmic forces linked our fates, it was your heart that whispered to mine, unveiling a truth that transcended mortal realms. In the act of saving you, a sacred dance between destinies unfurled, revealing the profound connection inscribed within the chronicles of time. Your heart told me the first time I saved you; your name is Liv, like life itself," Näcken revealed. In a timeless pause, his ethereal steps ceased, his gaze fixating upon Liv like a starlit enchantment. With a voice carrying the weight of countless whispers, he implored her, "Unveil the desires hidden within the chamber of your soul. Speak, and let the secrets of your yearnings merge into the cloth of our shared destiny."

"I yearn for you to embrace me, and seduce me," Liv confessed. Deep within her being, her heart galloped like a wild steed, its rhythm echoing the crescendo of desire gushing through her veins s. An age-old longing surged through her blood, yearning for Näcken's touch. As he drew her closer, his lips brushed against her neck, triggering a symphony of sensations that sent shivers cascading down her spine.

Näcken's hands, guided by an intuitive dance, traversed her petite form with a blend of tenderness and fervour. They traced the contours of her body, mapping out a journey of pleasure that left her breathless. Each caress became a brushstroke of passion, igniting flames of ecstasy within her. Liv, surrendering to the intoxicating moment, closed her eyes, allowing her other senses to heighten the pleasure that consumed her.

In the embrace of the untamed, nocturnal realm, Liv found herself entangled with a spirit of enchantment. The air crackled with electric energy, as if the entire universe conspired to bear witness to their union. Näcken's fervent kisses spoke a language of insatiable desire, a proclamation of his unquenchable hunger for her. The intensity of his passion mirrored her own, forging a connection of erotic fervour.

As Liv succumbed to the euphoric symphony of pleasure, she felt an irresistible urge to offer herself entirely to this extraordinary moment. In the depths of their union, she discovered liberation and a profound connection to the essence of her own being. Here, in Näcken's presence, she found a fiery passion that enveloped her, eradicating doubts and insecurities.

In the centre of their sexual moment, Liv could feel Näcken's longing reverberate through every touch and every kiss. His desire for her was palpable, an insatiable thirst that mirrored her own. Their passions entwined, merging into a dance of primal need and fervent devotion. It was a moment where time stood still, allowing them to revel in the divine ecstasy that their connection bestowed. As Näcken's lips brushed against hers, Liv moaned in pleasure, her world erupted in a kaleidoscope of sexual ecstasy.

With a potent surge of strength, Näcken's hands embarked on a journey of liberation, removing each layer of Liv's attire. His touch, infused with a primal vigour, conveyed a sense of reverence as the barriers between their beings dissolved. In his commanding grasp, Liv felt the tangible manifestation of

Näcken's power, an embodiment of his desire to explore the depths of her sexual fantasy. As Näcken's compelling touch unravelled the fabric that clung to Liv's skin, a symphony of anticipation played in the air. The raw intensity of his actions called out to the universe, kindling a fiery blaze within Liv's being. It was a dance of vulnerability and trust, where Näcken's strength served as a symbol of the profound sexual anticipation. Waves of pure delight cascaded through her being, electrifying every nerve, and setting her soul ablaze when Näcken's hands played with her clitoris. Gently he put his fingers inside of her, in that exquisite moment of sexual connection, time halted, and the universe seemed to be in a momentary hush. The touch of Näcken's lips upon hers ignited a plethora of sensations that defied description. She could feel his erected penis pushing hard against her body. It was as if a thousand shooting stars exploded within Liv, showering her essence with shimmering stardust.

Näcken's kisses emanated with an intensity that awakened Liv's deepest passions. Each press of his lips against hers was fuelled by a fervent passion that consumed them both, a manifestation to the depths of their shared desire. In his commanding embrace, Näcken assumed a decisive role, guiding their journey with an innate confidence that left Liv yearning for more.

As their lips merged in a rapturous dance, Näcken's touch exuded a magnetic force, asserting his dominance with an entrancing blend of strength and tenderness. He navigated the realms of pleasure with a resolute purpose, his every action embodying a powerful control that both exhilarated and thrilled Liv. It was a dance of fiery intensity, where the boundaries between pleasure and surrender blurred in an amalgamation of raw desire. His touch conveyed a hint of roughness, a primal energy that ignited Liv's senses, awakening her to a domain of unbridled euphoria. Yet, within the confines of their intimate union, there lingered a profound understanding, an unspoken agreement that violence had no place in their connection.

As Liv gazed into his mesmerizing, brown eyes, she uttered

primal sounds of pleasure. Liv's heart yearned to feel his penis inside of her, the anticipation surged within her like a wild river breaking free from its banks. Liv could scarcely contain the electric energy that coursed through her veins. Every fibre of her being trembled with a captivating mix of excitement and desire, threatening to spill over in a torrent of unrestrained passion.

His erection was massive and stiff, it stood before her, a masterpiece crafted by the hands of divine inspiration. Every inch, every contour, every detail, whispered of an artist's passion and devotion. It was a work of art that enflamed her sexual senses, inviting her to immerse herself in its magnificent presence. Every line and curve held a secret, a glimpse into the sexual adventure that awaited her. The anticipation that swelled within her chest threatened to engulf her, making her breath shallow and her heart race. She was a captive to the rapture that awaited her, her senses heightened and her spirit alight with an almost unbearable longing.

As she let her tiny hands caress his vibrant penis, a profound sense of honour washed over Liv, intertwining with a potent intrigue that captured her imagination. It possessed a size that was nothing short of perfection. Its proportions were meticulously crafted, forming an embodiment of harmony and balance. The perfection of its size illustrated eloquently the intention behind its creation. It was as if every dimension had been carefully considered, every measurement chosen with purpose. Liv marvelled at the precise balance it struck, evoking a sense of aesthetic pleasure that stirred her senses. It stood as a demonstration of meticulous design and flawless execution, she could not wait to have his pulsating penis within her exited body.

The air seemed charged with a hypnotic energy, as if the very universe conspired to heighten her senses. With each breath, the anticipation grew, Liv could feel herself getting really wet. With a graceful fluidity, Näcken spun Liv around effortlessly, as if the weight of the world had no hold upon her. As her body faced away, a tender shiver cascaded down her spine, a delicious premonition of the intimate connection about to unfold. Näcken's lips, guided by an invisible force, descended upon her from behind, lit a symphony of fire that burnt in every corner of her being.

As Näcken caressed her small breasts, the strength in his hands mirrored the untamed power of their passion, triggered a tempest of sensations that pulsed through every particle of her being. It was like a swirling vortex of stardust enveloped her, imbuing her essence with cosmic wonder, when Näcken put her down on all four on the moist ground. Liv gasped for air when Näcken embraced her from behind, he took a firm hold of his yearning limb and entered her body with passionate force. The world around her melted away, leaving only Näcken's erotic touch and the rapture of their electric sex. In the dance of their steamy encounter, Liv's heart soared to unimaginable heights when Näcken's penis filled her inside, intoxicated by the heady elixir of longing and enchantment. Every caress, every decisive press of Näcken's penis inside her, shouted a story of passion, exposing a truth that emanated a deep vibration within her, the boundaries of the physical world dissolved, and their souls fused in a celestial embrace. A tidal wave of pleasure surged through Liv's being, cascading like a melange of fireworks, igniting every nerve ending with an exquisite explosion of sensation. It coursed through her veins, electrifying her senses and engulfing her in a euphoric embrace that transcended the boundaries of time and space. As Näcken moved one of his hands between her legs to gently caress her clitoris, Liv surrendered herself completely to the elation that enveloped her.

Liv moaned loudly when Näcken took her from behind while he had one hand between her legs, still pleasuring her clitoris. It was a demonstration of Näcken's primal prowess, an expression of his ardour that left Liv breathless and yearning for more.

He moved with a mesmerizing rhythm, his strides carrying a harmonious cadence that spoke of strength and purpose. Each push inside of her took exuded a commanding presence, a testament to his resolute dominance, yet there was a grace in his motion, a deliberate intention that balanced power with finesse. His movements were a symphony of fluidity and control, a dance that resonated with both precision and passion. Each push and pull, a mark of his unfaltering determination. His pace was measured, not too forceful, allowing for a delicate balance between intensity and restraint.

As Näcken took Liv from behind, there was an undeniable magnetism in his movements, a magnetic pull that commanded attention and admiration. It was a captivating display of strength, a representation his self-assured nature. Yet, there was a gentleness in his firmness, a consideration for the needs and desires of his partner. In his motion, there was a perfect equilibrium, an artful blend of power and tenderness. His movements conveyed a resolute purpose, yet they were tempered with a sensitivity that clearly conveyed his profound understanding of pleasure. It was a dance of passion and control, where every movement was an invitation to explore the depths of desire. In the rhythm of his sexual pleasuring, Liv felt a magnetic allure, drawing her closer to him, captivating her with his confident presence. It was a manifestation of his prowess, a demonstration of his ability to navigate the delicate balance between dominance and reverence. His strides, strong and deliberate, carried an air of authority that set her body ablaze.

In a swift, yet gentle motion, Näcken spun Liv around, his strong arms lifting her with a tenderness that belied his commanding presence. As their bodies pivoted, a delicate dance unfolded, and Liv found herself lying on her back, her form embraced by the softness of the ground beneath her. Under the influence of passionate kisses, he entered her body. With a calculated thought, Näcken moved his pelvic a little bit higher. Every coordinated move resembled a passionate dance where his pelvic rubbed against her clitoris. He surged forward with pleasures determination, his strides devouring the distance with each powerful push. There was a captivating intensity in his sexual act, an unyielding drive that propelled him forward, unrelenting in his pursuit of his goal. Every move he made was infused with a fiery passion, a hunger that burned within him and radiated through his skin.

As Näcken made passionate sex with Liv, his muscles rippled with each forceful motion, a display of his strength and endurance. His body echoed with an unyielding energy, as if his very being was synchronized with the pulsating beat of his heart. His breathing became a fusion of exertion, intertwining with the raw power of his sexuality, creating a melodic harmony that dances in the forest.

Liv whispered out in pleasure, she put her hands on Näcken's buttocks and followed the swaying rhythm in his firm manoeuvres.

"Harder! " She moaned and Näcken complied.

Her soul danced with impatience, craving the taste of that elusive moment that lingered just beyond her grasp. Every fibre of her being strained against the constraints of time, willing it to accelerate, to bring her closer to the rapturous culmination of her desires. It was an assortment of anticipation, the crescendo building to a fever pitch, ready to erupt in a breathtaking climax. Liv could feel her entire body getting close to finish.

As Liv's eyes met Näcken's captivating gaze, a profound sensation rippled through her very being, unfurling the depths of her essence. It was as if a veiled portal had swung wide, revealing a universe brimming with emotions and long-dormant yearnings. Within Näcken's mystical eyes, she caught glimpses of timeless wisdom and indomitable strength, woven into the tapestry of his ancient soul. His gaze held the secrets of bygone eras, bearing the weight of innumerable tales and journeys. They served as windows to a realm where enchantment and marvel intertwined, mirroring the ethereal essence that defined him. Within their depths, Liv unearthed a vibrant mixture of hues, shimmering with an otherworldly luminosity that whispered of concealed realms and forgotten spells.

As Liv was getting closer to climax, a sense of exhilaration coursed through Näcken's veins, electrifying every fibre of his being. It was a dance of strength and passion, an ode to the sheer force of his will. Liv and Näcken climaxed together, their bodies melted into each other's arms, guided by an instinctual yearning to be as close as humanly possible.

With a tender touch, Näcken's fingers delicately weaved melodies through Liv's hair, while her gaze soared to the towering sentinels encircling them. "Even through a thousand lifetimes' quest," Näcken murmured, his voice a delicate rain upon the windswept tresses, "I would find none who could rival the resplendence that resides within you."

With each word, his lips imprinted upon her the essence of a myriad of sonnets, a symphony of devotion that reverberated within the chambers of her heart. "It feels as if I have wandered into a realm of fairytales. And yet, I see the path before me with crystal clarity," Liv whispered, her voice adorned with wonder and reverence. "I must return to the farm, but I will hurry back as swiftly as I can." She turned her gaze towards Näcken, her eyes aglow with the flickering light of infinite possibilities.

A gentle sigh escaped Näcken's lips, carrying the weight of longing that spanned eternity. "And I, bound by the infinite expanse of my love for you, shall forever stand as a sentinel of loyalty. Time itself shall bear witness to my everlasting commitment, as my words echo through the night, giving birth to luminosity within the veils of darkness. I will remain here, eternally waiting for your return."

In this sincere oath, Näcken's voice bloomed as a beacon of hope, casting a luminous glow upon the path that interwove their fates. Their souls, entwined like tendrils of destiny, embraced the poignant promise of their temporary parting. The night, adorned with stars that shimmered as celestial observers, bore witness to their eternal bond, a union etched within the very core of time. Näcken's words blossomed into the night, igniting radiant luminescence within the embrace of darkness.

CHAPTER 12

Beneath the embrace of celestial stars, on a night veiled in secrecy, Liv returned to the sanctuary of the forest, her heart burdened with longing. Amidst nature's sacred cathedral, she discovered her forbidden paramour, a divine revelation patiently awaiting her arrival. Näcken, adorned in the moon's gentle luminescence, faithfully claimed Liv's hand, an unspoken vow resonating in their touch, and guided her through veils of foliage, where whispers of shadows held secrets only comprehensible by the moon herself.

His countenance, an ode to the enigmatic mystique of the nocturne, bore the untamed locks of darkness, while his eyes, as profound as the ancient bark gracing the trees, mirrored the depths of their woodland dominion. In perfect harmony with the magnificent grandeur that enveloped them, his visage orchestrated a symphony of tranquillity and allure. Swept away by the melody echoing within her racing heart, Liv surrendered to Näcken's guidance, entrusting herself to the enigmatic depths of the forest's enchantment.

Hand in hand, they traversed the verdant empire, their words surrendered to the realm of silence, yet a silence born from profound comprehension shared solely by those willing to sacrifice all for each other's redemption. Time flowed like a murmuring brook as they ventured deeper into the forest, their connection's essence reverberating with each step.

After an ageless interval, their odyssey led them to the base of a nearby mountain, rising majestically like an ancient relic. Näcken, with a gesture tender yet resolute, beckoned Liv to ascend the rocky slope. Together, they climbed, ascending the heights with synchronized purpose, towards a small clearing that awaited them at the zenith of the mountain.

The panorama from high above was an enchanting spectacle, unparalleled in its grandeur. The moon, a radiant orb, bathed the surroundings in its tender, alluring glow. Each twinkling star, brimming with yearning, shimmered with envy, witnessing the timeless beauty bestowed upon nature.

"This is truly a realm of magic," she whispered, "I have never beheld such marvels before."

With a smile that mirrored the moon's gentle luminescence, Näcken invited Liv to join him upon a regal boulder, a throne amidst nature's dominions. As they settled upon its ancient surface, Näcken's slender fingers caressed the strings of his violin, birthing a melody as fragile as moonbeams. The ancient notes, an enchanting lament, unfurled and danced upon the mountaintop, their echoes lingering like whispers carried by the breeze.

The haunting strains of Näcken's violin became an ethereal enchantment, permeating the pores of their skin, integrating with their very essence. Like a mystical elixir, the melody seeped into their beings, traversing the pathways of their veins with seamless grace, forming a composition of solace within their souls.

As Näcken's nimble fingers created the intricate pattern of tune, Liv surrendered herself to the symphony, her eyes welcoming the tender caress of twilight. The music, akin to a celestial river, cascaded upon her senses, whisking her away to realms covered in secrecy. In the cradle of harmonious sound, she transcended the confines of her mundane existence, venturing into a realm where enchantment and elegance intertwined, adorning her spirit with an angelic peace. When Näcken cradled the instrument against their graceful form, a divine metamorphosis commenced. With each stroke of the bow, a constellation of captivating melodies burst into existence. The strings, resonating with a celestial purity, whispered secrets of ardour and yearning, casting a beguiling spell upon all who dared to listen. The forest and its inhabitants were enraptured by the enchanting hymn.

In the soulful presence of Näcken, it was as if the very essence of beauty itself found expression. His fingers danced upon the fretboard, gracefully navigating the labyrinthine path of notes, akin to a painter's brush tenderly adorning a canvas. Every nuanced expression, from the gentlest whispers to the soaring crescendos, painted vibrant strokes of emotion in the air.

As the music unfurled, time ceased its relentless march. The world stood still, seduced by the symphony that unfolded before their very eyes. The harmonies birthed a masterpiece of enchantment, transporting the listener to undiscovered realms. Hearts quivered in resonance with each tender vibration, their souls touched by the sheer magic emanating from skilful hands.

The music swirled and soared, carrying the weight of a thousand unspoken tales. It spoke of love's intoxicating dance, of heartache's poignant lament, and of the boundless yearning that stirs the depths of the human spirit. Näcken poured their seductive essence into the strings, transcending the realm of mere mortals. The notes seemed to flow effortlessly from his fingers, as if the music were a natural extension of his very being.

In that bewitching moment, the breathtaking beauty of Näcken's performance transcended the confines of time and space. It resonated deep within the core, awakening dormant emotions and igniting a celestial fire. Each delicate note, infused with Näcken's passion and virtuosity, served as a manifestation of the indomitable power of music to uplift, to heal, and to touch the sublime.

For what felt like an eternity, Näcken played while Liv listened, lost in the allure of the music and the captivating display of stars adorning the night sky. She felt as though she had finally escaped the shackles of her mundane existence and entered a realm of pure magic. Näcken continued to play, offering one melodic tale after another, until the night sky was bathed in the resounding echoes of their violin. As the final notes of the last composition faded away, tears welled up in Liv's eyes.

As the final chord hung in the air, a whispered surrender, Näcken gently placed his cherished violin aside. Liv's gaze, a mirror of her awakening soul, met his with a depth that resonated like the boundless cosmos. Yielding to the irresistible allure, Liv surrendered to Näcken's fervent kiss, an alchemical fusion of longing and passion. His hands, guided by the touch of a master, caressed her with a reverence akin to an artist cherishing his most treasured creation. In that stolen moment, their spirits entwined, harmonizing in a symphony of passion's unforgettable melody.

Liv's heart soared with ecstasy, a euphoria that swept through her being like a wild breeze caressing her soul. In perfect harmony with the rhythm of nature, she and Näcken gracefully lowered themselves onto the ground.

With the courage of a Valkyrie, Liv took command in their sexual encounter. Newfound confident fuelled her passion as she grabbed hold of Näckens penis and put herself on top of him. With fervent passion, she mounted his muscular body and started to ride him like an untamed demon. With every stride, she left behind the ordinary and ventured into the extraordinary. Her spirit danced upon the wings of the wind, carried by the wild embrace of nature. She revelled in the raw power of the moment, the adrenaline surging through her veins like liquid fire.

In the depths of her being, Liv felt the pulsating strength of life and the enchantment of the forest coursing through her bloodstream. She stood amidst the ancient trees, their towering presence embracing her with a sense of rootedness and resilience. As the gentle breeze whispered through the foliage, she could feel the delicate caress of nature's touch, awakening a profound connection that transcended the boundaries of her mortal form. The vibrant energy of the woodland creatures danced in harmony with her own, their movements a symphony of life's intricate rhythms. She breathed in the fragrance of earth and moss, a fragrant elixir that heightened her senses and ignited a primal awakening deep within.

Näcken's hands found their place upon Liv's hips, seamlessly tracing the contours of her body as they moved together in sexual harmony.

With the passion of a wild nymph, Liv put her legs backwards, her hips reached an angel where her clitoris got stimulated while fiercely riding Näcken's warm and sturdy frame. As Liv's delicate hands firmly grasped Näcken's strong shoulders, all constraints that once bound her were shattered, leaving her untethered to any inhibitions or doubts.

Liv's felt Näcken inside of her with a burning flame, a moment that unfolded precisely as she desired. In that passionate exchange, she exuded a regal air, for in that moment, she embodied the queen of her own destiny. There was no hesitation, no compromise, only the unyielding pursuit of her sexual pleasure. Every movement, a recognition of her autonomy and the unapologetic ownership of her passion.

Eager to climax, she urged herself to a swifter pace, feeling the exhilarating rush passion within her depts. Liv celebrated the sovereignty of her desires, unbound by external expectations or limitations. Each caress, each passionate moaning exchanged in the languid dance of their bodies, proclaimed her status as the mistress of her own fate. It was a declaration of self-empowerment, a confirmation of the realization that she alone held the power to shape her destiny. With each stride, she surrendered to the momentum, leaning forward as if merging her own body with the magnificent creature beneath her. Their shared purpose drove them forward, their spirits intertwining in a harmonious pursuit. In this passionate ride, time ceased to hold sway, as they traversed the open expanse with a singular purpose. Her orgasm came closer, with pleasures scream Liv climaxed. As she nestled against Näcken's chest, her heart found its home, beating in perfect harmony with his. The rhythm of their breaths intertwined, creating a symphony of tranquillity and belonging.

As the nocturnal symphony waned, Näcken, enveloped Liv's hand within his own, their fingers entwined like the delicate interplay of intertwined destinies. Descending from the awe-inspiring heights, their steps resonated with whispered vows, guiding them down the descent of the mountain. "In unseen realms, beyond mortal perception, dear Liv, lies a realm of wonders yet unfathomable," Näcken whispered, his voice a captivating melody of mystical allure. "I shall unfurl the enigmas concealed within the folds of existence and unveil before your eyes a medley of dreams yet unimagined."

Within the tumult of Liv's racing heart, Näcken's words reverberated like a tempestuous symphony, stirring the depths of her desires. The allure of unexplored domains beckoned to her, promising a voyage into the uncharted, an odyssey that would redefine the limits of her existence. Yet, amid the enthralling embrace of boundless possibilities, a bittersweet pang of guilt tugged at her soul, tethering her to the familiar shores of familial duty and the idyllic farmstead she called home. Sensing the turmoil within her, Näcken, with a gaze of understanding, began to speak, his voice a lullaby of wisdom and compassion.

"I empathize with your apprehensions, yet, find comfort in knowing that I shall forever be your champion, serenading your spirit with the ethereal strains of my violin. When the burdens of existence weigh heavily upon your shoulders, when the cacophony of the world becomes too deafening to bear, seek solace in the embrace of my melody. With each tender note, I shall weave a haven where time stands still, a refuge where you can immerse yourself in serenity and find respite from the chaos. My strings shall resound, beckoning you to my side, for I pledge unwaveringly to be your constant companion in the symphony of life."

"I yearn to spend every precious moment by your side. Though my duties call me to the farm, my heart longs to escape into this wondrous realm with you," Liv's voice, a melodic resonance of sincerity, reverberated through the humid air. Her words, untouched by artifice or pretence, carried the weight of truth, flowing like a stream unmarred by the currents of deceit. With resolute conviction, she bared her soul, casting aside the shadows of uncertainty and embracing the raw essence of honesty. Within Näcken's gaze, a profound melancholy found refuge, as if an ancient sorrow had taken residence in the depths of his being. It danced like elusive mist, entwining with his thoughts, unveiling a universe of intangible anguish. Each glance offered a glimpse into the depths of his pained memories, etched delicately upon the canvas of his countenance.

His eyes, once portals of vibrant hope, now carried the weight of unspoken sorrows. Within their depths, shadows waltzed with teardrops, their delicate choreography whispering tales of longing and heartache. A flickering flame, nearly extinguished, sought comfort amidst the expanse of his gaze.

Lines etched upon his brow, ancient runes of experience, bore witness to the burdens he had carried. Time had etched its story upon his face, mapping a life lived amidst the ebb and flows of joy and pain. Each crease and furrow told tales of battles fought, wounds healed, and losses mourned.

In the stillness of Näcken's presence, a quiet sorrow resounded, a haunting melody that echoed through the chambers of his soul. It murmured in hushed tones, beckoning a tender ache that lay dormant within. Like the delicate strands of a melancholic symphony, it tugged at heartstrings, evoking a storm of emotions coursing like a river through his veins.

Yet amidst the tempest of sadness that enshrouded him, a flicker of resilience remained. Deep within the recesses of his being, a sliver of hope persisted, refusing to be extinguished. It shimmered like a distant star, casting a faint glow upon the origin of his thoughts, an invitation to persevere despite the burdens that weighed upon his spirit.

Within the enigmatic depths of Näcken's eyes, one could discern a silent plea, a yearning for solace and understanding. It offered a glimpse into a labyrinth of emotions, where happiness and torment danced an intricate duet, forever intertwined. And though sorrow held its grip upon his thoughts, there resided within Näcken a profound beauty, born of vulnerability and resilience, awaiting discovery by those brave enough to venture into the depths of his soul.

"Though we traverse this earthly realm, we inhabit parallel planes, separated by the expanse of countless lifetimes. Mortal beings, with their fleeting existence, tread the stages of life with ephemeral footfalls. As time composes its infinite mosaic, a day shall arrive, not distant in the astral tapestry, when your existence shall fade, reduced to naught but a vanishing ember in the chronicles of history. Yet I, burdened with everlasting existence, shall persist, bound to an eternal symphony of sorrow. Within the recesses of my heart, pain twists and torments, an unrelenting tempest that knows no respite. It is you, dear one, who shall linger as the sole remnants of a bygone era, a cherished memory bound to me for the unending expanse of my achingly prolonged life.

Oh, how I shall yearn for the touch of your presence, the gentle brush of your essence against my weary soul. But alas, it is a cruel jest of fate, for your fragile mortal coil shall succumb to the march of time, while I, condemned to eternal existence, bear witness to the fading of countless stars and the crumbling of empires.

In the abyss of my eternal existence, memories of you shall become the ethereal sustenance that fuels my longing. Each fragment of remembrance, however fleeting, shall be cherished as a precious gem amidst the vast darkness of eternity. Through the pathways of perpetual solitude, I shall tread, haunted by the spectre of our shared past, forever grasping at the wisps of your presence.

As I journey through the endless epochs, the weight of your memory becomes my sole companion, an anchor amidst the vast sea of eternal melancholy. And though time may wane the vividness of your presence, leaving behind mere echoes of your essence, I shall cling to them with loyal devotion, for they are the only treasures I possess in this ceaseless expanse of my protracted existence.

Thus, dear one, we are ensnared in the cruel paradox of our disparate destinies. You, a fleeting ember amidst life's grand conflagration, shall diminish into the recesses of forgotten tales. And I, an eternal sentinel of sorrow, shall wander through the ages, cradling the bittersweet remembrance of our transient encounter, forever immersed in the tragic embrace of unending life ".

Näcken's melancholic words pierced Liv's heart like a sharpened blade. Gently, she caressed his face, becoming a vessel for his anguish, a conduit through which his pain flowed like a river of searing fire. Each tremor of his sorrow resonated within her, as if his wounds were etched upon her soul. Empathy, a compassionate thread intertwining their spirits, bound them in a shared understanding of profound suffering.

Through the alchemy of connection, she dissolved the barriers that separated them, transcending the limits of individual existence. His anguish became her burden, carried with tender reverence, as if cradling a fragile flame within her chest. The echoes of his pain vibrated through her being, unravelling the seams of her own tranquillity.

Through the everlasting bridge of empathy, she gazed into the abyss of his pain, her own heart mirroring the scars adorning his wounded soul. His anguish became a prism through which she experienced the profound depths of emotions, forging an unbreakable bond that defied the constraints of time and space.

"One of the most exquisite marvels of life is its fleeting nature, for it awakens within us a profound appreciation of every precious moment. And in this everchanging life, I hold a deep reverence for you," Liv's smile bloomed like a radiant sunbeam, illuminating the world with its playful glow. Her countenance became an enchanting fortress crafted from threads of joy and serenity. It was a celestial expression, infused with the whispers of dreams and the dance of boundless possibility. Her smile, a reflection of the sublime beauty of the universe, painted the canvas of existence with hues of warmth and resplendence.

"Now, lead me back, for the night grows late and I have lost all sense of time. I shall return in the days that follow," Through the enigmatic depths of Näcken's gaze, hidden secrets stirred, beckoning her to discover the mysteries held within. His eyes, akin to ancient gateways, whispered tales of forgotten enchantments and hidden wonders, enticing her into a realm beyond the boundaries of ordinary perception. With a knowing smile, he extended his hand, inviting her to walk through the labyrinthine embrace of the mystical forest.

Beneath the cloak of twilight's dominion, they commenced a quest through a realm bewitched, where ancient trees murmured forgotten wisdom and moonlit pathways twirled with the eternal radiance of dreams. The forest, pulsating with murmured enchantments, unfurled its verdant kingdom, guiding their steps as they meandered through a realm untouched by the passage of time.

As they ventured deeper into the heart of the enchanted woods, the air became imbued with the captivating fragrance of moss and dew-kissed leaves, while a symphony of unseen creatures serenaded their passage. Reality itself seemed to shift, revealing glimpses of hidden realms where magic and imagination converged.

Näcken, a guide in this enchanted domain, moved with a grace born of intimate familiarity with the forest's secrets. His footsteps, attuned to nature's rhythm, carved a path through the dappled moonlight and the gentle whispers of the breeze. He led her through the labyrinth of moss-laden stones and meandering streams, each step unveiling a new facet of the forest's enchantment.

Amidst the interplay of moonbeams and shadows, they traversed a dreamscape where time relinquished its hold, and reality intertwined with fantasy. The forest, a sanctuary of intrigue cradled them in its ancient embrace, murmuring tales of forgotten lore and untold possibilities.

CHAPTER 13

In the moon's affectionate graze, Näcken and Liv sought tranquillity in each other's existence, their bodies entwined like ivy, lovingly embraced by the gentle starlight. As the heavenly brilliance of the moon bathed them in its radiant luminescence, they surrendered to the symphony of the night, transcending the rhythmic pulse of time's ceaseless cadence. Their souls, entangled in a delicate choreography, pulsed with the rhythm of the universe, harmonizing with the nocturnal melodies that coursed through the mystical expanse. Amidst the whispering leaves and nocturnal secrets, an enchanting stillness descended, as if time itself had yielded to their plea and halted its relentless march.

In this suspended moment, the world around them blurred into obscurity, leaving only their entangled bodies and the symphony of their breaths intertwining with the murmurs of nature. The moon, like a celestial witness, poured its gentle radiance upon their joined forms, casting a silvery halo upon their shared sanctuary.

Under the celestial canopy where stars shimmered as witnesses to their intimate communion, Näcken and Liv revelled in the infinite possibilities of the present moment. It was a divine interlude, where their bodies melded into one another, entwined in a delicate balance of passion and tenderness that defied the limitations of mortal existence.

In this enchanted haven, time lingered, captivated by the sublime tableau they had become. Minutes flowed into an eternity, and the boundaries between night and day blurred, for they had discovered a timeless refuge, a haven where their love could flourish unrestricted by the constraints of temporal bounds.

Näcken and Liv embodied an eternal moment. Their bodies, interlaced in a display of desire and vulnerability, whispered secrets of love that resounded through the tranquil night. Time relinquished its dominion as they surrendered to the cosmic expanse of their shared existence, embracing a fleeting eternity that would forever reside within the depths of their souls. Liv turned to Näcken, her voice a gentle tremor.

"Lately, reflections on our love have been occupying my mind" Liv murmured, her voice tinged with a delicate quiver.

"I comprehend that we hail from disparate worlds, yet when we are together, I feel an undeniable sense of belonging, here in the embrace of the forest alongside you," Liv continued, her voice soft and vulnerable. "Never before have I experienced such an indescribable sentiment, and words falter in their attempt to capture its essence."

Näcken gazed at her with his deep, enigmatic eyes, and she glimpsed a glimmer of profound understanding in their depths. "No words are needed, dear one," he murmured. "Love, a celestial ember that sets our spirits ablaze, defies the boundaries of mortal comprehension. It eludes the grasp of language, slipping through the crevices of explanation like grains of sand through clasping fingers. Love exists as a resplendent and intangible force, igniting the very essence of our existence. It blossoms as a silent symphony, resonating through the chambers of the heart with a melody that surpasses the limitations of words. Love dances in the spaces between breaths, whispers secrets in the language of the soul, and paints the sky with hues of passion and tenderness. It is an enigma, etched into the fabric of human experience, thriving in the realm of emotion and vulnerability. Love, an ineffable connection, defies reason, yet forges a profound understanding that transcends intellect. Like a moonlit path leading to the depths of the unknown, love beckons us to surrender to its mysteries. It defies rationality, for its nature lies in surrender and acceptance. Love is not a thing to be grasped, but a presence to be felt, pulsating within our veins and permeating every fibre of our being. It remains an untouchable enigma, transcending the confines of definition. Love is an experience that defies articulation, an encounter to be felt with the fullness of our being. Love, in its essence, is an ineffable truth that resides in the sacred spaces between souls, an eternal flame that burns, unexplained yet undeniable. Love cannot be explained; it simply is."

As Näcken drew closer, a subdued suspense filled the air, enveloping them in a timeless grip. The world around them faded into insignificance as their lips finally met, igniting a passionate flame that danced between them. With a graceful movement, Näcken turned his gaze toward the violin resting nearby. As his hands delicately caressed the instrument's smooth curves, a sense of enchantment hung in the air. Liv watched in awe, her heart quickening with the promise of an imminent spellbinding performance.

The moment Näcken's fingers touched the strings, a profound stillness settled around them. The world was quiet in awe, poised to witness the magic about to unfold. As his hand glided over the bow, the wood came alive, murmuring secrets only music could comprehend.

Under the moon's shimmering governance, Liv found solace beside the tranquil lake. There, in the mysterious veil of night, she beheld Näcken, the enigmatic muse, as he composed melodies on his violin, infused with fervour and grace. Every inhabitant of this enchanted realm, captivated and spellbound, suspended their existence to marvel at his virtuosic prowess.

As Näcken's gaze met Liv's, his eyes, profound and mysterious, whispered countless secrets untold. His voice, a rasp tinged with seduction, enticed her senses, evoking an intoxicating drug that danced on the precipice of the erotic. In this divine encounter, the cosmic symphony of their souls harmonized, blending the elements of nature's serenade with the profundity of human desire. The ripples upon the lake's surface mirrored the tremors within Liv's heart, as Näcken's melody caressed the very core of her sexual longing. Time became an illusion, as the night itself elongated to savour this blissful union of music and passion. Liv, spellbound, surrendered herself to the enchantment, intertwined in the cadence that Näcken wove, transcending mortal imagination. In this realm of heightened sensation, the whispers of the wind carried their shared yearning, orchestrating a nocturnal ballet of desire. Näcken's fingertips, guided by an otherworldly force, danced upon the strings, conjuring melodies that screamed of hidden desires, forbidden pleasures, and the primal nature of the human spirit.

With the sweet melodies of his violin echoing in the air, Näcken gently placed the instrument aside, its strings still vibrating with the enchantment of his music. Drawing closer to Liv, he leaned in, his lips seeking the touch of hers in a tender dance of desire and longing.

With an unwavering passion burning in his eyes, Näcken's hands moved with purpose as he began to delicately remove Liv's clothes, one by one. The ambiance quivered with eagerness, as if every fibre of his being yearned to taste the beauty that lay beneath her veiled form. As each layer fell away, exposing the raw vulnerability of her flesh, Näcken's lips embarked on an exploration of her body, bestowing tender kisses upon her skin.

His kisses were a poem of desire, a rhapsodic dance upon the canvas of her being. With every caress of his lips, Liv felt the universe converge upon her, a celestial fusion of longing and ecstasy. Näcken's mouth travelled the contours of her body, leaving a trail of fervent kisses in its wake. Each touch was an illustration of his adoration, an offering of his soul's deepest desires. Näcken's kisses were a tender rebellion against the constraints of the mundane world, an expression of their shared yearning that defied societal norms. Each kiss told a story, whispered secrets of longing and whispered promises of untamed pleasure. As Näcken's lips travelled across her body, an orchestra of sensations swelled within Liv, crescendoing to the heights of rapture. His kisses painted an exquisite portrait upon her flesh, capturing the essence of their impassioned connection in brushstrokes of tenderness and longing. Lost in the labyrinth of their desires, Liv revelled in Näcken's touch, his lips mapping the landscape of her body with an unyielding hunger. In the sacred dance of their intimacy, boundaries dissolved, and they became vessels of passion, surrendering to the intoxicating rhythm of their mutual yearning. Every kiss was an affirmation of their shared vulnerability and an invitation to explore the depths of their passion without reservation.

Näcken slowly moved his lips down her body towards her legs, the passion burnt within, a radiant fire of desire. Anticipation hung in the air like a fragile veil, casting an enchanting spell over the atmosphere. It was a palpable energy, charged with a heady mix of excitement and longing.

With delicate finesse he started to lick Liv's clitoris, his tongue embarked on a gastronomic journey, savouring each morsel bestowed upon him. Time seemed to stretch as Näcken revelled in the exquisite pleasure of indulging in the sweet treats before him. With eager enthusiasm, he allowed himself to luxuriate in the euphoria that accompanied each delectable bite. As Liv's velvety clitoris touched his tongue, a symphony of flavours danced upon his palate, enchanting his senses. The sweetness enveloped his heart with a sense of fulfilment, as if he had stumbled upon a treasure long-awaited. Näcken savoured each mouthful, relishing in the satin-like surface that caressed his taste buds.

Seeing Liv lay there on her back, all exposed, bewitched by his tongue and mouth, gave him great pleasure and satisfaction. Her moaning filled Näcken's ears and intrigued his soul. His tongue moved in harmony with her yearning body, ready to explode in a wild orgasm. Liv's entire body moved in pleasure when Näcken's divine tongue caressed its way over her clitoris and vulva.

Taking his time, he explored the layers of her yearning delight, mindful to relish every intricate detail. The blissful sensation teased his senses, leaving a tantalizing trail along his nose as he continued his seductive journey. His tongue moved with a gentle swirl, tracing the contours of Liv's clitoris, seeking to embrace every corner and crevice.

Näcken was meticulous in his pursuit of pleasure, leaving no portion untouched by his attentive tongue. His taste buds revelled in the kaleidoscope of flavours, each one a delightful surprise that added depth and nuance to the experience. With reverence, he enveloped her life flower in his mouth, allowing its fullness to wash over him.

In a symphony of movement, his tongue swirled and danced, exploring every nook and cranny, ensuring that no essence went unnoticed. The pace quickened, driven by the desire to savour each moment before Liv climaxed. Näcken's commitment to relishing every second was unwavering, a proof of his devotion to this extraordinary pleasure.

With the last morsel gracefully embraced by his mouth, a profound sense of satisfaction washed over Näcken. The symphony of flavours and textures had reached its crescendo, leaving him satiated and content. It was a moment of pure bliss, a harmonious union of indulgence and fulfilment. Liv's entire body climaxed in a chock wave of electric energy.

Näcken, fixed his gaze upon her. His eyes shimmered with an allure as enchanting as moonlit ripples on a tranquil ocean, carrying the weight of untold stories and the fulfilment of long-awaited desires. Like celestial beacons adorning the night sky, they held a captivating mystery that beckoned and beguiled.

Within those radiant orbs, the tapestry of fulfilment unfurled, as if his very soul had discovered serenity and contentment. They spoke of dreams transformed into reality and whispered promises faithfully upheld, a reflection of a spirit at peace. With grace and tenderness, Näcken guided Liv back to the sanctuary of her farmstead.

CHAPTER 14

"I yearn to reveal unto you our ethereal realm, a hidden sanctuary transcending this mortal plane, traversed only by a scarce few souls," Näcken whispered, as the wind gently caressed his hair with a tender grace.

Näcken beckoned Liv to cross the obscured barrier that concealed their clandestine abode, where reality intertwined with the realm of dreams. His voice, like an ancient oracle's, resonated through the night, carrying the weight of unspoken marvels and inscrutable mysteries.

Within his words lay an invitation to undertake on a journey that surpasses the confines of mundane existence, delving into the depths of a celestial domain where nature and enchantment entwined in a harmonious dance. Näcken, guardian of hidden lore, extended an elusive promise, enthralling Liv into a realm where mortal hearts rarely tread.

As the breeze, nature's fervent messenger, delicately brushed against Näcken's dark hair, it whispered tales of cosmic splendours and unbridled beauty. His visage, bathed in an otherworldly luminescence, spoke of realms concealed from mortal eyes, where fantastical landscapes and celestial panoramas painted a picture beyond earthly comprehension.

Liv, standing on the precipice of her earthly existence, felt the allure of Näcken's enigmatic words tug at the strings of her heart. A longing surged within her, resonating with the melody of distant realms and echoing throughout her being. Captivated by Näcken's enchanting gaze, his eyes portals to a world brimming with undiscovered wonders, an irresistible yearning seized her soul.

Näcken, embodiment of ethereal wisdom, extended his invitation to Liv, offering her a glimpse into a realm where reality melded with dreams, and the extraordinary coexisted with the ordinary. The winds bore witness to their exchange, weaving a harmonious melody that carried the essence of the invitation, whispering promises of extraordinary encounters and sublime revelations.

Liv stood at the crossroads of her mortal existence, torn between the allure of the unknown and the familiar embrace of the earthly realm. Her heart fluttered with anticipation, tinged with an insatiable thirst for the extraordinary, as she pondered the fateful choice before her.

For within Näcken's invitation dwelled the promise of a clandestine domain, a sanctuary veiled in mystery, where the secrets of the cosmos danced with the whispers of the wind, and mortal hearts could find solace amidst the enchantment of celestial marvels.

"Where is this place?" Liv's curiosity sparked, her voice filled with wonder.

"Within this concealed haven, veiled from mortal sight, entrance is granted solely to those blessed by the hidden forces. Here, we dwell not amidst life's tumultuous dance, but in tranquil repose, where only the chosen may enter. In this sacred refuge, shielded from prying hands of the world, we discover solace and respite," Näcken answered, his words dripping with secrecy and enchantment.

"Will I encounter others like you there?" Liv inquired, her curiosity piqued.

"Indeed, within this legendary abode, the enigmatic ones find peace in their seclusion's embrace. They, whose existence remains veiled, seek the sanctity of solitude, venturing into this realm only when their souls yearn for tranquillity and serenity. It is a realm of breathtaking splendour, an alluring tapestry that ignites a fervent longing within me—a yearning to reveal its magnificence to you, my dear Liv."

As Näcken's gaze locked onto her, desire smouldered in his eyes, igniting a passionate inferno. In that moment, his invitation carried an undertone of intimate connection, a whispered promise to discover the secrets of their sanctuary and entwine their spirits amidst the mysteries of this captivating realm.

"Take me there," Liv insisted, her voice filled with determination.

In the depths of his gaze, Näcken posed a question that transcended mere words, reaching into the very core of Liv's being. "Do you possess the courage to surrender yourself to the unfathomable mysteries that lie ahead?" he inquired, his voice a gentle ripple upon a forgotten lake.

With his question, Näcken beckoned Liv to embark on a voyage where trust would become their lifeline, born of vulnerability and faith. It was an entreaty to cast aside the shackles of doubt and yield to the currents of destiny that entwined their fates.

Within that simple query resided the timeless flames of ancient legends, whispered by the spirits of forgotten realms. It carried the weight of countless tales where trust held the key to unlocking unseen worlds and uncharted dreams.

Standing at the precipice of uncertainty, Liv felt the weight of Näcken's inquiry deep within her being. It was a choice that would shape the trajectory of her existence, a leap of faith into the unknown. In the depths of her soul, she contemplated the profound implications of placing her trust in a being whose nature transcended mortal comprehension.

Näcken's gaze held a mosaic of emotions: hope, longing, and a glimmer of vulnerability that mirrored the trust he sought. His question, pregnant with profound implications, encapsulated the essence of their encounter, inviting Liv to release the safety of familiarity and embrace the enigmatic allure dancing in Näcken's eyes.

The air, teeming with excitement, bore witness to this pivotal exchange, as if holding its breath, eager to exhale in harmony with Liv's response. In this delicate juncture, trust became a hopeful bridge, spanning the immense space between their disparate worlds, beckoning Liv to place her faith in the enigmatic Näcken and surrender to a journey where truth and enchantment seamlessly entwined.

"With every essence of my being," Liv softly replied. Guided by Näcken's gentle hold, their entwined hands ventured into the depths of the enigmatic waters. Liv, breath held in expectation, surrendered herself to the liquid embrace as they descended beneath the aqueous veil. A chilling sensation, both invigorating and intimate, enveloped her flesh, the frigid touch of the depths soaring through her very core.

In that submerged realm, where trepidation lurked in the depths of her soul, Liv's lungs yearned for breath, and a tremor of unease threatened to consume her. Yet, in that momentous occasion, Näcken's arms encircled her, a steadfast anchor amidst the swirling sea, his touch radiating a calming warmth that quelled her tumultuous thoughts.

Together, they delved deeper, transcending the earthly confines of their former existence. The symphony of the lake, a lullaby of murmuring currents and aquatic whispers, cocooned them in a soothing embrace. A realm teeming with vibrant life unfurled before Liv's gaze, an ode to the unseen wonders that resided beneath the lake's glistening surface.

Amidst the shadows, a luminous glow beckoned, drawing Näcken and Liv closer to its ethereal radiance. In a fleeting instant, time bent, and space shifted, plunging them into an abyssal expanse of darkness. With eyes wide open, Liv beheld a newfound sight—a stretch of shoreline, caressed by crystalline waters, where onyx sands and stones mirrored the remnants of forgotten embers.

Majestic cliffs, adorned in obsidian splendour, stood as sentinels, encircling the beach like guardians of the mysteries enshrined within. Beyond the reach of the ocean, mountains asserted their dominion, their verdant meadows and lush forests unfurling like a seed nurtured by nature's gentle touch. The air, an elixir of serenity, brushed against Liv's skin, carrying with it the whispers of the waves, assuring her of a realm untouched by the inexorable march of time.

A myriad of life unfurled in this enchanting sanctuary. Birds took flight, their wings tracing graceful arcs across the sky, while creatures of the land drew near, their presence a gentle reminder of harmonious coexistence. As the sun, a bearer of hope, embarked on its ascent over the horizon, it bathed this hidden realm in resplendent light, illuminating every nook with the promise of fresh beginnings.

Within this idyllic haven, Liv found herself immersed in profound tranquillity, a place where time ceased its uncompromising stride. With each breath, she drank in the serenity that permeated the atmosphere, a soothing balm for her spirit. In this breathtaking domain, she felt an undeniable connection to the very essence of existence, an invitation to dwell in eternal peace.

Liv stood on the shore, her heart resonating with the rhythms of this mystical abode. The allure of this enchanted haven whispered promises of an everlasting journey, urging her to welcome the concept of infinity.

"It is a place of unparalleled beauty," Liv whispered, her voice a mere sigh upon the wind, as her gaze drank in the vista of this hauntingly mesmerizing realm. Her entire being trembled with an ineffable enchantment, carefully placed into the fabric of her soul.

In awe, she stood amidst the grandeur of this hidden realm, her eyes shimmering with the wonder of a starlit night, as she beheld the panorama that unveiled itself before her. A symphony of emotions danced upon her lips, yet words faltered in capturing the depth of her reverence.

The atmosphere itself appeared suspended, as if paying homage to the magnificence that unfurled before Liv's discerning gaze. She, a mere mortal, stood as a privileged witness to the revealed mysteries of a realm that exuded both ethereal splendour and sublime enchantment.

Her heart, an artwork upon which emotions painted their vibrant hues, surged with a whirlwind of gratitude, awe, and an insatiable yearning to immerse herself in the divine essence that permeated this sacred ground.

In this enchanting realm, every facet of Liv's soul resonated with an elusive harmony, a melodious whisper that carried ancient tales and bore the weight of forgotten dreams. It was as if the very landscape shared its secrets, unveiling the interplay of light and shadow, and revealing the profound mysteries that lay nestled within the depths of this mystical land.

Oh, how her soul longed to linger, to surrender to the seductive allure of this magical realm, where the serenity of the waves whispered ancient wisdom and the symphony of nature's spectacle enveloped her senses. For in this hauntingly mesmerizing place, Liv discovered an awakening, a profound connection to the very essence of existence itself.

With each breath of the enigmatic air, with each step upon the ebony sands, Liv bathed in the mysterious radiance, her heart forever captivated by the enchanting beauty that swirled around her. In this timeless sanctuary, she revelled in the tales whispered by the wind, the caress of the untamed waters, and the embrace of a realm where dreams and reality converged.

"Such is the nature of this realm," Näcken murmured, his words carrying the weight of eternity, as he stood by Liv's side, his gaze fixed upon the boundless expanse of the ocean. "A masterpiece evoked with roots of existence, where the essence of my being intertwines seamlessly with the depths of this legendary lake."

With each passing moment, Näcken's presence grew intertwined with the very fabric of this mystical haven, his essence flowing like a secret current that merged with the ripples of the water. He, the guardian of enigmas, beheld the vastness of the ocean, its infinite waves cradling the profound depths of his mysterious soul.

In that sacred juncture, Näcken and Liv stood as witnesses to the sublime union between self and surroundings, where the boundaries of their beings blurred into the landscape. Näcken, an integral part of this enchanted masterpiece, drew Liv closer to the intimate connection that resonated between his essence and the sprawling ocean before them.

The air whispered ancient secrets, carrying within it the echoes of forgotten tales. Näcken's very being, entwined with this hidden realm, mirrored the tranquil embrace of the lake—a reflection of serenity and depth. As his gaze lingered upon the expanse of the ocean, Liv caught a glimpse of the profound union between Näcken's essence and the captivating mystique of this timeless refuge.

"You mentioned the presence of the hidden ones who dwell here, tell me, who are they?" Liv inquired, her voice brimming with curiosity.

"We are the elusive ones, born from nature's sacred embrace," Näcken murmured, his voice a harmonious melody resonating with the umbles of ancient woods. "We are the ethereal spirits, guardians of sylvan glades, tranquil lakes, boundless oceans, and the wilds untouched. Our presence extends across the expanse of existence, embracing every realm, from the soaring peaks of majestic mountains to the nurturing arms of lush meadows.

These offspring of nature dwelled in a realm concealed from the mortal world, their essence veiled within the enigmatic depths of the unseen.

While some among our kind possessed the ability to manifest in tangible form, bridging the divide between realms, many remained as fleeting whispers, revealing themselves only in moments when the moon cast its gentle glow upon our rare dance. "

Näcken's gaze, suffused with ancestral pride, met Liv's, their shared heritage shimmering in his eyes. In that profound instant, Näcken embraced the legacy of their concealed lineage, an intertwined heritage pulsating with the heartbeat of ancient forests and the harmonies of untamed creatures. It was a pride born from their ancient duty as custodians and guardians, bound to preserve the delicate equilibrium of the natural world.

With each breath that passed between them, Näcken's gaze implored Liv to grasp the profound significance of their existence—their role as protectors, their divine connection to the very rhythm of creation. In that moment, Näcken's pride reflected the collective wisdom and strength of their kin, affirming their indispensable place in the heart of life itself.

"Why do most of your kind remain hidden?" Liv inquired, her voice a gentle murmur.

"For the hearts of mortals can be treacherous abysses," Näcken whispered, his voice chilling as it caressed the air. An icy veil draped over his countenance, casting a frosty hue upon his features. "Only those adorned with power and fortitude dare to unveil themselves, choosing to walk amidst the realm of visibility. Yet, mark my words, even in the unseen domains, we remain intertwined with the very essence of your world."

Within Näcken's words lingered a veiled warning, like a spectral mist, a reflection of the perils that dwelled within the human spirit. It served as a stark reminder of the shadows that could taint the delicate balance of existence, the innate capacity for destruction harboured within mortal hearts.

With measured resolve, Näcken unravelled the duality that governed their kind—their decision to manifest, a testament to their strength and prowess. However, an underlying truth persisted, whispered through the winds and echoed in the depths of forests—the hidden ones, concealed from mortal sight, exerted their influence, weaving ethereal threads into the very fabric of human existence.

Though unseen, their presence remained omnipresent, elaborately entwined into the lives of mortals. In the gentle rustle of leaves, the whispers of winds, and the serene symphony of nature, the hidden ones imparted their timeless wisdom, guiding the course of human destiny from the shadows.

Thus, within Näcken's solemn gaze, the weight of their concealed presence reverberated like thunder across the darkened sky, announcing the storm's arrival. —a reminder that their kinship surpassed mere visibility. Bound to the delicate equilibrium of nature, they stood as stalwart sentinels, guardians of harmony, and protectors of the intricate balance that interwove the myriad destinies of the world.

Näcken's composed countenance held a truth both cautionary and consoling—a reminder that while the hidden ones resided beyond mortal perception, their influence pervaded, an intangible force guiding the passage of human existence.

"What happens when you die?" Liv queried, her voice tinged with trepidation.

"What happens when you die?" Näcken echoed, his tone laced with a profound curiosity. "I am but a humble witness to the enigmas that shroud the mortal's journey beyond the veils of life," Näcken confessed, his gaze suffused with devout respect. His words, uttered with a piety akin to ancient verses, gently caressed the air, carrying the weight of eternity.

In Näcken's eyes, a glimpse of the enigmatic path that awaited mortal souls swirled with elegant grace. It was a path known solely to the spirits and guardians, those entrusted with the eternal custodianship of nature's breathtaking realms. When their enigmatic essence released its earthly vessel, they began their pilgrimage to the hallowed halls of Vatn lífsins—the realm where the river of life flowed.

In that solemn sanctuary, the spirits and guardians discovered everlasting serenity, their ethereal forms traversing the threshold of the next realm, braving the mysteries that awaited. Näcken, with boundless wisdom, comprehended that death was not a realm of punishment, but rather a blessed reunion with the domain they cherished and the kin who resided within.

Their journey into the beyond was not one of despair, but rather a divine union—a return to the very essence from which their spirits had emanated. Within the promise of that blissful reunion, Näcken and his kin discovered the eternal unity that transcended the transient veil of mortal anxieties.

"I both fear and yearn for the realm of death," Liv confessed, sorrow weighing upon her heart. "I fear that the words of the priests may bear truth, that an infernal fate awaits us all. Yet, deep within, I hold doubts. I do not embrace the notion of heaven or hell, but a fragment of uncertainty still lingers, haunted by the echoes of their teachings." Liv cast her gaze across the wide sea, her eyes clouded with melancholy.

"In the profound depths of introspection, all living beings contemplate their own existence, their souls entwined in a dance with the enigmas that separate life from the realm beyond. Fear, akin to a spectral apparition, clings to the hearts of creatures, for the safety of life is all they have known, and the unknown whispers hauntingly within their minds."

Näcken, with a tender touch and resolute conviction, clasped Liv's hand, turning her to face him. "Yet, fear not, my beloved," Näcken declared, his voice a melodic ode of eternal promises. "Even if the infernal gates themselves stood in our way, I would defy them to reclaim your essence. I would challenge the very demons, carrying you to the sanctuary of solace. My life, willingly offered, would shield you from the touch of wretched harm. In this world and beyond, there exists no limit to the lengths I would traverse for your sake."

From Näcken's words emanated loyalty and devotion, an everlasting vow etched upon the complex pages of his soul. In the presence of Liv, his purpose bloomed, as a stalwart guardian ready to venture into the darkest abysses to ensure her well-being.

Their bond, fortified by a persistent flame, flickered with resolute intensity, illuminating the shadows of uncertainty. Näcken's solemn pledge resonated through the chambers of their intertwined existence, an affirmation of the depth of his love, an offering of unwavering protection transcending the boundaries of love and life.

"You would defy the devil himself for me?" Liv smiled, though she found it hard to believe. Näcken drew nearer, closing the space between them.

"If a realm of infernal depths exists, surely its sovereign must be a spirit shrouded in shadows, a hidden one," Näcken spoke, his voice a solemn whisper that seduced the air. Within his words, the weight of eternal enigmas intertwined with delicate threads of truth.

Like a playful riddle veiled in mystery, Näcken hinted at the existence of a hellish domain, a realm where darkness reigned supreme, its very essence entwined with the concealed realm of the everlasting spirits. With a knowing gaze, Näcken peered into the depths of Liv's soul, as if acknowledging the profound interconnectedness that bound their beings.

Näcken unveiled the presence of an unseen puppeteer, a master orchestrator of malevolence, whose ethereal form resided in realms beyond mortal perception. A spirit, hidden and enigmatic, whispered secrets to the abyss and wielded influence over the echoes of damnation.

Näcken's words, suffused with haunting elegance, enticed the mind to wander through labyrinthine corridors of existence, to ponder the duality of light and darkness, of good and evil. In this evocative proclamation, he alluded to the possibility that even in realms beyond comprehension, the hidden ones held sway, their ethereal presence intertwining with the essence of existence.

"The devil is a fallen angel, a demon," Liv corrected gently.

"Demon, spirit," Näcken whispered, his voice a lament tinged with delicate sorrow. "Mere words bestowed upon the hidden ones by mortal tongues. They fail to grasp the essence of our being, the depths of our nature. We, the enigmatic guardians, surpass such limited understanding."

Näcken's gaze, adorned with bittersweet wisdom, met Liv's, embracing the profound divide that separated their realms. Names held no power in the realm of the hidden ones, mere fleeting echoes of mortal attempts to grasp the ethereal essence that eluded their grasp.

And yet, even in the face of the insurmountable separation awaiting them in the afterlife, Näcken's loyalty shone like a beacon in the darkness, never to dim. His words, infused with fervent passion, whispered promises of steadfast protection that transcended the layers of existence.

As Näcken's gaze roamed across the expanse of the boundless ocean, he acknowledged the ever-changing nature of their bond in the realms beyond. The hidden ones and mortals, destined to tread divergent paths, would forever be parted in the realm of the afterlife. Yet, in the face of this cosmic truth, Näcken's love, like the core of the earth, burned with unyielding heat.

His declaration traversed the winds, like a seashell tossed by the tides, following the rhythm of existence. In the realm where souls soared, where spirits whispered secrets and perils lurked, Näcken vowed to brave any treacherous domain, to confront any malevolent force, all in the name of preserving their connection. The yearning to safeguard Liv's soul resonated in every syllable, an eternal vow etched into the depths of his being. In this pledge, Näcken unveiled the depths of his love, willing to defy the cosmos itself to ensure her eternal safety and salvation.

"Would you truly undertake such a daunting quest for me?" Liv asked, her voice filled with gentle curiosity.

"With unwavering ardour, I shall face all obstacles in your name, engaging in battles fierce and unyielding, against infernal demons or ephemeral beings, embarking upon daunting journeys, traversing lands and ethereal realms. My affection for you knows no limits, boundless and resplendent as the cosmos itself," Näcken's voice, a tender serenade, whispered through the atmosphere. His words, like sweet poetry seducing the air. No demon's claws, no mortal's wrath could extinguish the fiery spirit that burned within him.

Through treacherous landscapes and uncharted realms, Näcken vowed to tread, a solitary figure braving the unknown frontiers of existence. Across the expanse of lands and the vast tapestry of realms, his love would guide his steps, forever faithful in its commitment, undeterred by the boundaries that sought to confine it.

"I feel like my soul is connected to yours in a way beyond life," Liv said, gazing at Näcken with eyes filled with adoration.

"Evermore entwined are our souls, for you dwell eternally within the profound depths of my heart. Time's indomitable march may pass, yet your essence shall forever grace my being," Näcken responded, his voice resounding with fervour. His locks of raven hue mirrored the grains of sand that lined the shores, an exquisite symphony of ebony and earth. As the sun's gentle caress bestowed its radiance upon the waters, his amber eyes gleamed like molten gold, casting a spellbinding enchantment upon all who beheld them.

"But I am a mortal," Liv said, her voice tinged with sadness. "One day, not too far from now, I will depart, leaving you behind."

"Inequity permeates existence," Näcken replied, his voice imbued with a profound understanding of life's caprices. "You have touched the very core of my soul, and though our destined path may be fleeting, our time together shall be cherished. Each passing second, I vow to stand unwaveringly by your side. Time, a force beyond our command, grants us only fragments, yet how we choose to infuse those fragments is our sole domain. And I, without hesitation, choose to immerse myself in your presence."

His lips met Liv's in a fervent union, in its fervour danced the sparks of his loyalty, resonating through countless dimensions. As Näcken's lips caressed hers, Liv could perceive the veracity of his every promise, an unbreakable bond that tethered their souls. In that moment, he lifted her delicately, settling her upon a rock adorning the shoreline.

Upon the enchanted shores, Näcken and Liv surrendered to unbridled love, the soulful ocean bearing witness to their sexual encounter. It was an act of desire and yearning, a dance of longing and passion, a connection surpassing life and realm. Their forms entwined harmoniously, and in tune to movements of the world. In seamless rhythm, their breath intertwined, their hears united, their souls embarked upon a shared odyssey.

Liv screamed out in pleasure, she poured the entirety of her being into this ephemeral moment, a moment of enlightenment, of the true self. Liv felt her purpose clearer than ever. Their sexual act was not just an act of the flesh, but an act of the spirit, two wonderers had bounded and now shared a future path. Together they enjoyed each other's bodies, they gave in to the ecstasy of experience another body unit with their own. As Liv climaxed, she felt the burdens of the world evaporate, replaced by an explosive universe within her being, a jubilant feast of cosmic sensations. With a tender touch, Näcken's fingers traced the contours of Liv's face, caressing her cheek with an exquisite gentleness.

"Forever, I shall be yours," he whispered, his words an eternal vow upon the altar of their shared destiny.

CHAPTER 15

Finn, with his suspecting gaze, perceived a stirring in the depths of Liv's being. A subtle transformation occurred, rendering her a vanishing silhouette, immersed in a realm of deep reflection. A profound sorrow draped her countenance, casting a shadow upon her soul. Finn, keen in his observations, couldn't escape the haunting sense of enigmatic chaos.

Yearning to unravel the mysteries enveloping her, he reached out earnestly, seeking answers within their relationship. Yet, Liv, a mistress of elusiveness, danced gracefully around the inquiries that tugged at Finn's heartstrings, skilfully eluding the tendrils of his concerned touch. Like stars obscured by city lights, his worries were dismissed, leaving him soaring aimlessly, like a kite without a string,

Under the moon's shimmering gaze, Finn lay imprisoned in a restless state, held captive by sleep's elusive grasp. Within the labyrinth of his mind, turbulent forces clashed, a tempestuous battle waged. A disquietude echoed deep within his being, for he sensed a shift, an uncertain alteration in Liv, his beloved. Like melting snow under the sun's gaze, her essence had transformed, invoking a disconcerting ache in his heart. No longer did she exhibit the hopeful seeds of affection that once rooted their souls.

Initially, a semblance of solace cloaked Finn's weary frame, embracing the absence of Liv's persistent yearning for his presence. Yet, as days surrendered to the tenacious march of time, apprehension slithered through his consciousness. A newfound vitality emanated from Liv's very core, exuding a resplendent radiance as if liberated from unseen restraints. She exuded vibrant joy, her spirit soaring toward unexplored realms, rekindling dormant dreams.

At first, Finn's spirit bore the weight of anxious anticipation, fearing Liv's impulsive actions following the loss of their cherished daughter, Gunn. Nevertheless, a semblance of tranquillity caressed his troubled soul, for his beloved appeared to find adventure in newfound ease. Yet, within the depths of his intuition, a lingering unease festered. Could there be another suitor, a lover, an intruder in their realm of affection? When Finn dared to glimpse into the depths of Liv's soul, he discovered a disheartening truth—her heart, once devoted solely to him, had strayed from its rightful home.

Fiery fury engulfed Finn's very essence, his rage swelling like a thunderous roar, echoing through the soul. Determination ignited within his core, an unwavering resolve to unveil this elusive rival and hold them accountable for their transgressions. Whispers of tales from the villagers, carried by the winds, had reached Finn's ears, troubling stories of wayward women entangled in forbidden love. Such a notion, a betrayal of Liv's faithfulness, became an unbearable burden that threatened to consume him entirely, for he couldn't bear the violation of their matrimonial bond.

Thus, in the ocean of stardust and constellations, Finn plunged into the abyss of a daring and hazardous expedition, a pilgrimage fuelled by an explosive fusion of entitlement and retribution. With fervent passion coursing through his veins, he vowed to uncover the enigmas veiled in Liv's newfound emancipation, to confront this unknown intruder who dared to trespass upon their intimate domain, and to demand justice for the devastation inflicted upon his wounded pride.

Amid the quiet haven of shadows, Finn's senses caught the delicate rhythm of footsteps, like whispered secrets caressing the air. He feigned slumber, hiding his watchful gaze beneath closed eyelids. Those tender sounds, as light as gossamer wings, glided past his tranquil form, bearing an unsettling melody. And with opened eyes, Finn beheld the image of his wife, venturing beyond the confines of their home. Before him, like a curtain drawn back, the truth was exposed —an insidious betrayal, woven deep within. For what other motive could guide a wedded woman into the nocturnal abyss, that deceitful mistress of shadows?

With anger and contempt, Finn adorned himself in garments that bore witness to his righteous fury. An unrelenting pursuit beckoned, an unquenchable thirst to discover the identity of the treacherous interloper who dared defile their sacred bond. Under a sultry eve, cloaked in a shroud of humidity, their clandestine rendezvous unfolded. Liv's footsteps led her towards the enigmatic calling of the forest, while Finn, concealed within nature's verdant refuge, yearned to unravel the truth. Why did she seek solace amidst the wooded depths?

Then, in that fateful moment, a tableau of terror materialized, searing through Finn's veins, transforming the lifeblood within into a chilling river. Näcken, sinewy and seductive, emerged like a spectre born from the darkest recesses of nightmares. His insidious presence entwined fingers with Liv's delicate hand. As they walked upon the path veiled by the ink-black night, fear pierced Finn's heart like an icy blade, constricting his very breath. Not only had she forsaken him for another man, but his cherished wife had succumbed to the sinister allure of a hellish demon!

A tempest of rage surged within Finn's essence, threatening to consume him in its fiery grip. His thirst for retribution surged, a tumultuous maelstrom demanding justice for the wounds inflicted upon his soul. Yet, amid the seething torrent of fury, a moment of clarity prevailed. Näcken, a creature of formidable power, capable of ensnaring the purest souls, had captured Liv within his diabolical web. She, perchance, remained an innocent victim, bewitched by his wicked charms. Regardless of the forces at play, the indisputable truth lingered—his cherished wife had allowed another entity to lay hands upon her, and for that transgression, she must atone.

Quietly, Finn embarked on their trail, a silent phantom whose heartbeat danced in harmony with the mystical whispers of the wind. He pursued their graceful figures, a spectral presence wrapped in the mystique of the twilight hour.

In the folds of this enchanted realm, he sought to unravel the secrets of their relationship, enraptured by the elegant ballet of their movements, as he traversed the forest. The silver cross, a guardian of unseen power, would shield and hide him from Näcken's sight. Finn beheld the sacred talisman, a shimmering silver cross that radiated a divine glow. It stood as a relic of unwavering protection, a gift bestowed upon him by the hand of fate, and a testament to his undying faith. Embracing its weight, he felt the intangible force of divine grace envelop his being, shielding him from the demonic clutches of Näcken's enchantment. Like a celestial key to the realm of sanctuary, the silver cross nestled against Finn's heart, a treasure forged in heavenly fires and imbued with the essence of divine intervention.

Within the depths of ebony's embrace, where a velveteen shroud enfolded the world, the night hushed its quiet breath, steeped in reverential awe. Yet, amid this enigmatic darkness, Näcken emerged as a luminary, an ethereal presence that bestowed upon the ancient woodland a supernaturally radiant glow.

His essence gleamed with an incandescent luminosity, as though the moon itself had spilled its magic upon his path. The forest, once swathed in obsidian veils, surrendered to his mystical aura, revealing its hidden secrets beneath his captivating gaze. Each step Näcken took illuminated the path before him, uncloaking the enchanting landscape of the nocturnal realm.

In his presence, the night transformed into a captivating spectacle, where shadows danced in breathtaking ecstasy and moonbeams wove through the foliage like celestial silk strands. The forest, once a realm of concealed mysteries, revealed its resplendence, awash in Näcken's ethereal radiance. Sharing mysteries with the breeze, the ancient trees basked in the glow of his otherworldly grace.

Stars, bewitched by his allure, shimmered with newfound intensity, mirroring the celestial incandescence that emanated from Näcken's very being. They bestowed their twinkling adoration upon him, granting divine favour upon this fabled figure traversing the nocturnal realm.

Creatures of the forest, from delicate woodland nymphs to elusive denizens of the night, stirred in reverence, drawn to Näcken's luminescent charm. Their eyes shimmered with pure light, reflecting the enchantment he exuded, as they surrendered to the symphony of his captivating presence. Beneath his otherworldly glow, the heart of the forest pulsated with resounding beats, enraptured by the poetic grandeur that Näcken bestowed upon the nocturnal kingdom.

Within Finn's chest, his heart throbbed with a hastened rhythm, fuelled by anger's fiery blaze. He felt an insistent need to discover their destination and unravel their intentions. Slowly, they ventured through the forest, and Finn kept a cautious distance, ensuring that Liv and Näcken remained unaware of his presence. Nervous and anxious, he resisted the urge to retreat, for he knew he could not turn back from this path.

Silently, Finn's heart composed a symphony of rage, its cadence an echo of fervent wrath coursing through his veins. Anger, an untamed tempest, propelled him forward with magnifying determination. The air crackled with the intensity of his resolve, driven by an unquenchable thirst to unearth Näcken's concealed destination and unravel the secrets intertwined within his wife's unholy bond with the enigmatic sorcerer.

Through the labyrinthine embrace of the forest, Liv and Näcken danced in mysterious harmony, their movements shrouded in shadows. Finn, a solitary phantom amidst the emerald forest, maintained a calculated distance, ensuring his presence remained veiled from their unsuspecting eyes. His footsteps, gentle as murmured secrets upon the mossy ground, echoed the tender dance of caution, skilfully weaving the delicate thread of secrecy between pursuit and revelation.

Tumultuous waves of nervousness and anxiety surged within Finn's core, threatening to dismantle his poise. Yet, from the depths of his soul, he drew forth a reservoir of fortitude, steadfast in his resolution. The weight of the unknown pressed upon his spirit, a burden he refused to cast aside, for within the embers of his curiosity, a path illuminated before him, unafraid to be trodden.

With each measured step, the forest whispered its ancient secrets, an ethereal choir of wisdom that caressed his senses. Rustling leaves murmured tales of clandestine rendezvous, while stoic oaks offered shelter from the tempest of emotions that sought to consume him. But Finn's resolute gaze remained fixed upon the figures ahead, his spirit aflame with fervent determination.

His heart yearned for answers, to unravel the enigmatic threads that bound his beloved to the hellish sorcerer. Upon the tightrope of emotions, Finn danced, suspended between desperation and resolve. To retreat, he knew, would be to surrender to the darkness of ignorance, a fate too heavy to bear.

Thus, with each determined step, Finn continued into the realm of uncertainty, his soul ignited by the flickering light of love and fury. Within Finn's being, a cauldron of betrayal seethed, molten lava coursing through his veins, scorching his very essence. Bound by enchantment's delicate threads or not, his beloved wife had forsaken their sacred bond, dancing with the shadows of the night, to seek solace in another's arms. Through the cloak of midnight hours, they traversed, their steps a whispered symphony of secrecy and hidden desires. At last, they arrived in a moonlit clearing, where beautiful moonbeams tenderly kissed the earth.

A ghostly sentinel, Finn concealed himself behind a sturdy tree, its trunk an anchor for his unravelling emotions. Näcken, orchestrator of this heart-wrenching tableau, drew closer to Liv, his seductive power radiating like a siren's call. Tension hung in the air like a thick fog as Näcken's lips sought hers, kindling an inferno of rage within Finn's core. His hands clenched with a fierce intensity, trembling with an overwhelming urge to confront the usurper of his affections.

Yet, amidst the hurricane of anger, Finn's spirit grappled with the sobering reality of Näcken's unfathomable might. Like an ancient deity, Näcken possessed powers that eludes the grasp of human minds, a force that danced on the precipice between enchantment and peril. Deep within his soul, Finn recognized that to challenge such a formidable entity alone would invite his own annihilation.

And so, while every fibre of his being yearned to charge forward and sever the bonds entwining his wife and the sorcerer, Finn exercised the utmost restraint. His gaze, ablaze with unquenchable fury, found calm in the wisdom of self-preservation. For he understood that to confront Näcken head-on would be to court certain doom, a treacherous dance with a predator of mystical realms.

The tempestuous waves of anger crashed upon the shores of Finn's resolve, threatening to consume him in a maelstrom of righteous fury. Yet, amidst the turmoil, a flicker of clarity emerged from the depths of his heart, reminding him of his own vulnerability in the face of Näcken's ethereal might. Bitter indeed was the realization, a surrender to the cruel truth of his own limitations. In the battle between love and vengeance, he chose the path of prudence, aware that to confront Näcken required strength yet to be unearthed.

With a heart aflame, the flames of thwarted fury dancing within, Finn exercised restraint, recognizing the peril that awaited should he cross paths with such a formidable entity. Within the depths of his gaze, a silent vow took shape—to gather the forces necessary to confront Näcken, to unmask the enchantment that held his beloved captive, and to reclaim that which rightfully belonged to him, regardless of the cost.

As Finn battled with the ghosts of his mind, Näcken started to undress Liv. Within Finn's tumultuous depths, a whirlwind of emotions collided, entwining him in a paradoxical dance of fervent sexual excitement and smouldering anger. **Swiftly Näcken turned Finn's wife around in a powerful motion and started to have sex with her.** At first, a sense of shame tiptoed through the corridors of Finn's conscience, like a ghostly spectre whispering tales of guilt. **Finn felt a strange feeling of both arousal and anger.** He yearned to cast aside this conflicted state of mind, for he wished not to revel in the strange allure of such emotions. But beneath the surface, a mysterious force beckoned him, compelling his gaze to linger upon the enchanting scene before him, **there was something erotic over watching another man have sex with his wife.** The juxtaposition of these intense sentiments stirred within him like tempestuous tides, threatening to consume his very being. An enigmatic sensation gripped his heart, both captivating and tormenting his soul, as he gazed upon the spectacle of his beloved wife having sex before his very eyes.

There was an allure, something profound erotic, an undeniable intrigue, in observing his wife from the shadows. It was a peculiar sensation, both captivating and unsettling, as he witnessed her in a realm unbeknownst to him, caught in the gravitational pull of a mysterious force. Excitement, like a kaleidoscope of vibrant hues, painted itself upon Finn's canvas of emotions. The forbidden tableau unfolding before his eyes became a delicious forbidden act. A fire within him flickered, kindling a sense of sexual curiosity that burned bright amidst the storm of conflicting emotions.

Yet, interlaced with this thrill of voyeuristic exploration, anger smouldered within Finn's soul like a dormant volcano awakening. It was a tempestuous flame, ignited by the betrayal that haunted the recesses of his heart. The sight of his beloved, entangled with another, fuelled the furnace of his fury, casting sparks that threatened to consume his very essence.

The intertwining of these seemingly incongruous emotions elevated Finn's tumultuous state to poetic heights, as if his heart were engaged in an intricate sonnet of passion and turmoil. His soul became a battleground of conflicting desires, the whispers of excitement and the roars of anger colliding in a symphony of chaos.

Within the depths of his being, Finn cradled a profound truth—a longing to comprehend, to unravel the enigmatic forces that ensnared his beloved. The peculiar allure that seized his spirit, despite the sting of betrayal, spoke of a love that surpassed the bounds of convention. It was this amalgamation of love and anger that wove a bittersweet melody, resonating through the chambers of his soul.

When he watched Liv in the realm of twilight's tender caress, blossomed like a radiant flower, he felt himself getting an erection. Every movement, every delicate sway of her form, whispered secrets of untamed joy, painting the night with strokes of celestial rapture. Her spirit danced upon the winds of elation, a symphony of laughter and grace that enchanted all who beheld her.

Her very being seemed to overflow with unabashed delight, a symphony of pure bliss echoing through the depths of Finn's longing heart. With every moaning she uttered, the earth quivered beneath her feet, as if nature herself delighted in her presence. Her moaning, like crystal cascades, reverberated through the enchanted forest, stirring the hearts of creatures great and small, who revelled in the enchanting melody that escaped her lips.

In the gentle embrace of moonlight's luminescence, Liv became a celestial muse, a living embodiment of euphoria's embrace. Her eyes, twin orbs of sparkling stardust, reflected the twinkling constellations above, unveiling the universe of joy that resided within her soul. With each breath, her radiant spirit breathed life into the night, illuminating the shadows with a soporific warmth that wrapped around the hearts of all who basked in her captivating aura.

Her infectious, pleasures screams rang through the air, like a chorus of songbirds serenading the moon, inviting the world to join in her sexual celebration. She wove her spell with grace and abandon, enchanting the very fabric of existence with her radiant presence.

In the depths of Finn's longing gaze, a tender ache bloomed, mingling with the splendour of admiration and a hint of bittersweet yearning. For in Liv's sheer enjoyment of Näcken's sexual power, he glimpsed a profound beauty that both delighted and pained his impassioned soul. It was a vision of joy and exhilaration that whispered tales of unadulterated enchantment, yet stirred the embers of longing within his heart.

As Finn beheld Liv's radiant countenance, his own spirit was caught in the tidal sway of her euphoria. He marvelled at her ability to immerse herself in the present, to find sexual pleasure with a demon. As Liv painted the night with her resplendent joy, Finn stood as a silent witness, his heart aflame with adoration and aching desire. Her radiance became a guiding star, illuminating his path with the promise of a passion that transcended the boundaries of time and space.

Finn started to pleasure himself, enraptured by the ethereal spell woven around him, ensnared in the delicate threads of the present moment. Time lost its grip upon his consciousness as he surrendered to the enchantment that swirled in the air. The barriers of inhibition crumbled, and he was swept away on the currents of his emotions, guided solely by the intoxicating dance of desire. He let his hand move up and down over his penis, caressing it like a whispering breeze, guided by the unspoken language of longing while beholding his naked wife's erotic encounter. Finn became captivated by the enchanting spectacle unfolding before his eyes. Each fluid movement was an erotic fantasy, painting the air with yearnful longing. In the crucible of exploration, Finn's spirit blazed with an insatiable curiosity. Liv's body, an instrument of poetry in motion, seemed to transcend the earthly realm, channelling the melodies of the universe through every exquisite gesture. **It did not take long for Finn to climax, t**he magnetic force of sexual desire intertwined with the pulsating rhythms of his penis, propelling him towards his orgasm.

In the aftermath, like a mist of melancholy, sorrow descended upon Finn. The burden of what he had witnessed pressed heavily upon his shoulders, threatening to crush his spirit beneath its weighty presence. Agonizing tendrils of anguish coiled around his heart, constricting his breath, as he grappled with the unfathomable truth that had unravelled before his eyes.

His soul recoiled at the sight of his beloved entangled with a creature of darkness, a demon that had insidiously infiltrated the sanctuary of their union. The betrayal pierced deep, cutting through the tender fabric of trust, leaving wounds that bled with the pain of shattered promises and shared experiences.

Within the abyss of despair, Finn's spirit faltered, consumed by the anguish that coursed through his veins. Betrayal's tendrils ensnared his very essence, squeezing the light from his being, as he struggled to comprehend the depths of his wife's transgression. It was a betrayal that surpassed the boundaries of mortal sins, a betrayal not only of their bond but also of the sacredness of their very souls.

Haunted by the knowledge of his wife's treachery, Finn found sanctuary in the darkness like a weary wanderer, seeking refuge from the harsh glare of reality. Shadows became his confidants, accepting his anguish without judgment, as he wrestled with the raw emotions threatening to overwhelm him. His spirit, once vibrant and aflame, now a vanishing illusion flickering, a mirage in the desert, burdened by the weight of love tarnished and defiled.

The echoes of their shattered marriage haunted through his mind, tormenting him with their bitter refrain. His heart bled from the wounds of a love betrayed, pain's tendrils entwined with his very existence. The foundation upon which their love had been built crumbled, reduced to mere ashes scattered by the wind, leaving behind a desolate landscape of broken dreams and fractured trust.

In the depths of his anguish, Finn grappled with the dual nature of emotions raging within. Anger burned in his veins, fuelled by the profound injustice of the situation. The sanctity of their love had been violated, tainted by the presence of an ungodly creature that dared to steal the affection rightfully his. Betrayal gnawed at his core, the bitter taste of deceit poisoning his soul.

Amidst such devastation, Finn's spirit wavered, weighed down by the magnitude of betrayal. The very essence of his being yearned for retribution, for justice to be served upon the unholy union that had desecrated their sacred bond. He became a wounded warrior, haunted by the echoes of his wife's transgressions, grappling with the darkness that threatened to drown him.

Swiftly, he hastened to the stable, where his faithful horse awaited, muscles taut with anticipation. With steady hands, Finn fastened the saddle upon the animal's sturdy back, forging a seamless bond between man and beast. Through whispered words of encouragement, he implored his equine companion to carry him forth with hasty speed.

Like a spectre in motion, the youthful creature darted through the veil of ebony night, a regal silhouette casting fleeting shadows upon the earth. The wind, an eager accomplice, told stories through the tangled tendrils of Finn's tousled hair, guiding him towards his fateful tryst. Time slipped away, until at last he arrived at a grand estate, an imposing edifice located on the outskirts of the village.

Urgently, Finn dismounted his noble companion, their breaths entwined in a symphony of synchrony. A cascade of purposeful steps propelled him towards the dwelling's beckoning threshold. The guardians of this nocturnal sanctuary, hounds of vigilance, erupted into a ferocious chorus of barks, their echoes shattering the silence. Within the depths of the dwelling, a solitary beam of light pierced the darkness, an invitation or a warning yet untold. Murmurs, delicate and elusive, teased his senses, hinting at enigmatic secrets.

With determined resolve, Finn's fingers poised for what lay ahead. Resounding raps upon the wooden door echoed with a resolute fury. And in response, the cacophony of canine baying intertwined with the discordant symphony of his own pounding heart. Illumination flooded the interiors, casting bright hues upon the anxious countenance of the solitary intruder. A clandestine encounter beckoned, and with unyielding purpose, Finn steeled himself to confront the mysteries concealed within those walls.

"Who dares to disturb my peace in the depths of night?" A stern voice responded with force. "I shall shoot and unleash the hounds upon you!"

"It is I, Finn," came Finn's calm reply. The man on the inside swiftly turned the lock.

"Finn?" he asked, perplexed. "What brings you to my doorstep at such an unearthly hour? Do you not realize the lateness of the hour?"

"I implore you, Father, I must speak with you," Finn pleaded.

"Cannot this wait until the morrow?" the Priest asked, growing annoyed.

"It concerns my wife; she has gone into the forest, ensnared by Näcken's wicked enchantments!" Finn cried out in despair. The Priest flung open the door.

"What? Näcken has beguiled your wife?" the Priest inquired.

"I witnessed her departing our home, and I followed her. Näcken appeared and led her into the forest," Finn spoke, his eyes brimming with tears.

"Fear not, my child," the Priest urged. "I know precisely what must be done. You have done well to seek my guidance."

"Thank you, Father!" Finn reverently kissed the Priest's hand.

"Were you spotted?" the Priest inquired, a glint of malice in his eyes. He had long awaited the chance to dispatch mercenaries into the forest, his desire to rid the realm of these malevolent creatures burning strong.

"No," Finn replied in hushed tones.

"Excellent," the Priest smirked. "Return home, my child, feign ignorance of these events."

"I am uncertain if I can bear such pretence," Finn confessed, his frustration palpable. "I desire to exact vengeance upon Näcken and make her face consequences." he continued.

"Fear not, my child, your desire for retribution shall be fulfilled. I promise you. But for now, return to your abode and act as if this blasphemy has not touched your awareness. I shall summon aid, and when they arrive, I shall reach out to you. I have a meticulous plan in place, patiently awaiting such an opportune moment."

"I carry a burden of shame, Father," Finn lamented.

"The weight of shame is not yours to bear. You have committed no wrong," the Priest reassured him.

"What shall befall my wife?" Finn queried.

"She has consorted with the devil's minions. There is no salvation for her. We must cleanse her through fire, for that is the sole means to salvage her tormented soul."

"But I believe in her innocence, I believe that Näcken's sorcery led her astray," Finn murmured with a heart heavy with compassion, his love for his wife still intact.

"Regardless, the only path to absolution is through the purifying flames," the Priest hissed with a venomous voice.

"I comprehend," Finn acquiesced, his voice tinged with resignation.

"Very well. Return now, and we shall delve deeper into this matter after Sunday's mass. Remember, you must carry on as if naught has occurred. Do not share your bed with your wife, for she is now tainted, impure, under the sway of Satan. And if doubt engulfs your spirit, seek solace in prayer. Should the weight grow unbearable, come to me, and I shall lend an ear," the Priest imparted, a smile dancing upon his lips. Finn nodded, mounting his steed in solemn silence. He rode back to the farm, an air of melancholy enveloping him, as he came to realize that he had lost Liv, and no effort of his could reclaim her.

CHAPTER 16

Liv, enchanted and spellbound, held her breath with bated anticipation as Näcken, in a graceful dance, led her through the water, revealing once again his hidden domain. The world transformed around her, as shadows engulfed her senses, shattered by a radiant light that bedazzled her eyes. Beholding her surroundings, she encountered a scene of serene beauty. A pure expanse of glistening snow adorned the earth beneath her feet, casting an aura of tranquillity.

Exploring her surroundings, Liv found herself standing in a profound valley, encircled by ancient, majestic mountains that whispered tales of time's ancient wisdom. A frozen creek meandered through this sanctuary, its icy waters flowing gracefully, a tribute to the frozen stillness of the land. Midnight had assumed its throne, and the celestial waltz of the Northern Lights harmonized with the twinkling stars, painting the velvety sky with a symphony of colours.

Amidst the frigid touch that clutched this realm, Liv remained untouched by its cold grasp, enfolded in a profound warmth that emanated from within. By her side stood Näcken, adorned in a flowing garment, his ivory-white hair gently cascading in harmony with the contours of his face. His profound gaze, filled with contemplation, delved into the depths of her soul, unveiling a calm assurance that surpassed worldly tribulations. His countenance exuded tranquillity and confidence, as if all the hardships of existence dissolved within the sanctuary of his meditative vow.

Näcken embraced Liv, a shield of protection and solace. Within the depths of his eyes, she glimpsed the boundless cosmos, the very source of life itself. In the shimmering pools of his gaze, her spirit discovered safety and purpose, resonating with the primal rhythm of creation.

"Why do I not feel the cold?" she whispered, her voice carried on the wings of curiosity and wonder.

"In this realm, my beloved," Näcken replied, his voice a symphony of enigmatic truths, "winter bends to your every whim. It need not ensnare you in its icy grip." Liv's gaze, drawn to Näcken's commanding presence, admired the sculpted contours of his form. Tall and gracefully lithe, his slender physique embodied strength beneath an elegant veneer, his broad shoulders a symbol of resilience. A tender caress graced her cheek as Näcken's fingertips brushed her with a gentleness that expressed a thousand words.

Within their connection, Näcken peered into the rich irises of Liv's eyes, a universe unto themselves. His gaze, suffused with tenderness and comprehension, sought the depths of her soul, traversing the hidden corridors of her being.

"Why have you brought me here once more?" Liv inquired, her chestnut hair flowing like a cascade down her back, a tapestry of warmth and earth.

"Here, my love, we find sanctuary, a refuge unburdened by the weight of your mortal existence," Näcken answered, his voice carrying the wisdom of ages. A tender embrace ensued as Liv's head found solace upon his chest, her ear attuned to the symphony of his heart's rhythm. Its cadence, a languid melody, surpassed the hurried beats of mortal pulses.

"I perceive the rhythm of your heart," Liv murmured, a radiant smile gracing her visage like the tender glow of dawn's first blush. "Never did I fathom that beings of immortality could possess such pulsations."

Näcken, beholding her innocent wonder, bestowed upon her a gentle gaze, his eyes shimmering with ancient enigmas. "Truly, my dear, I embody a spirit interwoven with corporeal existence. A fragile vessel of flesh and bone, vulnerable to the arrows and slings of mortality, yet blessed with an immortal essence that traverses realms. My form, distinct from your mortal coil, is bestowed with the breath of life, a sacred boon that unites us in this ethereal dance of being."

A reverent touch, akin to the northern wind caressing a sunlit meadow, graced the silken strands of Liv's hair, a gesture carrying solace and protection. "You mentioned that this realm belongs to the hidden ones, but what do they say when a human is present?" Liv's gaze, akin to a delicate wisp of starlight, followed the graceful passage of a creature traversing the realm with cautious grace. Its presence, a mere silhouette in the corner of this enchanted sanctuary, evoked a sense of vigilant guardianship.

"The ethereal inhabitants dwelling within these realms have yet to summon me," Näcken revealed, his voice carrying both reverence and defiance. "Perhaps, the celestial court mourns my transgression, for I have dared to invite a mortal into their hidden domain. Nevertheless, their disapproval wanes before the vastness of my devotion. You embody everything that I hold dear. To share my realm, my very essence, with you is a sacrifice I am willing to endure, disregarding their dissenting voices."

In his declaration, Näcken's voice resounded with resolute passion, his commitment everlasting, like the darkness before time itself started. For in his eyes, Liv was an unmatched treasure, a luminous jewel whose radiance eclipsed the judgments of celestial beings.

In the tranquil wonder of mutual epochs, Näcken Commenced a voyage of seductiveness, his lips a vessel of unspoken reactions as they met her aroused body. The caress of his breath against her skin was an erotic promise, a melody of longing composed in the language only lovers could fathom.

His fingers, blessed instruments of artistry, caressed Liv's body as if they were delicate strands of fate. Within the embrace of his hands, hands that bore the mark of time's caress and the touch of countless lifetimes, a fervent flame of passion's ardour ignited. With each touch, a constellation of notes was awakened within Liv as she gave into the divine touch of his hands. His hands, conduits of passion, seemed to dance across the surface of her body, their movements an intricate choreography that evoked the memories of places long forgotten and the echoes of emotions buried deep within.

With an air of unswerving assurance, Näcken enveloped Liv in his arms, a gesticulation that embodied the weight of wordless obligations and the elegance of a waltz unfurled in moonlit gardens. Lifted from the ground as if by the hands of fate itself, she surrendered to his touch, her heart dancing to the rhythm of his every breath. Näcken bore Liv across the threshold, traversing the realm of reality with the grace of a dreamweaver guided by the stars. In that enchanted realm, a bed of white flowers beckoned, petals like fragments of fallen constellations, strewn as offerings upon an altar of intimacy. He laid her down with a reverence that mirrored the adoration of a poet crafting verses to honour his muse. The fragrant blooms cradled their forms, an embrace that mirrored the intertwining of their souls.

With the fluid grace of a whispered sonnet, he released Liv from his grasp, each gaze lingering like a parting goodbye. And then, as if guided by the currents of an unseen ballet, he transitioned. With a seamless shift that emulated the meeting of two souls, he positioned himself atop her.

As his fingertips caressed her body, an alchemical connection blossomed, a union of soul and sound that transcended the physical realm. As his hands moved with the grace of a maestro conducting an orchestra of pleasure, the world seemed to fade away, leaving only the communion between passionate lovers. Her breath, once a seductive whisper, began to mimic the cadence of his erotic movements. In each inhalation, she drew in not just air, but the very essence of his erotic presence.

With a graceful descent, Näcken lowered himself into the space that destiny had carved, positioning his presence in the surface of their shared sexual encounter. As he settled, the distance between them seemed to melt away like morning mist beneath the caress of the sun's tender grace. In the intimate geography of their connection, he found his place behind her, his form an echo of her own, a silver imprint woven by the moon on the serene waters of an ocean.

As Näcken leaned in, a gravitational force stronger than any known drew him to her, their breaths mingling in a dance of unity, as if they were exhaling the echoes of their shared pleasure. His lips brushed against her neck and back, a connection that held the weight of pledges murmured amidst the silver-strewn night. Liv moved her body to the whispers of pleasure while she surrendered to Näcken's seductive hands.

In the chamber of harmonious enchantment, he caressed her breasts with hands that echoed with the ardour of a thousand love songs. His fingers, a blend of artist and alchemist, traced the contours of her breasts with a touch that bore the weight of ancient sonnets and fervent confessions. With every stroke, a tempest of melodies burst forth, like a torrent of stars cascading from the heavens to bless the earth. His movements were a dance of passion and technique, an intimate conversation with flesh and skin that resonated with the soul's deepest chambers.

Liv's fingertips alighted upon Näcken's penis with a touch as delicate as the fluttering of a butterfly's wings. Her hands, extensions of her very essence, bore the weight of a thousand caresses, each finger a storyteller in this wordless dialogue of touch. As her palms met the landscape of his penis, they traced the contours of strength and agility, a terrain where sexual dreams and erotic secrets intersected.

As the tempo of Näcken's breath quickened following the erotic caress of Liv's hands, he found himself drawn into the melody of their encounter, the music of their connection played out in the rhythm of his inhalations. With each drawing of breath Liv could feel him getting harder.

With a heart enkindled by an ember of passion, Näcken set his hands upon her clitoris, a serenade to the universe poised upon his fingertips. As his fingers danced upon her clitoris, they invoked not just passion, but a journey of the soul. Liv yielded to his touch, responding to his enthusiasm with a moaning that echoed his fervent spirit.

In the realm of erotic expressions, Liv parted her lips, and from the wellspring of her soul, a breath of pleasures sounds emerged, a symphony of desire carried by the currents of the heart.

Their bodies, ignited by a fiery passion, moved in a dance of ardour and grace—a flamenco that unfolded like a story written in the language of desire. His chest rose and fell with the rhythm of anticipation, a heartbeat that echoed in harmony with the pulse of the rapture that enveloped them. His hands, sculpted by the years of devotion to his calling, were instruments of power and tenderness, poised to weave a tale upon the canvas of her skin.

In the delicate interplay of energies, his senses became attuned to the soft echoes of her unspoken yearnings, Liv wanted to feel Näcken inside of her. The currents of their connection carried with them the subtle vibrations of her longing.

As Näcken's heartbeat echoed in the chambers of his chest, he felt the resonance of Liv's desires and parted her legs while entering her body. She gasped in pleasure, her longing, like a whispered secret, brushed against the edges of his consciousness, evoking a typhoon of emotions that swirled within him. With a grace befitting a lover's touch, Näckens hands undertook an odyssey across the expanse of Liv's clitoris. Her clitoris, a vessel of dreams and melodies, responded to his caress with a pulsating lusting, its swelling proportions a portal into a realm of havoc waiting to be unleashed.

His fingers, extensions of his soul's desires, danced upon Liv's clitoris, tracing a delicate path that mirrored the map of his heart's landscapes. With each press and release, a cascade of pleasure spread out like the sails of a ship catching the wind, a fragrant offering to the universe. Liv's moaning, an intimate companion to Näcken's artistry, sang in response to the tender call of his touch. His hands moved as if guided by a divine force, each stroke an utterance in a silent dialogue that only an artist could understand. The erotic passion flowed, not just from his fingertips, but from the very core of his being—a river of sentiments that meandered through the channels of Liv's body and resonated in the air like remnants of vows carried by the wind. As his hands navigated her clitoris, he created a story—an opus of longing and reflection, of triumphs and tribulations. The sound of er moaning, like a lover's breath, filled the forest, carrying with it the weight of his emotions, the beauty of his dreams, and the essence of his spirit. Näcken's hands were not just playing; they were conversing, exchanging secrets with her clitoris in a language that required no translation. Her clitoris, like a devoted confidant, responded to his touch with a sonority that reflected his intentions. In the luminal space of Näcken's seduction, time seemed to lose its grip, and he found himself immersed in a world where only Liv's pleasure mattered. His hands moved with the precision of a craftsman and the passion of a lover, each stroke an exploration, a revelation, an offering. Her horny calls, a savage storm of emotions, enveloped him, becoming an extension of his very essence.

He embarked upon a delicate ballet of contrasts, his touch upon her clitoris an embodiment of the fluctuation of emotions. Like a masterful painter wielding a brush, he shifted seamlessly between strokes of strength and gentleness, crafting a symphony that spoke of the profound interplay between light and shadow, passion and tenderness. With every stroke of his fingers, he conjured echoes of strength that resonated like the roar of waves crashing upon a shore, each stroke a declaration of his inner power. Liv responded to his touch with a resonance that reverberated through the air, an anthem of fortitude that spoke of his spirit's enduring commitment. The transition between these worlds—strong and soft—was seamless, an affirmation of his mastery over her clitoris. It was as if he were channelling the very essence of life's dichotomies, encapsulating the essence of yin and yang, of power and vulnerability, of the storm and the calm, all within the playfulness of his artistic hands.

In a symphony of longing and surrender, Näcken closed the distance between them, his lips meeting Liv's neck and ear. In the realm where souls entwine, he became attuned to a subtle transformation, a shift in the delicate currents of her being that whispered secrets of her approaching climax. It was as if the air itself had been charged with a new energy, a melody of sexual freedom that vibrated at a frequency he could not deny. Her aura pulsed with a vibrancy that was both exhilarating and mysterious, a dance of light and shadows that beckoned him to decipher its secrets. Like a celestial body adjusting its course amidst the limitless cosmos of the nocturnal heavens, he shifted his stance, a gesture filled with unspoken intentions and hidden desires.

"Why did you stop? " She asked.

"In this delicate hour of approaching climax, let the sands of time be patient a while longer." With the resonance of his voice, he summoned the ethereal magic that resided within his being, creating a symphony of intention and action that vibrated in the very air they breathed. In an act that transcended mere physicality, he lifted her—his touch a proof of his divine strength and her trust, a validation of the unspoken understanding that existed between them. His arms, like the embrace of a guardian angel, encircled her with a tenderness that bespoke of his appreciation.

With a touch that reverberated with purpose, Näcken gently leaned Liv against a venerable tree, as if engaging in a tender communion with the very core of the forest. Seductively, he entered her body. With each push and stride, the earth seemed to rise up to greet him, the soil responding to his presence as if whispering secrets only it could understand. His tempo was a rhythm, a heartbeat that synchronized with the pulse of the world around him. His muscles, sculpted by both time and intention, flexed and relaxed in harmony with the cadence of his breath. The wind, a gentle accomplice, played with the tendrils of his hair, caressing his skin like a lover's touch. Every inhalation was a communion with the air, every exhalation a release of energy that fuelled his passion. With each stride, he cast aside limitations, embracing the realm of possibility that stretched out before him like an endless opportunity. His breaths upon her neck became a chant, a mantra of determination that resonated in the very marrow of his bones. As Näcken continued to pleasure Liv, a fire burned within him—a fire of purpose, of passion, of the sheer exhilaration of being alive. His movements became a language, a declaration of his vitality, evidence of his connection with the magical world that enveloped him. In the delicate ballet between earth and sky, his pace unfolded like a verse in a timeless poem, each push an elegy to strength and assurance. With every stride, he etched a sonnet upon the landscape, an illustration of his mastery over the forces that bound him to the earth and propelled him forward.

Liv had her legs around his waist, she moved her hips with his pace. His gait, a dance of purpose and precision, painted a portrait of a man connected to his very core, his muscles a symphony of fluidity and grace. She could feel his upper body against hers in an erotic union.

Once more, the approaching climax echoed through Liv's senses, a primal instinct that stirred like a slumbering phoenix awakening from its dreams. Her pulse quickened, blending with the ancient echoes of sexual longing that had been imprinted within her core.

Amidst her pending climax, he yielded to the call of stillness—a moment of pause that became one with the tender pulse of time itself. The world, once a whirlwind of activity, stilled its voice in a breathless pause as he graced the continuum of motion with a momentary cessation. With a movement as fluid as a river's caress, he changed position—a transformation that held within its touch the quintessence of evolution itself. His form, once an embodiment of one posture, now emerged anew, a sculpture of limbs and lines that told a tale of change and growth.

Näcken allowed his essence to entwine with Liv's—a passionate union where his very being melded with her curves and contours. She became a vessel of trust, a willing disciple of his lead—a dance of souls that unfolded in the magical chambers of connection. He became a sculptor of motion, a maestro of angles—his body a brush painting the canvas of space with a symphony of shapes that echoed the language of his heart. With each gesture, each turn, each extension, he wove a tapestry of expression that danced between the realms of physics and poetry. His limbs, like verses of an unwritten poem, traced arcs and lines that seemed to transcend the limitations of the physical world. The air, a witness to his choreography, seemed to shimmer with the echoes of his movement, as if it were privy to a dialogue that resonated beyond the audible spectrum.

In the realm of dance, Näcken became a conjurer of angles—an enchanter who spun geometry into romance, who transformed degrees and lines into whispers of emotion. Every tilt of his head, every bend of his body, became a punctuation mark in a story that was both intimate and grand—a story told not with words, but with the tender language of motion.

As Näcken twirled and swayed, the angles of his body created an intricate mosaic, a mosaic that spoke of passion, of vulnerability, of the unspoken narratives that lived within his heart. With each shift of his weight, he seemed to unlock hidden dimensions, dimensions that held the power to convey emotions too nuanced for spoken language. Näcken's body, like a brush guided by unseen hands, painted the air with silhouettes of yearning, curves of exultation, and lines of ardour. It was as if the fundamental structure of existence responded to his movement—a movement that was both a manifestation of his erotic emotions and a portal to the realms of his soul.

"Please, let me climax! " Her plea a delicate invocation that soared beyond the boundaries of words. Liv's body was shaking from all the anticipation, her form became a vessel of quivers, a mixture of tremors that called out in the language of anticipation and sexual yearning.

"Let us linger a while longer in the embrace of this moment's gentle caress." Näcken became a bard of secrets, his voice a velvet caress that painted the air with the hues of erotic intimacy. Liv surrendered to the embrace of breath, her lungs like the wings of a fragile bird unfurling within the cage of her chest. With every inhalation, every gasp that quivered through her, she entered into a dance with the very essence of life. A tempest of yearning surged through her veins, an eruption of desire that painted the very canvas of her blood with shades of longing. In the embrace of her fervent longing, she was both the seeker and the sought, both the fire and the fuel.

Näcken continued to move her around, she was light as a feather compared to his immense strength. With every gesture, every twirl that unfolded in his hands, he became a conductor of their shared sexual dance—a dance that transcended mere motion, embodying the essence of their connection. As he continued to guide her with the gentle firmness of his touch, he became a guardian of their shared narrative—a narrative that unfolded through the poetry of movement. In the embrace of his steady guidance, she was both muse and melody, both partner and protagonist. Within the waltz of their shared existence, he commenced a symphony of motion—a crescendo that resonated through the tendrils of their connection. With a touch that seemed to harness the very essence of strength, Näcken's hands found solace upon Liv's hip, a touch that ignited a firestorm of sensations within the intimate alcoves of her being. Amidst the poetry of their dance, she surrendered her hip to the tender authority of his touch—an offering, a surrender that bespoke a profound trust. As he guided her hip with the grace of a maestro, he became a sorcerer of sensation—a conjurer who spun a web of desires with his hands.

With a grace that seemed to borrow from the very winds, his hands embraced her legs, guiding them through the air in a tender move that whispered of trust and surrender. As her limbs traced ethereal arcs, he brought her torso to rest upon his chest —a gesture that ignited an unspoken reverie, a reverie that shimmered like stardust through the cosmos of their entwined existence. Within the embrace of their passion, Liv surrendered to the caress of Näcken's guidance, her legs mere extensions of his intentions, her torso nestled against the fortress of his chest. As he swayed her legs and drew her close, he metamorphosed into an alchemist of motion—a weaver of movement and emotion, a conductor orchestrating the silent dialogue of their bodies. And as Näcken swung her legs and drew Liv close to his chest, their shared desire transformed into a hymn—a hymn of passion, of tenderness, and of the timeless harmonies that resound when two souls intertwine in the poetry of movement.

As Liv's heart raced and her breath quickened, she became a symphony of desire. She embarked on a whirlwind of movement, a dervish that spun faster and faster upon the hallowed stage of the enchanted forest—an erotic meeting that unfolded with the cadence of her heart and the touch of his inventive hands. With each movement, each twirl that carried her along the currents of rhythm, her form became an embodiment of swiftness, a vessel of momentum guided by the artistry of his touch. In the heart of their whirlwind, she surrendered to the symphony of their choreography, her body an instrument finely tuned to the melodies he sculpted with his hands. The world, a captive audience to their kinetic dialogue, seemed to slow its heartbeat, savouring the graceful display of their synchronicity—an elegant dialogue that celebrated the harmonious interplay between the tactile and the ephemeral.

The crescendo of their sex approached a symphony of movement that swelled with the promise of its impending culmination—a climax that stood at the precipice of its final, exquisite expression. As they approached the zenith of their choreographic creation, they became alchemists of sexual motion—a duet that crafted not just sexual desire, but an evocative narrative, a narrative that carried the resonance of their shared passion

And as they both climaxed, the celestial sphere froze in an instant of quiet waiting, savouring the harmonious notes of closure, of culmination, and of the timeless beauty that envelops a shared climax between lovers.

CHAPTER 17

In the divine asylum of Sunday's sanctuary, Liv struggled against the tides of drowsiness, determined to resist its seductive pull. Yet, an unsettling awareness tugged at her spirit, as the weight of the priest's gaze bore down upon her, laden with scorn and disdain. A tremor traced the graceful arch of her spine, like frost-kissed tendrils of an icy breath caressing her skin. The priest, a figure veiled in disquietude, exuded an aura of chilling detachment and unnerving unease.
Within the depths of her consciousness, Liv found herself entangled in a profound dissonance. Behind the guise of piety, the priest's countenance concealed a cryptic darkness that stirred apprehension within her core. An unsettling presence emanated from his very being, as if his soul languished in a desolate wasteland bereft of empathy and compassion, devoid of the gentle stirrings of benevolence.

In the sacred stillness of the church, Liv grappled with the enigma that lurked deep down in the essence of the priest. Shadows danced upon the walls, mirroring the wariness etched upon her face. For within the depths of her discerning gaze, she glimpsed the spectre of a man, his spirit imprisoned in frigid captivity, his heart ensnared in an unyielding grip. Though veiled by the mask of devotion, the priest's aura bore a mark of something unseen and disturbing. It whispered of a void, a dearth of warmth that left her soul adrift, yearning for the tender caress of compassion.

In the cathedral's divine glow, Liv became entangled in a symphony of disquietude, where the harmony of worship clashed with the dissonance of suspicion. The spectre of the priest loomed large, a mystery that shook the very bedrock of her faith, directing her through the complex mazes of doubt and apprehension as she sought respite in the endless expanse of the cathedral.

Upon the conclusion of the mass, Finn, a man cloaked in anger and contempt, beckoned Liv and their kin to retreat homeward, urging them to leave him to his solemn communion with the sly priest. As his directive echoed, a subtle unease tiptoed across Liv's consciousness, whispering insidious doubts into the recesses of her mind. Yet, she chose to suppress her disquiet, mindful of the perils that awaited those who captured the cunning focus of the priest. A shadowed memory danced upon the stage of her thoughts—a macabre tale of the priest and his brethren, their ruthless persecution of a young woman accused of consorting with the elusive forest spirit known as the Skogsåret, branded a witch. The echoes of that dark chapter lingered, a haunting refrain interwoven within the oral histories of her family.

Whispers, delicate as a spider's silk, spun by unseen hands, carried to her the murmurs of scepticism that veiled other lands and cities, casting doubt upon the existence of witchcraft and the malevolence ascribed to it. Yet, the priest, a zealous guardian of archaic beliefs, remained resolute in his conviction. To him, every trace of magic, regardless of its origin or intent, bore the stain of nefarious designs, a blight to be eradicated from the realm. Witch trials, though less frequent, endured within the confines of the region that held Liv captive. The priest, a harbinger of judgment and retribution, wielded his authority with uncompromising determination, perpetuating a legacy of intolerance and fear.

With hushed anticipation, Liv complied with the priest's decree, her heart quivering with trepidation, her thoughts swirling in a stormy tango of caution and deliberation. The echoes of a bygone era of persecution lingered still, and the priest, a messenger of antiquated beliefs, stood as a sentinel, his vigilant gaze casting an ominous shadow over those entangled within his sphere of influence.

Burdened by the weight of unease, Liv retraced her steps to the rustic haven, where tendrils of apprehension coiled tightly around her heart. Finn, the stoic pillar of their familial bond, bid his kin farewell with a determined nod, embarking on a solitary pilgrimage back to the church. Within those hallowed walls, a tapestry of resplendence unfurled—a grand cathedral, adorned in majestic splendour, where shards of luminosity descended from celestial heights, infusing the sacred space with an angelic radiance. Each beam, akin to liquid gold, flowed through stained glass panes, casting a kaleidoscope of hues upon the silent abode of devotion.

The light, a celestial messenger, pirouetted with grace, tenderly caressing every curve and crevice of the sanctuary. Orchestrated by divine hands, its gentle touch breathed life into the altar, bestowing upon it an otherworldly allure. Shadows danced in harmonious unity with the radiance, an exquisite ballet that crossed terrestrial thresholds. The air, steeped in reverential silence, bore witness to the spiritual interplay of light and shadow, a cosmic duet that whispered of enigmatic mysteries yet untold.

Finn, resolute in his purpose, crossed the threshold of the church once more, his steps muffled by the sacred hush that enrobed the holy grounds. With measured strides, he ventured further into the embrace of the sanctuary, its vast expanse paying homage to the grandeur of divinity. The hopeful glow enveloped him, anointing him with a fervour that mirrored his unwavering grit.

Within this cavernous sanctuary, where the divine manifested through the interplay of illumination and obscurity, Finn and the priest would converge, each performing their sacred dance amidst the solemnity of faith. The ocean of light unfurled, as if bearing witness to the enigmatic exchange poised to unfold within these sacred confines, murmuring tales of redemption and revelations yet to be discovered.

"Has your family returned to the farm?" inquired the priest, his voice a resonant murmur. Finn, weathered by the ceaseless march of time, responded with a solemn nod, his countenance etched with the lines of life's labours.

With the weight of the world upon his weary shoulders, Finn stood before the priest, a sentinel who had traversed the valleys of hardship and loss. Time, that tireless sculptor, had carved its marks upon his visage, each furrow an imprint of the trials and triumphs that had shaped his spirit. Like the grooves etched upon an ancient oak, his face bore the imprints of countless seasons, a testament to the unwavering fortitude that had carried him through life's tempests. His once piercing azure eyes, pools of untamed youth, now reflected the burdens he had shouldered, their faded brilliance a mirror of the journey travelled.

"Yes," Finn whispered, his voice carrying the weight of contemplation.

"Excellent. I have conversed with congregations in nearby villages, and they too share our beliefs regarding the tainted demons that lurk within the forest and the lake. Regrettably, many have turned away from our convictions, doubting the need to cleanse those who consort with the devil and his minions. But fear not, my child, for help is on the way. Mercenaries will soon arrive, lending their aid to our mission. The bishop shares our beliefs, for he too understands the abominable nature of these creatures! And there is more assistance to be sought. It is lamentable that the church is slowly forsaking the belief that the hidden ones are wicked and must be vanquished. We must purify the world of their presence! If we halt our hunt, they shall grow stronger, regaining their nefarious might. We have come so far, numerous witches, demons, and magical beings have already met their demise. To cease now would be to forfeit all that we have achieved. All that is evil must be cleansed by fire!" intoned the priest, his voice a symphony of concealed depths resonating through the sacred expanse. Veiled in his countenance was a cryptic smile, exuding the enigmatic allure of ancient secrets whispered between realms. Yet, within the depths of his being, a shadow of darkness stirred, as his whispered hiss pierced the sanctified air, a venomous murmur accompanied by narrowed eyes, betraying the lurking malice concealed within.

"Näcken is an exceedingly formidable creature," Finn's voice quivered with an undercurrent of fear, like a fragile note caught in a tempestuous wind. His words, laden with trepidation, carried the weight of a soul teetering on the precipice of uncertainty, seeking solace amidst the swirling shadows of the unknown.

"He is no match for our unwavering faith and our formidable arsenal," the priest's countenance blossomed with a smile, akin to moonlight gently caressing the petals of a delicate flower. His lips curved upward, revealing glimpses of enigmas hidden within. Within that cunning smile, slumbered secrets and whispered mysteries, while the elusive dance of light and shadow wove intricate patterns upon the tapestry of his visage. It was a smile that held the allure of forgotten tales and unspoken truths, inviting curiosity to wander through the labyrinthine corridors of the soul. "The mercenaries carry with them bullets of silver, one of the few things capable of harming Näcken and his fellow demons."

With a deliberate turn, the priest shifted his gaze, aligning his being with the trembling figure of Finn. As the priest faced Finn, his eyes peered into the depths of the man's quivering core, poised to unravel the enigma that lingered within. "However, there is a price. The church will aid you, but you must also pay a price, for the mercenaries come with a cost."

"Whatever it takes to save my wife's soul and vanquish that abomination!" From the depths of Finn's being, a tempest surged forth, igniting the embers of his voice with a chaotic inferno. Anger, a wildflower in bloom, unfurled its fiery petals, consuming the air with its volatile presence. Each syllable, like a crackling flame, carried the weight of smouldering resentment and scorned fury. "My family possesses the means to compensate the church for its troubles."

"Very well, I will summon you when the mercenaries arrive."

"What shall come to pass?"

"It is imperative that you maintain the guise of normalcy. Näcken may be a blasphemy, but he is not easily deceived or apprehended. Undoubtedly, he is formidable, and his magic is lethal. However, the mercenaries possess a weapon unlike any other, one they acquired in the holy land. It is said to wield tremendous power. No magical creature, demon, or spirit can touch it without perishing. If you pierce a spirit or demon with this blade, they shall be trapped in purgatory. And if the demonic Näcken is struck by this dagger, he shall forever be ensnared in purgatory, reducing the number of hidden ones in our world to worry about."

"Does this dagger truly possess such power?" Finn's voice carried a tinge of awe, his words evidence of the profound admiration coursing through his being. Like the delicate dance of autumn leaves in a gentle breeze, his voice swayed with an undercurrent of reverence, whispering a sacred incantation to the enigma before him.

"When the hidden ones meet their demise, they journey to their own realm of judgment. We know little of this place, but this dagger has been known to ensnare the hidden ones and banish them to purgatory. I would prefer they burn in the depths of hell, but for now, this shall suffice. The fewer of them in our world, the better."

"Why can't the dagger send spirits and demons to hell?" Enveloped in the priest's words, Finn found himself ensnared in the tale, his senses entangled in the labyrinth of wisdom spun by the persuasive figure before him. Spellbound, he posed his question, his voice a mere breath suspended in the realm of anticipation. Within his inquiry, the essence of his being intertwined with the threads of divine knowledge, merging the finite with the infinite, the seeker with the sought.

"Some say they are the hidden ones, the offspring of Adam and Eve who chose to dwell in sin instead of surrendering to God's will. They became different, cloaked in invisibility as they turned away from the path of righteousness. Their existence took a divergent course. I believe the dagger cannot send them to hell because they lack souls. Only those with a soul can truly lose one," the priest's voice resonated from the depths, tainted with a tenebrous disdain. Each syllable dripped with acrid venom, his words bearing a chilling frost that pierced the air with biting presence. His voice transformed into a vessel of repulsion, a tempest of revulsion that echoed through the church. Like an ancient curse whispered by a vengeful spirit, his words carried the weight of scorn and abhorrence, casting a pall of darkness upon the listener's heart.

"But were they not created by God?" Finn's voice, heavy with longing born from the depths of his being, ventured into the vast expanse of the unknown. Like a solitary wanderer beseeching solace from the cosmos, his words became a sacred hymn that caressed the edges of existence.

"The devil himself is a fallen angel!" The priest's voice ascended like a soaring phoenix, its timbre infused with an otherworldly resonance. From the depths of his being, his words emerged as celestial echoes, reverberating through the sacred space. With each syllable, his voice became a conduit for the forces stirring within, a tempest of divine authority that surged forth, shaking the very foundations of mortal perception. In that resounding moment, his voice carried the weight of a thousand sermons, a symphony summoning both reverence and trepidation, transcending the limitations of human utterance to touch upon the realms of the ineffable. "Just because something is created by God does not guarantee salvation."

"And what of my wife? Will salvation be granted to her?" Within the caverns of Finn's heart, the flame of love for Liv flickered, its gentle glow casting a tender radiance upon the labyrinthine corridors of his soul. Like a cherished relic suspended in the mists of time, the priest discerned the echoes of hesitation resonating within Finn's being. Ever attuned to the delicate currents of human emotion, the priest perceived the quivering doubts of uncertainty weaving their intricate dance through the core of Finn's spirit.

"You must be resolute, unwavering in your purpose," the priest spoke, his words resonating with an air of solemnity, his hand extended like a guiding light amidst the encroaching darkness. In his voice, a symphony of wisdom and foreboding unfolded, weaving a mixture of caution and prophecy. Like a sage of old, he imparted words that danced on the edge of divination, warning of the hidden perils that lay in wait, his voice a lantern illuminating the treacherous twists of fate. "To save your wife's soul from eternal damnation and spare her a lifetime in hell, she must be cleansed by fire and Näcken trapped in purgatory. There, he shall remain forever, and your wife shall stand before God, to be judged as we all must one day."

"But I confess, I struggle to comprehend," Finn's voice emerged, veiled in a perplexing mist, a whispered puzzle lingering in the spaces between uncertainty. Within the depths of his being, confusion swirled, entwining his thoughts in a bewildering dance. His words, fragments of a shattered dream, sought to untangle the mysteries that knotted his soul, their echoes carrying the weight of an unsolved riddle. In that moment of bewilderment, his voice became an elusive melody, harmonizing with the cosmic mysteries, yearning for clarity amidst the labyrinthine paths of his consciousness.

"If God created the spirits and demons, will He not one day pass judgment upon them?" The priest's countenance darkened, a storm brewing within, his visage resembling a sky pregnant with discontent. Like brooding thunderclouds, flickers of annoyance cast shadows upon his features. The priest's aura crackled with restlessness, his soul resounding with an irritable melody that danced upon the chords of frustration. His response, a lightning bolt piercing the sky, carried a subtle edge of impatience, glimpses of deeper turmoil concealed beneath the surface. It was as if his being recoiled from the intrusion, reluctant to reveal its secrets to inquisitive eyes.

"They shall face their reckoning in another realm." From the depths of his being, the priest summoned a voice imbued with resolute sternness, a sonorous proclamation that cut through the air. His words, like ancient stones hewn from the bedrock of conviction, bore the weight of moral authority, etching their mark upon their conversation. They brooked no dissent, commanding attention and reverence, a solemn invocation demanding the careful heed of all who dared to listen. "Yet if we can bind them in purgatory, it is a preferable path. Remember, should you harbour doubt, seek me out. God shall reward your unwavering concern as a devoted husband. Your wife's seduction by a demonic beast is not your fault. We must tread with caution, for many have fallen victim to Näcken's grasp. I have long awaited this opportunity. We have already trapped numerous of their kind in purgatory, and it shall be a gratifying task to bind one of their formidable beings to such poetic justice!"

"Rest assured, my path is unwavering," Finn declared, his voice a vessel of resolute tenacity, each word an oath that entwined his spirit with blind loyalty. "My loyalty shall forever be bestowed upon God."

In response, the priest's countenance adorned itself with a knowing sparkle, a subtle curl of amusement seamlessly blended into the cobweb of his expression. His lips, shaped by a playfully wise curve, exuded a satisfaction that whispered of hidden truths. Like a mischievous flame flickering in his eyes, his enigmatic smile alluded to the labyrinthine depths of his understanding, hinting at a concealed agenda. Within that intriguing smirk, the priest embodied the duality of master and puppeteer, his gaze an invitation to curiosity, concealing the true intentions that lay veiled in the depths of his being.

"Fear not, my child, for we shall reconvene next Sunday. In the coming weeks, help shall arrive, and together we shall vanquish the offspring of darkness," the priest proclaimed, his voice an anthem of righteous conviction that resounded through the sacred space.

CHAPTER 18

Two suns had gracefully danced through the sky, casting their gentle glow upon the earth, and Liv felt herself irresistibly drawn to the enchantment of the woodland realm once more. A subtle unease lingered within her core, a whispered hymn of transformation that stirred the very air itself. Seeking solace and understanding, Liv had gone to share her burdens with Finn, yet his distant demeanour shielded him from her tender longings, his words barely a murmur swallowed by the infinite distance of his preoccupations. And now, as she set foot in the realm of ancient trees, Näcken materialized before her, a beacon of familiarity amidst the whirlwind of her thoughts.

The lines of concern etched upon Liv's countenance did not elude Näcken's discerning gaze, for his eyes were attuned to the delicate subtleties of her heart. With a voice as serene as a clear sky painted with wisps of delicate clouds, he inquired, "What weighs upon you, my beloved?" His words bore an unspoken vow, a melodious promise that pledged protection in the face of her fears.

"I cannot fully fathom," Liv's voice trembled upon her lips like a fragile snowflake quivering beneath unspoken secrets. Her gaze, heavy with a mournful melancholy, cast wistful glances toward the distant homestead, as if tethered by ethereal threads to the echoes of her past. Her voice echoed a myriad of whispered longings, an orchestration of emotions entwined with the flickering dance of nostalgia. It was a tender entreaty, a fragment of her soul seeking solace amidst the tempestuous winds of uncertainty, as she stood at the crossroads between devotion and the beckoning unknown. "It is merely an unfamiliar sensation that has enveloped me."

From the depths of his voice laden with ancient wisdom, Näcken's words flowed like a gentle caress of moonlit waves upon the shores of understanding. His voice, a vessel of timeless insights, bore the weight of profound truths, resonating with the subtle currents of profound awareness. Through his utterance, celestial tendrils of guidance unfurled, enfolding Liv's restless soul with compassionate certainty.

"One's intuition," Näcken spoke with the cadence of a tender breeze, "is a sacred compass, an illumined guide that navigates the intricate corridors of existence. When doubt takes root and whispers of unrest stir within, it is imperative to heed the murmurs of your spirit. For intuition, delicate yet steadfast, perceives what the heart may overlook. Trust the faint whispers carried by the wind, for they often veil the secrets concealed from mere mortal eyes."

In those profound words, Näcken unveiled the mystical waltz between intuition and sentiment, illuminating the path where intuitive guidance melded with the melodies of the heart.

"I sense an ominous stir." Liv's voice fluttered from the depths of her being, a delicate melody tinted with sorrow, each note carrying the weight of unspoken foreboding. Her words, adorned with the melancholy of twilight's lament, bore the burden of countless concealed sorrows that danced on the fringes of her awareness. Like a mournful sonata, her voice became an instrument of longing, seeking harmony amidst the enigmatic tides of her emotions. "Finn has undergone a transformation; I suspect both he and the priest know about us."

From the core of his resolute being, Näcken's voice reverberated like a guardian's plea, draped in tones of unwavering concern. Each syllable, steeped in ancient wisdom, carried echoes of protective devotion, encircling Liv's anxious form. Näcken's words became a shield of vigilant care, poised to ward off encroaching shadows seeking to engulf her essence. "If the tendrils of truth weave such a tapestry of doubt," Näcken whispered, his voice a solemn lullaby, "then peril looms in the recesses of your path. A spectre of danger lingers, eager to entangle your unique spirit in its web of deception." His words, akin to a celestial chorus of caution, resonated through the woods, their potent vibrations akin to a guardian's embrace, safeguarding her from unseen threats.

"But if they held knowledge of truth, would they not have locked me away and pursued you already?" As Liv's gaze met Näcken's ethereal form, her eyes, windows to her soul's depths, emanated a radiant warmth akin to the gentle hum of a well-loved lullaby sung in the dark. In that tender exchange, her heart, a melodious symphony of devotion, whispered secrets of affection entwined with her very spirit. It was a gaze brimming with tender ardour, an offering of love's unadulterated essence, bestowed upon Näcken like a fragrant blossom surrendering to the caress of a sunbeam.

His presence, akin to a serene oasis amidst the arid desert of uncertainties, enfolded her in a cocoon of unconditional acceptance. It was a gaze that carried the weight of the universe, wordless verses of devotion written in the language of soulful connections, where the unspoken desires of her heart found a haven within the safety of Näcken's enchanting being.

Within the depths of his being, Näcken's voice unfurled like a hidden spring, its mellifluous cadence carrying echoes of ancient wisdom. With a touch of solemn grace, his words crafted a poetic tale, unveiling the intricacies of his nature. Each utterance, akin to a carefully woven verse, painted a portrait of caution amidst the tapestry of human artifice.

"In the realm of mortal hearts," Näcken pondered, his voice a tender whisper upon introspective winds, "cunning oft wields its art with mastery. Amidst their dance of desires and deceit, one must tread with watchful eyes, for shadows of treachery may lie veiled beneath guises of innocence." His words, enshrouded in protective counsel, murmured of a sanctuary beyond human bounds, where the light of love could blossom freely.

"Remain by my side," Näcken beseeched, his voice a haven of devotion, "and embrace a life liberated from mortal intricacies. Here, fear shall be banished, and the spectres of adversity quelled by my unwavering guardianship. Together, we shall forge a fortress of love, dwelling amidst the very essence of our boundless affection until the final breath graces your days within this enchanting realm."

Within his offer lay the allure of an eternal sanctuary, where the currents of mortal existence would yield to a realm of timeless ardour. Näcken's words, akin to a seductive symphony, enticed Liv to shed her earthly burdens and find refuge in a love unbound by mortal confines.

"I desire nothing more than to intertwine my life with yours," Liv whispered, her touch as delicate as the brush of moonlight upon Näcken's cheek. In that tender connection, their souls danced, entwined in a timeless embrace of affection and understanding. Her caress, suffused with the warmth of tender devotion, graced his skin like a fleeting stroke upon the canvas of their intertwined destiny. The world around them dissolved into insignificance, as if time halted to witness the communion of their souls.

Within that tender gesture, Liv's touch transformed into a gentle serenade, a symphony of unspoken desires and uncharted dreams that reverberated through Näcken's very essence. Their touch, a sublime communion of hearts, carried the weight of lifetimes, the memories of countless stories etched upon their intertwined destinies. It transcended mere physicality, evoking a profound understanding that spanned realms known and unknown.

"I perceive your steadfast determination," Näcken murmured, his voice a whisper that echoed through the foliage, acknowledging the depths of her unwavering spirit. As his gaze met Liv's, a spectrum of admiration shimmered within his eyes, reflecting the brilliance of her unyielding essence. "Your resistance, even when peril casts its frigid shadow upon your very existence, exemplifies the unquenchable flame that burns within you. Your fortitude, forged in the crucible of resolute conviction, becomes a guiding light that ignites the embers of my deepest admiration."

A fleeting tremor of concern graced Näcken's countenance, for he recognized the fragility of her mortal form, vulnerable amidst a realm rife with shadows and uncertainties. His voice, tinged with a note of tender protectiveness, resonated like a promise from a guardian spirit, shielding her from encroaching darkness. "Yet, my heart trembles with an apprehension that eclipses the radiance of our love. Within the confines of the farmstead, I am but a spectre, bereft of power to shield you from the malevolence that prowls in the shadows."

In his words lay the poignant truth, an acknowledgment that his ethereal presence could not fend off the perils that lurked beyond the sanctuary of their shared existence. Näcken's reverence for her indomitable spirit intertwined with the somber realization that his protection could not extend to the boundaries of their mortal abode. It was a lament for the limitations imposed by their divergent worlds, a demonstration of the relentless grasp of fate that held their destinies in precarious balance.

"If necessity demands, I shall summon every ounce of strength to safeguard my being and seek refuge by your side," Liv declared with unyielding courage, her voice a hymn of resolute determination that pierced the air. Her words, adorned with the hues of unwavering resolve, reverberated throughout their shared realm. Her voice carried the weight of countless battles fought, a mark of the fortitude coursing through her veins.

"I shall not yield," she affirmed, her voice a resounding symphony of defiance and bravery. "Even in the face of daunting peril, I refuse to relinquish my stance."

Within her courageous words, a symphony of unyielding resilience and unflinching willpower unfurled, resonating across their shared domain. It was a confirmation of her determined commitment to remain faithful to her principles, even amidst adversity. Liv's resolute voice, akin to a guiding star amidst encroaching darkness, illuminated the path she had chosen, beckoning Näcken to stand alongside her in unbroken solidarity.

Liv's resolute proclamation breathed vitality into the nature of their connection, infusing it with a fortitude capable of withstanding any tempest. It stood as proof of the profound depths of her spirit, a resounding call that stirred Näcken's very soul. In her inspirational courage, she embodied the essence of their shared odyssey, reminding Näcken that their love was forged in the crucible of everlasting resolve, unyielding in the face of uncertainty.

"Do you dare risk your very existence by venturing here to witness my ethereal presence?" Näcken's voice, carrying a blend of concern and caution. Like a melancholic melody whispered by the breeze, his words held the weight of solemn wisdom. "Within the safety of your farm's embrace lies a sanctuary where you may find respite from the perils that dwell beyond."

In his inquiry, a tender apprehension wove threads of protectiveness and care. Näcken, ever mindful of the delicate balance between their worlds, implored her to consider the gravity of her choice. His voice, a somber lullaby murmured across moonlit ripples, urged her to return to the haven of familiarity and seclusion.

"For in these mystical realms, where shadows intertwine with secrets, danger slumbers within each whispered breath," he continued, his words like a delicate raindrop landing on calm waters. "To remain concealed, shielded from prying eyes, may grant you the mantle of safety that guards against harm's ceaseless pursuit."

His voice, though adorned with a touch of melancholy, overflowed with a resolute desire to safeguard her from the fangs of uncertainty. It carried a plea rooted in his profound understanding of the fragile nature of mortal existence, a plea to shield the precious flame that burned within her from the impending gloom. Näcken yearned to shelter her from the tempestuous currents that roared beyond the boundaries of their union, cherishing her presence as a unique jewel amidst an ever-shifting expanse.

Yet, beneath the layers of his plea, an undeniable current of longing surged, a yearning to hold her close. Näcken, torn between his desire to ensure Liv's safety and his longing to revel in her presence, found solace in the hope that she would heed his words and embrace the sanctuary offered within the farm's warm embrace.

Näcken had vowed, solemnly, to release Liv if it was her desire, yet within the depths of his being, an abyss of emptiness yawned—a void that could never be filled without her. The notion of a life bereft of her cast a somber pall over his existence, a haunting reminder of the hollowness that would forever shadow his days. Her departure, should she choose it, would render his world devoid of colour, stripping away the vibrant hues that once adorned each passing moment. In the absence of her luminosity, the days would lose their lustre, and the nights would transform into an endless expanse of solitude. He carried the weight of his silent ache, a stoic guardian of the vacant chambers within his chest. For even as he had vowed to release her, his heart would forever echo with the remnants of her name, murmuring fragments of a love that could never be extinguished.

"No," Liv's voice interjected with a resolute tenacity, cutting through the atmosphere like a sword carving through swirling mist. Her interruption bore the weight of a thousand battles, refusing to be swayed by the cautionary whispers that lingered in Näcken's words. "Never," she declared, her voice infused with an indomitable spirit.

Her interruption, born of fierce defiance, disrupted the delicate equilibrium between prudence and adventure that hung in the air. Liv's voice, akin to a clarion call summoning the untamed unknown, resounded with the courage of a Valkyrie warrior.

"I shall not be content to remain concealed," she pressed on, her words portrayed her undaunted persistence. In her interruption, a symphony of rebellion and yearning rose, casting aside the chains of fear and embracing the untamed whispers of destiny. Liv's resolute voice, like a beacon of untethered desire, illuminated the path she had chosen, inviting Näcken to stand alongside her in the battle to come.

"Even if they extinguish my flame, so be it, for I refuse to dwell in fear and succumb to a life of pretence. I shall persist in coming here, for every fibre of my being yearns for you, but I tremble, for I know not what they might do unto you."

Together, they commenced a harmonious journey, facing the tumultuous melody of life's uncertainties. Bound by a shared longing for the extraordinary, they merged their souls together, crafting a symphony that danced upon the precipice of the unknown, forever entwined in the audacious pursuit of their shared destiny.

"You have yet to fathom the depths of my essence," Näcken's once serene eyes transformed into ebony orbs of enigma. "I am eternal, a being that assumes myriad forms, wielding powers capable of unleashing devastation and anguish upon those who dare challenge me or lay a finger upon those I hold dear. Within me resides potent abilities, formidable and awe-inspiring, and I shall not hesitate to quell any flame that dares scorch your tender existence. Bound within me lie incomprehensible strengths, and I shall bring ruin upon any who inflict harm upon you. I am not a creature driven by aggression, impulsiveness, or violence, yet I possess the capacity to wield death and sorrow as instruments of retribution against those deserving my righteous wrath! I shall not waver in safeguarding you or myself, employing every ounce of my prowess. No obstacle shall evade my resolve, no adversary shall elude my vanquishing, no realm shall defy my conquest, no monstrosity shall withstand my taming, for you, and for the preservation of your well-being, I am eternally your champion," Näcken's words, ablaze with fervent ardour, resonated through the ethereal tapestry.

A veil of mystery draped his countenance as he spoke, his voice a low, resonating timbre that sliced through the reigning silence. His proclamation, forged from a fusion of strength and protectiveness, resounded with the weight of his eternal existence. Näcken, not driven by inherent aggression, impulsivity, nor drawn to violence, possessed the capacity to wield death and sorrow as instruments of retribution against those deserving of his righteous fury. With every fibre of his being, he pledged unwavering devotion to safeguarding Liv, poised to confront any obstacle, vanquish any adversary, and conquer every realm that dared encroach upon their sanctuary. Even the most formidable of monsters would bow in submission to his commanding presence, for he was her unyielding champion, forever bound to her safety.

As Näcken's impassioned words caressed Liv's receptive ears, she found herself swept away by a tidal wave of overwhelming emotions, crashing upon the shores of her being. His affection, akin to a tempestuous storm of ardour, enfolded her in its exhilarating embrace, leaving her breathless and utterly enraptured.

Näcken's gentle touch traced the contours of Liv's body, spurring a whirlwind of inner reactions. The soft caress of his fingertips sent shivers of delight streaming across her skin, awakening a fiery longing that pulsed within her veins. Emboldened by desire, Liv ventured lower, her lips yearning to taste the expanse of Näcken's sculpted abdomen. With tender reverence, she pressed her kisses against the taut canvas of his muscular stomach, bestowing a trail of affectionate devotion. In a dance of passion and surrender, her lips journeyed downward towards his penis, guided by an invisible magnetism that drew her closer to the core of her desires.

Gracefully, Liv held his penis between her lips, its contour caressed by her warm breath. With each exhale, his manhood danced in harmony with her sighs, as if whispering secrets of the natural world. As his foreskin brushed against her tongue, a subtle sweetness enveloped her senses, infusing her being with pleasure. The fragrant aroma mingled with the taste of her lips, creating a symphony of sensations. In this intimate gesture, Liv became a conduit between the realms of nature and human existence. With his penis delicately held in her mouth, Liv revelled in the poetic fusion of nature's gifts and her own embodiment.

Näcken tilted his head back in pleasure, his countenance bathed in a breathtaking glow. From his lips flowed ancient words, whispered with a melodic resonance that stirred the depths of Liv's soul. Though she did not comprehend their meaning, their mystical essence permeated the air, weaving a spell that enveloped them both.

Liv felt an intoxicating surge of empowerment pumping through her circulatory system, there was something deeply erotic over pleasuring Näcken orally and hearing him moan in ecstasy. The world around them faded into insignificance as Liv indulged in the rapture of exploring his body, traversing the landscape of his form with a thirst that only passion could quench.

As Liv heard the noses of pleasure coming from Näcken's mouth, she instinctively adjusted her own movements to synchronize with his rhythmic desire. Every touch, every caress, and every sucking motion was aimed at fulfilling his desires. She revelled in the delight that gleamed in his eyes and the way his body responded to her every move. With devoted intention, she explored his body, seeking to uncover every secret pleasure that lay within. Her fingertips traced a path of tantalizing anticipation, evoking shivers of ecstasy. Liv revelled in the power she held to ignite his senses and triggered a fire within him, all to satisfy Näcken's sexual longing.

In her pursuit to please him, Liv became attuned to his every reaction, attuned to his every sigh and moan. She became an artist of pleasure, crafting a combination of stimuli that drove him to the heights of bliss. Each breath, each sigh, and each shared moment further fuelled her determination to bring him untold pleasure. Liv basked in the knowledge that she held the key to his pleasure, knowing that her touch could elicit the most profound responses. She delighted in the knowledge that her devotion was reciprocated, that her efforts to please him were met with equal fervour.

Sometimes Liv's movements were swift and eager, driven by an insatiable craving to consume. Other times, she slowed her pace, allowing the flavours to unfold on her tongue, savouring the essence of Näcken as it melted into a delightful sweetness. Liv felt a euphoric rush when Näcken's penis moved around in her mouth. With each passing movement, she relished in the playfulness of her movements, varying the speed and intensity to heighten her enjoyment.

The flavours danced upon her tongue, an exquisite collection of tastes that sent shivers down her spine. It was a sensation that enveloped her senses, captivating her with its delectable essence. Each morsel was a delight, a perfect harmony of flavours that left her craving more.

With each lick, a delightful sensation washed over her, evoking a growing sense of horniness deep within. She felt herself getting wet while she continued to lick the top of Näcken's penis. As Liv indulged in its divine treat, a warmth spread through her, illuminating her face with pure delight. It was as if the world around her faded into the background, and all that mattered in that moment was the simple pleasure of his penis. The act of sucking became a playful dance, a small act of bliss that brought her immense satisfaction. She relished in the happiness that circulated within her blood, savouring every lick as if it were a precious gift.

Liv yearned to fully immerse herself in the desirous task of bringing him to the edge of climax. In her pursuit, she surrendered her own desires, focusing solely on his needs and wants. She craved to wholly engross herself in the task of pleasing him. With each breath, Liv seized the chance to satisfy him.

When Näcken moaned out in ecstasy Liv felt herself getting even hornier, she started to touch herself with one hand while she continued to pleasure Näcken.

Liv was overcome with sexual desire, finding immense joy and fulfilment in her commitment to Näcken's orgasm. The experience was a delightful blend of amusement and satisfaction, as she wholeheartedly dedicated herself to his desires.

Liv revelled in the knowledge that she could make him horny, she revelled in the knowledge that he yearned for her body, she revelled in the knowledge that he was turned on by her performance. It was a delicious feeling, knowing that her presence ignited a deep desire within him. The thought of being the object of his longing brought a surge of confidence and power to her being.

Liv adjusted her speed, finding a rhythm that suited her desires, as she felt Näcken's penis swelling and pulsating in her mouth.

She embraced the freedom to explore different tempos, allowing her body to respond to the moment.

She sensed his proximity to his desired outcome, a palpable energy that permeated the air. The anticipation built within her, mirroring his intent and purpose. With each passing moment, Liv could feel him drawing nearer to his climax. That knowledge ignited an even greater sense of excitement within her, her garments clung to her body, drenched by her wet flower.

In the final moments before Näcken reached his goal, she found herself fully present, immersed in the intoxicating dance of desire. Liv felt his final movement burst into a waterfall in her mouth. She waited for Näcken to empty his seed in her mouth. Her mouth came alive engulfed in a crescendo of senses. Liv savoured the juicy sweetness, relishing in the burst of flavours that danced upon her taste buds. She cherished the lingering taste on her lips and the memory of the pleasure she had just experienced.

Liv retreated a single stride, creating a minuscule distance between herself and Näcken. "Where are you headed?" Näcken's voice, like a gentle melody, caressed the air, as his enigmatic eyes held her captive. "In this realm of yearning, my soul dances to the rhythm of your presence, longing for your body. I yearn to indulge in your sugared delights, to taste your sweet symphony upon my lips. With each delicate morsel, a dance of beauty shall enchant my senses. Let your wet essence melt upon my tongue, releasing its saccharine melody, a symphony of flavours that serenade my desire. Oh, the bliss of that tender surrender, as my taste buds awaken to your divine sensation, and my heart rejoices in the euphoria of confectionery bliss. " He whispered, his words carrying the weight of erotic, desire and passion.

In a passionate embrace, Näcken lifted Liv from her earthly worries, cradling her delicately within the circle of his arms. With utmost care, he gently lowered her onto the cool, verdant ground, creating a pleasures haven where he could pleasure her.

With a flourish of purpose, he moved with unshakable purpose and parted her yearning legs.

"I am already wet " Liv whispered. "Passion took over my soul when I committed to pleasuring you. "

" I am captivated by the depths of your devotion, and how effortlessly it intertwines with my own desires. " With a languid grace, Näcken's lips embraced her delight, capturing its essence upon his tongue. Each delicate lick, a dance of seduction, invoked a cascade of sensations that stirred Liv's senses. His tongue, like a maestro's wand, conducted an orchestration of pleasure, savouring every nuance and infusing it with a seductive allure.

Näcken, consumed by a divine yearning, surrendered to his sexual desire. His lips and tongue, adorned with the whispers of ancient melodies and the touch of ethereal dew, commenced a sacred pilgrimage across Liv's legs.

With every breath she inhaled, the air transformed into a potent elixir, infusing her being with an exhilarating surge of vitality. Her heart, a relentless drum of passion, pounded within her chest, synchronizing its rhythm with the pulse of the earth beneath her feet. As her pace quickened, Liv's senses heightened, she yearned to feel Näckens tongue all over her.

Näcken's tongue spun in a delicate pirouette, tracing endless circles upon Liv's clitoris, as he played with his hands inside of her. Each delicate touch left a trail of starlit stardust, igniting a sonata of reactions that danced upon her flesh, invoking a crescendo of pleasure that bloomed in the depths of her being.

Ensnared within the relentless grip of passions burning desire, Liv could not contain herself. As his lips, dipped in the nectar of desire and steeped in the ambrosia of longing, brushed against her clitoris, bestowing tender kisses that spoke of reverence and adoration, she was getting ready to climax. With every passionate press of his lips, Näcken sought to etch an indelible memory upon Liv's clitoris, an exquisite mosaic of passion and yearning.

Liv gave in to temptation and let the orgasm explode through her body like derailing train.

With a mesmerizing grace that defied earthly boundaries, Näcken lifted Liv aloft, his embrace a sanctuary of strength and tenderness, where love's ethereal dance found its sacred stage.

"Oh, how my heart yearns to dwell beneath the enchantment of the veiled night sky, to stretch our shared moments into an eternal moment," Näcken confessed with a serenity that echoed like whispered melodies on the breeze. His words, carried by the currents of the unseen, were gentle invitations to a realm where time itself ceased to exist. "Yet, I sense the ethereal presence of the ancient ones, the timeless guardians who beckon me. Fear not, my love, for I shall guide you back to the sanctuary of the farm, cradled within the arms of safety. And then, with a heaviness that weighs upon my very core, I must retreat into the realm of my kin, surrendering to the call of ancestral ties."

His voice, a tranquil river of reassurance, bore the weight of profound understanding. Näcken's duty to his lineage, his kinship with celestial forces that guided his ethereal existence, found solace in the words he spoke. Though the impending parting loomed near, he exuded an aura of calm resolve, a steadfast commitment to honour the bonds that tied him to his ancient kin.

"You have ignited a flame within my life that I never knew existed," Liv's voice, a tender melody woven with the essence of stardust, let her words dance upon the air with grace. A smile, akin to a budding rose kissed by the golden hues of dawn, graced her countenance, illuminating the depths of her soul. "I am eternally grateful for everything you have bestowed upon me."

Hand in hand, they embarked on a tranquil voyage toward the culmination of the verdant woodland, a realm where mysteries intertwined, whispering secrets to those who dared to listen. Bathed in the magical glow of moonlight, Näcken, his heart overflowing with longing, bestowed upon Liv a kiss of profound depth. In that tender hold, a symphony of love soared, entwining their souls in a communion of affection and passionate desire.

"In the realm of beauty's kaleidoscope, your radiance outshines the brightest stars adorning the heavens. Your presence, like a captivating sunrise, paints the world in hues of enchantment, mesmerizing every gaze that dares to behold your breathtaking form. Deep within the recesses of my soul, a symphony of admiration swells, for your allure transcends earthly comparisons. With every glance directed toward you, my heart trembles, for your visage holds the power to eclipse the beauty of a thousand moonlit nights." As Liv reluctantly parted from Näcken's words, a sense of awe wrapped around her essence, flooding her being with sublime grace. Meanwhile, Näcken stood in tranquil contemplation, his gaze steadfastly fixed upon the retreating figure of Liv.

The wind moving in languid motion, breathed with delicate veneration, and the atmosphere underwent a subtle metamorphosis, as if nature itself sensed the profound significance of this ethereal encounter. Beside Näcken, a figure materialized—a being steeped in ancient wisdom and unwavering power. Näcken, recognizing the presence of this venerable entity, maintained his watchful vigil over Liv, for he knew the identity of his silent companion.

The ancient one, his eyes brimming with profound insight, allowed his gaze to linger upon Liv. A communion of spirits took place, an exchange of unspoken truths and unuttered desires. In that moment, the ephemeral bridge between mortal and ethereal realms drew closer, forged by the enigmatic hand of destiny.

"Behold, dear Lythandir," the ancient one began, his voice resounding like a symphony of celestial whispers, "it lies within your very essence to enchant and captivate mortal souls, drawing them into your embrace of enchantment. Yet, heed my words, for caution must be your eternal companion, as our kind is not destined to partake in the fragile constitution of human love. Alas, it seldom culminates in a harmonious symphony of hearts."

A reverberating warning, adorned with the wisdom of ages past, cascaded through the calm air, resonating with the weight of eternity. The ancient one, a sage of unparalleled sagacity, sought to impart the gravity of his words upon Näcken's soul.

To this solemn admonition, Näcken, his voice a gentle caress, replied, "She is not a mere mortal, for in saving her, a mystical alchemy of destiny transpired. A part of my essence, my very magic, flowed into her delicate vessel, intertwining our fates irrevocably. Fate's whims have united us, weaving our souls together in an eternal dance of enchantment, forever bridging the divide between us. It is not by choice, but by the hand of mystical providence, that she has become an eternal fragment of my being, and I, an eternal fragment of hers. Our destinies melded by the very fabric of enchantment."

In his proclamation, Näcken laid bare the immutable bond forged by forces beyond mortal comprehension. Their intertwined existence, an acknowledgment of the ethereal realm's intervention, wove a narrative of transcendence that surpassed the boundaries of mere human emotions. It was a bond consecrated by the interplay of magic, forever binding their souls in a celestial union that defied the constraints of time and human frailty.

"Then, perchance, I shall release her from this mortal coil, liberating you from the shackles that confine your heart," resonated the ancient one's words, piercing Näcken's being like a thousand sharp-edged stars. Yet, as Näcken reacted instinctively, propelling himself towards the ancient one, his essence aflame with fury, he soon discovered the insurmountable power that resided within the venerable entity. In an effortless display of supremacy, the ancient one subdued Näcken, his grip unyielding as he pinned him to the very earth that bore witness to their struggle.

"In that case, Baelgrim, I beseech you, end my existence in this very moment!" Näcken pleaded, his voice laced with desperation. The mere thought of losing her, his soul's predestined companion, was an agony he could not fathom enduring. Knowing full well the ancient one possessed the ability to extinguish his life effortlessly, Näcken acquiesced, surrendering to his captor's hold, poised on the precipice of capitulation.

The ancient one peered deeply into Näcken's eyes, unearthing a reflection of his own ancient soul within them. "Verily, it is the truth," he murmured, a trace of empathy tingeing his voice. "Her essence, an eternal flame, resides intertwined with your being. We, the denizens of enchantment, diverge from humankind, for we would not inflict harm upon an innocent life." With a gesture of release, the ancient one relinquished his grip upon Näcken, allowing him to rise from the earthly plane.

"Yet, you tread upon treacherous ground," the ancient one cautioned, his tone imbued with somber wisdom. "Too many of our brethren have succumbed to the malevolence of humanity, their existence extinguished by the cruel hands that fear our supernatural essence. The days when we coexisted alongside mortals in harmony have faded into the mists of oblivion. Thus, we seek solace within the embrace of forests, lakes, and the very elements of nature itself, finding sanctuary from their ever-looming presence. Soon, we shall leave this world, vanishing from the physical realm, never to return in corporeal form."

In the melancholic timbre of the ancient one's voice, lay the sorrow of a world lost to the ravages of humankind's fear and ignorance. Their collective fate, forever intertwined with the whims of mortals, compelled them to retreat to the mythical abodes of nature, relinquishing their physical manifestations.

The encroaching era foretold a future wherein the enigmatic beings of magic would become naught but whispers, forever concealed from human comprehension.

"Should they dare encroach upon my sanctum, I shall unfurl the tempest's fury upon their doorstep!" Näcken declared, his voice resounding with an undeniable power that sent shock waves through the heart of the forest.

His words hung heavy in the air, woven with the threads of defiance and unyielding determination. Yet, the ancient one, bearing the weight of eons upon his shoulders, interjected with a somber reminder. "Though they may stand as an army, we, the guardians of enchantment, dwindle in number with each passing day. Most among us choose to retreat into the embrace of our ethereal realm, forsaking this profane abode that mortals claim as their own."

In the ancient one's voice, a cautionary tale unfolded, its undertones laced with a potent blend of vigilance and care. The impending storm loomed, casting shadows upon the path that Näcken fearlessly trod.

"Behold," Näcken responded, his tone infused with a pride unyielding. "My powers remain undiminished, a force to be reckoned with. I shall wield whatever means necessary to safeguard both my existence and hers, for our destinies are forever intertwined."

With relentless resolve, Näcken cast aside the notion of surrender, his love for her serving as an indomitable flame that ignited his spirit. The ancient one, his voice carrying the weight of sincere benevolence, sought to illuminate the perils that lay ahead.

"I offer you this warning, not out of a desire to witness your demise," the ancient one murmured, his voice a blend of wisdom and compassion. "For humankind possesses weapons forged from silver, along with other formidable abilities, whose depths you may never fathom. It is within your safety to retreat to our ethereal realm, relinquishing this realm that teeters on the edge of darkness."

Näcken, unyielding in his loyalty and devotion, rejected the ancient one's counsel without hesitation. "Nay," he declared, his voice resonating with steadfast resolve. "I shall not abandon her, for she is the very breath that ignites the flame within my soul. In her embrace, I have found solace, and I shall stand unyielding, shielding her from the tempest that looms."

Thus, the battle lines were drawn, as Näcken chose love's arduous path, casting aside the veil of safety and embracing the tempest that awaited, all for the sake of a love that defied reason and risked the fragile future of their intertwined fates.

"Whispered among the hidden brethren, I have heard the murmurs of your transgression, bringing her, a mortal, into the sacred embrace of our ethereal realm—an act forbidden, defying the ancient laws that bind us," lectured the ancient one, his voice a river of wisdom cascading through the corridors of time. He spoke not from malice, but from duty bound by the echoes of countless ages.

With a voice that resonated like the hymns of ancient lore, the ancient one continued, "I, tethered to you through the strands of our shared past, shall offer naught but a warning. Yet, should you transgress these sacred boundaries once more, the harbingers of consequence shall be unleashed upon your very soul. Our ethereal kin, the myriad creatures that dwell within this realm, find no solace in the presence of mortals, their hearts aflutter with trepidation. You must honour and safeguard this fragile kingdom."

Acknowledging the ancient one's words with utmost reverence, Näcken replied, his voice an understanding caress, "Indeed, Baelgrim, I shall revere the sanctity of our ways, honouring the sacred boundaries that have guided us through the eons."

Curiosity now danced within the ancient one's eyes as he inquired, "Does she possess a love that compels you to risk your eternal essence, to defy the currents of immortality?"

With ironclad loyalty pouring through the ventricles of his heart, Näcken responded, his voice laced with devotion, "She is not merely a mortal to me, but the breath that animates my immortal soul. In her presence, I have discovered a love that transcends the boundaries of existence—a love worth surrendering all that I am, all that I was, and all that I shall be. It is a devotion that surpasses reason, a bond that defies the constraints of time and space. For her, I would traverse the realms of eternity itself."

In his proclamation, Näcken bared his soul, revealing the depths of his feelings. The ancient one, a witness to the fervour burning within Näcken's being, contemplated the boundless power of love, recognizing the flame that could ignite even the most eternal souls.

"The sight of you surrendering your essence for the sake of a mortal taints my heart with sorrow," intoned the ancient one, his voice carrying a weighty disdain. "Nevertheless, should you ever yearn to return to our ethereal realm, the gate shall remain open. But tread with caution, for whispers upon the wind foretell of a sinister relic possessed by humanity—the midnight dagger—an artifact capable of ensnaring the hidden ones in the limbo of purgatory."

With steadfast resolve, Näcken assured, "I shall remain faithful and unwavering in my devotion."

Piercing through the air, the ancient one's voice dripped with curiosity and reproach as he questioned, "What sets her apart from the countless souls you have enchanted? I have witnessed you captivate many men and women, yet none have woven themselves so deeply into the fabric of your being that you forsake all reason and even contemplate an assault upon my person."

A serene smile curved Näcken's lips, his voice a serenade of boundless passion as he unravelled the enigma of their connection. "Her heart, an ethereal beacon, speaks to mine in a language known only to our intertwined souls. I can hear the echoes of her essence resonating within me, intertwining our destinies like two disparate worlds converging in celestial harmony. To protect and serve her has become my calling, as our fates merge in a dance of interwoven destinies. Bound we are, inextricably linked, her allure captivating my thoughts and seizing dominion over my mind. Forever shall her memory linger, an indelible imprint etched within the deepest recesses of my immortal soul."

Within Näcken's words, love encircled its affectionate twigs, a celestial melody that echoed through the hallways of their connection, transcending the boundaries of time and space.

Caution whispered within the ancient one's voice, his words laced with genuine concern. "Be vigilant, for the path that lies ahead remains shrouded in uncertainty. The design of her destiny holds untold secrets, and the trials you shall face may surpass even the realm of imagination." Vanished as swiftly as the fleeting breeze, a mysterious spectre he became, akin to a hushed wraith that traverses the nocturnal veil, withdrawing from Näcken the company they had momentarily shared. Solitude enshrouded the desolate woodland, tenderly cradling him amidst the serenity of the night's embrace.

CHAPTER 19

Liv awakened abruptly, emerging from a realm of slumber with a surge of unease. A whirlwind of panic engulfed her, as a phantom hand encroached upon her senses, obscuring her sight and muting her voice. Once liberated, her limbs now found themselves ensnared by the ruthless embrace of obscurity, rendering her powerless. Within her chest, her heart stirred, a tempest of trepidation, echoing the tumultuous symphony of her distress.

Violently, she was wrenched away, torn from her bed and thrust into the abyss of the unknown. Foreign whispers, echoing in an alien tongue, reached her ears, igniting an inferno of anxiety that coursed through her veins like wildfire. Questions, like spectres of doubt, plagued her thoughts. What cruel design had orchestrated this nightmarish destiny? To what forbidding realm were they spiriting her away? Liv's lungs threatened to burst as her screams pierced the air, yet her futile resistance met the icy indifference of her captor. His strength, a monstrous apparition, dwarfed her feeble attempts to break free, reducing her struggles to faint whispers against an unyielding tempest.

Bound by ropes that ensnared not only her body but also her spirit, Liv strained against her confines, each motion a defiant act against the shadows that sought to claim her. Yet, another figure, a silent accomplice, responded to her desperate cries, coming to the aid of their comrade. They skilfully wove additional strands of captivity around her quivering form, entwining her essence within a prison of helplessness. As they carried her beyond the threshold, the touch of humid air brushed against her skin, whispering of the untold horrors that lay ahead.

Summoning the depths of her resilience, Liv drew a breath, inhaling the strength and fortitude residing in the profound recesses of her being. She steeled herself, a valiant warrior in the face of adversity, pledging to remain strong against this malevolence. Regardless of the trials awaiting her, she would erect an unyielding fortress, a beacon of courage amid encroaching shadows.

"Where are you going? And for what reason do you steal her away?" Greta's voice quivered with apprehension, her words a plea for enlightenment amidst the swirling chaos.

"Greta!" Liv's voice resounded, a frightened melody threading through the abyss of uncertainty. Though her vision was veiled, her heart recognized the soothing cadence of her dear friend's voice. "Escape! Depart from this place and seek shelter!"

The priest, his voice an eerie symphony tainted by violence and an insatiable thirst for crimson, dismissed Greta's desperate inquiry, shrouding his words in enigma. "It is of no consequence to you."

"Finn?" Greta's voice betrayed her confusion, mingling with the sprouts of uncertainty that cloaked the somber night.

"Finn? Are you there?" Liv's voice carried a flicker of hope, reaching out in search of the familiar solace that Finn's presence often bestowed.
"Return indoors, Greta. I shall handle this, fear not," Finn's voice caressed Greta's ears, his tone strained yet unwavering.

"Finn, do not let them do this to me! Do not let them take me away" Liv pleaded, her voice a tapestry woven with desperation, her struggle against the binding ropes a symbol to her unyielding resolve. But her resistance proved futile as one of the men, with an unrelenting grip, swiftly placed her into a waiting carriage.

"All shall be well, Liv," Finn's voice echoed, burdened with the weight of their shared hardships. "This torment shall soon conclude."

"What do you mean?" Liv demanded, urgency lacing her words as she sought answers in the shroud of night. "Finn? Finn!" Yet Finn's response remained a haunting silence, offering no answers amidst her mounting distress. Faint murmurs of conversation among the men, accompanied by the rhythmic hoofbeats of horses in motion, shattered the stillness of the nocturnal realm, where even summer's gentle touch clung tenaciously to the land.

In a solemn procession, cloaked in secrecy, the priest and Finn advanced, their footfalls whispered secrets upon the earth. Liv, ensnared within the veils of night, strained her senses, attuned to the somber symphony of darkness, seeking fragments of truth that floated upon ethereal winds. With every fibre of her being, she yearned to catch glimpses of their destination, for she knew all too well the dreadful fate that awaited her—a flickering flame of life imperilled by the priest's sinister intentions.

The night's embrace enveloped Liv, its smooth touch a proof to the clandestine nature of their voyage. She stood upon the precipice of escape, her determination flickering like a solitary star amidst the ebony expanse. Every rustle, every distant whisper of the night held the potential to unmask her captors' designs, granting her a fragile thread of hope. The echoes of their footfalls, though muted by the shroud of darkness, divulged secrets that pirouetted upon her ears, teasing elusive fragments of knowledge.

Alert to the impending peril, Liv's heart danced to a frenetic rhythm, a symphony of survival resounding within her chest. Undeterred by the weight of her plight, her spirit yearned for liberation, for the opportunity to elude the clutches of the priest, whose twisted desires hungered for the annihilation of her very essence.

As the moon cast its enchanting glow upon the landscape, Liv's determination surged, an indomitable force coursing through her veins. In the depths of her being, she harboured a solid conviction—an unspoken vow to safeguard the flame of her existence. Each breath she drew, saturated with the fragrance of freedom, fanned the embers of her spirit, kindling a fervent blaze in her heart.

Within the symphony of night, Liv sought her deliverance, unravelling the concealed mystery of whispered secrets, tracing hidden trails through the labyrinthine darkness. For she understood that the path to freedom was cloaked within the realm of murmurs, and with every passing moment, her resolve grew stronger, vowing to seize her chance at liberation, to defy the cruel hands of destiny that sought to extinguish her life.

CHAPTER 20

After eons had elapsed, the stallions ceased their unwavering march, their hooves yielding to the sacred hush that enfolded the tableau. Liv, her senses heightened to their zenith, became acutely attuned to her surroundings. In an instant, the shroud obscuring her vision was violently torn asunder, baring her captor's countenance—etched with terror and wrath, bearing witness to the malevolence that stained his very essence. Liv's searching gaze swept across the enigmatic vista, and her heart skipped a beat as her eyes beheld a ghastly tableau—a bonfire, poised to devour her final form. The dread that had gripped her soul now teetered on the precipice of grim actuality: the priest, a sinister puppeteer, intended to offer her as a sacrifice to the insatiable flames.

Summoning every vestige of her strength, Liv waged war against the fetters that ensnared her, her spirit aflame with indomitable defiance. She shrieked, convulsed, and writhed, determined to resist even in the face of imminent demise. The resilient flame of her spirit refused to be extinguished easily, for she would not grant the priest the satisfaction of witnessing her succumb to fear. With devoted courage, she stood poised to confront her final moments, unyielding and undaunted.

"You may scream and struggle to your heart's content, for there is no saviour who shall rescue you," the priest sneered, revelling in the cruel spectacle that unfolded before him. The men bound Liv to a sturdy stake at the heart of the pyre, while Finn, tormented by a tempest of conflicting emotions, stood beside the malevolent priest.

"Finn, help me!" Liv beseeched, her voice quivering with desperation and a flicker of hope.

"The only path to salvation for her soul is through the embrace of the devouring flames!" the priest declared, his gaze fixated on Finn. Though sorrow lingered in Finn's gaze, he remained silent, burdened by the weight of his torment. A henchman, brandishing a fiery torch, approached Liv with menacing intent. "Have you any final words before you face your creator?" the priest taunted, his voice dripping with contempt.

"I do not tremble before you!" Liv proclaimed with unyielding clarity, her voice resonating with resolute conviction. "I shall meet my end with valour! Your attempts at manipulation shall not sway me! I shall not yield!"

"Very well," the priest sighed, a hint of disappointment tinging his words. He gestured to the merciless lackey to ignite the pyre and consign Liv to her doom. Aware that her final moments were imminent, Liv refused to surrender to despair. Instead, deep within her heart, hope blossomed—a fervent belief in a reunion with her beloved Gunn in realms beyond. Yet, in a twist of fate unforeseen, the zephyrs whispered a change, caressing the air with an icy breath. The fire upon the henchman's torch froze, crystalline frost cascading to the earth in a shattered spectacle.

"Sorcery!" the priest gasped, his accusation tinged with fear. "She is a sorceress!" And in that pivotal juncture, a figure materialized from the heart of the verdant forest—a saviour amid the tumultuous maelstrom. Näcken, adorned with an otherworldly aura, had descended to rescue Liv from her impending doom.

His gaze, ablaze with a foreboding amber glow, emanated an unearthly luminescence, reminiscent of a wrathful spectre. His tresses, akin to fiery tendrils of a conflagration, cascaded with an unbridled brilliance. His hands, clenched in a furious coil, unveiled the turbulent tempest that raged within his very core. Draped in a robe steeped in the scarlet shade of spilled life and adorned with obsidian footwear that whispered secrets of the shadows, he exuded an aura of formidable might. As the mercenaries quivered and their voices melded into a chorus of dread, a malevolent smile twisted upon the priest's visage.

Liv, her heart thundering within her breast, met Näcken's gaze, her fear mirroring the depths of her soul's trepidation. She could not fathom the notion of losing him, for he was her beacon of guidance in this labyrinthine darkness. The mercenaries, a ruthless force numbering beyond a dozen, stood poised with weapons of annihilation in hand. Finn and the priest, bearing firearms unfamiliar to Liv's eyes, appeared as harbingers of impending doom. The crack of gunfire rent the air, the initial shot directed at Näcken. Yet, with an ethereal grace and swiftness that defied mortal bounds, Näcken moved, effortlessly evading the projectile as if he were but a whisper of the wind.

"End him!" The priest's voice resonated with a perverse craving, his countenance contorted by ravenous desire. And in response to his insidious decree, a chorus of malevolence erupted from the mercenaries, their weapons unleashing a symphony of lethal projectiles upon Näcken.

However, undeterred by the onslaught, the spirit of the lake transcended the mortal realm with a divine elegance. Like a celestial dancer amidst a tempest of malevolence, he defied the rain of bullets, weaving through the storm with a grace that mirrored the fluidity of rippling waters. Each step bore witness to his refined determination, his resolve unyielding in the face of encroaching shadows.

With the grace of a swaying reed in the twilight's embrace, Näcken descended upon the first mercenary, his presence elusive yet undeniable. In the breathless moment between heartbeats, he moved as a whisper, swift as a fleeting dream, and laid the warrior low, effortlessly snapping his neck. The mercenaries, driven by their greed and consumed by the allure of their coveted prize, found themselves ensnared in the labyrinth of Näcken's celestial artistry. Each step he took was a symphony of celerity, a ballet of dignified grace that shattered their feeble attempts at concentration. With a commanding gesture, Näcken forced his hand through the chest of one mercenary, ripping out his bleeding heart. His hand, an embodiment of raw strength, bore the weight of countless eons, resonating with the echoes of forgotten legends.

As the mercenaries brandished their weapons, their hands trembling with fear, their fingers tensed upon the triggers, releasing a volley of thunderous intent. Their bullets were but feeble whispers against the nature of Näcken's unparalleled agility. Like spectral apparitions, the projectiles danced through the air, trailing ribbons of impending doom, yet unable to penetrate the flesh of Näcken's boundless swiftness.

As the mercenaries unleashed their gleaming arsenal of swords and knives, an opus of metallic fury pierced the air. The glint of cold steel, a reflection of their intent, danced like errant stars amidst the gathering darkness. Yet, Näcken stood resolute, a figure bathed in an aura of tranquillity that belied the chaos around him. Their blades, once symbols of dominion and devastation, met Näcken's folkloric presence with a resounding chorus of futile resistance. With each swing and thrust, their efforts unravelled like delicate threads in the hands of fate. The mercenaries' eyes widened in disbelief, their confidence crumbling like ancient ruins beneath the weight of Näcken's insurmountable prowess. The clash of steel against steel reverberated through the stillness, a discordant symphony played out on the stage of their vanishing aspirations. Each strike, once propelled by vengeful fervour, dissipated into the void, devoured by the maw of inexorable destiny.

Within the realm of mortal comprehension, Näcken was a tempest incarnate, a force woven from the fabric of ancient wrath and relentless determination. His presence surged with an intensity that defied containment, his essence radiating an aura of commanding might that sent tremors through the hearts of those who dared stand against him. He moved with the predatory precision of a hunting tiger, as he removed the spine of one of the mercenaries, his movements a rhapsody of calculated violence.

In their pursuit of domination, the mercenaries witnessed the depths of Näcken's ferocity when he slit one mercenary's stomach wide open, an unquenchable inferno that consumed all who dared challenge his dominion. His violence was a sonata of chaos, an unrestrained torrent that swept away their feeble illusions of control. Their futile attempts to ensnare him only served to expose the futility of their endeavours, leaving them ensnared in a web of their own making.

As Näcken, a tempest of unstoppable might, whirled through the battlefield, one warrior, driven by desperation and a touch of fate's caprice, managed to graze Näcken's mythological form with a glinting blade. As the blade met Näcken's flesh, breaching the boundary between mortal and immortal, he violently crushed the man's skull.

The mercenaries' attempts to capture him were naught but futile gambits, mere echoes in the tempest of his wrath. With every elusive maneuver, Näcken taunted them, his very existence a reminder of their mortal frailty and insignificance.

One by one, Näcken seized their fates, ending their lives with a violent grace. His movements, a choreography of untamed fury and calculated precision, possessed an otherworldly magnetism that drew the mercenaries into a dance of obliteration. With every encounter, Näcken's celestial essence clashed against their mortal limitations, toppling their resolve like a fragile house of cards. Each mercenary, with quivering limbs and blood-stained hands, succumbed to the inexorable tide of Näcken's relentless onslaught. His fists, imbued with the unyielding might of supernatural power, blazed through the battlefield like scorching comets, obliterating their feeble defences with a ruthless efficiency. Their bodies, once vessels of misguided bravado, crumbled beneath the weight of Näcken's indomitable force.

The mercenaries, once confident in their pursuits, now succumbed to a maelstrom of confusion and desperation. Like leaves caught in a tempest, their resolve wavered, their collective focus scattered amidst Näcken's whirlwind of mastery. His speed, a torrential storm of brilliance, overwhelmed their defences and left them gasping for stability. Like a master conductor guiding an orchestra of failure, Näcken beckoned the mercenaries deeper into the labyrinth of their own inadequacy. Their weapons, once symbols of dominance, became heavy burdens in their grasp, mere extensions of impotence and despair. Each strike met with vacant air, as Näcken eluded their reach like a distant dream, leaving them grasping at shadows of their own creation.

With a measured grace that defied the tumultuous symphony around him, Näcken slowly pulled the helmet from a mercenary, unravelling the shroud of anonymity that cloaked the mercenary's countenance and ripped his entire face off.

His wrath, a tempest of cosmic proportions, tore through their ranks with a primal hunger, leaving naught but shattered remnants of their former selves in its wake. With every fallen mercenary, Näcken's legend grew, his name etched in the chronicles of myth and terror. The carnage he wrought became a memoir of destruction, resonating through the ages as a reminder of the futility of mortal arrogance. The echoes of their screams and pleas crawled through the battlefield, a chilling reminder of Näcken's indomitable power.

And in the aftermath of the tumult, as the dust settled upon the scarred battleground, Näcken stood amidst the remnants —a visage of primeval strength and unworldly wrath. The mercenaries, defeated and shattered, bore witness to the furious dance of a being whose essence was ungraspable to mortals. In that perilous encounter, Näcken penned a sonnet of devastation and violence, a haunting masterpiece that would forever be whispered in reverent tones of fear and wonder.

Finn, his visage etched with trepidation, beheld the supernatural spectacle unfolding before his eyes. Fear coiled within the depths of his gaze, like a sinuous serpent, as he witnessed the undeniable might of Näcken. Beside him, the priest, a vessel of divine authority, observed the chaos with mounting fury. Indignation blazed within his eyes, stoked by a righteous anger that smouldered deep within his soul. The realization seared through his consciousness like an infernal blaze, for he comprehended the futility of the mercenaries' quest, the sheer impossibility of slaying this enigma that stood before them.

In the sacred recesses of his spirit, the priest's unshakeable faith took root, intertwining with the unsettling truth that unfurled before his very eyes. As Näcken's infernal presence blazed with otherworldly radiance, the priest's gaze pierced through the cloak of illusion, discerning the darkness that veiled the creature's celestial form. His convictions aligned with the harrowing reality—he beheld Näcken, a diabolical spirit of immense power, an embodiment of malevolence itself.

In the crucible of desperation, where hope teetered upon the precipice of oblivion, the priest's trembling hands sought solace in the icy embrace of his rifle. Each furrow etched upon his brow and every heartbeat echoing the cadence of uncertainty, he gripped the weight of his weapon, a conduit for his faltering resolve. The rifle, an extension of his desperate will, became a vessel for the priest's defiance. Its steel frame murmured tales of resistance, forged in the crucible of righteous fury. With every loaded round, a shard of his spirit melded with the ammunition, channelling the fervour of his faith and the flickering ember of hope.

In a sublime symphony of ethereal might, Näcken's celestial essence merged, entwined with the tapestry of mortal existence. With a touch that resonated both grace and fervour, his hands, like fleeting moonlit tendrils, sought purchase upon the quivering form of an unfortunate mercenary. In that suspended moment, the laws of gravity seemed to yield to the enigmatic will of the water spirit. With resolute purpose, the rifle's barrel transformed into a portal, from which a sliver of lead ventured forth, propelled by whispered hopes from the desperate. The bullet, a harbinger of mortal constraint, found its mark amidst Näcken's fabled form, piercing the skin of his celestial being. The wound, a blemish upon his radiant essence, marred eternal perfection with a transient stain—evidence of the cosmic dance of sacrifice and consequence.

Within the confines of nature's sanctum, Näcken's celestial embodiment bowed to the overpowering force of gravity, cascading upon the verdant bed of emerald grass. A gasp, galloping through the serene air, accompanied the collision of his ethereal essence with the terrestrial realm. In a crescendo of surrender and suffering, each laboured breath became an overture of agony, whispering tales of anguish etched into the quintessence of his mythical being. A silver bullet, crafted with exquisite precision and imbued with mortal intent, had found its mark amidst Näcken's form—a weapon honed to perfection, with the sole purpose of rending the ephemeral veil and forging a path of devastation through the water spirit's intangible existence. Now, as the bullet traversed his bloodstream, Näcken bore witness to the insidious poison of destruction unfurling within.

Finn, seduced by treachery's allure, ventured forth with a dagger poised to sever the fragile thread binding Näcken's supernatural being. Like a spectre of deceit, he moved with stealth and malice, his intent concealed within the shadows, yearning to pierce the very core of the water spirit's vulnerability.

Yet, within the wounded depths of Näcken's celestial form, a resilient spark of vitality endured. Though the sting of the silver bullet echoed through his supernatural veins, his essence flickered with an indomitable spirit—a defiance transcending the realm of mortal afflictions. With sublime grace and unyielding resolve, Näcken, wounded yet unbroken, eluded Finn's treacherous designs.

In the crescendo of fate's intricate design, Näcken, injured yet ablaze with glorious power, seized Finn by the throat. The water spirit's hand, a manifestation of dominant strength, encircled Finn's neck like an unyielding vise, constricting the flow of life's vital elixir. Finn's world narrowed to the primal instinct of survival, his gasping breaths a symphony of desperate struggle against Näcken's merciless grip. The water spirit's eyes, once tranquil pools of enigma, now burned with an intensity mirroring the inferno of their clash. Näcken, wounded but resolute, held firm to his celestial dominion, his grasp an acknowledgement of the volatile interplay of mercy and retribution. As Finn's vision blurred and the edges of consciousness threatened to dissolve into the abyss, a tempest of emotions churned within Liv's trembling soul.

"Cease this madness!" Liv's voice erupted with a fervent plea, her cries carrying a potent blend of frustration and desperation. "Spare his life! Let him live!" Her words, infused with a loyalty that defied the encroaching darkness, resounded through the air, resonating with Näcken's very soul. His gaze, a tender fusion of determination and affection, shifted from Liv to Finn—a man ensnared in the clutches of fear and uncertainty. Näcken released his grip on Finn, guiding him gently to the ground with a touch as soft as a soothing whisper amidst the chaos. Bittersweet pain flickered in Finn's eyes as he surrendered to unconsciousness, his spirit battered yet tenaciously clutching to the fragile threads of survival.

Näcken's focus returned to the priest—a vessel of nefariousness and twisted desires. Within his being, a defiant rhythm pulsed with every beat of his heart, urging him forward. The priest, consumed by his vindictiveness, once again aimed his weapon, a futile endeavour to vanquish the unconquerable spirit standing before him. Yet, in a breathtaking display of grace and swiftness, Näcken eluded the venomous intent, a wisp of ephemeral existence traversing the boundaries of time. In the fraction of a moment, he closed the gap between himself and the priest—a manifestation of retribution and guardianship.

"You... " In the pregnant pause between the priest's exhaled breath and the shaping of his next damning words, Näcken twisted his neck and killed him rapidly.

As the priest exhaled his final breath, surrendering to the gruesome clasp of mortality, his life force dwindled, a flickering flame extinguished upon the altar of existence. In the wake of his departure, the earthly realm, once adorned with serenity and vibrant beauty, transformed into a solemn tableau of crimson tragedy. Where lush blades of grass had once embraced the moon's gentle caress, now bore witness to the evanescent nature of life, painted in the hues of warm blood. Näcken, amidst this mournful concoction of spilled existence, stood resolute, his robe billowing like an ebony river merging with the sacred tide of crimson. As Näcken surveyed the aftermath of the priest's demise, his gaze lingered upon the blood-stained grass—a poignant reminder of the fragile foundation underlying even the most idyllic landscapes.

With urgency threading through his every motion, Näcken swiftly approached Liv, his ethereal presence enfolding her like a protective shield. In one graceful motion, he unravelled the cruel bindings that had ensnared her, liberating her from the chains of fear and despair. As Liv rose, her form trembling beneath the weight of the harrowing ordeal, Näcken's arms embraced her, offering solace amidst the chaos that had unfurled.

Locked in their gaze, Liv discerned the anguish etched upon Näcken's countenance. Concern mingled with tenderness in her voice as she voiced her apprehension, her words carried on the breath of gentle whispers. "You are wounded," she murmured, her voice a delicate blend of worry and care.

Aching with the pain threatening to engulf him, Näcken summoned his dwindling strength, his voice heavy with the precariousness of his state. "You must aid me in extracting these accursed bullets," he implored, blood staining his words as it trickled from his lips. Urgency coloured his plea, for he knew the silver bullets, infused with malevolence crafted to ravage his very essence, posed a dire threat. Weariness began to weigh upon him, his vitality diminishing as he beheld the safety of his beloved Liv, finding solace in the knowledge that she had been spared from the cruel embrace of harm.

" I shall spare no effort to rescue you," Liv vowed with courageous devotion, her commitment a resolute flame that flickered in her heart. With delicate hands, she sought solace upon Näcken's shoulders, tracing the contours of his enchanting form with a touch as tender as a lover's caress. Beneath her fingertips, she felt the soft texture of his skin, affirmation of his otherworldly nature. His once fiery locks, now transformed into a colour of rich mahogany, framed a countenance that exuded an enigmatic allure.

As their eyes locked in an intimate understanding, Liv found herself immersed in the depths of Näcken's enigmatic gaze, now aglow with hazel hues that mirrored the mysteries of his immortal soul. Within those depths, she discerned an eternal promise, a steadfast spirit that would forever dwell within their shared realm. In his allegiant gaze, she glimpsed a devotion that surpassed the boundaries of death and despair—an unyielding commitment to safeguard her well-being, even at the cost of his own life.

In that fateful moment, an unfathomable agony etched itself upon Näcken's countenance, marking lines of torment upon his once serene visage. The pallor of his skin faded to an ashen grey, while his once supple bones turned petrified, as if transformed into unyielding stone. Emerging from the shadows, Finn revealed his treachery, plunging the blade of the accursed night dagger deep into Näcken's defenceless back. A tremor coursed through Näcken's being as he sank to his knees, his life force ebbing away with each fleeting breath. His eyes, shining with eternal love, pierced into Liv's horrified soul—bereft yet steadfast, regret mingling with the profound adoration that now seemed cruelly destined to be severed by death's unforgiving hand.

Within the depths of Liv's shattered heart, a torrent of shock and sorrow surged forth, threatening to consume her very essence. Once again, destiny had snatched away a cherished soul, forever intertwining their spirits in an unbreakable bond. She crumbled to her knees, enfolding Näcken's cemented form in her trembling arms, her touch a desperate plea to halt the inexorable descent into eternal slumber. As Näcken drew his final breath, the ethereal essence that had ignited their love dissipated, leaving behind an indelible monument of hardened stone.

Standing defiantly behind them, Finn revelled in his malevolent triumph, radiating disdain with every pore. With a contemptuous gesture, he cast aside the accursed weapon, allowing it to be claimed by the unforgiving earth. Liv's anguished cries pierced the air, a lament of agony piercing through the surrounding darkness. Through tear-stained eyes, she met Finn's gaze, her ire unleashed in a tempest of anger and frustration. No longer could she contain the tumultuous storm of emotions raging within her wounded heart—the betrayal and loss entwined in a maelstrom of despair.

"What monstrous act have you committed?" Her voice resounded with a poignant mix of anguish and frustration, echoing through the hollow expanse of the night.

"I have liberated you from this devil, I have freed you from his demonic grip!" Finn retorted, his words charged with determination, poised to justify his actions.

"He never forced me, I was never under any kind of spell!" Liv stood tall, her gaze unwavering as she confronted Finn. "Näcken has saved me in ways that words fail to capture."

"That is merely Näcken's enchantment speaking. The priest believed it would fade with his demise, yet it seems he was mistaken." Disappointment etched its mark upon Finn's face, regret colouring his voice. Consumed by her emotions, Liv unleashed her pent-up fury upon Finn. Her screams haunted through the night, an explosion of anguish and despair. "Hold your tongue, woman!" Finn pushed her away, sending Liv sprawling to the ground. Amidst the chaos, she tightly gripped the dagger, her fingers trembling with anger. Pointing it towards Finn, he questioned, "Are you planning to take my life?" Finn's laughter swirled with derision, his eyes gleaming with misplaced confidence. "I am your husband, we have children together, and you have sworn loyalty and devotion to me."

"You had intended to kill me!" Liv's voice resonated with profound betrayal and pain.

"It is the only way to save your soul!" Finn advanced towards Liv, his steps resolute and purposeful. "I cannot bear to witness your soul consumed by the inferno of damnation. Can you not comprehend? It is the only recourse, the sole beacon of hope to preserve your very being. Do not burden me further with resistance," Finn's voice trembled with the weight of his conviction. As he closed in, Liv steeled herself, resolute in her determination to deny him the taking of her life.

Then, like a miraculous spectre, a veil of mist unfurled across the expanse. Hoarfrost seduced the valley in its enchanting splendour, adorning the world with an ethereal touch. Emerging from this celestial shroud, the ancient one materialized beside Liv. His countenance, dark and majestic, stood tall like a colossal figure, while his flowing white hair shimmered like moonlit silk. His piercing blue eyes held a delicate balance of clarity and enigma, casting an irresistible allure. The presence he emanated sent shivers down Finn's spine—a palpable aura of primal strength and untamed grace.

Clad in immaculate white garments, which danced with the caress of gentle breezes, the ancient one demonstrated the harmonious fusion of power and elegance. Finn's body stiffened upon beholding this majestic entity, for he recognized in him a kindred essence, akin to that of Näcken. Yet, something set them apart—an intangible distinction that rendered this supernatural being untouchable. Deep within his bone marrow, Finn understood that he could not contend with such a transcendent spirit, for this being was unlike any he had encountered or heard of.

"Depart from this realm and forsake this sacred ground forever," the ancient one's voice resonated with a haunting timbre, carrying the weight of countless ages as he fixed his gaze upon Finn. Trepidation took root within Finn's chest, intertwining with his every fibre, compelling him to flee, his footsteps hastening, never daring to cast his eyes backward.

The ancient one then turned his attention to Liv, who still clutched the dagger with unyielding resolve. His eyes, beacons of wisdom, held a profound understanding as they met Näcken's gaze, and with measured grace, he settled beside his kindred spirit. A gesture of reverence and tenderness followed, as the ancient one reached out, his touch gracing the petrified countenance of Näcken.

"Behold, witness the consequence of love's delicate dance," the ancient one whispered, his voice a lamentation interlaced with empathy. From his sorrowful eyes, a solitary tear, liquid gold, descended upon the earth, its touch awakening a flourishing garden of ivory blooms, their petals intertwining with Näcken's ethereal remnants. Turning his gaze towards Liv, the ancient one beheld her with a mixture of compassion and solemn wisdom. "Within your grasp lies a weapon forged to wound the very essence of magical creatures. It has cast your beloved into the purgatory of eternal confines, forever ensnared within its unforgiving embrace. Many of my kin have suffered a similar fate, their spirits eternally entwined within the tapestry of my immortal soul." His words flowed forth with fervent poeticism, resonating with a depth that stirred the very core of one's being. "Should you choose to follow me into our hidden realm, veiled from mortal eyes, you may safely relinquish the dagger to a haven where no human hand shall ever unleash such destiny upon a fabled being."

"Here, take it," Liv whispered, extending the dagger towards the ancient one. Yet, a shiver of trepidation coursed through the ancient one's essence, causing him to retreat, taking a step backward, fearful of the potent artifact's touch.

"Alas, I dare not grasp it, for even the slightest contact would ensnare my very soul, binding it to the horrific powers it holds. Nonetheless, now that we possess it, we may securely confine it within our realm, far from the cruel desires of mortals," the ancient one replied, his voice trembling with caution and reverence.

"I will help you bring the dagger to safety," determined, Liv fixed her gaze upon the ancient one, her eyes burning with steadfast determination. "But you must bring him back to me," she implored, her words infused with an unyielding demand.

"I perceive the burden of sorrow etched upon your spirit, young one," the ancient one murmured, casting a compassionate gaze upon Liv. "You have nurtured love for one of our kind, and I shall not inflict further harm upon you. Yet, I possess no power to summon him back; he dwells beyond my reach, eternally lost."

"Is there no way to bring him back?" Liv beseeched, her voice a plaintive plea carried by the winds.

"His soul lies imprisoned within purgatorial confines, ensnared by the dark influence of the dagger. Whosoever it pierces, into that realm they are thrust. If you were to plunge it into your own heart, your very essence would journey to that self-same domain," the ancient one disclosed, his voice heavy with the weight of truth.

"Then I shall do so!" Liv declared, her spirit ablaze with firm resolve.

"Refrain from hastiness, mortal!" the ancient one cautioned, his voice resonating with a blend of concern and wisdom. "Purgatory is a realm that rejects the intrusion of souls such as yours. The dwellers within shall strive to expel you, and the path back from that unfathomable abyss is fraught with perils untold. Many have succumbed to its labyrinthine depths, never to find their way back."

Undeterred, Liv met the ancient one's gaze, her eyes ablaze with courage, her spirit resolute. "I shall find a way, I shall guide his soul back to my reality," she declared, her words carried on the wings of bravery.

"However," the ancient one interjected, interrupting Liv's resolute proclamation. "There may exist a grievous toll to pay. Upon your return, the wounds inflicted by the dagger upon your delicate form are unknown. Death may beckon, drawing near. The price of rescuing your beloved may come at the expense of your own existence. You shall not meet an immediate demise upon your return; instead, a variety of unexplored pain shall envelop your being, its duration unknown, until it ultimately claims your very life. Furthermore, should you pierce yourself, you must hold fast to the dagger, for if you release your grip, the tenuous connection to this realm may sever, consigning you to an eternal limbo," the ancient one conveyed with a solemn countenance, each word weighed with the gravity of the impending sacrifice.

"I understand, I accept the dangers that might lie ahead" Liv responded, her voice serene and resolute. The ancient one regarded her with astonishment.

"You are willing to wager your own mortal coil to salvage one of our kind?" he queried, his voice laced with curiosity and awe.

"I do not fear death or pain. If there is a chance, then I must seize it. If there is a way to bring him back, then I must try. What worth does my life hold if I am not willing to risk it for something I believe in?" Liv's voice echoed with conviction, her words an anthem of faithful determination. A momentary pause embraced the air as she absorbed the weight of her resolve. "And upon my return, I shall bring the dagger into your realm," she declared, her eyes fixed upon the ancient one with fervent devotion and a promise sealed within their depths.

"Very well," he acknowledged, his voice carrying a solemn authority. "I shall remain steadfast here, guarding your earthly vessel as your spirit journeys through the veiled recesses of the unknown. I shall not waver from your side," his words rang with genuine truth, sincere in their commitment. Liv nodded, her gaze still flickering nervously towards the dagger. Its craftsmanship was a marvel to behold, its blade gleaming with a keen edge, while remnants of Näcken's blood lingered upon its surface like a poignant reminder of the trials endured.

In a moment of profound resolve, Liv drew a breath, as if gathering the strength to face her deepest trepidations. Fearlessly, she pierced her own being, the blade meeting her tender flesh. A shudder coursed through her veins, as if icy rivulets of blood froze within, while her heart raced with unbridled intensity. In an instant, darkness engulfed her, and her consciousness swiftly slipped away.

CHAPTER 21

As Liv surfaced from slumber, the world greeted her with a pulsating ache that resonated deep within her head. Beneath her, grains of sand caressed her body, their touch tangible. She surveyed her surroundings, finding herself perched within an arid expanse, a desert stretching to the horizon. Majestic dunes and towering peaks encircled her, while the sky, devoid of the sun's radiance, donned a cloak of fiery orange. No foliage, no creatures, no trace of water met her searching gaze

Curiosity tugged at Liv's heart, propelling her on a solitary journey through the vastness of this desert realm, a quest to unravel its secrets. With each step, the landscape unfurled memories from her own existence, scenes from her life playing out before her eyes, each one distinct and poignant. Liv pondered, recognizing this realm as a purgatory, where souls confronted their transgressions and sought redemption, where the path to heaven or hell awaited discovery. To navigate this realm, she resolved to cling fiercely to her own life, wary of the perils lurking within introspection's treacherous embrace.

With relentless persistence, she focused on the recent chapters of her journey, tightly grasping cherished recollections while eschewing reflections on her missteps. Among these memories, one shone with undeniable clarity—the passionate bond she shared with Näcken, a profound connection that delved into the depths of their souls, baring their true essence. She believed that this bond held the key, a guiding light amidst the enigmatic labyrinth that surrounded her. Liv continued her stride, harnessing the essence of Näcken's presence, shutting out distractions that sought to divert her purpose.

The concept of time grew nebulous, lost in an ocean of simultaneous occurrences stretching into infinity. Hunger, thirst, fatigue, and sleep dissolved into illusory whispers within this realm. It was a place where the soul lingered, vulnerable to the clutches of an endless loop. After an eternity that felt both fleeting and everlasting, Liv found herself standing before a wall of polished marble. Though she couldn't fathom why, an undeniable intuition told her that the souls of the hidden ones resided beyond this barrier. Placing her hand upon its surface, she pressed her ear against the cool expanse, its touch sending a shiver through her being. "How can I transcend an obstacle that is no obstacle?" she whispered, her voice carried away by the desert wind.

Turning to her left, Liv beheld the presence of a small fox, a creature embodying youthful spirit and animated life. Its tail wagged playfully, a silent invitation to acknowledge its existence.

"You must release your attachment to pain and sorrow, surrendering to love, acceptance, and harmony. The painful ways of the past can no longer guide your steps if you wish to ascend this wall," urged the creature, its words weaving through the chambers of Liv's mind. The voice, an embodiment of feminine grace, resonated within her being. And in that moment, Liv's countenance bloomed with a radiant smile, for she recognized the spirit of Gunn, her beloved daughter, as her guide. She was not alone in this unknown realm.

With profound resolve, Liv inhaled deeply, exhaling a torrent of anger, fury, and burdensome sorrows that had clung to her heart. Within that breath, a wondrous transformation transpired—the marble wall, once insurmountable, began to yield. Before her awestruck gaze unfurled a mesmerizing sight—a multitude of souls, like luminous beacons, emerged in myriad forms, their brilliance illuminating the expanse. It was a vista of breathtaking magnificence.

Tranquillity enfolded Liv, entwining her essence with this sacred realm. The connection she felt was profound, forging an indescribable bond that beckoned her to linger. Reluctant to depart, she yearned to bask in the embrace of this transcendent place, where the symphony of souls whispered secrets and tales of forgotten dreams.

"Remember the ancient one's wisdom," implored the fox, its unwavering gaze fixed upon Liv. Within its eyes, a shimmering reservoir of timeless knowledge seemed to reside.

In the sacred stillness, Liv's senses attuned to the profound secrets held within this ethereal realm. The whispered echoes of forgotten ages resonated in her soul, the ancient one's voice echoing like a distant melody. It spoke of truths that transcended time, guiding her along the path of enlightenment and illumination.

As the fox stared into the depths of her being, it ignited a fire within her spirit, awakening a dormant reservoir of courage and resilience. Through its inspirational gaze, Liv felt the weight of history and the echoes of countless journeys. In that moment, the ephemeral veil between worlds grew thin, and she found herself entwined in a tempest of timeless wisdom and enigmatic purpose. With reverence, Liv heeded the fox's words, treasuring the ancient one's teachings as precious jewels within her heart.

"Do not lose yourself in the allure of this realm. It is indeed captivating and beautiful, but it is not your place to remain," the fox cautioned.

"And you, my child," Liv whispered, her gaze tenderly fixed upon the fox. A supernova of emotions danced within her eyes, their depths reflecting the immensity of her affection. "If I stay here, I can be with all these enchanting souls, and I can have you by my side for eternity. In this realm, you are here, close to me. What more do I need?" The air grew hushed, as if on the cusp of something momentous for the fox's response. Liv's words lingered, their resonance mingling with the whispers of the ageless wind. Within the fox's delicate gaze, an unspoken understanding unfolded, a connection that transcended the boundaries of words. In that unspoken language of the heart, Liv could sense the echoes of reciprocated affection, a love that spanned realms and conquered mortal constraints.

Yet, as their eyes met, the fox's gaze shimmered with a blend of compassion and playful wisdom. Its untamed spirit seemed to whisper a truth beyond the grasp of immediate desires—a truth that resonated with the depths of Liv's soul. The allure of eternal companionship clashed with the realization that the journey of the heart demanded more than the sweet solace of a single realm. With a bittersweet smile gracing her lips, Liv extended her hand, inviting the fox to join her on what might be her final journey.

"I know your heart yearns for answers," the fox spoke softly, its voice carrying the weight of whispered echoes. In its eyes, ancient wisdom gleamed untamed, gazing upon Liv with affectionate tenderness. "My love for you, dear mother, transcends the bounds of life. And I promise you, we shall reunite in the realm beyond, but we cannot linger here. I have waited for you, and now it is time for us to depart. Follow my steps, and I shall guide you back to the world and the promises that await." The air grew heavy, as if carrying the depths of their emotions. Liv's spirit trembled, caught between the heavenly allure of eternity and the vibrant pulse of mortal existence. The fox's words, a gentle caress upon her soul, spoke of an eternal union, of a love that would endure beyond the veil of life's transient dance. A longing as ancient as time itself surged within her, yearning to be reunited with her beloved daughter.

Liv's heart swelled with an overpowering blend of hope and

trepidation. She knew that to heed the fox's call was to accept the uncharted path, relinquishing the comforts of this transcendent realm and returning to the realm of the living where death and failure might be waiting. And yet, the fox's reliable guidance beckoned her forward, promising the fulfilment of a destiny entwined, an unbreakable bond that transcended the limitations of time and space.

With courage and sorrow in her heart, Liv extended her hand, her touch mirroring the fox's determination. In that loving union, their spirits entwined, they embarked upon a journey that would traverse the realms of both mortality and eternity. The fox, a beacon of light and love, led the way, its pawprints etching a trail of destiny upon their road. Step by step, they ventured forth, their hearts beating in synchrony, guided by a love that would span the ages.

For in the depths of their souls, they knew that the promise of their reunion would not be fulfilled in the ethereal realms alone. It awaited them in the essence of the afterlife, in the intricate dance of joy and sorrow, and in the eternal embrace of a love that had endured the ravages of time. Together, they would navigate the realms, side by side, united by an unbreakable bond that whispered of a destiny stronger than death itself. And as they went forth, the symphony of their love resounded through the grasp of purgatory, an eternal melody that reverberated through eternity.

"What of Eric and Per? Are they with you? Are they still alive?" Liv's voice trembled with a mixture of sorrow and concern, her heart burdened by the weight of unanswered questions. Silence descended like a heavy mist, casting an air of melancholy around the sacred space. The fox, with eyes as ancient as time, regarded Liv with a depth of understanding. In its gaze, a reflection of empathy and compassion flickered, like the eternal flame of remembrance.

"They are not with me, nor are they in the realm of death.

Their spirits remain upon the earthly plane. You need not worry. All shall be well, and you can release your burdens," the fox murmured, its voice a tender lullaby that caressed the ache within Liv's heart. Within its gentle tone resonated a serenity born of ancient wisdom, an assuring calm that danced through the calm air. In those whispered words, the weight upon Liv's soul began to lift, like tendrils of mist dissipating beneath the radiant dawn. The fox's presence emanated a contagious tranquillity, its soothing voice a beacon of solace amidst the storms that raged within.

With every fibre of her being, Liv endeavoured to trust in the fox's serene guidance, releasing the grip of worry that had clung to her heart. As she exhaled the burdens that had consumed her, a profound stillness settled within her being. The fox's words, like inspirational mantras, floated through the depths of her consciousness, casting ripples of serenity that merged with the very essence of her existence.

"So it is true," Liv spoke softly, her voice carrying a hint of melancholy. Her gaze traversed the galaxy of souls stretching before her, an ocean of ethereal beings whose luminescence illuminated the realm. Each flickering light held an untold story, an existence intertwined with eternity. "In the afterlife, I must choose if I shall spend it by your side or his," Liv whispered, her voice carried by the winds that danced through the realm of souls.

"Why would you think so?" the fox questioned, its voice flowing with a gentle rhythm. "You may not have the power to choose your realm in life, but in death, you transcend time and space. How else could we explain that purgatory holds these spirits? Death is both the same and different for all of us. It is nothing and everything, the singular force that unites us, regardless of our life's journey. Your heart will only be lost and separated from everyone if you believe it to be so and allow it to happen."

A solitary tear traced a delicate path down Liv's pale cheek, a crystalline testament to the depths of her emotions. Her eyes met the fox's gaze, a profound sense of serenity enveloping her being. With a resolute breath, she drew strength from the wellspring within, intertwining her essence with the collective life force that surrounded her.

In that sacred communion, Liv began the transformative quest, embracing the souls that pulsed with ethereal radiance. Every step she took resonated with the harmony of interconnectedness, as if the souls themselves became extensions of her own spirit. She became the vessel through which their stories flowed, the embodiment of their hopes and dreams.

And as Liv turned away from the sea of souls, her footsteps imprinted a path of incandescent light upon the arid desert floor. In a mesmerizing procession, the souls followed in her wake, their collective presence illuminating the realm with a divine radiance. Together, they wove a symphony of existence, a soulful ballet that celebrated the unity of entwined souls.

As Liv beheld the obsidian stone, its somber presence amidst the vibrant souls surrounding her, a sense of reverence filled her heart. She turned to the fox, gratitude and contentment shining in her eyes, a gentle smile graced her lips.

With graceful determination, she reached out and caressed the obsidian surface, a gesture symbolizing her sacrifice bringing these souls back into the earthly realm.

The fox, a silent witness to her journey, regarded her with eyes gleaming with pride and affection. In the harmonious connection of their shared understanding, a profound bond flourished, transcending the boundaries of the seen and unseen.

Hand in paw, Liv and the fox stood before the obsidian monolith, their spirits entwined in a dance of destiny. Together, they ventured into the unknown, unaware of what might lie ahead. In their union, the realms of the living and the afterlife converged, weaving a tale of acceptance, resilience, and the eternal cycle of entangled souls.

"I will be reunited with you soon," Liv whispered tenderly, her fingertips tracing the cool surface of the obsidian stone. Her touch ignited a surge of transformative energy, bridging the divide between realms. Purgatory's grasp relinquished its hold, freeing her spirit to return back to the earthly plane.

In a sublime blink of time, Liv emerged from the depths of purgatory, her essence seamlessly merging with her corporeal form. The night enveloped her like a faithful cloak, a sanctuary of shadows whispering secrets to the stars above. Standing as a stalwart guardian, the ancient one remained unwavering, preserving her earthly vessel, their connection unbroken by the passage of time.

With an anticipatory breath, Liv's soul descended upon her physical being, infusing her senses with a tremor of astonishment. Her eyes fluttered open, like a phoenix reborn from the ashes, the nocturnal sky transformed into a spectacle of resplendent radiance. The once-shadowed valley burst forth in an explosion of light as the spirits she had led from purgatory met the earthly realm. Each ethereal presence danced and shimmered, casting a myriad of hues upon the land, as if the very essence of existence rejoiced in their return.

In awe, the ancient one stood witness, his wise eyes wide with wonder, beholding the convergence of realms before them. In the luminous spectacle created by Liv's sacrifice, his steadfast guardianship found affirmation, as the radiant theatrics unfolded.

With the valley aglow in the spiritual radiance of her triumph, Liv inhaled the essence of newfound possibility, her senses alive with the fragrance of peace. Their collective brilliance infused her with strength, their spirits forever intertwined with her own. In their wake, the valley flourished, bathed in the iridescence of uncountable spirits.

"As destiny ordained, you have fulfilled your sacred vow,

uniting my long-lost kin," marvelled the ancient one, his eyes shimmering with awe as they beheld the divine congregation of liberated souls. Amidst the luminous spectacle, Liv's strength waned, her body weakened by the crimson flow from her wounded abdomen.

"Lead me to your realm so that I may place the dagger there before the last vestiges of strength forsake my mortal form," Liv implored the ancient one, her voice getting weaker by the words.

The ancient one nodded, his touch gentle yet resolute upon Liv's shoulder, as she clung tenaciously to the instrument of her sacrifice. In a dance of ancient sorcery, they traversed the veils, transcending the boundaries that separate realms, arriving in the sacred abode of the fabled spirits.

With deliberate purpose, Liv placed the dagger upon a weathered wooden stump, its significance etched upon the fabric of her soul. As the ancient one wove intricate gestures, thorns sprouted from the earth, encircling the weapon—a testament to the price she had paid. "Now," the ancient one murmured, his voice a delicate whisper carried by the wind, "allow me to return you to the realm of the living, that you may bid farewell to Näcken, your beloved, one final time."

The embers of Liv's heart flickered, tendrils of pain coursing through her dying body, threatening to extinguish her spirit. With trembling hands, she fought against the encroaching chill, seeking to stem the flow of her life's essence. Yet, the veil of mortality grew ever thinner, her essence slipping away like long lost whispers carried upon the gentle breeze. With unwavering grace, the ancient one guided her back to the valley.

"Their journeys, too, shall come to fruition," the ancient one responded, his voice resonating with wisdom and serenity. "In the grand splendour of existence, each soul finds its way back to its earthly vessel, for the cycles of life and death intertwine like the ivy's embrace. Fear not, dear human, for the remaining souls, scattered across realms, shall be reunited with their mortal forms in due time."

Liv, her eyes shimmering with a blend of hope and concern, pondered the destiny of the countless spirits she had encountered on her ethereal odyssey. The weight of their longing pressed upon her heart, urging her to seek answers from the ancient one, the guardian of cosmic truths.

The ancient one, his countenance veiled in both solemnity and solace, offered a comforting embrace in his response. "As your spirit found its way back to your earthly vessel, so too shall the others find their destined return. The tapestry of destiny is woven with intricate threads, and the enigma of existence knows no boundaries. Guided by unseen forces that shape our cosmic dance, the souls shall be drawn back to the realm of the living."

A profound sense of interconnectedness grew within Liv, as if the souls she encountered were kindred spirits, united by an unquenchable yearning for wholeness and reunion. Though the path ahead may be shrouded in mystery and the passage of time an expansive chasm, the ancient one's words reverberated with a soothing certainty, breathing peace into her grief-filled soul.

With a tranquil nod, Liv accepted the unfolding secrets of destiny, surrendering herself to the enigmatic currents that guided the souls' pilgrimage. She recognized that their stories, akin to celestial constellations, would converge upon the canvas of mortal existence, each star interconnected with purpose and significance.

"Behold," spoke the ancient one, his voice resonating with the weight of countless epochs. "The souls, long held captive in the clutches of time, shall embark upon a joyful odyssey to reclaim their once-forgotten vessels. Some have languished in ethereal bondage for centuries, suspended betwixt realms, and now, they stand at the crossroads of existence. The choice is theirs to make, to resume the dance of life or to embrace the infinite touch of death."

As the ancient one's words wove his mystic spell, a radiant light emerged from the distant horizon, traversing the air until it alighted upon Näcken's once vibrant, now petrified form. The luminescence intertwined with the somber hues of his stony countenance, and a wondrous metamorphosis unfurled. With each passing moment, the shackles of dark enchantment yielded, relinquishing their hold to the resurgence of Näcken's awakened consciousness. Like an echo of newfound liberation, a silver bullet, once embedded within his form, descended gracefully, coming to rest upon the warm ground.

Bewildered, Näcken's gaze oscillated between the ancient one and Liv, his eyes a tempestuous whirlwind of emotions. A wave of relief cascaded upon Liv's pallid visage, a delicate flush of life ebbing as death tightened its grip within her attenuated veins. In the throes of exhaustion, she surrendered to the frailty, descending towards the cradle of the earth. It was then that Näcken, swift as a flowing river, caught her fading form within his arms, cradling her with a tenderness that mirrored their love.

Amidst this poignant tableau, the fox lingered nearby, its coat adorned with untamed hues, its tail swaying to a mystical rhythm. With eyes the colour of earth's fertile soil, it observed the unfolding scene, perceiving the delicate balance between life and death that eluded mortal comprehension. A sage guardian, it stood witness to the unfurling act of destiny, its silent presence, proof of the profound secrets hidden within the cosmic dance.

In Näcken's anguished gaze, Liv discovered solace and reassurance, even as the twilight of her existence threatened to consume her. With a tender touch, she lovingly caressed his face, her fingertips tracing the lines that told their shared history. A gentle smile graced her lips.

In that ephemeral moment, the cosmos itself paused, enraptured by the force of their love. Liv and Näcken stood as one, defying the relentless march of mortality. Though burdened by the weight of their finite existence, their spirits soared, entangled in a dance that transcended the confines of time.

"I love you, and I am grateful that I could restore your soul and set things right. I never intended to bring these troubles into your life," Liv whispered, her words carrying a vulnerability that resonated through the luminous expanse. Näcken met her gaze, his eyes a wellspring of depth and enchantment, capturing her essence within their earthy brown hues. They shimmered with an iridescent spark, reminiscent of the very moment their souls first intertwined.

"The memory of you," Näcken spoke, his voice a tender caress upon her soul, "is forever etched upon the foundation of my heart. No matter where your spirit roams, whether in distant realms or unseen dimensions, I shall embark on an eternal quest, traversing the corridors of time until I find you. Distance holds no sway over the ceaseless pursuit of our union. Even if your countenance were to change, adorned with a different guise, my soul would recognize the essence that resides within. Across countless lifetimes, I will search for you, unwavering in my devotion. For love, dearest Liv, transcends the boundaries of language. Our souls are forever intertwined, and without your presence, I am a mere fragment of existence, forever incomplete."

With a yearning that defied mortal comprehension, Näcken pressed his lips to Liv's pallid, azure hue. It was a kiss that bore witness to their shared pain, a sacred merging of souls where each breath exchanged deeply illustrated their eternal bond. As their lips gently brushed against one another, a symphony of emotions surged within their beings, weaving their destinies together and sealing their love.

Näcken turned to the ancient one, guardian of realms and keeper of ancient secrets. His eyes, filled with an impassioned plea, implored the timeless being for assistance. "I beseech you, Baelgrim" he pleaded, his voice tinged with desperation, "Save her, for within her fragile vessel resides the very essence of my being. Without her, my existence would be naught but a hollow shell, adrift in an eternal void. Spare no effort, ancient one, in your divine intervention. Let her grace this world once more, for I cannot fathom a reality devoid of her presence by my side."

A profound silence settled upon the realm, the weight of Näcken's plea hanging in the air like an unbreakable enchantment. The ancient one, his countenance adorned with timeless wisdom, regarded Näcken with a blend of compassion and unwavering resolve.

"Ah, dear Lythandir," the ancient one spoke, his voice resonating with the echoes of ages past. "You yearn for a miracle that eludes even the most skilled weavers of fate. The power of transformation lies within my grasp, but the delicate balance of existence must be honoured. The cycle of life and death, intricate and unyielding, dances with purpose and intent. It is not for me, nor any guardian of realms, to alter its divine course." His gazes turned to Liv, her form delicate and vulnerable, yet a celestial radiance emanating from within. "She has embraced her destined path, acknowledging the transient nature of mortal existence. To prolong her life, even though the infusion of immortal essence, would condemn her to an eternal struggle. The human lifespan, though fleeting, carries a sacred grace. It is a melody that unfolds, inviting us to savour each precious note before it gracefully merges into the eternal symphony of the cosmos."

Näcken's voice, tinged with shadows, intertwined with the ancient one's wisdom. "But what of our love, our eternal bond? Can it not transcend the boundaries of time and mortality? Shall we not defy the very laws that bind us?"

Softening their gaze, the ancient one recognized the depth of Näcken's anguish. "Love, in its divine essence, surpasses all boundaries. It weaves threads of connection that span lifetimes and realms. Yet, dear Näcken, even the most profound love must face the reality of impermanence. It is the delicate nature of mortal existence that infuses our encounters with an intoxicating sweetness. To seek immortality in the name of love is to yearn for an eternity marred by sorrow and longing, for the fates have decreed our paths to diverge."

Näcken's voice resonated with desperation and resolve. "If you cannot save her, then grant me the choice to merge our eternal essences. Let her become one with my spirit, her soul forever entwined with mine."

The ancient one, his deep eyes reflecting the vastness of the cosmos, held a mournful gaze. "Such a union, though tempting, would be an illusion. Her essence, tethered to mortality, would be engulfed by the weight of eternity. It would be a path strewn with thorns, where her very being would fragment and be lost in the abyss of time. Such is the price we pay for the fleeting beauty of human existence."

As Näcken absorbed the ancient one's words, a melancholic acceptance settled upon his countenance. He embraced Liv, cradling her delicate form with a tenderness born of unwavering devotion. Their souls, forever embroiled, found solace in the bittersweet truth of their love. With a lingering touch, Näcken whispered words of adoration into Liv's ear, pledging eternal fidelity even as the shadows of parting loomed.

"Behold, fair one, should I bestow upon her a shard of your very essence, a lament would arise from the ancient depths. As you surrender your eternal breath, a withering of your immortal frame shall commence, akin to the mortals' fate. Endowed with the blessing of timeless existence, we traverse betwixt realms, untouched by the hand of age or affliction. We do not tire, nor crave respite, for magic courses through our ethereal veins. Yet, should I transmute your essence, you shall forfeit your passage between worlds. Your power and aptitude shall endure, yet you shall be ensnared within this realm, our domain. What impels you to relinquish all for a mere mortal? Shall the allure of love overshadow the boundless wonders that grace your immortal being?" The ancient one's voice trembled, carrying the weight of eternity's burden. His eyes, brimming with unfathomable wisdom, locked with Näcken's unwavering gaze. "In the realm of immortality, where time dances on the edges of eternity, the allure of mortality remains an enigma, a momentary flame that both captivates and unsettles," the ancient one spoke, his voice carrying echoes from countless epochs. "To surrender the infinite expanse of eternal life for the delicate beauty of a mortal soul is a choice that defies logic, a symphony of selflessness that reverberates through the fabric of existence."

Näcken's countenance, steadfast and suffused with a love that could stir the heavens, locked with the ancient one's gaze, unyielding in its commitment. "Within her mortal essence resides an ineffable radiance, a constellation of emotions that stirs the depths of my immortal heart. Her transient existence holds a profundity that transcends realms, a sacred melody that reverberates within the very core of my being. I cannot forsake the intoxicating touch of her mortal embrace."

Approaching Näcken, the ancient one, his presence shimmering with the essence of bygone epochs, wore an expression of awe mingled with trepidation. "To relinquish the gift of immortality, to traverse the path of mortality, is to surrender the timeless dance of realms and tread a labyrinth fraught with uncharted perils. You, Näcken, bear the eternal flame coursing through your veins, traversing unseen boundaries and partaking in the cosmic ballet of wonders. Why surrender it all for the fleeting existence of a mere mortal?"

Näcken's voice, infused with courage and tenderness, resounded throughout the ethereal expanse. "Her mortal existence, though fugacious, possesses an iridescent essence that eclipses the infinite. In her presence, time unravels, and I am consumed by a love that defies the boundaries of existence. Without her, the realm itself would lose its radiance. For this divine connection, I would willingly relinquish my eternal existence, knowing that a life with her is worth a thousand lifetimes of immortality. Grant her restoration, and let us transcend into our ethereal realm, where we may dwell in serenity and tranquillity for the remaining fleeting days, entwining our souls in an eternal dance. And when the time of reckoning arrives, hand in hand, we shall confront the embrace of death," pleaded Näcken, his voice filled with longing.

"Why should I permit her existence within that realm, and why would I grant you solace when you no longer belong among us? What form would you assume? Neither wholly human nor fully among the hidden ones, forever caught between realms," countered the ancient one, a touch of sorrow weaving through his words.

"For her, I would forsake all, sacrificing the remaining days of my immortal existence to bask in the tender warmth of her arms for a mere few decades. There is no life where her delicate essence falters. Only darkness prevails, and willingly would I descend into the abyss. Without her, I am adrift, a lost soul yearning for solace. I cannot bear the thought of losing her. Should she perish in this realm, my very essence shall journey forth into the next, for within the depths of my heart, her absence leaves no room for life," Näcken declared with fervour and genuine sincerity. The ancient one, moved by the fervent affection Näcken held for the mortal, felt a stirring within his ancient heart.

"For ages untold, I have known you, and now I discern the unwavering resolve that guides your path. Though it brings me sorrow to witness the fate you have chosen, I am not devoid of compassion. If this be your true desire, I shall extend my aid," spoke the ancient one, his voice touched by profound melancholy.

Amidst the ethereal glow suffusing the sacred space, Näcken's devoted gaze met Liv's dying form. The weight of eternity pressed upon his shoulders, and yet, in that moment, doubt and hesitation were but distant echoes. With a voice resonating with loyal conviction, he proclaimed, "In the depths of my being, I hold an unshakable certainty."

A tremor of fragility coursed through Liv's feeble form, rendering her voiceless. As the ancient one, a guardian of realms, approached the entwined pair, a solemn hush settled upon the verdant ground. With hands weathered and wise, the ancient one gently graced Liv's brow and Näcken's cheek. Eyes closed, they became conduits of cosmic energy, vessels through which the magic of worlds flowed.

Within the sacred embrace of their touch, Näcken felt a searing anguish, a pain that pierced every fibre of his being. His essence, once ablaze with immortal power, now convulsed and withered within his mortal vessel.

Through the labyrinthine corridors of his torment, Näcken sensed the rise and fall of his fading essence, a sacrifice that reverberated with the weight of cosmic destiny. The enchantment danced within his veins, entwining with his very soul, as his essence surged forth like an untamed tempest. It surged, a wild river, from his body to intertwine with Liv's, seeking to breathe life into her ebbing form.

Within the sanctuary of that magical exchange, Liv, suspended between life and death, gasped with newfound breath as a supernova of energy cascaded into her bones and flesh. The hurricane of vitality, a symphony of renewal, coursed through her essence, mending the torn fabric of her existence. And with each surge of life's current, the wound upon her stomach closed.

As Näcken lifted Liv, their souls entwined in a union of resilience, he enfolded her in his arms with an embrace overflowing with devotion. In that embrace, passion ignited, the flames of their desire burning brighter than the very stars. A tender, impassioned kiss sealed their bond, an eternal affirmation of their shared path.

Amidst the tableau of love and rebirth, the fox, a silent witness to their blooming union, beheld the transcendental beauty of their love, its gaze a reflection of the timeless enchantment that wove between mortal and immortal hearts.

"Whenever you are ready, I shall come for you and guide you through the other side," the majestic creature whispered, its voice carried upon the wind's gentle caress. With a graceful flick of its tail, it dissolved into eclipsing mist, leaving behind naught but an essence of otherworldly mystique.

"What happened?" Bewildered and yearning for understanding, Liv turned to the ancient one, her eyes searching for answers within the depths of his timeless gaze. The ancient one exuded an aura of never-ending wisdom, a conduit between realms, bridging the gap between mortal existence and ethereal domains.

With measured words, the ancient one spoke, his voice a melodic blend of resonance and reverie. "The choice now lies before you, dear soul, veiled within the delicate threads of destiny. You may opt to linger in this mortal plane, where life's echoes whisper upon the breeze. Alternatively, you may embark upon a profound voyage into our realm, a realm unfathomable to the human heart. But choose wisely, for once you tread upon the chosen path, there shall be no turning back. And henceforth, my aid shall be withheld, for the tides of fate are relentless and demand unwavering commitment."

The burden of choice pressed upon Liv's tender heart, as she stood at the crossroads of destiny. Earthly bonds tugged at her spirit, their familiarity beckoning her to linger in the realm of mortal connections, where fleeting joys bloomed like fragile blossoms. Yet, the ethereal realm whispered seductive secrets, promising a love that knew no bounds and a world untouched by suffering.

In the midst of this profound reflection, Näcken's voice, urgent yet gentle, filled the air. "Beloved, forsake the strife of this world," he implored, his eyes ablaze with faithful determination. "Together, let us escape this torment, seeking solace in a sanctuary hidden from prying eyes. In that sacred realm, our love shall shine undimmed by fear or persecution. If we remain here, pursued relentlessly, our souls shall know no rest. Let us embark on a journey to peaceful realms."

Echoes of barks and frenzied voices reached Liv's ears, a chilling reminder of imminent danger. Torches flickered, casting eerie shadows that danced closer with each passing moment.

"And what of my children?" Liv's voice trembled with concern, torn between maternal duty and the fiery love that bound her to Näcken.

"Their wings have spread wide, my love, as they soar upon their own destinies," Näcken reassured, his gaze filled with unwavering affection and understanding. His words brought solace to Liv's troubled heart, and she turned to the ancient one, seeking guidance in this fateful hour.

"Guide us to your realm," Liv implored, her voice resolute. The ancient one, a repository of timeless wisdom and untold secrets, smiled with benevolence.

"Follow my steps," the ancient one beckoned, leading them through the veils of reality. Hand in hand, Näcken and Liv embarked on a transcendent journey, leaving behind the encroaching mob and the perils of mortal existence. They dissolved into the ethereal realm, their fate sealed at the threshold, forever bound by the cords of their love.

Days melted into years, and years into decades, as they traversed the path of eternity, their hands clasped in unwavering solidarity. Näcken's once youthful visage embraced the lines of age, his eyes tenderly gazing upon Liv's weathered face, a tribute to the life they had shared.

"Now, my love, the time has come for our next voyage," he

whispered, his voice a pacifying elixir. Their hands entwined, a poignant reminder of the vow they had made. "Remember, I shall embark on an eternal quest to find you, to reclaim you in my embrace. My search shall persist, unyielding, until our souls intertwine once more."

Liv's smile blossomed, radiant as the setting sun, as she clung to Näcken's hand. By their side, the faithful fox materialized, a symbol of eternal loyalty and solace. Together, they ventured forth into the realm of infinite possibilities, their hearts forever entwined in a dance of love and transcendence.

"Come, dear mother," the creature's voice whispered, a tender melody that caressed their souls. "Do not fear, for I shall guide you. In my presence, you shall find solace, and together we shall traverse the ethereal realm." With Näcken's hand firmly clasped in hers, Liv began her final odyssey, traversing the ethereal threshold that separates mortal existence from the afterlife. Hand in hand, they embraced the unknown, casting aside the weight of mortality and surrendering to the embrace of the unseen.

Their grip tightened, their spirits merging and intertwining as they crossed into the uncharted expanse of eternity. The world they left behind faded, its echoes dissipating in the mists of forgotten memories. United in love, accompanied by the steadfast fox, they soared, their bond unbreakable, forever woven into the tapestry of everlasting existence.

Made in the USA
Middletown, DE
14 January 2024

47851691R00169